Notorious man . . .

Everyone knows about Dylan Moore—his brilliant talent and his pleasure-seeking ways—but no one knows the torment that lies beneath his reckless veneer. Only one woman gets a glimpse of the forces that drive Dylan's soul, a woman who haunts his dreams and evokes his passions as no other ever has before.

Disgraced and destitute, Grace Cheval wants nothing to do with the seductive man who desires her. When Dylan offers her a position as governess to his newfound daughter, she knows his true intentions are dishonorable. Yet she finds this charismatic man hard to resist, and she returns his passionate kisses with a fire that matches his own. Can Dylan dare hope that this proud, spirited beauty will melt the ice around his heart?

Avon Books by
Laura Lee Guhrke

AND THEN HE KISSED HER
SHE'S NO PRINCESS
THE MARRIAGE BED
HIS EVERY KISS
GUILTY PLEASURES

LAURA LEE GUHRKE

HIS EVERY KISS

An Avon Romantic Treasure

AVON BOOKS
An Imprint of HarperCollinsPublishers

This is a work of fiction. Names, characters, places, and incidents are products of the author's imagination or are used fictitiously and are not to be construed as real. Any resemblance to actual events, locales, organizations, or persons, living or dead, is entirely coincidental.

AVON BOOKS
An Imprint of HarperCollins*Publishers*
10 East 53rd Street
New York, New York 10022-5299

First Avon Books paperback printing: October 2004

Avon Trademark Reg. U.S. Pat. Off. and in Other Countries, Marca Registrada, Hecho en U.S.A.
HarperCollins® is a registered trademark of HarperCollins Publishers Inc.

Printed in the U.S.A.

10 9 8 7 6 5 4 3

For my father, William Guhrke,
for being the only person in our family
with musical talent, and for
giving me my appreciation
of classical music.
I love you, Dad,
but since I can't
carry a tune in a bucket,
why couldn't you have passed
your singing voice on to me?

Acknowledgments

My thanks to Ms. Terry Rogers for all her help during the writing of this book. Ms. Rogers, who holds a Bachelor of Arts in Music Education and has taught piano for ten years, gave me valuable assistance on the musical aspects of this story. Terry, you have my heartfelt gratitude.

Prologue

London
1827

He was going mad. Damn that noise, that agonizing noise. It was a high-pitched whine that seared his brain like fire, an incessant, unwavering sound that was slowly driving him insane. If only he could make it stop. But it never stopped.

Dylan Moore flung back the sheet with a curse and got out of bed. Naked, he crossed the bedchamber and pushed aside the heavy brocaded draperies to look out. The sky was pitch black, making the hour sometime between midnight and dawn, and only the lamp at the corner illuminated the empty street below. Except in his own mind, everything was silent. He stared out the window, hating every human being in London

1

who could enjoy the silence, who could sleep when he could not.

His movements awakened Phelps, and the valet entered from the dressing room, a lit candle in his hand. "Unable to sleep again tonight, sir?"

"Yes." Dylan exhaled a sharp sigh. Three months now. How many more nights could this go on, this sleeping for only minutes at a time? His head was throbbing in painful protest at the never-ending noise and the lack of sleep, and he leaned his forehead against the window, fighting the impulse to smash his head through the glass and end this torture.

"The laudanum that Doctor Forbes prescribed . . ." The valet hesitated at the fierce scowl his master turned on him, but concern impelled him to persevere. "Perhaps I should prepare another dose?"

"No." Lying in bed waiting for the opiate to take effect was an intolerable idea. Dylan turned away from the window and strode past his valet toward the dressing room. "I'm going out."

"I will awaken Roberts and have him bring your carriage around front for you."

"I don't want my carriage. I am going for a walk."

"Alone, sir?"

"Alone."

Phelps could not have thought that walking around London alone in the middle of the night was a good idea, but his expression conveyed no opinion of the matter. Dylan was a man who did what he pleased, and it was not his valet's place to question the wisdom of such a course. "Yes, sir," Phelps said and began helping him dress.

Ten minutes later, Phelps returned to bed at his orders, and Dylan went downstairs, the lit candle in his hand illuminating his way through the darkened house. He entered his study, walked to his desk, and opened the drawer. He stared at the pistol for a moment, then picked it up. A man dressed in expensive clothing roaming the city alone at night was asking for trouble, and it was wise to take precautions. He loaded the weapon, then slipped it into the pocket of his long black cloak and left the study. He passed the music room on his way to the front door, and something made him pause. Perhaps a walk was not the distraction he really needed. He hesitated, then turned and entered the music room.

Until the accident, he had spent many of his waking hours here. A moment of carelessness, a fall from his horse, the slamming of his head against a rock, and everything had changed. It had taken two days for his left ear to stop bleeding and a fortnight to recover from the concussion. During that time, he had hoped the ringing in his ears would go away, but it had only seemed to worsen. During the month following his recovery, he had entered this room every morning as if to work. He had sat down at the grand piano pretending that nothing was wrong, telling himself over and over that his affliction was temporary, that he had not lost his gift, that if only he tried, he would be able to write music again. Finally, he had given up in despair, and he had not entered this room since then.

He walked slowly to the immense Broadwood Grand piano, staring at the glow of his candle reflecting off the polished walnut top. Perhaps in the past three months, some magical transformation had taken place, and when he put his hands on the keys, the music would come again. He could at least try. After placing the candle in the carved walnut holder meant for that purpose, he propped up the lid of the piano and sat down on the bench.

Dylan stared down at the keys for a long moment, then ran his fingers over them in the notes of a minuet, the first piece of music he had ever written. Not bad for a seven-year-old boy, he conceded. But in the intervening twenty years, he had composed nineteen symphonies, ten operas, and so many concertos, waltzes, and sonatas that he couldn't possibly count them all. He had been born into wealth, and from his music he had achieved not only more money but fame and critical success as well. Yet he knew it all counted for nothing. It was the music that mattered. It was the music that he loved.

He glanced at the scribbled sheet music before him, staring at his own writing as if it were that of a stranger. It was from *Valmont,* his latest composition, the opera he had written based on the scandalous novel *Les Liaisons Dangéreuses.* He had finished the work the day before that shattering autumn ride through Hyde Park.

He had written the opera in less than a week. Music had always come so easily to him. He had always been able to hear melodies in his mind; they had poured from his consciousness onto pages with ease, a gift he had always taken for granted. With brutal clarity, he suddenly acknowledged the truth. *Valmont* was the last thing he had written, the last thing he would ever write. Why not admit it? He couldn't hear the music anymore. The whine in his head drowned it out.

Four different physicians had told him the damage was permanent, that he was fortunate to still be able to hear, that he would get used to the noise. His fingers crashed down on the keys, and he rose to his feet. Creating music was the passion of his life, the purpose of his existence. Now the gift was gone. He would never get used to it.

He blew out the candle and left the house. A heavy fog had descended, the curse of winter in London, and he walked mindlessly through it, concentrating on the tap of his boots against the cobblestones. He walked without any conscious direction, only realizing where his footsteps were leading him when he found himself standing in front of the Charing Cross Palladium.

The once popular concert hall had long ago given way to the more opulent Covent Garden. The owner had little interest in attempting to regain for the Palladium its former eminence, but Dylan had conducted his first symphony here a decade ago, when the Palladium's popularity had been at its height. The place was little used now, and he could not help a grim smile at the irony. How appropriate. A has-been concert hall for a has-been composer.

A faint light filtered out from beneath the double entrance doors, and Dylan frowned. Why should there be lamps lit inside the building at this hour? He pulled on the handle of one of the doors and found that it was unlocked. He stepped inside.

"Is anyone here?" he called, but his voice

echoed through the place and died away with no reply. He crossed the wide foyer and passed through one of the arches that led into the theater itself. Several stage lamps were flickering, and their light revealed a mop and bucket on the floor of the stage, but there was no person in sight.

Dylan called out again, but he still received no answer. Probably the charwoman had forgotten to extinguish the lamps and lock the doors before leaving. Forgetting to lock the doors was a forgivable offense, since there was nothing to steal. With no productions in work, there would be no props, costumes, or musical instruments in the theater. But the burning lamps were another matter. Left unattended, they could start a fire.

He walked down one of the aisles, thinking to extinguish the lamps before he departed, but when he reached the orchestra pit, he stopped. The pit was empty, save a wooden baton on the floor, left behind by the last conductor. He stared at it for a moment, then descended the steps into the pit and picked it up from the floor.

He rolled the baton between his palms, remembering the first time he had conducted here, the critical acclaim and success that had followed. Soon it would all be gone. Already people were beginning to talk about his dark moods and his headaches. Though only four doctors and his valet knew of his affliction, he did not see how he could hide it forever. When the music stopped coming after two decades of prolific composing, people would know. Soon it would be common knowledge that Dylan Moore, England's most famous composer, had lost his musical gifts.

Music was his life. Enraged that what he loved so dearly had been taken away, he flung the baton, and it clattered across the wooden floor of the orchestra pit. Without music, what would he do? Must he suffer this intolerable affliction forever? Spend the rest of his days listening to one sound, a sound that never changed, never wavered, and never ended?

There was one way to stop it. The thought penetrated him like a bone-chilling wind, and Dylan knew the real reason he had brought the pistol with him and why his footsteps had led him here. It was fitting that he should die now, at the height of his fame, in the concert hall where he had achieved his first success, before critics could shred him and friends could—God forbid—pity him. He slipped a hand into the pocket of his cloak and pulled out the pistol.

Dylan closed his eyes and lifted the gun, positioning the end of the barrel directly beneath his chin, his purpose to obliterate once and for all the sound that seared through his brain with such monotony. He cocked the hammer. It was so simple. One squeeze, then silence. Blessed, heavenly silence.

The music caught him by surprise. He froze, recognizing the unmistakable first notes of one of his own violin sonatas, a playful piece of music that floated to him from the left side of the stage. He opened his eyes and glanced in that direction, startled to see a young woman standing there, a violin in her hands.

Dylan watched as she began to walk across the stage. She played as she walked, and the lighthearted strains of the music did not falter as she came to a halt in the center of the stage, only a few feet from him.

Dylan studied her in the lamplight that gleamed on her rich, golden-blond hair and the brass buttons of her dark green dress. She was tall, slender but shapely. Graceful, too, swaying as she played, as if caught in a gentle breeze. Her face was turned a bit away from him, the side of her jaw pressed to the chin rest of her instrument as she performed his own music for him. She played very well for a woman so young, but it was not her skill with the violin that fascinated him. She had a touch of the West Country folklore about her, the mystery that evoked memories of his Devonshire childhood and tales of wood nymphs, pixies, and magic. His fancy caught for the moment, he lowered the pistol in his hand.

The music stopped.

She lowered her instrument to look down at him standing in the orchestra pit, and Dylan caught his breath. Never had he seen a lovelier woman in his life. She had all the usual requirements of beauty—oval face, well-proportioned features, creamy skin, very kissable lips—but her beauty was not what made something twist inside him, something sweet and painful like the sharp sting of a meal's first bite.

No, it was her eyes. Huge eyes of an indescribable, light green color, they were as cool and peaceful as the shade of a willow tree. There was no coquetry there, no feminine interest, just a tranquil, steady gaze with a hint of sadness. She was young, a bit short of twenty perhaps, and yet those eyes seemed ageless. Those eyes would be beautiful when she was eighty.

Her gaze remained locked with his, but she said nothing. Slowly she lowered her instrument, and for a long moment, they stared at one another. In the silence, past the whine in his head, Dylan suddenly heard something else, a vague bit of music that hovered on the edge of his consciousness, the opening notes of a new composition. He struggled to bring them to the forefront of his mind, but like the mist outside, they were impossible to take hold of. The more he strained to hear them, the further they slipped away. After a moment, the notes of music disappeared and only the whine remained.

The woman watched him for a moment longer, then her gaze lowered to the pistol in his hand. "I'd rather you didn't," she said. "I am the charwoman here, and it is my responsibility to keep everything tidy. If you shot yourself, I would have to clean up the mess."

Her comment was so prosaic, so practical, and so unlike any idea of a mystical wood nymph that Dylan almost wanted to laugh. "Very true. How does a charwoman learn to play the violin?"

"All very unpleasant for me," she went on without answering his question, "since I've never been able to stand the sight of blood. There would be the devil of a row over the stains on the floor— blood does not come out of wood, you know— and I would be sacked on the spot for allowing Dylan Moore to shoot himself."

Her voice was an educated voice, hardly that of a charwoman, with the unmistakable hint of a

Cornish accent. West Country. He'd been right, then. Her voice was rich, low-pitched, so soft that it could arouse any man's erotic imaginings. How could a mere charwoman have a voice like that? "You know who I am," he said, "yet I do not know you. Have we met before?"

"Of course I know who you are. I am a musician, after all. I saw you conduct in Salzburg last year, so I recognized you at once."

This was ludicrous. Charwomen did not attend concerts in Salzburg or play the violin. He had to be dreaming. Before he could ask any questions to help him make sense of it all, she spoke again. "If you killed yourself, I would lose my position because of your action, and with no recommendation to help me find another situation, I would become destitute. Your death would bring pain to others as well. What of your family, your friends and acquaintances? The owner here would have a worthless piece of property on his hands, for no one would wish to lease this theater again, and certainly no one would have an interest in purchasing it."

As she enumerated the consequences of his suicide in a rather obvious attempt to make him feel guilty, the loveliness of her voice began to lose its charm for him.

"Your relations," she went on, "would have to live not only with the grief of your death but also with the disgrace of your suicide. But then, your concerns are more important than anyone else's, and I am sure the consequences to others do not matter to you in the least."

The consequences to others had never even occurred to him, and the censure behind this impudent young woman's mock sympathy rankled. "It is my life," he pointed out, scowling at her. "Why should I not end it if I wish to?"

Her expression became even more grave as she gazed down at him from the stage. "Because it would be wrong."

"Indeed? And who are you to preach the morality of it to me? My guardian angel, my soul, my bloody conscience?"

"It would be wrong," she repeated.

"Damn it, woman, I have the right to take my own life if I wish to do so!"

She shook her head. "No, you do not. You may be needed for something important."

He did laugh then, a harsh sound that echoed through the theater. "Needed for what? Saving damsels in distress, perhaps?" He mocked her, mocked the earnestness in her voice, the patient gravity in her eyes. "Slaying dragons? Needed for what?"

"I don't know." She moved forward and jumped down from the stage into the orchestra pit, landing beside him. Tucking her violin and bow beneath her arm, she reached out her hand and curled it around the barrel of the pistol. She pulled the gun gently from his grasp, as if knowing he could not fight her for it without the possibility of injuring her, as if knowing he would not take that risk. She turned away and pointed the weapon toward the empty seats until she had eased the hammer back into place, then she put the gun in a pocket of her gown.

"That's rather futile, don't you think?" he chided. "I have many more pistols at home."

She shrugged. "Everyone has free will. If you

try again to kill yourself, I cannot stop you. But I do not believe you will try again."

He was surprised by the matter-of-fact tone of her voice. "You seem very sure of that."

"I am. I have heard enough about you to know you are not that sort of man. Not really."

"Heard about me, have you?" He could not help asking the inevitable question. "What sort of man am I, then?"

"Arrogant," she answered at once. "Arrogant enough to believe that the world of music will be diminished if you are not in it. Willful. Obsessed. Your work takes precedence over everyone and everything else."

An unflattering opinion, he supposed, and brutally accurate.

"You are also very strong," she added, "strong enough to find courage to live, I think."

He didn't know if she meant that, or if it was merely said to encourage him to change his mind. "You think a great deal for a charwoman."

She ignored that. "Now that the darkest moment has passed, you will find all sorts of excuses not to use suicide to end your suffering."

Dylan didn't need her to talk about his suffering. "You know nothing of me but what you have heard. You do not even know the reasons for my choice."

"No reason is good enough to justify suicide."

Her moral rectitude was beginning to have the irritating quality of a sermon. "An opinion gained from your years of experience, no doubt," he shot back.

She looked away. "Why?" she murmured, sounding exasperated, almost angry. "Why are all of you so wretchedly tormented?"

He raised an eyebrow at the unexpected question and the tone of her voice. "All of us?" he repeated.

"Artists. Musicians, actors, painters, poets, composers. It isn't really necessary, you know."

"You are a musician."

"I play competently, and that is all. I am not a virtuoso. I do not have the brilliance of a true artist." She returned her gaze to his face, and Dylan knew this woman and her eyes would haunt his dreams for a long time to come. "But you do," she said. "You have the touch of greatness."

"That is all in the past. I will never write music again."

She did not ask him why. Her mouth formed a rather ironic, twisted smile. "Yes, you will. One day."

She had no idea what she was talking about, but before he could argue the point, she turned away. Pulling her violin and bow from beneath her arm, she mounted the steps out of the orchestra pit, then stopped on the stage and turned to look at him. "Put out the lamps when you leave, would you?"

She retraced her steps toward the left wing of the stage. Dylan watched her go, remaining where he was for several more moments, still wondering if he were caught in some sort of strange dream.

Suddenly, out of nowhere, he heard that mysterious bit of music again, and he closed his eyes, straining to hear it. A few notes of a new composition danced with tantalizing promise just out of his reach, but he could not grasp them, he could not keep the melody. It vanished into nothingness once again. He opened his eyes, but the woman who had brought him that moment of music had vanished.

"Wait!" he called to her. "Come back!"

He ascended the steps and followed her, but when he reached the back of the stage, she was nowhere in sight. He strode down the corridors, calling to her, pulling back the curtains of each dressing room he passed, but he did not find her in any of them. When he reached the back door and opened it, there was no sign of her in the mist that swirled through the alley behind the theater. "I do not even know your name!" he shouted.

There was no reply. The woman and her violin had disappeared, and the notes in his head had departed with her. He strained to hear them again, but they were drowned out. He was alone again with his tormentor.

Dylan clamped his hands over his ears, but it was a futile gesture. He could not blot out the noise in his brain with his hands. There was only one way to stop it, but it was too late for that now.

With a roar of frustration and rage, he slammed his fist against the door, hardly noticing the pain. She was right. He had lost the impetus to end his life, and he cursed her for taking from him the easy way out. Now he knew his fate was to live with this torture until he went mad.

Chapter 1

London
March 1832

The ostrich plume was tickling her nose, and
there was nothing Grace Cheval could do
about it. She slid the bow across the strings of her
violin, trying to concentrate on the allegro of Vivaldi's *L'Autunno*, rather than on the huge feather
that had come loose from her hat and fallen forward across her cheek. She prayed she wouldn't
sneeze.

The feather wasn't her only problem. Ballrooms
were always too warm, especially at these
crowded charity affairs. Worse, the ball was Fancy
Dress, and the costume she had been given to
wear did not help. The heavy velvet doublet of a
highwayman made playing her violin for an entire evening a tiring business. The combination of

15

doublet, plumed hat, and leather mask made her feel as if she were in an oven. As she played, Grace shook her head several times, trying to get the ostrich plume out of her face without missing a note of the music, but it was a futile attempt. The silly thing insisted on falling right back down again to tickle her nose.

Vivaldi finally ended, much to her relief. As the couples who had been engaged in the quadrille left the ballroom floor, she set her violin and bow in her lap, then lifted her hands to yank the ostrich plume out of her hat. When it came away, she tossed it aside and turned her sheet music to the Weber waltz, which was the last dance of the evening. She lifted her violin once again as one of her fellow musicians leaned closer to her.

"You only got half of it," he told her in a low voice. "The other half is poking straight up out of your hat."

"Rot," she shot back as she tucked her violin beneath her chin. "You are such a liar, Teddy."

"I'm not lying," the young man answered, settling the laurel wreath of Caesar more firmly into his chestnut brown hair before lifting his bow to the cello between his knees. "Sticking up like that, it looks like a house chimney, only fluffy."

Grace raised her own bow. "I can always tell when you're lying. Your ears get red."

He gave a chuckle as they began to play. Grace had performed at so many balls during the past three years that she knew most published waltzes by heart, and that enabled her to have a look at the dancers as she played.

Queen Elizabeth danced by, along with her partner, Henry the Second. Helen of Troy was next, with a man whose costume was merely a black evening suit and long, gold-lined black cape. He made her think at once of Faust's devil, Mephistopheles. The two made a striking pair, for the woman's white toga was an eye-catching contrast to the man's dark clothes and coloring. As the couple swirled past her, she noticed that his black hair was long and tied back, an odd thing, many years out of fashion, yet not quite in keeping with his costume. He wore no mask, and her glimpse of his face caused her hand to falter in surprise. Her violin hit a strident note. She recovered herself, and the pair moved out of her line of vision, but Grace knew she had not been mistaken in her recognition of him.

Dylan Moore.

She would never forget the night she had met the famous composer, and she doubted most other women would forget either. A compelling man, tall, with eyes of true black. Meeting his gaze had been like looking into an abyss where no light could penetrate the depths. A man with a resolute jaw that said he usually got what he wanted, and a cynical curve to his mouth that said he was easily bored by it afterward. A man of breathtaking genius, wealth and position, a man who seemed to have everything life could offer, a man who had put the barrel of a pistol beneath his chin.

She could still remember the sick lurch of her stomach as she had watched him from behind the heavy velvet curtain of the Palladium that night five years ago. She had played her violin then, too, hoping the notes of Moore's own music would not be drowned out by a pistol shot.

Etienne had taken her back to Paris only a day later, and she had not seen Moore again, but she had heard a great deal about him during the five years that had followed their strange encounter. Everyone from Paris to Vienna and back again had been eager to discuss the latest news about England's most famous composer. There had been plenty of it.

His tempestuous love affair with the actress Abigail Williams was the stuff of legend, an affair begun when he had jumped down from his box at Covent Garden and carried her right off the stage in the midst of a play, ended when she had found him in bed with a beautiful Chinese prostitute he had supposedly won in a card game. He had lived openly with half a dozen women during the past five years, including a Russian dancer and the illegitimate daughter of an Indian rajah.

In addition to news about Moore, there was gossip. It was said that a riding accident had affected his brain and he was slowly going mad. It was said that he drank and gambled to excess, used opiates, smoked hashish. It was said he went without sleep for days at a time, fought countless duels but only with swords, and rode his horse at breakneck speed no matter whether he was riding on the Row or jumping fences at a country house. It was said there was no dare he would not take up, no challenge he would let pass, no rule he had not broken.

Moore and his partner moved in front of her again, only a few feet away this time, and Grace sucked in a deep breath, startled by the change in him that five years had wrought. He still had the same wide shoulders and lean hips she remembered, the body of a man skilled at sport, but his countenance had changed. His face was still a handsome one, but it bore the unmistakable lines of dissipation and neglect, lines carved indelibly into his forehead, the corners of his eyes, and the edges of his mouth, lines that should not have existed on the face of a man just two years past thirty. She realized with a flash of anger that the gossip must be nothing less than the truth. The man had always been rather wild, but now he looked as if he had become exactly the shameless libertine gossips whispered about.

Grace did not know what had prompted him to contemplate suicide five years before, but she remembered her own conviction that he would not make another attempt, and it seemed she had been right. Instead of choosing to die, he had clearly decided to go to the opposite extreme, living hard and fast, as if trying to gain every bit of sensation out of each moment.

Despite his declaration to her that he would never write music again, it would seem that he had. His opera, *Valmont*, published four years ago, was still playing in opera houses all over England and Europe. His Nineteenth Symphony last year, while not as highly acclaimed as his previous work, had still been a smashing success. But he did not produce music with the fevered energy of earlier days, and during the past year, he had published only one sonata.

Too busy, perhaps, she thought, noting how closely he held Helen of Troy as they waltzed, how he leaned down to murmur in her ear. Scandalous behavior, especially at a public ball, and so in keeping with his reputation.

At that moment, Moore glanced in her direction, and she lowered her gaze to her sheet music, grateful for the hat that shaded her eyes and the mask that shielded her face. When she looked up again, he and his partner had melted into the crowd of dancers once again, and she was glad of it. She knew he was not her business, but it did not keep her from a sense of frustration that she had saved a man's life so that he might squander it on debauchery and excess.

The waltz ended, the couples left the floor to move toward the supper that awaited them, and the musicians began to pack up their instruments. As Grace tucked her violin and bow in their velvet-lined case, she put Moore out of her mind. His life, or the wasting of it, was his own affair.

She placed her sheet music on top of her violin, then pushed down the lid of her case and fastened the buckles of the leather straps. She picked up the case by its handle and used her free hand to grab her music stand. "I will meet you and the others out behind the mews," she told Teddy. "This room is much too warm, and I need some air."

He nodded. "Next time we play a Fancy Dress ball, I will see if I can find you a more comfortable costume," he said with a grin.

"Do," she agreed with fervor as she turned away. "Bring me a bit of cold tongue and ham from the supper, would you, Teddy?" she requested over her shoulder as she moved toward the door out of the ballroom. "That is, if you can sweet-talk any from the serving maids on your way out."

Grace departed from the ballroom, leaving the

male musicians to their usual practice of flirting with the maids who assisted with the supper, caging a free meal of the leavings and stealing a kiss or two. Turning away from the grand staircase that led down to the front entrance of the public ballroom, she walked to the far end of the corridor. Like servants, hired musicians took the back stairs. She went down to the ground floor, then slipped out into the cool, moonlit night.

As she crossed the line of carriages that clogged the alley, Grace nodded to the drivers, who waited to take vehicles around front when the evening's festivities ended. She continued on through the stable mews to the alley behind, where she would wait for Teddy. He lived near her own lodgings in Bermondsey and would see her safely home.

Grace set her violin case and music stand beside the brick wall that separated the stables from the street beyond, then began to remove some of the stifling clothes of her costume. She doffed the hat, letting her long, straight hair fall down her back, then she pulled the mask from across her eyes and removed the doublet, glad when she was down to the breeches, boots and white linen shirt that were all that remained of her costume.

Though it was early spring, winter still lingered. A light, chilly wind drifted through the alley, and the cold air felt refreshing on her sweat-tinged body after the stifling atmosphere of an over-crowded ballroom. Unfortunately, the breeze brought with it the unpleasant smells of London. Even in Mayfair, even when it was cold, one could not escape the mingled odors of the river, rotting garbage, and coal soot that permeated the air.

She closed her eyes, turning to lean her back against the alley wall, inhaling the smells that swirled around her with distaste, wishing she could go back to the English countryside of her girlhood—sleepy summer air, the sound of the ocean, the hum of bees, and the scent of roses, but that wasn't possible. One could never go back, and ruined women couldn't go home again.

Etienne had promised to show her the world, and he had. She thought of all the beautiful, exciting places her husband had taken her during their marriage. Paris, Salzburg, Florence, Prague, Vienna . . . all the European capitals, where Etienne had been the darling of aristocratic, wealthy patrons, and his paintings had been their adored possessions.

There would be no country summers, no roses, and no home for her now. The earnings of an orange-seller who played her violin at parties could not even pay the rent on her tiny room and put food in her mouth, much less find her a home. "Someday," she vowed to the night air, giving voice to her dearest wish, "I shall have a home again, a cottage of my own in the country. Cream-colored," she added, "with slate blue shutters and a garden of roses."

"Might I suggest a few window boxes of bachelor buttons, geraniums, and ivy as well?"

That amused question interrupted her daydream, and Grace opened her eyes to find the unmistakable form of Dylan Moore only a dozen feet away from her. "And perhaps," he added, "a horse chestnut tree?"

He stood by the stable wall, his long hair loose now, the cloak hanging from his powerful shoulders like a shadow, and his white cravat glimmering between the folds of midnight black. "Do you talk to yourself often?" he asked.

"Only when I do not realize someone is eavesdropping."

Moore made no apology for that. "At last, I have seen my charwoman again." He took a step toward her. "I tried so hard to find you. I searched everywhere. I went back to the Palladium, but you had left your post without giving notice, and no one there knew where you had gone, nor anything about you. In any crowd, I scanned face after face, desperate to see yours. I observed every woman I saw scrubbing a floor. I studied the face of every violinist I came across. I even made inquiries of the Musician's Livery. All to no avail."

"Why did you search for me?"

"To tell you how much I hated you, of course."

The words were lightly spoken, but Grace sensed he meant them. "Hate me?" she repeated. "But I saved your life!"

"Yes, and how I cursed you for it." He took another step toward her, and the movement brought him out of the darkness and into the glow of the streetlamp behind her. "Sometimes," he went on, "I tried to convince myself that I had conjured you in a dream, that you were a fancy wrought by my deepest longings, and that I would never see you again because you did not exist. Yet I could never quite accept the notion. I wanted so badly for you to be real. As hard as I tried, I could not keep hating you, even though you saved my life when I did not want to be saved."

"But now, with the passage of time, are you not glad you lived?"

"Glad? God, no!" His vehemence startled her. He lowered his head, pressing his palms against his skull as if he had a headache. "Dear God, no."

There was such genuine anguish in his voice. Grace looked at him, feeling a tug of compassion, and she ruthlessly shoved it away.

Artists.

Her husband had sucked so much compassion out of her that she had little of it left. Tormented artists no longer held any charm for her. "Poor fellow," she said. "Wealth, fame, connections, success, good looks, and talent. How you must be suffering."

He lifted his head, shaking back his long hair like a restless stallion, but when he spoke, that careless drawl was back in his voice. "But I do suffer, ma'am. Life is so deuced exhausting."

She gave a disapproving sniff. "I have no doubt, the notorious way you live it."

"Been paying attention, have you?"

He sounded quite pleased at the discovery, and that angered her again. "Enough to know that you live as if you have a death wish, sir. Laugh if you like, but I see nothing amusing about that. If I was wrong about you, if you would still prefer to die, then what are you doing standing here now, talking to me?" She was tired of this, tired of attempting reason with men of artistic temperament. She had escaped that prison long ago. "It would be a simple matter to kill yourself. Why have you not just done it?"

"Because of you!" he said with such passion that Grace was startled. Several quick strides, and he was standing at arm's length from her. "Do you not yet understand? Because of *you*."

He brought his arms up on either side to trap her. Grace tensed, feeling a sudden glimmer of fear. She flattened back against the hard brick behind her and lifted her chin to look straight into his eyes. Light poured over them from the streetlamp on the other side of the wall, and in that golden glow, his eyes were opaque, like a night sky without any stars. "You cannot lay responsibility for your life or death at my door, sir."

"Can I not?" He leaned closer, close enough that his warm breath caressed her cheek in the cool evening. "You—your face, your voice, your eyes—God, your eyes. The music that surrounds you. These things have haunted me these five long years. The hope that I would someday find you again, that I would hear the music of you again—these hopes have enabled me to get through my days, one by one."

"Me?" Grace shook her head, stunned. "Why me? What music?"

He pulled back a bit and did not answer. The sounds of traffic passing in the noisy street beyond echoed through the alley as they stared at one another in silence. Grace waited, not daring to move, not knowing quite what he would do if she did. The spring wind brushed past them, lifting a tendril of her long blond hair across her face.

That caught his attention. He lifted his hand to pull the strands away before she could do so, and something changed in him. His body relaxed, and his expression softened to a tenderness she had not seen in his face before. "You are as lovely as I remember," he murmured as his knuckles brushed her cheek. "So lovely."

The way he spoke flustered her, and she felt the

spark of something completely unexpected, something she had thought long dead inside of her. Physical desire. It came to life again in an instant, evoked by the caress of Moore's hand on her cheek.

Grace drew in a sharp breath, trying to shove that feeling away, but she could not. It felt like warm sunshine spreading through her body after the cold darkness of winter. She had forgotten this—she had forgotten what a man's touch felt like. When his fingertips moved along the side of her face and he tucked the tendril of her hair back behind her ear, she almost turned her face into his palm to kiss it. Almost.

"What do you want of me?" she asked, trying to maintain some sort of rational thought, but the heat of his body so close and the powerful rush of her own feelings were making it hard to think straight. "Are you trying to seduce me?"

"Seduce you?" he repeated thoughtfully, running the tip of his finger back and forth along the curve of her ear. "I can think of nothing that would bring me more pleasure. You intoxicate me."

"You are a torrid man, aren't you?" Grace started to look away, but he slid his hand into her hair to keep her gaze on his face. She stared at him, at his dark, passionate eyes and his sensuous mouth. It was ridiculous, she knew, that a virtual stranger could make her feel this way, as soft and warm as caramel in the sun. His caress was melting her on the spot. She should duck under his arm and run away, yet she could not seem to move. "This is absurd," she scoffed, but her voice came out low and thick, the voice of a woman being seduced and enjoying it. "You do not even know me."

"I feel as if I know you." The pad of his thumb caressed her temple. "I hear music when I look at you."

Grace gave a half-laugh at that cliché. Surely this man could do better than that. "Of course you do."

Those mocking words seemed to ignite something inside him. He moved again, tilting her head back as he leaned into her, pressing her against the wall with the sheer weight of his body. Her heartbeat quickened, and she felt her insides begin to tremble at his aggressive move. Not with fear, she realized to her chagrin, but anticipation. No wonder Dylan Moore had bedded so many women. He had such a talent for getting them there.

He bent his head, and before she could think, she was parting her lips to take his kiss. A lush, open-mouthed kiss it was, one that sent shimmers of pleasure through her entire body, pleasure so startling she cried out against his mouth.

He caressed her tongue with his own, deepening the kiss. As if her body had a will of its own, Grace gripped the edges of his cloak in her fists, rose on her toes, and met his kiss with the shameful eagerness of a strumpet. So long since she had felt this way. So long since she'd felt this craving for a man's kiss, his touch, his body. She felt so keenly alive at this moment. She let go of his cloak and wrapped her arms around his neck, pressing closer to the hard wall of his body.

He made a rough, ardent sound against her

mouth. His hand left her hair to move in an inex-
orable slide down the side of her throat, over her
collarbone, to her breast. He paused there for only
a second, just long enough to feel the thudding of
her heart against his fingertips through her linen
shirt before moving further down to stop at her
waist. He pulled her away from the wall and
wrapped his arm around her, then yanked her
upward off the ground until her hips were
pressed to his.

This was madness.

Grace turned her face away to break the kiss,
panting. She slid her arms down from around his
neck, but he did not let her go. He continued to
hold her tight against him, his lips against her
hair, her feet dangling a few inches off the
ground. It was impossible to ignore the hard and
intimate feel of his arousal, and she was mortified
that she had let a man she barely knew put her in
this position, a man who by his own admission
had once hated her. She returned her gaze to his,
trying to gain control of her turbulent emotions.
"Let me go."

He relaxed his hold, but only enough to let her
body slide down until her boots hit solid ground.
"I heard music in my head the first time I saw
you. When I saw you again in that ballroom, the
music is how I recognized you. Despite that silly
mask and hat, despite Weber's waltz and all the
talking voices, I knew it was you by the music I
heard in my head."

"You are a composer," she said in a breathless
rush. "You hear music all the time, I daresay. How
significant is that?" She flattened her palms

against his chest, feeling hard muscle beneath her hands as she tried to push him away.

It was like pushing a wall, and he did not move. "More important than you can imagine."

His arm began to ease its hold on her even as another voice, an outraged male voice, entered the conversation. "Get away from her!"

Grace looked past Moore to see Teddy striding around the corner of the stables in their direction. He was still wearing his costume, but under his arm was a burlap bundle of food. In his hands, he carried his cello case and music stand. He dropped them as he approached, his stride quickening.

Moore turned to glance at Teddy over his shoulder, but he did not seem at all perturbed by the angry young man. "I would not dream of fighting your gallant," he said, that sardonic amusement back in his voice as he returned his gaze to her. "Especially when he is wearing a toga."

Moore pressed another kiss to her mouth, a quick one, then he let her go, moving a good distance away and allowing Teddy plenty of room to come between them.

The younger man clenched his fists as he stood in front of her, facing Moore. "Are you all right, Grace?" he asked over his shoulder without turning to look at her.

Teddy was barely eighteen, but he was prepared to defend her against a man who topped his height by a good six inches and outweighed him by at least four stone. Grace laid a hand on his arm. "I am perfectly well, Teddy," she answered and looked at Moore over the younger man's shoulder. "He was just leaving."

Moore bowed to her. "I bid you good night," he said, still ignoring the young man who had come to her rescue. He turned away and started back toward the public assembly rooms, but then he paused and looked back at her over one shoulder. "You spoke of responsibility earlier," he said. "The Chinese say that if you save a man from death you are responsible for his life. We shall see each other again, Grace. I swear it."

She watched as he turned and strode away, the edge of his cloak flaring and twisting behind him in the breeze, its gold satin lining glimmering in the streetlight.

How appropriate that such a man should choose to be Mephistopheles at a Fancy Dress ball, she thought. She had saved his life with the best of intentions, but as Dylan Moore blended into the night shadows and disappeared, she wondered with foreboding if good intentions did indeed pave the road to hell.

Chapter 2

She was real. Dylan leaned back against the seat of his carriage and closed his eyes. During these past five years, he had almost come to believe that he had imagined her that night at the Palladium, that he had somehow conjured her out of the desperation in his soul, a muse to sit on his shoulder like a bewitching pixy, taunting him with nothing but a series of notes and the sweet promise of a symphony. She was real after all.

The moment he had seen her again, he had heard that same bit of music. If only he could remember those notes, hear them clearly enough to write them down, but though he tried, he could not bring them back. They were drowned out by the noise in his mind that made his head ache and the sound of traffic as his carriage made the slow crawl around Piccadilly Circus.

The music would not be lost, however, not this

time. He had found his muse, and with her, the music. Now he knew enough about her that it would be easy to locate her, and that was the only reason he had let her get away. He knew just how to find her again.

Grace, with those light green eyes and that tawny blond hair. A woman of extraordinary beauty and surprising passion. When he had pinned her against that wall and kissed her, she had recognized what was in his body, known what it meant, enjoyed it. So had he. No timid virgin, this muse of his. No, she was a woman who had known a lover's touch and savored it. If he made love to her, he could only imagine what music the sweet heat of her body would inspire. He intended to find a way to make that happen.

The carriage came to a halt in front of a gaming hell in Soho. It was one Dylan particularly favored, because, with its tinny pianoforte, pretty bawds, and crowds of men, it was noisy enough to drown out every other sound in his brain. It was also ethical enough not to weight the dice, mark the cards, or water the liquor. Most important of all, it was always open for business. At half past two in the morning, Dylan's evening had barely begun.

Luck favored him on this occasion, and he walked away from the baccarat tables six hours and two bottles of brandy later, richer by three hundred and seventeen pounds. Not that it would last, of course. Next time, he would lose it all and then some, but it never really mattered to him if he won or lost. Gambling was a distraction, and that was the important thing. These days, he lived for diversions and distractions, anything that would keep him from letting the whine in his head drive him mad.

It was just past nine o'clock in the morning when Dylan arrived at his own home in Portman Square, not an unusual time for him. Though it was not a large house, Dylan had amused himself by filling it with as many modern conveniences and comfortable luxuries as possible. Another diversion, for in truth, the only material thing that mattered to Dylan was his piano.

Though his body was tired, he was not home to seek his bed. He never slept well, and after the events of this evening, he knew any attempt to sleep would be futile. He left Roberts waiting out in front of the house with the carriage, for he intended only to bathe, shave, and change out of evening clothes, then depart again.

When his butler, Osgoode, opened the front door, Dylan had only taken one step inside the black-and-white tiled foyer before the servant said, "You have had a visitor, sir."

Dylan handed over his cloak, hat, and gloves. "When?"

"She came about two hours ago."

"She?" Though there were several women at present who might be inclined to call on him at such a scandalously early hour, he doubted that the only woman who piqued his interest at this moment was one of them. "Who was it?"

"A nun, sir. A Catholic nun."

Despite his headache, Dylan could not help laughing at that. "A nun coming to call on me at any time of day is unbelievable, but at seven o'clock in the morning, it is ridiculous," he said as he crossed the foyer to the stairs. "Does she expect to find contributors half-asleep and hope to collect more for her charities that way?"

"She did not come to collect for charity, sir," the butler called after him. "She came to deliver something to you."

"Oh, yes?" He threw the words carelessly over his shoulder as he climbed the stairs, uninterested. "Religious tracts, I suppose."

To his astonishment, the butler followed him up the stairs. "Begging your pardon, sir," he said, panting as he attempted to keep up with Dylan, whose long legs and impatience had given him the habit of taking stairs two at a time. "It is of far greater significance than that. I believe you should see for yourself. At once."

Dylan paused at the first floor, his hand on the polished rosewood cap of the wrought-iron stair rail as he turned to stare down at the servant who had halted several steps below him. This insistence was impertinent in the extreme, and Osgoode was never impertinent.

"Indeed?" Dylan murmured and started back down the stairs. "Your insistence makes me curious. What is it this nun has brought me?"

The butler waited until they were back down in the foyer before he answered. "It is a rather difficult thing to describe, but the nun called it a gift, sir. Although she also said it is something that has always belonged to you."

Riddles amused him. "You intrigue me, Osgoode. Bring it at once, then."

"Yes, sir."

The butler turned to go toward the back of the house, and Dylan crossed the wide foyer to open the pair of doors that led into the music room. He walked to the piano and pushed back the walnut lid to reveal the ivory keys beneath. It had been so long since he had even attempted to play a piece of music. Almost hesitantly, he placed his hand on the keys and pressed half a dozen of them in slow succession. That was it, he thought, a bit stunned. That was what he had heard from her.

He did not know why, when he looked at that woman, he heard these notes, or why there was a black void after them where a melody should be. He did not know why that woman seemed to bring him the only hint of music he had heard in five years. But there was one thing he did know. This time, he was not going to let her get away.

A slight cough broke into his thoughts, but Dylan did not glance up from the musical instrument before him. "Well, what is this gift a nun has brought me, Osgoode?" he asked as he played those notes again.

The butler did not answer, and Dylan looked up to find that the servant was not there. Instead, he saw a much smaller figure standing in the doorway. It was a little girl.

He straightened from the piano, staring at the child. Though not very familiar with children, he figured her to be about eight or nine years old. She was dressed in a blue-and-green plaid dress with a white collar and stockings, and there was a woolen bundle clutched in her arms. He knew he had never seen this child before in his life, but her long braids and big, round eyes were as black as his own. Dylan let out a curse worthy of a sailor.

The girl came into the room. "I don't think I want a father who swears."

Father? He swore again.

The child's black brows knitted in a dubious frown, making it clear to Dylan that he wasn't quite up to snuff in her opinion. "Since you are rich, am I going to have my own room?"

Dylan did not reply. Instead, he stepped around the girl and out of the music room to find his butler hovering nearby. "Osgoode, come with me."

The butler closed the doors of the music room, shutting the little girl inside, and followed his master across the foyer to the drawing room opposite. "Yes, sir?"

Dylan heard a squeaking sound, and he looked across the foyer to see that the doors to the music room were once again open. The child's face was peering at them from around one of the doors, her small fingers curled over the wooden edge. He closed the drawing room door to shut out her curious gaze, then turned to his butler. "Who in Hades is that?" he asked, jerking one thumb over his shoulder.

"I believe her name is Isabel, sir."

"I don't care about her name! I want to know what she is doing here. Have you lost your sense, man, to be accepting stray children brought to my door by nuns?"

His rising voice caused Osgoode to give him an apologetic look. "Sister Agnes said Isabel was your daughter, and the child would be living here with you from now on. She spoke as if it had all been arranged in advance."

"What? I have made no such arrangement."

"I tried to convince the good sister of that," Osgoode hastened to assure him, "knowing if it were true, you would have told me of Isabel's arrival. But the sister explained she had come all the way from St. Catherine's Orphanage in Metz to bring your daughter to you. Her ship returning her to the Continent was leaving within the hour and she had no time to wait—"

"I don't care if she joined the British Navy and was bound for the West Indies. I have never seen this child before, nor even heard of her, and you are correct that if I had made such an arrangement, I would have told you of it. Good God, what were you thinking? Any woman could dress up as a nun, wait until I am not at home, and drop her child here for me to care for. I would not be the first gentleman in such a circumstance."

"Isabel does look like you, sir."

"What does that have to do with anything?"

"I am sorry if I have given offense," the butler said, looking pained at the very idea, "but I did not know what else I could do. Sister Agnes refused to take the little girl away with her, nor would she wait until you returned. I could not shove such a little thing outside into the London street, could I, sir? To be at the mercy of all manner of ruffians and villains? Not your daughter."

"She is not mine!" Dylan roared. "Did this nun provide any proof of my paternity? Any proof at all?"

Osgoode gave one of those irritating little coughs butlers always use when they are about to impart news their masters do not wish to hear. "She left a letter and asked that it be given to you." He reached into his jacket pocket and pulled out a folded sheet of parchment. "I assume the proof is mentioned there."

Dylan took the letter from the servant's hand, broke the wax seal, and unfolded it. It was from the Mother Superior of the Order of St. Catherine, a convent and orphanage in Metz. The Reverend Mother stated that the child, Isabel, born in 1824, was the daughter of a French woman named Vivienne Moreau who had died of scarlet fever six weeks before. On her deathbed, Miss Moreau had sworn an oath to Mary, Holy Mother of God, that the father of her child was Dylan Moore, the English composer. Since the young woman was making her final confession to God, the Reverend Mother had added, she would not lie.

"Of course not," Dylan murmured at that sly line, thinking that nuns must be starting to cultivate a sense of humor, a twisted one at that.

He continued to read. Miss Moreau had also assured the Reverend Mother that Moore was a wealthy man who would take full responsibility for his child's upbringing and care. She had also provided enough money for passage to England so that Sister Agnes could deliver Isabel directly into his hands. That was all. There was no offered proof or connection to him whatsoever.

Dylan folded the letter and shoved it into his pocket, then turned away from Osgoode and began to pace, repeating the woman's name in his mind.

Vivienne Moreau. The name sparked no sense of recognition. He tried to think back nine years. Two years after Cambridge, and he'd been on the Continent, touring the European capitals to perform his piano pieces and conduct his symphonies. He'd been twenty-three then, cocky with the phenomenal success of his third symphony, randy as hell, and swimming in women. These days, he always provided himself with a

supply of French letters, but back then, he had
been too young and careless to bother with the
protection such sheaths afforded. He could have
fathered a child and never known about it. He
had probably fathered several.

On the other hand, he might never have known
this Vivienne at all. If he had, why would the
woman wait so long to claim his paternity for her
daughter? It could all be the fabrication of a
woman desperate to ensure her child's future. He
was famous throughout Britain and Europe.
Knowing his wealth and his success—and his
reputation, he was forced to admit—any woman
could decide to claim him as the father of her
child and demand his support.

The Reverend Mother had made no reference to
a place, date, or meeting. Nor had she mentioned
any objects or letters that would establish a connection. In fact, with the exception of her coloring, there was nothing to prove this child was his.
Without proof and with no memory of the
woman, he had no intention of taking on this obligation. He would arrange for the adoption of the
girl to some family in the country, but that was all.

His decision made, Dylan started out of the
drawing room. The moment Osgoode opened the
door for him, Dylan discovered that the child was
no longer peering around the door across the
foyer. Instead, both doors to the music room were
wide open, and she was seated at his immense
piano, playing an unusual piece he had never
heard before. The music flowed from the instrument beneath her fingers with an ease and ability
far beyond her years.

Dylan walked to the music room and paused in

the doorway, listening until she had played the final note. When she turned and looked at him as if waiting for his judgement on her ability, he gave it. "You play exceedingly well for a little girl."

"I play exceedingly well for an adult," Isabel answered, not one for false modesty. He almost wanted to smile. Impudent, this child.

"You speak excellent English," he told her.

"You are English. Mama thought I should learn to speak it well, since you are my father."

She fell silent, and the pause was awkward. She spoke of his paternity with absolute conviction. Unlike her, he was not so certain. Could a man ever be certain?

He glanced at the woolen bundle she had opened on the carpet and its contents—a pile of sheet music. "I do not recognize that piece you just played," he said, "but it is unique and quite beautiful. Who composed it?"

The child looked up at him, her big, black eyes unblinking. "I did."

For the wealthy and privileged, making a morning call meant arriving after three o'clock in the afternoon. Dylan, however, had never been a man thwarted in his objectives by something as trivial as convention, and there was a call he needed to make as soon as possible.

Leaving the pint-sized version of his own musical gifts to Osgoode because he didn't know what else to do with her, Dylan bathed, shaved, changed into fresh linen and a morning suit of clothes—black, as his perverse fashion sense always dictated—and departed the house, leaving instructions with the butler to put the child in the suite of rooms on the third floor that had once been a nursery, and to have the cook get her something to eat.

Just past eleven, he arrived at Enderby, the estate of Lord and Lady Hammond just outside London. The viscountess was at home, he was told, though she might not be receiving just now. This last bit of information was imparted with a tactful, but pointed, glance at the grandfather clock in the foyer and a gesture toward the calling card tray, but Dylan had no intention of simply leaving his card. He said he would wait to see if she would receive him.

The servant knew the composer was a friend of Lady Hammond and her brother, the Duke of Tremore, and that they considered Dylan to be almost a member of their family. He accepted Dylan's cloak, hat, and gloves, which he handed off to a maid before leading the other man up an immense staircase and into the drawing room.

The drawing room at Enderby was a wholly feminine affair. Its upholstery and draperies in delicate pastels of pink and celadon, its intricate white plasterwork and floral trompe l'oeil, proclaimed more loudly than any words printed in the scandal sheets that Lord Hammond was seldom in residence here, or anywhere else his wife happened to be. Viola's estrangement from her husband was in its eighth year now, and no one even discussed it anymore. Her brother had often commented that if he had his way, Hammond's head would be on a spike on London Bridge. Dylan had never admitted either to Anthony or Viola that he was well acquainted with the renegade viscount. Birds of a feather, and all that.

They'd shared tables and consumed a great deal of brandy at many gaming hells over the past few years. Viola was a topic they had never discussed.

Dylan flung himself into a striped brocade chair and pinched the bridge of his nose between his thumb and forefinger. The whine was loud this morning, so loud that it was like a white-hot pain through his skull. Headaches were a malady to which he had long ago become accustomed. He lowered his hand and reached into the inner pocket of his jacket for the small, blue vial that he always kept with him. Pulling out the cork, he took a swallow of laudanum, then recorked the bottle and put it back in his pocket. That would help until he could get some sleep.

One day, even the opiate would no longer work, nor would the women, the brandy, the hashish, or the gaming hells. A day would come when all the reckless things he did just for the hell of it would no longer divert his attention from the unwavering noise. That was when he would go insane.

Unless the music could save him. He had not written a single new piece in five long years. To keep down the gossip, he published an old composition every once in awhile, but that was all.

If he could only compose, his life would once again have purpose. That woman, Grace, held the key, though he did not know why. He had never believed in muses before. He had never needed one before. All Dylan knew was that he had to find her. More than that, he had to keep her with him until he could write the composition she had inspired. Always ambitious, he hoped for a symphony, although a sonata or concerto was a more likely possibility. At this point, anything he could manage to write would be a miracle.

Thoughts of music brought to mind the piece played by the child, Isabel. Quick and tricky, it would have been quite difficult for most people to play. If indeed the girl had composed it, then perhaps his blood did flow in her veins.

With that thought, Dylan raked back his hair with a sigh. There was no perhaps about it. He might not remember the mother, but the child was his. Though everything in him wanted to deny it, he knew the truth. He had known it from the moment he had heard her play, from the moment he had looked into her proud, imperious black eyes as she had claimed the piece her own. He felt a wave of pity for her. With him for a father, God help her. He was no sort of man for such a role. He could barely take care of himself.

He'd send her to relatives in the country until she was old enough for school. She certainly could not live with him.

"Dylan!"

The exclamation of greeting had him rising to his feet as Lady Hammond entered the room. Viola was as feminine as her surroundings, with her small, shapely figure, creamy complexion, honey-colored hair, and delicate features. Looking as lovely as sunrise in an apricot-colored morning gown, she held out her hands to greet him as he crossed the room to her.

"It is barely eleven o'clock," she said with a smile, followed at once by a pretty yawn. "Only from you, darling, would I accept a call at this ungodly hour."

She accepted the kisses he pressed to each of her cheeks with all the ease of their long acquaintance, then seated herself on the white chintz settee opposite the striped chair in which Dylan had been sitting when she'd entered the room. "What brings you here?" she asked.

"My apologies for the timing of my call," he answered, resuming his seat, "but I assure you that this is a matter of vital importance. You were one of the lady patronesses for that charity ball last evening, I believe."

"The one for London hospitals? I did not feel very well and was unable to be there, but yes, I was one of the patronesses. Did you attend?"

The question held a hint of surprise, for charity balls were not really in keeping with Dylan's idea of amusement. Though he did not often go to such events, he knew Viola always put him on the invitation lists because his famous name impelled any music lover or scandal-sheet reader to attend in the faint hope of meeting him, and thereby raised more money for whatever charity was involved.

"I did," he confirmed. "A whim, I suppose. If I do not occasionally appear at one of these things, rumors start to circulate that I've finally come a cropper. I came to see you because I want to know who that violinist was last evening."

"Violinist?" She laughed. "Only you, Dylan, would call at this hour to inquire about the musicians at a ball and call that important."

"I am interested in one musician in particular. She was one of four violins, costumed as a highwayman with a mask across her eyes."

"A woman?"

"Her name is Grace. How can I find her?"

"Heavens, I don't know," Viola cried in lively amusement. "What is this all about? A female violinist costumed as a highwayman. How intriguing! Did she play so beautifully that you want her for your next concert, or do you simply want her?"

An appealing idea, but he pushed it aside for the moment. "Neither," he lied and met Viola's laughing hazel eyes with a serious gaze of his own. "My dear friend, this is more important to me than you could possibly imagine."

Viola knew nothing of his affliction, but something of the desperation he felt must have shown in his countenance, for her amusement faded. "I could ask Miss Tate. She would know, I daresay."

Rising to her feet, the viscountess walked to the bellpull against the wall and gave the rope a tug. Within moments, a footman came running. "Stephens, please have Tate found at once, and send her to me."

It was about five minutes later that Viola's personal secretary entered the room.

The viscountess asked her to find out about the musicians from the ball the night before, and the secretary departed, returning moments later with a sheet of paper in her hand. "The octet was hired from the Musicians' Company of the City Livery, my lady," she said, handing the paper to Viola. "These are the names."

Viola dismissed Miss Tate and scanned the list. "Are you certain you went to my charity ball? All the musicians there last evening were men. The four violinists were Cecil Howard, Edward Finnes, William Fraser, and James Broderick."

"Viola, I met her. I spoke to her." *Kissed her*, he added to himself, for the memory of his muse was still vivid in his mind, the soft warmth of her skin, the feel of her body in his arms, the passion that had revealed itself the moment he had touched her. "She was dressed as a man, but she was very much a woman, believe me. I must find her."

Dylan looked at Viola, noticing the hint of concern in her expression at the vehemence of his last words. Given his deepening moodiness and increasingly volatile behavior during the past five years, he knew Viola had a tendency to worry about him far more than was necessary. "I am quite well," he told her. "I can assure you I have no need to conjure women in my imagination."

"Of course not!" Viola came to stand beside his chair and laid a gentle hand on his shoulder. "But I cannot help being concerned about you, about your—" She paused, trying to define what she meant.

"Eccentricities," he supplied, "might be a tactful way of putting it."

Her hand squeezed his shoulder. "Anthony and Daphne are worried about you as well. And Ian—"

"Ian?" Dylan laughed at the mention of his older brother as he rose to his feet. "Ian is far too busy gadding about the Continent to worry about me. He's at some congress in Venice at the moment, a diplomatic crisis of gargantuan proportions. Good thing he was the good boy and became an ambassador. The family doesn't need two black sheep."

He took the list of names from Viola's hand and

put it in his pocket, then he lifted her hand to his lips and kissed it. "Thank you, Viscountess. I owe you a debt of gratitude."

"But I have done so little."

"On the contrary." He let go of her hand and bowed, then started for the door. Though he could never explain it to her, Viola had just done more for him than she would ever know.

Chapter 3

The rain was pouring down as Grace lugged her orange basket across the new London Bridge. She spent her days selling oranges on the corner of Ludgate Hill and the Old Bailey for a penny apiece, and on cold, wet days like this, it was a hard job indeed. She was glad to be headed home.

The basket was nearly full, and that meant she still didn't have enough money this week to pay Mrs. Abbott. Because of last night's ball, she had been able to give her landlady half the three weeks' back rent she owed, and she had promised to pay the remainder on Friday, along with the full rent for next week. An empty promise at the moment, since she had no more than sixpence in her pocket.

Sixpence would cut no ice with Mrs. Abbott.

The landlady had only let her remain this long because, during the previous six months, she had paid every penny owed every week. She was also quiet, didn't entertain gentlemen in her room, and didn't complain. Mrs. Abbott's beneficence would not last beyond Friday, only two days away.

Grace had felt fear seeping into her mind all day, fear that had grown with each person who had passed her by today, for on a day like this people were more concerned with getting out of the wet than buying her oranges. Grace's dark mood was not helped by her lack of sleep the night before, since the ball had prevented her from getting more than two hours of that precious commodity.

As Grace turned onto St. Thomas Street toward her lodgings in Crucifix Lane, she wrapped her cloak more tightly around herself against the rain. Her room wasn't a very good one, for it was only a tiny garret on the edge of a rookery slum, but at least it was clean, respectable, and had good, strong locks. Most important, it was hers, at least for two more precious days.

She shuddered to think what would happen to her if she could not pay what she owed. Mrs. Abbott would turn her out, and she'd have no choice but to move to one of those horrid boarding-houses again, where women were crowded together like sardines in tins. She could pawn her violin, the only thing of value she had left, but that would not save her in the long run, since music was her most profitable form of income when she could get the work. That wasn't often, since she was not a member of the Musician's Livery.

She had none of the money her brother had given her when she had gone home last autumn. Her mother and father were dead, and James had been the only surviving member of her family who had even agreed to see her. The visit had not been a success. He had told her to leave Still-mouth and never return. She suspected he had given her the money only to get quit of her as quickly as possible.

Grace tightened her grip on her basket and quickened her steps against the wet weather and the deepening darkness. She did not want to sell her violin or move back into a sardine tin. The idea of prostitution made her sick with fear. Her only other option was to write to James and beg.

Or she could pose.

Grace had never had any modest illusions about her looks, nor any conceit. She was beautiful, and she accepted it, just as she accepted other irrefutable facts of life. Her beauty was what had first caused the great Cheval to fall in love with her, beauty that had impelled Etienne's friends and pupils to constantly ask if they could paint her. There must be artists in England who would be willing to do the same. She would have to pose nude, of course, since she required more than the usual payment of a free meal and indecent suggestions. To pay Mrs. Abbott, she needed cold, hard sterling.

She had never posed without her clothes for anyone but Etienne, and the idea of doing so made her uneasy, especially since she would have to deal with forceful male expectations that had nothing to do with art, but it was a far better choice than prostitution.

Her stomach rumbled with hunger. A few bits of tongue and ham from the ball last night and an orange from her basket this morning hadn't been enough to sustain her through an entire working day. She pressed her free hand to her midsection. As she traced the hard, unmistakable lines of her ribs beneath her wool cloak and gown, Grace realized that not many artists would want to paint nudes of her now. They liked their models with lush, generous curves, and she was so thin.

Grace resumed walking. Tomorrow, she would write to James, but it would take longer than two days for her to receive the money, even if he sent it. In the meantime, she would try to earn money posing. If that did not work, she would have to pawn her violin. If James refused to send her money, prostitution would be the only choice she had left.

To distract her mind from such grim circumstances, Grace thought instead of her cottage in the country. As she walked, she envisioned its thatched roof, fat dormers, and blue shutters. On dark, dreary days like this, when she was afraid to think of the harsh realities in her life now, it helped to believe finding such a place was possible. It had been so long since she'd had a home.

She and Etienne had traveled all over the Continent, back and forth to England, going anywhere his whims to paint had taken them. At first, their life together had seemed like such a grand, romantic adventure, and the first two years had been the happiest of her life. She could not pin down just when everything had started to go wrong, but sometime in their third year together, the dark side of her husband's temperament had begun to show itself. Etienne had become hell to live with, but God, how she had loved him. Far longer than she should have.

He was dead two years now, and it was very hard for Grace to remember what had prompted a respectable Cornish girl of seventeen to disgrace her family and run off with a Frenchman she'd known only a week. Looking back on it years after the love had died, the fact that Cheval had been captivated by the color of her eyes didn't seem quite so romantic any more.

It was dark by the time Grace turned into Crucifix Lane. As she walked toward her lodging house halfway down the block, she noticed the luxurious town coach nearby, but she was too preoccupied with her own thoughts to wonder what such a vehicle was doing in her neighborhood. She paused before the front door of her lodgings, reluctant to go in and face the inevitable confrontation with her landlady, but she was already soaking, it was cold, and she couldn't afford to catch a chill. Grace gave a resigned sigh and pulled her door key out of her pocket.

A hand touched her shoulder. Startled, she jumped with a cry of alarm as the key slipped from her fingers. It hit the cobblestones with a clink as she turned around to find herself face-to-face with Dylan Moore.

"You!" she cried, not knowing if it was panic at his sudden appearance that surged through her, or relief that he wasn't some thug bent on stealing her precious oranges. "What are you doing here?"

"I came to see you, of course. What else would I be doing in Bermondsey?"

Grace stared at him as the rain poured over them both, as the wind whipped at the edges of his cloak and hers, and she remembered his words that they would meet again. She tightened her grip on the handle of her basket, dismayed by how quickly his prediction had come true. "How did you find me?"

"Your friend Teddy is a member of the Musician's Livery." Moore bent to retrieve her key from where it had landed beside her feet. Key in hand, he straightened again. "The fellow did not wish to tell me anything about you, but he changed his mind when he saw the shine on a sovereign. His heroic attempts to protect you wilted in an instant, and he gave me the direction of your lodgings."

Grace was not surprised. After all, Teddy was as poor as she. "You paid him a quid to find me? Whatever for?"

Instead of answering, he held out the latch key to her and said, "Might we continue this discussion indoors, where it is warm and dry?"

She did not move, and he went on, "I have a business proposal to discuss with you."

A business proposal from a man. She knew what *that* meant.

He heard her sound of derision. "I only want you to listen to what I have to say," he told her.

"Listening?" she countered. "Is that what the fashionable people are calling it these days?"

A smile curved his mouth at that question. "I simply want to *talk* with you. I will pay you for your time." He took in her worn wool cloak and orange basket and added, "You seem to be in need of the funds."

"You are going to pay me just for listening?" she repeated with skepticism, remembering the night before. Talking with her was not the only thing he wanted to do.

"Just for listening. I give you my word." He shoved a wet strand of hair out of his face and glanced at the shabbiness around him. "A fiver would go a long way in this neighborhood."

That was an unarguable point, and it seemed like an answer to her prayers. Five pounds would pay all that she owed her landlady and give her enough extra for some decent food. Besides, the cold wind was slicing through her wet clothes, and her teeth were beginning to chatter. She capitulated. "Very well," she agreed and pushed the key into the lock.

Moore followed her into the foyer of the lodging house and closed the door behind them as she started toward the stairs. Over her shoulder, she whispered, "I shall give you fifteen minutes."

He laughed out loud, and she turned around, pressing her hand to his mouth in a frantic effort to quiet him. "Hush," she said with an apprehensive glance down the corridor that led to Mrs. Abbott's drawing room.

"I'm not sure fifteen minutes is worth five pounds," he murmured against her palm, his laughter still evident in the black eyes that looked into hers over the hand against his mouth.

His voice made the idea of listening to his offer sound illicit in itself, and his lips were warm against her skin. She jerked her hand back, then turned it palm-up with a pointed look at him.

He pulled a flat money purse of black leather from a pocket inside his cloak, but before he could open it, they were interrupted.

"Evening, missus."

Grace grimaced at the vinegar-voiced greeting and turned around as the short, steel-haired land-lady emerged from the corridor.

Mrs. Abbott glanced at Dylan, who returned her scrutiny with careless amusement. She took a long, shrewd look at the money purse in his hand, then she ran her gaze up and down his tall form, studying his expensive, well-cut clothes and finely tooled boots, and she did not seem to mind that he was dripping water all over her floor.

After a moment, she returned her attention to Grace, and when she spoke, her voice was still briskly businesslike, but there was a hint of con-ciliation in it as well. "You know the rules, ma'am. No gentlemen in the rooms. And with the money you still owe me, plus this week's lodgings yet to pay, I can't be making an exception for you, can I, now?"

Even as she asked the question, Mrs. Abbott slid Dylan a sly glance. Grace opened her mouth to speak, but before she could do so, Moore was pulling out a five-pound note.

"I fully comprehend your dilemma, my good woman," he said, holding out the money to her. "This will overcome all your objections, I imagine."

Grace watched in dismay as Mrs. Abbott snatched the fiver Moore had promised her from his hand before she could say a word of protest.

"Indeed it does, sir," the landlady assured him, her manner becoming solicitous.

"No, wait!" Grace cried, her heart sinking. "It is not at all what you think. This man is not—"

"Good," Dylan cut her off as he spoke to the landlady and tucked his money purse back inside his cloak. "This lady's debt to you is now discharged, and her rent paid through the week. You may keep the rest for yourself, provided I am allowed to come and go from here as I please."

Grace made a sound of outrage. She was ignored as Dylan and Mrs. Abbott exchanged glances. "We understand each other, do we not?" he asked the landlady.

"Yes, indeed. Would you be needing anything in the morning, sir? Hot water, of course, and tea. Would you care for breakfast? I can bring up hot, buttered toast. Bacon and kidneys, too, if you like."

Dylan glanced at Grace, casting a look over her form. He clearly found her in need of feeding, for he turned back to Mrs. Abbott. "Nothing for me, but you may bring a full breakfast for her tomorrow, if you would. Whatever she wants." He smiled at the woman. "I like to make her happy."

Mrs. Abbott smiled back. "I understand, sir."

"Excellent," Dylan said. "Now leave us."

The smirk on the landlady's face remained as she curtsied, and Grace burned with humiliation. "Now look what you have done!" she cried the moment the landlady was out of sight, wanting to smash an orange over his head.

"I paid her because it was expedient. Nothing more. Why do you care what she thinks?"

"Because now she'll be thinking I'm available

for any man she wants to send to my room,"
Grace shot back, nauseated by the thought. "As
long as she gets a share of it."

"No, she won't. Not now."

"Why? Because you paid her three pounds
more than I owed her so that you may come and
go as you please? You had no right to do that, and
I still expect to be paid that other three pounds."

He made a sound of impatience. "Which room
is yours? I will not stay down here and have your
salacious landlady listening to our conversation."

"If she is salacious, that is your fault. Thanks to
you, she thinks I am a prostitute!"

"No, she thinks you are a kept woman."

Grace gave a humorless laugh. "And there is a
difference?"

"Most certainly. Kept women are more expensive. They are also exclusive. Since you are being
kept by me, you are safe from any other gentlemen callers your landlady might send your way,
for the time being at least. Give me your key."

He was right, of course. Grace handed over her
key. "Top floor. And I am not being kept by you.
Nor shall I be."

Moore did not reply. He ascended the stairs
with her in tow until they reached her tiny room
at the top. He unlocked the door, and both of
them stepped inside her room. He closed the
door behind them and turned the bolt, then
handed the key back to her. "There, now we may
have some privacy."

Since that was just what made her wary, she did
not take her gaze from him as she set her basket on
the wooden seat of the room's only chair, a ladder-
back, ramshackle piece with peeling paint beside

the door. She hung her cloak from a hook on the wall and put her key in the pocket of her skirt.

He removed his own wet cloak and tossed it over her orange basket. He removed his gloves as he took a look at his surroundings, at the beamed attic ceiling above his head and the spare, dilapidated furnishings, including the narrow bed under the window, with its rusting iron frame and thin straw mattress.

He dropped the gloves on top of his cloak, then removed his coat. He tugged at his cravat, untying it, and reached for the top button of his shirt.

"You presume I have accepted your illicit proposal, even before you make it!" Grace cried. "I never had any intention of accepting it. Get out."

"I presume nothing," he answered, ignoring her order to leave. "Grace, you have no idea how irritating a high collar and cravat can be when they are soaking wet. Since I paid for this time, I intend to be comfortable during it. That is all." He unfastened the other two buttons of his shirt, smoothed his waistcoat, and straightened his cuffs. "Perhaps we should sit down?"

"When my bed is the only seat in the room? I think not."

He shrugged and stepped around her. "Stand if you like, but I have had no sleep for two days, and I intend to sit down."

Tense and wary, she watched as he suited the action to the word, and her growing apprehension must have shown in her face, for something almost gentle came into his handsome, ravaged countenance. "Grace, I gave you my word."

She flattened back against the door. "Get to the point."

He settled back on the bed, resting his weight on his arms, and he said the last thing in the world she would have expected. "What do you know about being a governess?"

Chapter 4

Grace stared at the disreputable man sprawled back on her bed. "A governess?"

"Yes, to my daughter." He gave her a wry look. "You seem surprised. Expecting an offer of a different sort, were you?"

"If I did, you could hardly blame me for it. Do you really have a daughter?"

"Yes. Isabel is eight years old."

"But—" She broke off and gave a half-laugh. It was so ludicrous, especially given what offer she had been expecting. "You know nothing about me, yet you would entrust me with your child?"

"You saved my life, so the least I can do is rescue you from destitution. The musicians I interviewed who knew you all gave the highest opinion of your character."

"But how do you know I am qualified to be a governess?"

"I know you play the violin, so you probably had music tutors. You read sheet music. You told me that you saw me conduct at a concert in Salzburg. Though you have worked as a charwoman and now sell oranges on the street, I doubt your circumstances have always been as dire as they are now. I can discern from the way you move, the way you walk, and the way you talk that you are a woman of the gentry. From Cornwall. I can hear it in your accent. You had a governess yourself as a girl, I should think."

Grace listened to these conclusions about herself, all of which were true. It was a bit disconcerting to know that a man, especially this man, should be able to draw such an accurate assessment of her. "I did not know I was so easy to read."

"Not that easy. I am a man who pays attention."

"To women. Yes, I am aware of that." She could not help being curious about his situation with his daughter, and she asked, "Does it not usually fall to a child's mother to hire a governess?"

His expression did not change. "Isabel's mother is dead."

"Surely you could find a qualified governess amongst your acquaintance, or hire one from an agency. Why offer the post to me?"

"Because I want to."

"I daresay that is always a good enough reason for you."

That made him smile. It was a smile of wicked humor and thoroughly dishonorable intentions.

Grace had seen the world; she'd been married to a passionate, worldly man. She knew everything there was to know about physical love between a man and a woman, but for some inexplicable reason, Dylan Moore's smile made her blush. *Heavens,* she thought with dismay, *I haven't blushed since I was a green girl.* "Governess, my eye," she muttered.

He moved, stretching out along the length of her bed, resting his weight on his elbow and his cheek in his hand. With that disheveled hair all around his shoulders and the evening shadow of a beard on his face, with those enigmatic dark eyes and their opulent black lashes, with that smile, he looked every bit the hedonistic devil described in the scandal sheets. And he knew it. The man had no shame.

"Grace." He said her name soft and low, as if testing the sound of it on his tongue. It was as lush as a caress. She felt her blush deepening, her tenseness easing into something else. As unexpectedly as last night, heat stirred inside her.

"I am a virtuous woman," she blurted out without thinking.

He didn't blink an eye. "I never said you weren't."

Grace folded her arms and took a deep, steadying breath, wanting to bite her tongue off for saying what should never have to be said. "If I agree to be your daughter's governess, what wages are you offering?"

That smile vanished, much to her relief. He sat up straight on the bed. "Before we discuss it, I must tell you there is a catch. In addition to your duties with Isabel, there is something else I demand in return for what I will pay you."

Her reply was a cynical twist of her lips. "Mm—hmm."

"This is only employment at will from my point of view. Meaning I can sack you if I wish, but you will not be free to resign."

Her eyes narrowed. "That is not employment. It is slavery."

She watched as he glanced around her little attic room. Observant devil that he was, Grace knew that nothing about its shabbiness would escape his notice. He was seeing the two worn dresses hanging from hooks on the wall—the only two dresses she owned other than the ugly green plaid on her back. He was noticing the small amount of coal left in the bin beside the fireplace. He was feeling the cheapness of the mattress and threadbare blanket beneath his body, remembering her inability to pay her rent.

He was pointing out the obvious without saying a word, but no matter what he was offering, she would not agree to be dependent upon his whim for her survival. "I will not consent to anything of the sort without a time limitation."

"Very well." He looked at her for a moment, then he said, "One year. At that time, I shall pay you the full wages I owe you, whatever we agree them to be. You get nothing until then, for I will not have you get a month or two of sterling in your pocket and leave me."

"Why? Are . . . umm . . . governesses in such short supply these days?"

"Suffice it to say, when I am paying for things, I like them my way."

Grace didn't want to dance around the issue. If he was making an honorable offer, she would accept it. If not, she would write to her brother. "What do you believe you will be paying for?"

"A governess." When she did not reply, he went on, "Since you seem to wish for plain speaking, I will confess I came here with a different offer in mind, but you are clearly not amenable to the idea of being my mistress." His smile became winsome, meant to sweeten. "I give you fair warning that I am going to attempt to change your mind on that score, but in the interim, I am offering you a post as governess to my daughter instead."

"I see. At least you are honest. If you make these attempts to change my mind, as you put it, and I continue to refuse you, what then?"

"Then you refuse." His dark eyes narrowed a bit. "I won't force you, if that is what you fear."

He certainly hadn't needed to force her last night, she thought with chagrin. "Why me?" she asked. "A man like you has no trouble finding a mistress."

"You are not just any woman. I told you last night, I hear music with you."

"You were just saying that," she scoffed. "You did not mean it."

"But I did mean it. When I am with you, I hear music. You inspire me."

Oh, God. She closed her eyes and saw herself on a Cornish hillside with another man, a man who had wanted the very same thing of her. A man with blue eyes, not black, looking at her over the top of a canvas on a cliff above the sea.

My muse, Etienne had always called her. Etienne Cheval, the greatest painter of his day, who had believed that a commonplace English girl from an unremarkable country family was the wellspring from which he could draw all his inspiration and brilliance, who had blamed her and broken her heart when it had not worked.

"You need not look as if I am leading you to your execution," Moore said, breaking into her thoughts.

His dry comment caused Grace to open her eyes. Etienne's image disappeared at once, vanquished by the much more dominating presence of the man right in front of her, a man dark and ravaged, and very much alive.

"Why does Dylan Moore need a muse?" she asked.

"Why do you loathe the idea of being one?"

Grace looked at him, helpless to explain. She felt history repeating itself, and she did not know why. She was nothing like what an artist's lover ought to be. She was practical, serious-minded, moral, and not exciting at all. It was so strange, she thought, that not one but two men of genius could see the same thing in her, something that captivated their imaginations and inspired them to create works of art. She did not understand it, for she was so very ordinary.

Muses, she knew, did not exist. Her dismay vanished, leaving only a deep, bruising tiredness. "It doesn't work, you know."

Something painful flickered in his expression, but in less than a second, his face was once again unreadable. "Yes, it does. It has to."

Grace sighed. A blocked and frustrated artist in a dry spell who wanted an easy way out of the drought. Though this was an ideal opportunity to escape the dire straits in which she found herself, accepting Moore's offer would be like wrapping herself in chains. She wanted nothing to do with artists and their art. "Thank you for your offer, Mr. Moore," she said, shaking her head, "but I must refuse. I cannot give you what you want. You promised me five pounds for listening, two of which you gave my landlady on my behalf. I would like the other three now, please. Then I would like you to leave."

She expected him to refuse to pay her, or sulk and argue and ask tiresome questions about her reasons, but he did none of those things. He sat there and studied her, his deep-set eyes unwavering in their scrutiny. Grace waited, but the seconds came and went and still he did not stir.

"I would like you to go," she said, breaking the uncomfortable silence.

"Slate blue shutters," he murmured, his intense gaze still on her face. "And lots of roses."

Those words hit her like a punch to the stomach. Grace sucked in a deep breath at having her deepest desire quoted back to her. Damn the man.

"A cottage in the country with a garden," he went on. "If that is what you want, Grace, I can provide it."

Of course he could. She should have known a devil would tempt her with what she wanted most.

"I happen to have just such a cottage," he went on. "The shutters are not blue, I'm afraid, but that can be remedied. And, if memory serves, there are plenty of roses in the garden."

She pressed a hand to her forehead, thinking of her disgraced family and Dylan Moore's fame. If she lived with him, even as a governess, people would still think the worst. On the other hand, her reputation was beyond amendment, and what did it matter? What was left of her family had already rejected her. It would be stupid to refuse an offer such as this. So, so stupid. She felt herself beginning to crack. "Please tell me this cottage is not in Cornwall," she said.

"No, Devonshire, actually," he answered. "It sits on an estate I own there. It is yours if you work for me for the coming twelve months. The same terms still apply, however. You cannot leave unless I tell you to go, and I will not pay you until the end of that year. Then I will deed the cottage to you and pay you all wages I owe you."

"What are these wages?"

"Is one thousand pounds acceptable to you?"

"A thousand pounds? As one year's wages for a governess? You must be—"

"Mad?" He moved unexpectedly, straightening and rising from the bed in the taut, fluid motions of a predatory animal. As he crossed her tiny room, Grace took an involuntary step back, and her heel hit the door behind her.

"I am not mad. Not yet, at least." He halted with scarcely a foot of space between them. "I want you, I have made no secret of it. I hope with time to make you feel the same and become my mistress in truth for as long as it is agreeable to us both. If that happens, I will give you far more lavish gifts than a mere cottage and a thousand pounds, believe me. If you choose to be nothing more than a governess for the coming year, then that is your choice. Be aware that I would never make an offer as generous as this to any other woman to be merely a governess. This is for you alone."

"Why me?" she cried out in frustration, asking

the question not only of him but of the great
Cheval as well. Etienne, who could not answer
her, who had never been able to answer her.

Moore, one of the most brilliant composers
who had ever lived, could not answer it either. A
hint of her own bafflement crossed his face. "I
don't know," he said in a hoarse whisper. "I cannot explain it."

Grace stepped around him and crossed the
room to put more distance between them. How
could she accept? How could she not?

She turned to look at him over her shoulder.
The fine linen sleeves of his white shirt and the
gold buttons on his black-and-beige striped waistcoat looked so expensive and elegant against the
pitted, dingy wall of her flat. He expected her to
do what all his money and position and talent
could not do. Take away his desperation. She
would fail, and he would hate her for it, but that
could not be helped. He had made himself her
only honorable chance to have a life beyond the
edge of destitution, and she was going to take it.
"I accept."

"It is done, then." He walked around her to the
door, fastening shirt buttons as he went. He
pulled his cravat from the chair, turned up his
high collar, and wrapped the damp strip of silk
around his neck.

"What sort of education do you require for your
daughter?" she asked as he moved to the tin-
framed mirror on her wall near the door. He knotted his cravat, bending to see his hands reflected
in the distorted glass as she went on, "I can in-
struct her in violin, but as I am not accomplished
with piano, I fear—"

His abrupt shout of laughter stopped her. He straightened, giving her a wry glance as he pulled his coat from the chair and shrugged into it. "Isabel is a better composer than I was at her age. She plays the piano exquisitely. Violin instruction would not go amiss, I daresay." He paused, frowning in thought. "Unless she already knows how to play the violin. Given her talents, that would not surprise me."

"You don't know if your own daughter plays the violin?"

"No." He did not elaborate. "I leave it to you to select an appropriate curriculum for her. I would imagine you know more about what a little girl needs in the way of an education than I do." He pulled his card from the pocket of his coat and tossed it on top of the oranges in her basket. "I hope you can begin your duties tomorrow," he went on, placing three one-pound notes in her basket as well. "I will expect you at eleven o'clock."

"This is so absurd!" she cried, still unable to quite take it all in. "Paid like a mistress to do a governess's job."

"Absurdity is part of life, is it not?" He slung his cloak around his shoulders and reached for the handle of the door.

She watched him open it and walk out. "What if you find me a horrible governess?" she called after him.

"It does not matter in the least."

"So being your daughter's governess is merely a pretext to install me in your household? It really has nothing to do with her, does it?"

He stopped and turned to look at her in the

doorway. "No." With that, he departed and closed the door behind him.

Grace stared at the door after he had gone, bemused. Her feelings about what she had just done were bewildering and contradictory. On the one hand, she was so relieved to have employment, food, and a secure roof over her head that it made her weak, and the notion that a home of her own and a thousand pounds awaited her at the end of one short year was almost too good to be true. It seemed unreal.

She was not worried about being a governess. Having been the oldest of seven, she knew enough about looking after children to deal well with one eight-year-old. It was her employer who worried her. Dylan Moore was a man obsessed with his music and in the throes of thwarted creativity. He was willful, arrogant, and as changeable as an English spring day. She glanced at the bed, imagining him as he had been only moments ago, his long, powerful body sprawled across the mattress, studying her with those black eyes, smiling. He was darkly seductive to women.

I hear music when I look at you. You are my muse.

He believed that, and she knew what such a notion meant to an artist. She stood there for a long time, thinking of Faust, who had sold his soul to a devil in order to gain his greatest desire. In accepting Moore's offer, she could not help but wonder if she had just made the same mistake.

The rain had softened from a downpour to a light drizzle by the time Dylan's carriage pulled into Portman Square. Once inside the house, he handed Osgoode his cloak and informed the butler that his daughter's governess would be arriving at eleven o'clock the following morning. He then ordered a bottle of brandy sent up to his room and asked about Isabel.

"One of the maids put her to bed over two hours ago, sir."

"Excellent," Dylan answered and started upstairs, relieved. He might be the child's father, but he had no idea what to do with her, and he was glad he wouldn't be the one to raise her. Most parents in his general acquaintance did not raise their own children. They put them in the care of nannies, tutors, and governesses, then sent them off to school, just as he intended to do. After his mother's death when he was a boy, he had seen his own father for only a few minutes a day. That had become two hours twice a year after he'd been sent up to Harrow. If he had to be a father, he intended to be a typical one.

By the time Dylan reached the second floor and started down the corridor to his room, Phelps had already been informed of his arrival. Dylan found his valet waiting by the door of the bedchamber, watching his approach in horror. Before he was halfway down the corridor, the poor fellow was lamenting the wet clothes and hair that would surely bring his master down with the ague.

Dylan walked past Phelps into his bedchamber, ignoring the valet's well-meant suggestion that he really should begin wearing a hat and carrying an umbrella when he went out. The servant assisted him out of his damp clothing, and since it was only ten o'clock, the valet suggested several evening suits from which he might choose, but Dylan stopped him.

"The weather's too foul tonight," he said. "I shall stay in."

He changed into a pair of Cossack trousers, then slipped on his favorite dressing gown, a garment of heavy black silk embroidered with red dragons. When he left his bedchamber, he encountered a footman coming along the corridor with his brandy. He plucked the bottle from the tray as he passed the servant and went downstairs to the music room, where he walked straight to the piano.

He lit a lamp and sat down on the bench, staring at the single sheet of composition paper that rested on the music stand, a sheet that contained scarcely a dozen notes. Because of Grace, there would be more to follow, though he could not explain what made him so certain of it.

Dylan took another swallow of brandy and rested his free hand on the keyboard. Closing his eyes, he played the notes several times, striving to shut out all the other noise as he focused his concentration on the woman and the music that invaded his imagination whenever she was near.

"Why do you play those same notes over and over?"

He opened his eyes and turned his head to see Isabel stretched out in the brown velvet chaise longue that rested in a darkened corner of the room. Her white nightgown gleamed in the shadows. When she scooted forward on the chaise longue and into the light of the lamp on the piano, he could see that firmly ensconced in one side of her mouth was a peppermint stick. He didn't even know there were comfits in the house.

He frowned at her. "I thought you were in bed."

She frowned right back at him, unintimidated. "Your valet woke me up," she said in martyred accents as she brandished her candy stick at him. "I can't very well sleep when he is wailing on and on about your soaking wet hair right across the corridor from my room, can I?"

"What are you doing in a room across from mine? Your room is in the nursery, on the third floor."

"I moved. There isn't any furniture on the third floor."

"The servants should have brought furniture from another bedroom."

"I told them not to bother with all that. I don't like the nursery. It's too hot up there."

Dylan wanted to laugh at the lie, but he guessed that a father was expected to look stern about things like that. "It is not hot this evening. It is, in fact, quite cool outside."

"Maybe so," she answered, "but in a few months, it won't be, and it would be silly to sleep all the way up there now and have to move later, don't you think?"

If Isabel had already managed to persuade the staff to let her sleep in a room that was not part of the old nursery, Dylan suspected she was capable of far more troublesome antics down the road. Grace would have her hands full. "I've hired you a governess."

"Ugh." She made a face and chomped down on her candy stick. "How horrid!" she said around the bits of peppermint in her mouth. "Can't I have a majordomo instead?"

"Only princesses have majordomos. Other little girls have nannies and governesses."

"I know, and it's so rum. I'd rather be a princess. Then I could order everyone about. Even you." She brandished the stubby end of her peppermint stick at him. "Give me a proper bedroom, or I shall lock you in the Tower," she intoned with as much majesty as an eight-year-old could summon. He grinned, and she stuck her candy stick back in her mouth. "Besides," she went on in an ordinary voice, "governesses are awful. They are dowdy and dull. They are always making you do sums, and they twitter and fuss when you don't mend your stockings."

Dylan took her word on that. "This governess isn't anything like that."

"Is she pretty?"

Pretty? Hardly the word for a woman who had haunted his dreams for five years. "I suppose she's pretty," he answered as he lifted the bottle of brandy to his lips.

"Is she your mistress?"

He choked. "For God's sake, how do you even know about such things? Never mind," he added at once, realizing that this was hardly a topic one discussed with a child. "I think you should go to bed."

"You can tell me." She rested her chin on her cotton-covered knees, sucking on her candy and eying him with a wise sort of skepticism. He didn't want to know how she had acquired it.

"She is not my mistress," he answered, telling himself his answer was the truth, at this moment anyway. "And we are not going to talk about this again. Go to bed."

She slid off the chaise longue, but instead of going toward the door, she moved to stand beside him. "I'm not tired. Can't I play piano with you? We could do duets."

He shook his head, but she persisted. "I would keep up, I swear I would, Papa."

Papa. He did not even like the word. It implied affection that she could not possibly feel for him. It implied responsibility he did not want. He should tell her not to call him that.

She put a hand on the keyboard and pressed a few notes at random. "I made that up just now," she said. "I like it. I think it's a serenade, don't you?"

"Perhaps."

"You have an estate in the country, don't you?" she asked and played a few more notes. "Fruit orchards. Pears and apples. It's in a place called Devonshire. I read about it." She stopped and met his gaze. "I've read all about you."

Dylan didn't know what to say. Most of what was printed about him wasn't what a child should be reading. Feeling suddenly awkward, he looked away from her gaze, staring down at the small hand on the piano. He watched as she put her other hand on the keyboard and began to improvise on her little serenade.

"Can we go there some time, Papa?" she asked. "I've never been to the country."

"Isabel—"

"It would be nice to go to the country and have a pony."

There was a mournful note in her voice, and when he looked over at her, her eyes were so hopeful, so wistful.

Without thinking, he leaned close to her and gave her a kiss on her temple, the same careless gesture of affection he would give any female with inconvenient expectations. "I have work to do, and you need to go to sleep. We'll talk about ponies some other time."

Reluctantly, Isabel walked away from the piano. "If I don't like my governess, can I sack her?"

"No."

She paused by the doors. "Would you sack her for me?"

He told her the truth. "No."

"Mistress." She nodded, looking far too wise for an eight-year-old. "Just what I thought."

With that, she departed, and Dylan watched her go, feeling chagrined by the child's assumption, though he could not find fault with it. It would be the truth if he had his way.

It was disconcerting to hear a little girl talk about such things, and he doubted they were even supposed to understand the concept of mistresses. But then, what did he know about little girls?

Nothing, he answered his own question. All the more reason for her to go to school when the year was over. It was for the best. If she were not so gifted, he would ship her to relatives as he had originally intended, but her musical ability should be nurtured. Her talent warranted a music conservatory in Germany or Italy.

I've read all about you.

Isabel's words stirred something inside him, a sense of disquiet at what she must have read. He was the man that he was. He hardly needed to apologize for it, and he ruthlessly shoved any sense of disquiet aside.

His plan was all for the best. During the coming year, Isabel would have Grace to look after her, he would have Grace with him, and Grace would gain for herself a secure future. Dylan finished off the brandy, telling himself it was the perfect solution for all of them.

Chapter 5

When Grace arrived at Dylan Moore's home the following day, she did not have any idea what to expect, but knowing what she did about the owner of the house, she concluded that nothing about her new situation could surprise her. In that, she was mistaken.

"Are you my father's mistress?"

The abrupt question rang down to the foyer from overhead, interrupting the butler's introduction of Grace to the group of servants gathered around her. All were silent as Grace tilted back her head to look up at the child leaning over the wrought-iron stair rail above her. No introduction was needed here.

Isabel had the same dark eyes as her father, the same willful jaw line, and, obviously, the same ability to speak in a forthright fashion when necessary. She stood on her tiptoes, her braids hanging down, the painted blue-and-white sky of the dome behind her head a sharp contrast to her black hair.

Grace was not a woman easily shocked, but such a question from a little girl was rather shocking. She lowered her gaze to the impassive face of the butler, Osgoode. She cast a look around her at the various members of the household. No one said a word. The perfect servants who knew their place, all of them were now behaving as if they were part of the wallpaper. She did not know if they had formed the same opinion of her as Isabel, but Grace knew she would have to dispel such notions by her behavior, not her words.

"Osgoode?" She looked at the butler, then at the small valise near her feet.

He took the hint at once and signaled for a footman to take her valise upstairs. The younger man obeyed, and the butler returned his attention to her. "The master wishes to see you this afternoon at four o'clock," he told her with a bow. He left the foyer, with the rotund little housekeeper, Mrs. Ellis, right behind him. The maids and remaining footmen also dispersed, leaving Grace alone with her new pupil.

She looked back up at the child hanging over the rail. "I am Mrs. Cheval," she said. "You must be Miss Isabel Moore." She paused, then added, "But perhaps I am mistaken. I was told by her father that Isabel was a young lady, and young ladies do not ask indiscreet questions."

The child straightened away from the rail and started down the stairs. "The only questions that aren't indiscreet are about the weather, the roads, or people's health." At the bottom of the stairs, she added, "It's the indiscreet questions that help you find out things."

There was enough truth in the child's words that Grace felt a smile tug at her mouth.

Isabel came to a halt in front of her, tilting her head back. "Are you going to give me an answer?"

"I certainly am not. People of good breeding do not answer such questions as that."

"My father answered it. He said you're not, but I'm not sure I believe him."

"Don't you believe your father when he tells you things?"

Isabel shrugged. "Adults lie," she answered in a matter-of-fact way that was oddly pathetic. "I have to find out if my father is the sort to tell lies." She paused, and her eyes narrowed in an almost accusing stare. "You might tell lies, too."

Grace did not know what to make of the child's statements and questions, but as she looked into Isabel's face, she realized one thing. Despite the cynicism of her words and her worldly-wise manner, this little girl was very apprehensive about her new governess. "I don't tell lies."

"We'll see," Isabel answered with skepticism. "If you are his mistress, I'll find out soon enough."

"This is not an appropriate topic for discussion, and I believe you know that already. Also, a matter of that sort is your father's own business."

Something hard crossed Isabel's face, something that should not have been on the face of a little girl. "You're wrong!" she cried out with such vehemence that Grace was startled. "It's my business, too. I'm not letting this sort of thing happen anymore."

So that was it. Mistresses coming and going. Grace felt a wave of compassion for the child, who had a rake for a father, no mother at all, and clearly no upbringing. Looking directly into her eyes, Grace said, "It will not happen because of me."

"Humph," was the child's only reply, making short shrift of Grace's assurances.

Changing the girl's opinion would take time, and she made no further attempt to change it now. "I should like to see the nursery," she said. "Will you show it to me, please?"

Isabel's jaw set and she crossed her arms. "You might as well know I don't want a governess."

"Want one or no," Grace answered cheerfully, "you have one."

The child turned away and started for the stairs. "If that's really so, it won't be for long. You won't stick it. They never do."

Grace only intended to stick it for one year. "They?" she echoed as she and Isabel started up the stairs. "How many governesses have you had?"

Isabel paused, and Grace stopped beside her. The child counted silently on her fingers, then looked up at her and smiled. It was a wicked smile, just like that of the man who had sired her. "You're the thirteenth. Lucky you."

Heavens, Grace thought, *the acorn and the oak. What have I gotten myself into?*

Sleep was a precious and unpredictable commodity for Dylan. Achieving it usually required a bit of assistance. Last night, even though he had gone two days without any rest and downed nearly a bottle of brandy, he had been unable to quiet his mind enough to lay his head down. Even by sunrise, he had not been able to sleep without the help of a pipe of hashish and a few sips of laudanum.

When he awoke, Dylan paid the price for all that help. For some idiotic reason, Phelps decided to open the draperies, and the clatter of rings sliding across a wooden rod woke him. He opened his eyes, and the bright sunlight sent shafts of pain through his skull like needles. Today just had to be one of the rare days when England had bright, brilliant sunshine.

Dylan turned onto his stomach with a groan. "Christ, man, what are you doing?" he mumbled as he covered the side of his face with a pillow. "Shut those damned things."

"Good day, sir," his valet greeted him with the irritating cheerfulness of those who knew nothing of overindulgence or its consequences. "Would you care for breakfast?"

Breakfast? Dylan's tongue felt glued to the top of his mouth, his body felt drier than the desert, and the thought of food made him want to retch. "No," he said through clenched teeth. "If I catch even a whiff of kippers in this room, I shall make you a footman and hire myself a new valet. Now let me have my rest."

"My apologies, sir, but it is now quarter past three, and you do have that appointment at four o'clock. I assumed you would wish to bathe and shave beforehand, so I have had a bath drawn. It is waiting for you."

Dylan didn't care about bathing, shaving, appointments, or much else at this moment. All he wanted was to return to sleep, the only quiet refuge he had. He buried himself deeper into the bed linens and struggled to fall back to sleep, but it was too late. Already, his companion was there to torture him, humming along like a faulty tuning fork that never quite hit perfect pitch. He groaned again and reached for a second pillow, pressing it against his ear, but his attempt to shut out the whine was useless.

"Shall I tell Mrs. Cheval you wish to postpone the appointment?"

He knew no one by that name. Besides, in his present condition, even a woman wasn't enough to stir him. "Who?"

"Isabel's governess. I believe you told Osgoode last evening that she would be arriving this morning and that you wished to meet with her at four o'clock to discuss her duties."

So Cheval was her surname, he thought groggily. It had never occurred to him she might be married. That bed in her flat was only big enough for one. Even if she was married, she had lived alone. She had to be a widow, or perhaps she had separated from her husband. No matter her current situation, she was a woman of experience. His favorite kind.

Half-asleep, Dylan focused his sleep-drugged senses on her, and that made him smile. Grace. Her name suited her. His fist tightened around a handful of feather pillow as he imagined her slender body in his arms, felt again the plump, perfect shape of her small breast beneath his palm. The whine in his brain receded as arousal took its place, as he remembered the soft, immediate yielding of her mouth and the welcoming eagerness of her kiss. He had not expected to awaken such desire in her so suddenly the other night, but the surprise had been a sweet one indeed.

No other man had touched her in a long time. He was certain of that, and he hungered to remedy it. If she were here beside him now, he would find all the secret places that gave her the greatest pleasure, exploiting them until she couldn't bear it, until he entered her and the only sounds he could hear were the frantic cries of her climax.

"I could tell her you are ill," Phelps's dignified voice called out from the dressing room, ruining the most luscious, erotic fantasy Dylan had ever had. He forced down his erection and vowed that soon, it wouldn't be a fantasy.

After a few minutes, he pushed aside the pillows and the counterpane and got out of bed. The moment he did, he felt his head exploding, and he pressed his hands to the sides of his skull.

Phelps entered from the dressing room just in time to see his grimace of pain. "Perhaps a dish of tea?" the valet suggested. "With mint. It does help when you drink it, sir."

Tea was the last thing he needed. "Phelps, I hate tea," he mumbled, rubbing his palms over his face. "You have worked for me for thirteen years. You know how much I hate tea."

"A chamomile tisane then? Or coffee?"

A chamomile tisane sounded worse than tea. Coffee, at least, sounded . . . tolerable. "Yes, have coffee sent up. I'll take it in the bath. And send a maid to tell Mrs. Cheval I shall meet with her in the music room." Naked, he walked across to the dressing room and into the chamber beyond it, where a huge copper tub had been filled with steaming water.

After a bath, a shave, and coffee, Dylan felt considerably better. The clock struck four as he walked to the music room, where Grace was waiting for him. He paused in the wide doorway to watch her.

She was standing behind his piano and had not noticed his arrival. She was looking at the scribbled sheet music on the stand. As he watched, she played several notes in succession. Bits and pieces of herself caught on paper. He wondered what she would think of that if he told her.

This was the first time he had seen her in daylight, and the sun did no disservice to her skin, for it looked as soft and luminous now as it had the night before. The sunshine caught all the gold and caramel glints in the braided crown of her hair, a simple fashion, with none of the absurd adornments now in vogue. No feathers and ribbons sticking out, none of the frizzy curls made by hot tongs, and none of those stupid sticks with fruit on them. Though the absence of such decoration was probably due to her destitution, he was glad of it, for her hair needed no adornments. If it were down, it would be like liquid gold in his hands—thick, heavy, shining.

Dylan's imaginings of an hour ago came back to taunt him, and they were much harder to set aside when she was standing right before his eyes. He entered the room.

She caught the movement and looked up. Her eyes were an even more clear, translucent green than he had thought, a color enhanced by the deep maroon shade of her dress, one of two he had seen hanging in her flat. It was threadbare and a bit loose on her slender frame, emphasizing just how close to the bone she had been living.

"Not accomplished with piano, you told me last night," he said as he closed the doors behind him. "Yet you do play."

"I'm sorry," she said, and drew her hand back from the piano. "I am aware that a composer's instrument is sacred territory. I did not mean to invade it."

"Do not make yourself uneasy, for I am not so temperamental as that." He moved to stand beside her. "If you wish to play, there is sheet music in the cabinet."

He gestured to the mahogany map cabinet directly behind them, where he kept published sheet music, but she shook her head. "I meant what I said, and I would not torture you with my attempts at piano. I always preferred the violin."

"You must keep your violin here in the music room, so that you may practice when you have the opportunity. Perhaps we might play together."

The idea did not meet with her enthusiasm. "I believe you wished to meet with me to discuss the matter for which I was hired," she reminded him, sounding just as a nursery governess should— prim, brisk, and efficient, prompting him to an immediate desire to tear down that demeanor.

"So I did." Dylan sat down at the bench and gestured for her to do the same. As she obeyed, he added, "What sort of play do governesses engage in?"

She gave him a look of reproof. "I thought you wished to talk about Isabel."

"Of course," he said in pretended surprise, still watching her as he began to press the piano keys before him in idle fashion. "What else would we be discussing? Do you not intend to have play-time in your curriculum?"

"For her, yes." A blush flared in her cheeks as he laughed, and she looked away.

"I am glad to hear it," he said. "Play is impor-tant."

"Your daughter seems a very intelligent girl."

"Too clever by half," he agreed and continued to press keys at random. He closed his eyes and focused all his senses on the woman beside him, waiting, hoping to hear something, some hint of music.

He could feel her presence so close to him; it was almost as if they were touching. His eyes closed, he turned his head slightly toward her and caught the scent of something. He inhaled deeply, savoring the light, delicate fragrance of pear oil. It reminded him of Devonshire and home.

"Isabel is quite talented at the piano," she said. "Did you teach her?"

"No." Dylan didn't remember that scent on her skin in her room last night, nor had she been wearing it the night before in the alley. He opened his eyes and cast her a sideways glance from beneath his lashes as he played, moving his hand two octaves up the scale with deliberate in-tent. "I like your perfume," he said, his forearm only an inch or two from her breast as he toyed with piano keys. "Why do you not wear it all the time?"

Her serious profile did not change at the com-pliment. "It is soap, not perfume."

"My estate mills pear soap. So does my brother's."

"Yes. The maid who brought it so I could refresh myself mentioned that." She would not allow herself to be flustered by his closeness or the intimacy of the subject, it seemed. "Mr. Moore," she said, without looking at him, "if you do not wish to talk about your daughter, I shall leave you to your music."

She started to rise from the bench, and he spoke to stop her. "If you move, Grace," he said pleasantly, "I shall fire you."

She sank back down beside him. "That is blackmail."

"Blackmail is a rather harsh way of putting it," he answered, looking over at her, smiling as he continued to play. "I prefer to call it leverage."

"Please do not—" She broke off, bit her lip, and turned her head away from him. After a moment, she said, "I would prefer not to discuss intimate subjects such as my toilette with you."

God, he loved the sound of her voice. Even when she tried to sound disapproving, she really could not manage it. He wondered if she knew that. Her voice was soothing, melodic, like listening to a woodland stream. Closing his eyes as he played, he said, "Very well. We shall discuss whatever subject you would prefer."

"The nursery is empty," she said, "and Isabel has informed me that her room is on the second floor. A little girl should sleep in the nursery. Would it be acceptable for me to move Isabel up there? Her nanny would sleep there as well, of course."

"Move her if you like, but she doesn't have a nanny. You'll need to hire one."

"Very well. May I also purchase suitable furnishings for the nursery?"

"Such as?"

He listened as she reeled off a list of all the things a child's nursery required—furniture, book shelves, a tea table, slates, primers, books, games, puzzles, maps, and as she spoke, the noise in his head began to fade. He stopped playing and merely listened to her talk.

"Isabel has very little in the way of clothes," Grace went on. "She has but two day dresses, and a third reserved for Sunday. I should like to take her to a dressmaker. Would that be acceptable?"

"By all means. Have Osgoode arrange accounts for Isabel at the proper modistes and purchase for her whatever she needs. And furnish the nursery any way you please. See Osgoode for a list of shops in Bond Street where I have accounts. As for sleeping arrangements, I hope you like your own room?"

"It's lovely."

"Is there anything you need? If so, you only need ask Osgoode or Mrs. Ellis."

"Thank you." Once again she diverted the topic from herself. "I wish to determine a course of study for Isabel, but to do that, I need to know what her education has been up until now."

"I do not know. I suppose you could ask her."

"I did."

Given his own experience thus far, it was not hard to guess the outcome of Grace's conversations with his daughter. "And?"

"She did not want to talk about what she had already been taught, but she did not hesitate to tell me what she wishes to do from now on. She does not want to learn mathematics, and she quite rebelled at collecting butterflies or learning German. As for other feminine accomplishments, let us say she was not enthusiastic. She wants to play piano and compose. That is all."

"Has she played for you?"

"Oh, yes. A sonata, two concertos, and a serenade, all her own. She says she is beginning work on a symphony."

Dylan felt a glimmer of pride, which was rather an odd thing, since he barely knew the child. "She is a very talented girl."

"Yes, she is, but I suspect her greatest talent may be that of getting her own way." She paused, then added in a wry voice, "It seems she takes after her father in more ways than one."

He laughed at that. Unexpectedly, she did, too. He stopped playing and turned to her, appreciating the smile that lit her face. "That is the first time I have seen you smile." Before he could even think, he was lifting his hand to touch her again.

That smile vanished as his fingertips grazed her cheek. He paused, looking into those extraordinary eyes, eyes as green and lovely as spring. Spring, and starting afresh, and all things new again. If only he could be renewed.

His fingers were calloused from a lifetime of pounding on piano keys, but her skin felt so soft against them. He flattened his palm against the side of her face, cupping her cheek. His thumb brushed against her lips. That delicious scent of pear invaded his senses, and the noise in his head receded to a faraway hum, then it disappeared altogether. For a few blessed moments, he heard nothing at all.

He closed his eyes. He stopped breathing. He did not move. So long since he had heard the sound of silence, he had forgotten what it was like. It was like heaven.

She opened her mouth against his thumb. "Hush," he said in a harsh whisper. "Not yet. Don't ruin it."

Dylan felt every breath she took against his thumb, waiting. He wanted to draw music out of her and put it on paper. He wanted the taste of her, the feel of her, the peace that would come afterward.

He could hear the noise coming back. Desperate to keep it at bay, he slid his thumb beneath her jaw and tilted her head back to kiss her. The noise grew louder, but the moment he touched his lips to hers, it ceased to matter. Christ, she was sweet. Honey on his tongue.

"No."

The word was muffled against his mouth, but he heard it, and he opened his eyes as Grace slid away from him, off the piano bench and out of his reach. He watched her back away from him and move to the other end of the long Broadwood Grand. She stared back at him without speaking.

"Grace," he said, his voice as soft as he could make it. "Come back."

She shook her head, took two steps back, then turned away. She flung the doors open and departed. He let her go.

In her wake, she left behind that pear fragrance

and something else. Without thinking, he put one hand on the keys and pounded out a quick, hard series of notes, not the notes he always heard with Grace, but instead the austere tones of C minor. He realized he had just created the opening of the first movement of a symphony. The masculine theme. The music Grace had inspired five years ago was the feminine theme that would follow it.

Of course, he thought, and crossed to his writing desk for quill, ink, and staff paper. He returned with them to the piano and began improvising on the notes he had just played.

The idea seemed so obvious now. The masculine and the feminine. He would use them throughout not only the first movement but also the entire piece. A symphony written to be like a love affair.

It was an excellent idea creatively, but he craved the reality even more. Even while he worked, Dylan could not stop thinking about Grace, about the scent of her skin, the shape of her body, the taste of her kiss. Over and over, he tortured himself with thoughts of her, but if he had ever harbored any doubts that she would inspire him, they were gone by the end of the day.

Dylan set down the quill and stared at the scrawled sheet music spread across the top of his piano. He had a basic structure for the first movement, the first tangible evidence that he could still compose, but he would gladly have given it back to the gods for another moment of her, and her kiss, and the silence.

Chapter 6

Filling a suite of five empty rooms required a long shopping list. Grace pulled the pencil from behind her ear, and, at the bottom of her list, she added two armoires.

"I don't see why I have to sleep up here," Isabel said, standing next to her and sounding quite aggrieved that both her governess and her father were in agreement that a little girl of eight belonged in the nursery.

"Think of it this way," Grace said, using the wall as her writing surface as she penciled in a blackboard and chalk below the armoires. "You do have the largest suite in the house."

She glanced at Isabel just in time to see the little girl's face brighten. "That's true," Isabel agreed. "It is even bigger than Papa's. But that's only because if I had brothers and sisters, I'd have to share. Can you put staff paper on the list? Stacks and stacks?"

"Your father said to buy whatever we needed. I think it is important to have stacks and stacks of composition paper."

"Me, too."

"As do I," Grace corrected and continued perusing her list. As talented as she was, a child of Isabel's intelligence required a more substantial education than most other children to keep her from becoming bored, and she needed interests beyond her music. To her growing list, Grace added a set of watercolor paints and supplies, a child's dinner service and tea set, and an abacus.

Isabel looked at the list. "Why do we need a fishing net?"

"I thought we could go to Hyde Park and fish some of the tiny insects out of the ponds. If we got a microscope, we could look at them very closely."

"Why would we want to?"

Biology was not very appealing to Isabel, Grace could see. She changed tactics. "Going to parks is necessary so one can enjoy the fresh air."

"I've been to parks all my life. They all look the same."

Grace looked at the child. "Do they?" she asked, noticing that Isabel seemed very forlorn all of a sudden.

"I'd rather go to Papa's estate in the country. There are ponies there. Molly told me."

"Molly?"

"Third housemaid. She said Papa's estate is called Nightingale's Gate, and it has orchards. Apples, pears, plums. And the house is right on the sea. I've never even seen the sea, well, except to cross the Channel."

"The sea is wonderful," Grace told her. "I grew up in Land's End."

"Land's End? That is at the very, very tip of England, isn't it?"

"Yes, it is. You could look out over the ocean from my parents' house." Grace was overcome by an unexpected wave of homesickness, and she pushed it away. Showing Isabel the list, she asked, "Can you think of anything else we need?"

Isabel read through the list again and shook her head. "No. There's an awful lot to buy already, isn't there? We shall be shopping for days."

"It puzzles me that there is nothing up here. I know you have had quite a few governesses, so why is the nursery empty? Had you been sent up to school?"

"No, I have always had governesses, until the nuns anyway."

"Nuns? Is your family Catholic?"

"Mama was, I think, but she never went to mass or anything. Papa is English, so I don't think he is a Catholic. In fact," she added, looking up at Grace with a thoughtful frown, "I can't see Papa being anything. Can you?"

Not unless being a hedonist is a religion. "So, if you have had governesses, why is there nothing up here?"

Isabel's eyes widened in surprise. "Didn't my father tell you? I only got here three days ago. I was born in France, at Metz. My mama died three months ago. Scarlet fever, and I had to go to the convent. Sister Agnes brought me here to live with Papa, and I like it much better. I don't think my father was expecting me."

"You have only been with your father three days? He did not tell me any of this."

"I had never met him before I got here, but I knew a lot about him. The newspapers are always writing stories about things he's done. Did you know he won a prostitute in a card game? She was his mistress before you."

"Isabel!"

"He smokes hashish, too. I saw him, the other night. He has a glass pipe in his room. It's blue."

How did the child even recognize hashish? Grace wondered how to respond to comments like this from a little girl. She thought of what her own childhood governess would have done, but that was no help, for she doubted Mrs. Filbert had ever needed to deal with a child like Isabel or a man like Moore. "That will be enough, Isabel."

The child looked at her with deceptive innocence. "Does it bother you?"

Grace guessed that getting under her skin was the child's objective, and she lied. "No, but it should bother you. I thought you didn't want your father to have mistresses, yet you talk so freely about them."

Isabel frowned at her, obviously unhappy that her governess wasn't responding in the expected way.

"Besides," Grace went on pleasantly, "these are not appropriate topics for a young lady to be discussing with anyone, and it grieves me to think that when you are in society, you will be shunned for saying such outrageous things."

"Papa says outrageous things, and he isn't shunned."

That was true, but Grace wasn't about to discuss the details. She turned toward the wall, flattened out the paper, and added draperies and carpets to her list. "Your father is an artist. Artists are . . . different."

"I am an artist, too!"

"Perhaps, but you are a girl, and it is different." Grace paused, her hand tightening around the pencil, staring at the wall. "It is a horrible thing for a girl to be shunned by society. If you knew what it meant, you would cease this sort of talk."

She thrust the pencil behind her ear again and turned to the child, adding, "I have read about your father, too. I know as much about his reputation as you do. But it has nothing to do with either of us."

Isabel frowned, staring up at her. After a moment, she said, "Why did you really come here?"

"I needed work."

"Because you are poor. I can tell by your dresses. They are awful."

Grace smiled. "Thank you."

Isabel bit her lip and was silent for a moment, then she exhaled a sharp sigh, looked away, and said, "That was rude. I'm sorry."

"I accept your apology."

"You're far too nice, you know," Isabel told her, taking refuge in the offering of sage advice. "It doesn't do for a governess to be so nice."

"Thinking you shall walk all over me, are you?"

"Yes." Unexpectedly, Isabel smiled at her. It

was devilish and beguiling, and at that moment, she looked so much like her father that Grace was startled. "That is exactly what I was thinking."

"You should give in now, then," Grace countered, laughing. "Since I can tell what you are thinking, you don't have a chance."

Isabel's smile faded, and she looked at Grace thoughtfully. "I don't understand you. You aren't anything like my other governesses."

"And you are not like any child I've ever met before. In many ways, you are a great deal like your father."

Isabel looked pleased. "You really think so?"

"Yes. What was your mother like?"

The little girl turned away with a shrug. "I hardly ever saw her, unless she was giving me a present or taking me somewhere in the carriage. She did that sometimes, if she wasn't sleeping in the afternoon."

Isabel walked to the window to look out, as if uninterested in the subject of her other parent, but it had only been three months since the woman's death, and Grace was not fooled. "You must miss her."

Isabel turned sharply at the question. "No, I don't. I hardly even remember what she looks like. I never saw her. Why would I miss her?"

The vehemence of the reply told its own story. She missed her mother. Badly.

Grace walked over to the window. "Why don't we go into the other rooms and see what we need to buy to furnish those, hmm?"

Before the child could reply, a footman entered the room.

"A note for you from the master, Mrs. Cheval," the young man said as he crossed the room. He held out the folded sheet of parchment to her with a bow. "He asked me to wait for a reply."

"What does it say?" Isabel asked, moving to stand beside Grace as she broke the seal and unfolded the note.

"A young lady does not inquire about the private correspondence of others," Grace said gently and lifted the letter higher to keep it away from the child's curious gaze. She scanned the few lines written there, lines that were scrawled across the page as if a drunken spider had gotten into the inkwell.

Grace,

I have need of your company this afternoon. Be so kind as to meet me in the music room at four o'clock.

Moore

It seemed that yesterday's meeting was to be a daily occurrence, and though she was not surprised, she did not welcome it. Too many ghosts, she thought. Too many expectations.

Too much seductive charm.

Hush, Moore had said, touching her face. *Don't ruin it.* What on earth had he meant? Ruin what? It was as if all he wanted to do was sit there with her in the quiet and listen, as if there would be music. And then he'd kissed her.

She touched her cheek where he had touched it

and felt herself getting warm. What was it about him that affected her so? She'd met other powerful, brilliant men. Was it Moore's tortured creativity that fascinated her, that drew her to him like a moth to a flame? If so, she needed to give herself a dunk in cold water before she got scorched by the fire.

"Why do you keep rubbing your cheek like that?" Isabel asked.

Grace jerked her hand away from her face and looked up to find Isabel right beside her. "Am I?" she asked, discomfited to hear her voice come out in a breathless little rush.

"Yes." Isabel looked up into her face, staring, frowning. "You don't have a pimple," she assured her. "No spider bite or anything."

"I'm glad to hear it," Grace answered and doused any notion that Moore was charming. He was a shameless man, wild and unprincipled. Hadn't she learned by now? Artists cared for their art more than they could ever care for any person. Even for a brief amour, even if he heated her blood and made her ache, she did not want a man like him, not any more. Not ever again.

She had been alone so long, and when he had touched her and kissed her, it had seemed as if he had never felt skin so soft or tasted lips so sweet, but it was not real. He might treat her as if she were the only woman in the world, but he was still Dylan Moore, and she knew enough about him to know that on some other night, some other woman would be the only woman in the world.

Grace turned to the wall, laid the note out flat

against the plaster, and retrieved her pencil. Directly beneath his words, she wrote her response.

Sir,

I apologize for the informality of this reply, but I am currently without proper paper and ink. I have made the arrangements of Isabel's schedule with the household. From three o'clock until five, she has lessons with me in German. Her dinner hour is five o'clock. After that, she and I have play time until she goes to bed at eight. Therefore, I fear I cannot meet with you at your suggested hour. I respectfully request we postpone this meeting until tomorrow morning. Perhaps nine o'clock?

Mrs. Cheval

She refolded the sheet and handed it to the footman. He took it and departed with another bow, and she put Moore out of her mind. She returned her attention to her shopping list, discussing the furnishings with Isabel.

"Are we going to have any games?" Isabel asked.

"We are."

"Smashing! Like what?"

"I thought perhaps battledore and shuttlecock, hide and go seek, and blindman's bluff would be fun."

Isabel's nose wrinkled with obvious contempt. "Those are for little girls."

Grace pressed her lips together, trying to hide a smile. "What games would you like?"

"Cap-verses. Crambo. Backgammon. Chess."

Isabel was probably better at those evening games for adults than most adults were. "We shall do them all," she said and added a chess set and a backgammon board to her list. "Now, let's talk about furnishings for your room."

She started toward the largest of the four bedrooms in the nursery, but Isabel's voice stopped her.

"I like my bedroom downstairs."

"It is a very nice room, but since it is not in the nursery, it won't do."

Isabel began trying to argue that she was old enough for a proper bedroom and wanted to stay where she was, but before Grace could remind Isabel that her father's orders matched Grace's own, the footman returned.

He carried a silver tray, and on it was a note from Moore, a few sheets of blank paper, and an elaborate desk set, complete with ink, quill, and other letter-writing materials. She pulled Moore's reply from the tray and read it.

Grace,

No gentleman of consequence rises at the ungodly hour of nine o'clock in the morning, especially not in London during the season, a fact of which I am sure you are well aware. As to the responsibility for my daughter's dinner and bedtime, these duties are part of a nanny's job. I have already given you leave to hire one. Therefore, I shall anticipate your arrival in the music room at four o'clock.

Moore

Her reply to him was quick and scrupulously polite.

Sir,

I am sure you would wish me to hire a qualified nanny. This will take several days at least. I recommend this meeting be postponed until Monday.

She sent the footman off again, and before Isabel resumed pleading her case, Grace said, "I appreciate your reasons, Isabel, but it is customary for young girls to sleep in the nursery until the age of fourteen, and you are eight. Therefore, you shall sleep here. You father has instructed me to hire a nanny—"

Isabel's groan only interrupted her for a moment. "—and after I do so," Grace went on, "the nanny will sleep up here as well. Until you are fourteen, the nursery is the only appropriate room for you. Your father said the same."

Children were so persistent. Isabel began arguing the point again. She wanted a big girl's room, and she was not concerned with how things should be done.

Neither, it seemed, was her parent.

I could not bear a postponement, Grace, for I crave your company. I have four maids. Pick one to assume the nanny's duties until you hire one. I expect your company at four o'clock.

Grace stuffed the letter in her pocket and looked at the footman, who was standing by the door, waiting for her reply. She gave in to the inevitable. "Tell Mr. Moore I shall meet with him as he has requested."

The footman once again departed. Grace returned her attention to Isabel and bedroom furnishings, trying to put Moore out of her mind. But she felt the warmth of his touch on her cheek all day long, and told herself sternly that she wouldn't let him get away with anything like that again.

When she entered the music room that afternoon, Moore was already there. He rose from the piano bench as she came in, and the moment he saw her, he shook his head, frowning. "Grace, that gown is a horror. Send it to the dustbin, I pray you."

Grace came to a stop on the opposite side of the piano and glanced down at herself. She was wearing the gray dress today, a thin wool garment that covered her from her throat to the floor, and its white collar and cuffs were yellowed and frayed. "It is rather a fright," she agreed, looking up, "but I only paid a few pence for it."

"I can well believe it. I want you to go to a dressmaker first thing tomorrow and buy some pretty gowns for yourself. Charge them to me."

She shifted her weight from one foot to the other. She did not want to look pretty for him. She did not want to feel pretty with him. That was dangerous territory. "It would not be proper for you to buy my clothes."

"You are living unchaperoned in a bachelor's house. Does the propriety of clothes matter to you?"

She seized on another excuse. "Your daughter already thinks I am your mistress. What will she think if I allow you to buy my clothes?"

"That you are sensible?" he suggested. "Get some new gowns, Grace. That is an order. I don't want my daughter's governess going about looking like a scullery maid's dishrag."

"When your acquaintances meet me, they will not believe for a moment I am your daughter's governess."

"Even worse. I would never allow my mistress to go about in a gown like that one." He sounded appalled, but there was a teasing hint of a smile in his eyes. "Grace, think of my reputation. People would be horrified to think I would treat my mistress so cheaply."

"Oh, all right!" she gave in, exasperated. "I shall buy some new clothes. I insist you deduct the charges from my salary."

"Are you always this prudish?"

"Are you always this indifferent to propriety?"

"I am." His grin was unapologetic. "I am the black sheep of my family, much to my brother's dismay. I pay little heed to the conventions of society. By the way, since I am paying for these gowns, nothing that resembles this one in any way." He gestured to the dress. "Only you, Grace, could don a gown as hideous as this and still be beautiful enough to make a priest weep."

A blush flamed in her cheeks. "Do you always give women such compliments?"

"Yes."

"Why?"

His answer was rueful. "Because they usually work."

Grace could not help it. She burst out laughing. "Really, you have no shame!"

"At least I have earned a smile from you, so I am unrepentant."

"Are you ever repentant about anything?"

It was his turn to laugh. "Rarely," he admitted and gestured for her to sit beside him on the piano bench, but she turned away, pretending not to notice. She moved instead to a chair several feet to his right. Sitting there was safer than sitting beside him. He couldn't kiss her again and turn her insides to melted caramel if she was out of his reach.

To her relief, he did not quibble about it. Instead, he resumed his own seat, turning slightly on the piano bench to face her. "Since we met, I have learned one thing about you at least. You are not vain."

"But I am. I have my petty vanities, just as everyone does."

"How I should like to discover them."

"You won't."

"Won't I?"

She felt a jolt of excitement at the softness of his voice and the determination behind it, but she pretended to be unmoved. "They are not worth such scrutiny, I assure you."

"But if I find them, I can exploit them shamelessly."

Before she could think of a reply, he turned toward the piano and began to play scales. She lowered her gaze to his hands as his long, strong fingers moved over the keys in what was almost a caressing way, slow, deliberate, and with full appreciation of what he was doing.

At first, he played them in the ordinary way, one note after the other, in perfect order. But then, after a few minutes, he began to change direction. His right hand moved up the keyboard and his left hand moved down, forming the mirror image of major and minor as his arms extended toward each end of the piano. Then a reversal, and he quickened the pace from quarter tones to eighth tones as his hands moved back to middle C, then faster still as he moved again toward the ends of the piano.

He shifted, and his hands played in parallel motion this time, adding accidentals. Grace watched, fascinated, as he shifted into harmonic and melodic minor scales, then circles of fifth. He dallied with those for awhile, then shifted again, this time from scales to modes, and his fingers moved faster, hit harder. Ionian mode, then Dorian, Phrygian, Lydian. It was somewhere in the Lydian mode that she stopped thinking about the individual notes he played and just listened, staring at the frenetic movement of his hands in fascination. Time seemed to stand still, and modes became bits and pieces of melodies strung together, one after the other. Some she recognized, but many she did not. They were probably of his own invention.

Grace didn't know how much time passed, but when his left hand stilled and his right hand shifted back to the most basic scales, she sensed he was nearly finished. As he played the light and happy C major, he turned his head to look at her, and his long hair touched the keyboard beside his thumb. Smiling at her, he hit the final notes, a playful, teasing trio of do-si-do.

"Show-off," she accused, trying not to laugh. "Ordinary scales too dull for you?"

His hands slid away from the keys. "I do my scales daily because I have to, but I have always hated them, even as a child," he confessed, shaking back his hair as he turned toward her, his expression like that of a schoolboy caught misbehaving. "I spent a great deal of time finding a way to make them more interesting."

"And drove your music tutors raving mad, I daresay."

"No. They were usually out of the room long before that, writing resignation letters to my mother."

"You should be worried then. Isabel is so much like you, I might do the same."

"Ah, but you can't. Remember?"

Grace tensed at the gentle reminder of their arrangement and the fact that if she left before he told her to go, it would be without her pay. "Should I be concerned about that?" she asked, forcing lightness into her voice.

"Very concerned." He turned back to the piano and began plucking at keys in random fashion as he had done yesterday. "I am far harder to handle than my daughter."

Grace could well believe it, but she much preferred to keep their conversation on the child. "As you requested, I have left Isabel in the care of your maid Molly Knight. I shall visit the agencies when I take Isabel shopping tomorrow. I intend to begin interviewing nannies as soon as possible."

"Excellent."

He said nothing more, and Grace frowned. "You seem to have little interest in the upbringing of your daughter."

"Do I?" He continued to play the piano without looking at her. "Perhaps that is because I am not accustomed to the role."

His words confirmed what Isabel had already told her, and there was really only one conclusion to be drawn. He had never had any interest in the child. "I see."

Dylan looked over at her, his brows drawn together in a frown of his own as if irritated by her bland reply. "Isabel's mother had died. The child appeared on my doorstep, and that was the first moment I learned of her existence. I had never been told of my paternity. It was a shock."

"And now?"

"I am—" He paused and looked down at the piano keys. "I do not know quite what to do with her."

"That is understandable. I imagine most fathers in your situation would feel that way at first. But why did Isabel's mother not tell you of this long ago?"

"If you are asking me for an assessment of the character of Isabel's mother, I am afraid I cannot give you one. I do not remember the woman."

"Not at all?"

He shrugged. "It was a long time ago. During my salad days."

"From what I hear," she said dryly, "all your days are your salad days."

He laughed at that, oblivious to the sting in her words. "Not so. These days, I prefer a steady diet of dessert."

She could almost fool herself into thinking that when he smiled, it was for her alone. It made her feel like the passionate, adventurous girl who had longed for things far beyond country life, country dance, and marriage to a country squire. That girl had believed a big, exciting world was out there to be seized, enjoyed, and savored for all it was worth, and that a man who could knock your senses awry and turn your heart into mush could make it all happen for you.

That was what made Dylan Moore so dangerous to women. In his dark, dark eyes and sinful smile was the heady promise that when you were with him, life could always be dessert.

She reminded herself that she was no longer that girl, foolish and passionate and so terribly vulnerable. She was a woman now, a woman shaped not only by romance, love, and adventure but also by hard times and harsh realities, and the struggle to keep balance. She had learned her lesson. Life was not kind to those who broke the rules. Grace drew a deep breath. "I should be sick on a diet of desserts," she answered. "Sweets do not tempt me."

"No?" He rose from the piano and she tensed, her hands clutched together in her lap as he moved to stand behind her chair. He rested his hands on the chair back and leaned down, close to her ear. "What does tempt you, Grace?"

"Plain dishes," she said firmly. "Porridge. Boiled beef and cabbage. Things like that."

"Spoken like a very efficient, proper governess." He laughed softly, his breath warm, so close to her ear. "I don't believe it for a moment. You feel as I do about the food of life."

She turned in her chair to look at him over her shoulder. "I certainly do not."

"If you did not, you would not kiss as you do."

She jerked in her chair. She would not, she would not ask him how she kissed.

He told her anyway. "You kiss as if it is the first and last time you will ever be kissed."

She swallowed hard. "I think you misjudge me, sir. Unlike you, I choose not to give in to every impulse I feel, indulge every whim I think of, and commit every outrageous act I can. It's called restraint. You might exercise it sometime."

Her words, so horribly sanctimonious to her own ears, seemed to amuse him. "My very own little puritan," he murmured. "You speak of restraint. Where was it the other night when you kissed me so passionately?"

"I did not kiss you," she corrected at once. It was technically the truth. "You kissed me."

"Then your restraint must be what impelled you to fling your arms around my neck and kiss me back."

She turned her head and frowned at him. Insufferable man. "I did no such thing!"

"Yes, you did. At least be honest enough to admit it."

"I did not even know you!" she cried, horrified because she remembered in vivid detail just how unrestrained she had been. She looked away. "I did not intend . . . that is, I was not . . ." Her voice trailed off. "It was a momentary weakness," she conceded. "I wasn't thinking clearly."

"Grace, you flatter me. I had no idea my kisses have such power over you that you cease to think."

"I did not say that."

"Forgive me. I thought you did." He leaned a bit closer. "Besides, you think too much."

He touched her cheek with his lips, and she leaned sideways to evade him. "Around you, sir, thinking would seem to be a wise idea."

Moore moved to kneel beside her chair. He took her chin in his hand and turned her face toward his. "Why?" he asked as he moved even closer to her.

Grace could feel her resolve slip a notch at the closeness of his mouth, the touch of his hand on her face, but she came to her senses and turned away. "Please do not behave dishonorably toward me."

He chuckled, blowing warm breath against her cheek as he remained beside her chair, his fingertips moving across the side of her throat to the nape of her neck. "Stealing kisses from beautiful women is dishonorable? God, I am forever damned."

"You gave me your word," she reminded him and jerked herself to her feet, dismayed at how wrenching it was to tear herself away. Once there was a safe distance between them, she turned to face him. "I demand that you honor it."

He stood up. "Have I broken my word? Tell me how."

"You just did."

He folded his arms and tilted his head, looking at her with an expression of pretended perplexity. "Did I miss the part where you said no?"

"You did not give me the opportunity to say no!"

"You had plenty of opportunity. You just chose not to exercise it."

Another truth. "I expect you to behave as an honorable gentleman," she said, trying to maintain some control over the situation.

"I am struggling as best I can," he said, not trying very hard to look contrite. "But whenever you are near me, I lose my head. And you cannot deny that you feel a similar passion for me."

"What I feel at any particular moment does not signify!" she cried. "I don't live as you do, jumping from sensation to sensation, living only for pleasure and the pursuit of it." She paused and took a deep breath. "To you, I am only the latest in a long line of women, a line where there will be many more after me."

"Is that what this is about? Feminine pride?"

"No, it is about you. I cannot give you what you want! You want more than my body, more than my company. You want something no one else can give you, not even me."

"What is that?"

"The ability to be brilliant over and over again."

He did not move, but something in his face told her she had hit the mark. And it hurt him. For a long moment, he just stood there, then he turned away, muttering an oath under his breath. He walked away, moved around the room in a restless sort of way. Without looking at her, he said, "How many times must I tell you that you are my muse? That I hear music with you?"

"Muses do not exist. The music is all there, inside yourself. Why can you not see it? You do not need me."

"You know so much about creative art, do you?"

"I know more about it than you could possibly imagine." An image of Etienne flashed through her mind, and the seven frantic, sleepless days and nights he had spent covering the walls of their rooms in Vienna with layer upon layer of black paint, all because he could not paint anything else. She wrapped her arms around herself, suddenly cold. "You cannot get your creative inspirations from me. Or any other woman, for that matter."

Moore gave a laugh and turned to face her. "Is that what you think? That I seek out women only so that I can create music?"

"I think it is possible."

"If that is what you believe, then you know nothing about me. I seek out women for the pleasure and distraction their company provides me. You are different. You are—" He broke off, raking back his long, black hair with a sigh of frustration. "I cannot explain it."

"If I am so different, then do not treat me as you treat other women."

"How should I treat you? Do not even suggest I should regard you as just another member of my household staff."

Grace proposed the only option she could think of. "Can we not simply be friends?"

Chapter 7

"**F**riends?" Dylan had never heard anything so unappealing in his life. He didn't want to be Grace's friend. He wanted to hold her in his arms, drag her down beneath him, kiss her, touch her, stoke her body to a fiery heat, and put any notions of friendship out of her head.

He wanted to be her lover. Friendship was a pathetic and completely inadequate substitute. Damn it all, he was not composing a divertimento, which was the only sort of piece that could be inspired by something as insipid as mere friendship. He was composing a symphony, for God's sake—a grand passion, a love affair, not background music for a dinner party. Unfortunately, his *inamorata* in this particular love affair was not cooperating.

He forced himself to say something. "Cannot lovers also be friends?"

"I meant we should be friends in the ordinary sense," she answered. "Platonic friends."

He told her the truth, and he told it bluntly. "For a man, being friends with a woman without the hope of more is a pointless exercise, not to mention intolerable."

"Many people of opposite sexes are friends just for the pleasure of company. They discuss interesting topics of the day. It is all part of civilized society and intellectual conversation."

"I comprehend the concept, thank you," he said in a wry voice. "You mean we should be indifferent acquaintances. Forgive me if I feel little joy at the prospect. For one thing, I seldom find interesting topics of the day to be interesting. For another, I don't see how a muse who is merely my friend could be all that inspiring. And third, I cannot promise to remain true to such a friendship, for I shall still steal your kisses whenever I can. You see? I am not a good friend for a woman to have."

She ignored that. "Have you never had a woman for a friend?"

"No." He paused, then amended, "Let me be fully accurate. There are two women in my life that might be described by your notion of friendship. One of them is the Duchess of Tremore, who is the wife of my dearest friend. The other is Tremore's sister, Lady Hammond, whose husband is also a friend of mine. Platonic friendship is the only possible option for me with either of those women. There are certain rules about that sort of thing."

"Rules?" Grace shook her head in disbelief. "I did not realize you played by any rules."

"A man does not attempt to turn his friends into cuckolds. There are some conventions," he added dryly, "that even I will not break."

"Perhaps one of those conventions should be that your daughter's governess can never be more than a friend to you. Is that so hard for you to accept?"

Dylan cast a lingering glance over her body, and erotic imaginings of her flashed across his mind. "Impossible, I would say."

"A pity, then. Friendship is all I can give you."

She sounded so certain of her statement that he wanted to pull her into his arms again and make it a lie. Her passionate response to his kiss in the alley was still vivid in his mind. She wanted him as much as he wanted her, and friendship entered into it only because she did not want to want him. Women just had to make these things complicated. Though he hated to admit it, that was part of their charm.

"Very well. Friends it is, then." He lifted her hand in his and pressed a kiss to her knuckles. "For now," he added and let go of her hand. "Dine with me tonight."

She looked away, then back at him. "I do not think that is a good idea."

"Friends dine together, do they not?"

"Of course, but—"

"Dining together usually means conversation on interesting topics of the day?" he went on, using her own words against her.

"Yes, but—"

"To me, that sounds very much like intellectual conversation, keeping company, and civilized society. Would you not agree?"

Grace frowned, knowing she had just been neatly trapped, but he would not let her find a way to wriggle out of it. He took her cheeks in his hands and leaned forward to plant a kiss right between her frowning brows, then he let her go. "Excellent," he said as if she had accepted his invitation, then he turned away and started toward the doors. "I shall meet you this evening in the drawing room, and we shall go in to dinner together. Eight o'clock."

"And if I don't come?" she called after him. "Shall you burst into my room and carry me down as if I were Abigail Williams on the stage?"

"No," he flung back over his shoulder, laughing as he opened the doors out of the music room. "I'll bring dinner to you and we shall picnic on your bed. God knows, I would prefer it that way."

He left the music room, and he could not remember the last time he had felt this exhilarated by any woman's company. Being friends first was a new experience for him. Her declaration that she would never be able to give him more than friendship was a challenge. Dylan loved new experiences, a challenge was always irresistible, and never was a very long time.

Grace was in over her head. She stared at her reflection in her bedroom mirror and wondered what on earth she'd been thinking to propose a compromise of friendship. Being friends with Dylan Moore was like being friends with a tiger. They might keep company for awhile, but eventually, he'd have her for supper.

She reminded herself that no matter what he might try, all she had to do was say no. She could say no. She ought to say no. The trouble was that when he kissed her, when he touched her, she didn't want to say no, and clever devil that he was, he knew it. He had sensed her aching loneliness that night behind the mews, and he was now exploiting it. She was letting him. She *liked* letting him. It was the heady, dizzying dance of romance, a game she had not played for so long that the thrill of it was almost irresistible.

Growing up, she had said no to so many things. She had been a good girl, a sensible girl, a respectable girl. Then Etienne had come, she'd gone rather mad, and *no* had ceased to exist for a long, long time. In exchange for that, she had received joy, adventure, love, and soul-deep heartbreak. Being good was so much easier, so much safer. So much more sensible.

Grace glanced at the clock on her mantel. Ten minutes past eight. If she lingered here too long, he would carry through with his threat. She tucked a stray tendril of hair back into the coil of braid on top of her head. She smoothed the dark red wool of her skirt, adjusted her sleeves, and pulled on her only pair of evening gloves, reminding herself with each of these actions that this was only a meal shared between friends. If he made any improper advances, all she had to do was throw his agreement to platonic friendship in his face and walk away.

Grace went down to the drawing room, where Dylan was waiting for her. He wore impeccable evening dress, but his hair hung loose about his shoulders as if he were some lawless highwayman from the previous century. Though it might be a deliberate affectation, it was an effective one.

The contrast of elegance and dishevelment was striking, and it suited him so well that any woman would find it attractive. She did.

"I am sorry to be late," she said as she entered the room, hoping she did not sound as skittish as she felt.

"Please do not apologize," he said. "That you came is far more important."

"Did you think I would not?" She gave a nervous laugh and berated herself for it at once. Lord, what was the matter with her? He was not going to ravish her at the dinner table. On the other hand, he might. One could never be sure with him. "After what you threatened to do, I could hardly refuse."

"Even if that is the only reason you came, I am rewarded. Though I must confess I had a preference for the picnic."

The image of it flashed across her mind, an image of both of them camped out on her bed, naked, with a basket of food. It was so sudden and so vivid in her mind that her insides began to quiver, and her imagination ran on a wild tangent about what he could do to her with strawberries.

"Shall we?"

The soft question sent waves of desire through her entire body. *Yes*, she wanted to say and bit her lip.

He turned, offering her his arm.

"Oh," she said, staring at him, fighting to come to her senses. "Dinner."

He began to smile, the wretched man. "Yes, dinner. I even told them to serve it in the dining room."

Why hadn't she brought her fan down with

her? She needed it right now. Grace turned to take his arm, but when she felt the hardness of muscle through his shirt and evening coat, she just could not fight her own imagination.

He could carry a woman just about anywhere, she thought as they left the drawing room. *Off a stage. Down from her room to the dinner table. To heaven and hell and back again.* After all she had learned about life, why did journeys of that sort still hold any appeal for her?

To distract herself, she felt compelled to say something, and she chose the tried-and-true— and very safe—subject of the weather as they walked to the dining room.

Though he had already made clear his loathing of mundane conversation, he answered in a most serious and attentive manner that the warming temperatures of April would be most welcome after the cold winds of March. But those laugh lines at the corners of his eyes gave him away as he added, "Despite the heavy rains we have had, I am told the state of the roads is excellent for those just now arriving from the country."

Grace pretended not to notice. "That bodes well for the season," she said as they entered the dining room, where Osgoode and two footmen awaited them.

The dining room of Dylan's home was small by the standards of his social circle, for there was only space for ten at table. The ceilings were low for a dining room, giving the room a feeling of intimacy. Like all the other rooms of his house, this one was intended for luxury and comfort, not necessarily convention. The thick carpet was of a lavish Turkish design, but the colors of gold, blue,

and aubergine were muted. The walls were color
washed in ecru, the white moldings were commonplace egg and dart, and the white marble fireplace was simply carved. There were only two
paintings, landscapes by Gainsborough, and the
only mirrors were located behind the wall
sconces, their sole purpose to reflect light. There
were no gas lamps in the room, only the soft
golden glow of candles. It was a room meant for
guests to feel at ease, though it could not soothe
away the quivery combination of nervousness
and anticipation inside her.

A footman pulled out her chair, and after she
sat down, Dylan took his seat to her left at the
head of the table. The moment they were seated,
he leaned toward her in a confidential manner, as
if they were at some fashionable dinner party and
he was about to tell her an interesting piece of
news. "Have you heard that hostesses have finally
taken up the issue of swords at balls?"

She took a deep breath, grateful that he was
playing along with her desire for innocuous conversation. She began pulling off her gloves. "Have
they?"

"Yes. It has been deemed at last that a military
gentleman must hand over his sword at a ball if he
intends to dance. If he does not do so, no hostess
or patroness shall invite him again."

"That is exciting news indeed," she answered.
"And such a relief for the ladies, to know we shall
no longer be poked by some lieutenant's annoy-
ing scabbard during a quadrille."

The moment she said it, she realized how it
sounded, and she choked back a laugh, turning
her face away.

"I could say something very naughty just now," he murmured.

"Don't." She shook her head and yanked her serviette from her plate. She pressed the piece of linen to her mouth, muffling her laughter. "Don't say a word."

To her relief, he obeyed. After a moment, she was able to look at him again. "I am glad," she said with a little cough as she smoothed her serviette across her lap, "that the fashionables have finally decided the matter."

"Vitally important, I say." He paused. "Especially to the virtue of ladies."

She gave him a glance of reproof, then turned her attention to the footman waiting by her right with the first course. When the servant presented her with the soup, Grace found herself staring down at the dish in utter bewilderment. Porridge?

Bewildered, she glanced back up at the footman, but his expressionless face told her nothing. She took another look at the silver-edged soup plate in front of her and saw that she had not been mistaken. It was porridge. She glanced at Dylan and noticed that the servant was placing vichyssoise in front of him. Though he was staring down at his own plate and she could not look into his eyes, Grace could see his mouth, and she watched as one corner began to curve upward. Suddenly, the memory of her own words came back to her.

Plain dishes. Porridge. Boiled beef and cabbage. Things like that.

This time, she could not stop it. Laughter bubbled up inside her and spilled out like overflowing champagne as she remembered that conversation. "You are an impossible man!" she said between gasps of laughter. "Truly impossible to tease me so."

Dylan looked up from his own soup. That tiny smirk was gone, replaced by such innocent perplexity that she could not stop laughing. "Grace, Grace," he chided, "how can you say such a thing? I am only thinking of your preferences."

Still laughing, she said, "Because of the soup, I surmise that several more courses of wholesome food await me in the kitchen? Boiled beef and cabbage perhaps?"

"You did express a fondness for that particular dish."

"So I did. Pray tell me, what courses are you having?"

"Tail of lobster for the fish, my personal favorite, though I am certain you would not care for it. I know your preferences rebel against such rich food. Although"—he paused, laugh lines deepening as he looked at her—"I heard that Mrs. March did prepare two lobsters. She does know how much I favor that particular dish."

"Two lobster tails for one man? Such extravagance."

"Is it not? I believe Mrs. March has also prepared for me a saddle of lamb, and one of beef, baby carrots, and asparagus. For dessert, I asked her to make two of my favorites, a lemon torte and a chocolate soufflé. Not that the desserts would be of any interest to you, of course."

She looked over at his vichyssoise, then at her own porridge. She cleared her throat. "I believe I am changing my opinion on gastronomic matters, and coming round to your way of thinking," she said gravely.

"Are you indeed?" When she nodded, Dylan signaled to Osgoode. "I believe Mrs. Cheval has changed her mind," he said.

It was clear the butler and footman both knew what he meant, for Osgoode waved the footman toward the door of the dining room, and a few minutes later, she was also being served a bowl of the chilled potato and leek soup.

She picked up her spoon and smiled at him. "Do you know what the worst thing is about you?"

"Now, this is a splendid topic for conversation between friends. Continue."

Still smiling, she said, "You are a scoundrel, and by all rights, I should dislike you. But I cannot. Every time I think I dislike you, you do something that changes my mind."

"Thank you." He tilted his head to one side, seeming to reconsider. "I think."

His pretended doubt widened her smile. "It is a backhanded compliment, I know, but it is true. I want to dislike you, but I can't."

"Why should you want to dislike me?"

"Because I should."

"Do you always do what you should?"

"Yes," she lied.

"If that is true, Grace, you are missing a great deal of what life has to offer."

"Perhaps," she said, not adding that she had already seen a great deal of what life had to offer, and most of it had not been worth the price. She deliberately reverted to small talk. "I read in the *Times* this morning that the British population is now estimated to be nearly fourteen million people."

Dylan lifted his eyes toward the ceiling with a sigh. "Grace, please do not give me such dull subjects. Let us discuss something interesting. Politics, for instance."

She smiled, playing along. "If you insist upon so much excitement, I can oblige you. The Reform Bill is finally expected to pass the House of Lords this spring."

As the meal progressed, conversation became a game, with each of them trying to outdo the other by presenting the dullest news possible. By the time dessert arrived, they agreed Dylan had won for his announcement that Lord Ashe had fainted at the news that his second cousin once removed was in fact marrying a man in trade. Both of them proclaimed it shocking as a footman presented them with chocolate soufflé and lemon torte.

She studied the tray, trying to make up her mind.

"Are you certain you wouldn't prefer a plain, boiled pudding?" Dylan asked, watching in amusement as she wavered, unable to decide.

"No," she answered, giving him a gentle kick under the table. "I shall have both."

"Both?" Dylan looked at her as if shocked. "But Grace, boiled pudding is easier on the digestion. Much more sensible to have that."

"I am being sensible," she told him as two dessert plates were placed in front of her. "Since I cannot make up my mind, the only sensible thing to do is have both."

"My wicked ways are rubbing off on you," he warned her as the footman presented him with two plates as well. He devoured both desserts quickly, with the careless enjoyment of someone accustomed to such luxuries. She was not so hasty.

Grace alternated between the two, taking a bite or two of sweet, smooth chocolate soufflé, then following it with a bite of tangy lemon torte. She could not remember the last time she had tasted anything this good. The only sweet she'd had in months was sugar for her tea, and even that tiny luxury had stopped quite some time ago. Dylan was leaning back in his chair, seeming fascinated simply to watch her eat. Finally, she set down her fork with a satisfied sigh.

"You still have a bite left," he pointed out, gesturing to the chunk of lemon torte still on her plate.

She looked at it and started to pick up her fork, then changed her mind. "I cannot," she groaned. "I am too full. If I have that last bite, I shall be sick. It has been so long since I have dined like this."

Osgoode and the footman took away the dessert plates and set out fruit and cheese. Osgoode presented Grace with a selection of dessert wines, and she chose sherry. The butler then poured a brandy for Dylan, and all three servants left them alone in the dining room.

Dylan lifted his glass, looking at her over the rim. "Now that dinner is over, I think we should leave trivial subjects aside and talk about something important."

Grace looked at him with suspicion. "Why am I feeling that you have a particular topic in mind?"

"Because I do. I want to talk about you. I want to know how a girl of Cornish gentry, who has seen me conduct in Salzburg, became a charwoman. How a woman who obviously came from breeding is reduced to selling oranges on the street. Grace, what happened to you?"

She wished she knew the answer to that question. She looked at him helplessly. "Many things have happened to me, things I choose not to discuss with anyone. My past is a painful subject for me. Please do not ask me about it."

"Very well," he said quietly. "Then we shall have entertainment instead. What would you like?"

Relieved, she said, "Why don't you play the piano for me?"

"I'd rather you play your violin for me."

"For you?" She shook her head. "Never."

"Do not talk as if you have never played for me before."

"Only once, and it was the only thing I could think of."

"To stop me, you mean?" He stared down into his glass, silent for a long time. Then he said, "You were right, you know." His voice held a strange, soft note. Even sitting only two feet away, Grace had to lean forward to hear him. "I never tried again. I thought of it. I contemplated where, how, and when. I even loaded the gun once." He would not look at her, but instead kept his gaze on his glass, his thick lashes lowered. "I never managed to get the barrel to my head. I kept hearing your voice telling me it would be wrong."

Grace did not know what to say, so she said nothing.

He swirled the contents of his glass and took a swallow, then leaned back and looked at her. "When you practice your violin, what music do you choose?"

She smiled sweetly at him. "Mozart."

"Mozart!" Dylan straightened in his chair, set his glass down, and looked at her as if appalled. "That shallow fellow who never composed a truly meaningful piece in his life?"

"Sorry." She tried to look apologetic. "I love Beethoven, too, but he is harder to play."

"Worse and worse! What ever happened to loyalty? You are supposed to be my muse, remember?"

"The truth is I don't like to play your music."

"What?"

"Well, your pieces are extremely difficult! They are so intricate they tire out the musician. Really, you are more complicated than Beethoven. Do you know how difficult it is to play your Violin Concerto Number 10? I can never play it correctly."

"You sound like a student, Grace. The soloist should always play a concerto from the heart. The only correct way is the way you feel it should be."

"Playing a piece is all about the musician's feelings, is it?" she said, smiling, glad she got to tease him now. "Then why are you so difficult to work with?"

"We have never worked together," he said with certainty as he leaned forward to pluck a grape from the basket of fruit on the table. "I would remember if we had. In any case, I am not difficult. Who has been telling you such monstrous lies?"

"Only everyone! Why, every musician I know who has worked with you in orchestra complains how hard it is to satisfy you."

"Being the soloist for a concerto is very different from playing in the orchestra, and you know it perfectly well. Besides, musicians in orchestra always complain."

"We do not."

He picked up another grape and nibbled on it. "Do, too."

She grabbed a grape for herself and gave him a *humph* of indignation. But before she could argue with him further, he spoke again. "Where have you played orchestra, Grace? Not in England."

"No, Vienna and Salzburg. Paris, too. As you know, the Continent is much less prickly about having women in the orchestra. In England, they make it so difficult. Musician's Livery and all that."

"Silly, if you ask me," he said, taking another bite of his grape. "I would put you in my orchestra."

"Even if that were true, you could not get by with it. There would be no end of a fuss from the men. Unless I donned a gentleman's evening suit, put on a false mustache, and cut off my hair to fool the other musicians."

He gave a shout of laughter. "You couldn't fool them if you tried. I saw that highwayman costume, remember? As for cutting your hair—" Dylan broke off, and his amusement faded as he glanced at the braid coiled on top of her head. "As for cutting off your hair," he said with slow, deliberate emphasis, "it would be a travesty. Do not even consider it."

"I appreciate the compliment, but I do not need your permission."

"Humbling me again, are you, Grace?"

"I am trying." She looked at him again, doubtfully this time. "I do not think it is working."

"But it is," he said as he popped the last bite of his grape in his mouth. "I assure you I am quite humbled by you. Alas, it is not me you adore, but Mozart—"

"That is not fair!" she protested. "I like your music, truly. I only meant—"

"Like it? Is that all?" He looked so seriously vexed, and yet she knew from something in his eyes that he was teasing her again. "God save me from the day when the only emotion my music evokes is liking. You see, Grace, how you can humble me without even realizing it."

"Absurd man!" she cried, laughing. "What is it you want of a muse, then? You want me to sit beside you all the day long and tell you how wonderful you are, is that it?"

"Yes," he said, laughing with her. "Yes, I do."

"As if that would truly inspire you! You would just become conceited and complacent and would never write another thing."

"I would tell you how wonderful you are if you played for me," he said, turning the tables on her.

"As you already pointed out, I have played for you."

"Five years ago."

"And at the ball only a few nights ago."

"In an octet. I want to hear you play solo."

She made a wry face. "I am no virtuoso."

"I prefer to judge that for myself." He stood up and held out his hand. "Play my Violin Concerto Number 10 for me."

"What?" No more teasing. He was serious now. Dismayed, she shook her head. "No, no. Oh, no."

"Why not? Friends play for each other."

She bit her lip and looked down at his outstretched hand. In desperation, she searched for an excuse. "I can't do a violin concerto. I've no orchestra to accompany."

"I shall accompany you on piano," he said, taking that lame excuse away from her.

Grace started to panic. She did not want to play in front of him. This was Dylan Moore, after all, not some hostess giving a dinner party who needed musicians. She had never been chosen to be the soloist. It was not even as if she had ever hungered for it. "No, please, I would rather not. It would be far better if you played, and I could listen. That would be so much better, more entertaining for both of us."

He shook his head, unsmiling, still holding out his hand. "Grace, I am not going to be auditioning you."

"I have not played as a soloist. And when I played for you alone, my only goal was to stop you from—" She broke off, then said, "You know what I mean. I wasn't thinking about the music. I just caught up my violin and started to play."

"Then do it again now."

She did not want to do it. There was something so unnerving about the idea of playing for him. His music was beautiful and complex, and she was not skilled enough to do it justice.

"I shan't laugh," he promised, "if that is what you fear. I shan't be critical."

When he took her hand and pulled her to her feet, she let him. Reluctantly, she went with him into the music room and let him send a footman to her room for her violin case. She wanted to ask him for the sheet music, but soloists weren't supposed to need the sheet music. She took up her instrument and moved to stand beside where he sat at the piano. "You won't like it," she said.

"What I like doesn't matter. You are the soloist. You are in charge. Now play."

He began, and so did she. He made it easy for her, not deviating from the music as he had originally published it, giving her the freedom to do whatever she wanted with the violin. She played with every bit of concentration she had, sure that without the sheet music, she would forget and skip a section or two along the way. Within each cadenza, she used his notes, and added variations of other soloists. If she were a virtuoso, she would have invented her own on the spot, but she couldn't, not like this, not with him listening. She made do.

At the end, all she could do was sigh with relief that she was done, and wait for him to say something. He had promised he wouldn't make fun of her or shred her, so whatever he said would be nice and innocuous and terribly insincere.

"Grace, what was all that reluctance? You play beautifully. Though a bit more confidence in yourself would not go amiss."

"Thank you," she said, shifting her weight uncomfortably, "but you perceived how I borrowed each cadenza."

"But you improvised within it."

"To make it easier!"

Dylan shook his head, not believing her. "Play your cadenza of the first movement again."

She complied, but in the midst of it, he stopped her. "Right there!" he said. "That is an example. You were improvising on Paganini's version. You did that little trill in the middle, and trills usually only go at the end. What you did was beautiful and just right. I love it there."

She drew a deep breath. "You don't have to lie to me."

"I'm not. You had a dozen of those little innovations, and each one is unique and right."

Dylan rose from the piano bench and turned to her. She glanced sideways, not daring to look at him and see a lie in his eyes. "I think if you trusted yourself more," he said, "you could invent your own cadenzas, and you wouldn't even need my notes to do it."

"You are not just saying that?"

"Not even to get you into bed."

She almost laughed, then something in his eyes stopped her. Neither of them spoke, and she felt a growing tension between them, thick and heavy. She could not seem to move. The clock on the mantel began to chime, but when the chimes had died away, she could not have said what the time was. She could not look away from those black, black eyes.

"It is getting late."

His voice broke the strange spell. She swallowed and looked at the clock. Midnight. "Yes," she answered, feeling awkward all of a sudden. "I should go up."

He bowed to her. "Good night, Grace."

"Good night."

He walked with her to the closed doors and opened one door for her. She started to step past him and go through the doorway, but then she stopped and turned toward him. "I think you were wrong about yourself," she said. "I think you could be a true friend to anyone, even a woman."

He took her hand, kissed the gloved back of it, and slanted her a grin that was anything but good and true. "Are you saying you trust me?"

She smiled back at him. "Not for a moment."

With that, she left him. As she went upstairs to her room, she realized she might be in worse trouble now than she had been before. She had invented the idea of being friends as a compromise with him. She had to stay a year, and the only sane thing was to keep distance between them, but she wasn't feeling sane.

She was feeling as if she were headed for the edge of the earth—where the dragons were, where she could believe love and a love affair were the same thing, where she could play with dragon fire and not come away scorched.

Grace closed her bedroom door behind her and leaned back against it. She had been right about one thing when she'd gone downstairs four hours ago. With this man, she was in way over her head.

Chapter 8

The following afternoon, Grace discovered that Dylan Moore was not the only one who found it difficult to abide by rules. His daughter seemed to have the same problem. After an entire day of shopping, Grace could fully appreciate why Isabel was on her thirteenth governess.

"Isabel, we are not going to argue about this," she said, pausing in the foyer as the two footmen who had accompanied them to the shops brought in armfuls of bags and boxes from the carriage. "You now have plenty of toys among which to choose. You do not need exotic pets from the Argentine. When you are in the country, you shall have animals to play with. In the meantime, if you want to see animals, we shall visit the zoo."

Isabel's face bore a fierce resentment. "My other governesses let me have pets."

"Good for them," Grace countered and con-

cluded from the child's scowling face that she was
no longer considered too nice to be a governess.
She handed her cloak, hat, and gloves to the maid
waiting to receive them and turned to the butler,
who stood by her in the foyer, awaiting her instructions. "Osgoode, the furnishings I selected
are being delivered within the week. Would you
see that they are placed in the nursery when they
arrive?"

"I keep telling you, I don't want to be in the
nursery!" Isabel wailed.

She had seemed to accept the nursery situation
the day before, but not today. Impervious to this
caprice on the part of her pupil, who was tired,
hungry, and, most of all, cranky, Grace pulled two
bags from the pile on the floor. "I'll take these,"
she told Osgoode. "Have the rest of these pack-
ages sent up to Isabel's room in the nursery."

"Yes, of course." The butler proceeded with di-
recting the efforts of the footmen who were bringing in the results of their shopping trip as Isabel
began to cry. Grace took one shopping bag by its
twine handle and went to the music room, decid-
ing that she had had enough of this. Isabel followed her, protesting more loudly the closer they
got to her father.

A footman opened one of the doors into the
music room and Grace went in, the angry, crying
child behind her. Dylan had risen from the piano
and was halfway to the door, probably because he
had heard his daughter sobbing. He stopped
when they came in.

Isabel ran to him at once. "Papa!" she cried,
flinging her arms around him. "Oh, Papa, I hate
her! She is so awful. Please help me!"

Grace nodded to him, ignoring the infuriated child, who was clinging to him like a lifeline. She walked past both of them to the chaise longue and placed the shopping bag on the brown velvet cushion. "Good afternoon," she greeted him sweetly as she pulled off her gloves and tossed them aside. She dug through the shopping bag and pulled out a handful of embroidery floss and a handful of ribbons. She turned to Isabel, one in each hand. "Which would you prefer to begin with, embroidery or trimming a bonnet?"

His daughter's loud wail caused Dylan to give Grace a long, thoughtful look, then he pulled Isabel's clinging arms from around his waist and sat her down on the piano bench so that she was facing Grace instead of the keyboard. He waited a moment, but when Grace remained standing, he sat down beside the child. "Stop crying, Isabel," he ordered. "At once, now."

The little girl's sobs died away to angry hiccoughs. She folded her arms and glared at her governess with a fierce scowl on her tearstained face. Not the least impressed, Grace ignored it and turned to put the floss and ribbon back in the shopping bag now that she had made her point.

"Mrs. Cheval," Dylan said in the sudden silence, "I think you should tell me what this is about."

"Certainly," she said. "Isabel does not want to sleep in the nursery. She does not want to do her lessons. She does not want to learn to embroider cushions, or decorate bonnets, or speak German, or do mathematics, or read, or go to Hyde Park. She does not want to take her baths, or eat her meals on time, or get up in the morning. Her attempts to quarrel with me today have been futile, and therefore, she is angry. In short, sir, your child is having a tantrum."

"I am not!" Isabel cried out, wiping away angry tears with her hands.

Dylan gave a sigh and raked back his hair, clearly appreciating the fact that Grace was placing the responsibility of his fatherhood directly in his hands.

"I don't want to learn embroidery and do bonnets," Isabel told him. "Those are stupid things. I don't want to learn mathematics and German. All I want is to write my music and play games and have fun."

An unexpected grin caught at Dylan's mouth, and Grace frowned at him. "Don't you dare encourage her."

"But deuce take it, she is so much like me, isn't she?"

At this moment, Grace did not think that was necessarily something to be proud of. "Isabel needs a well-rounded education appropriate to a young lady. Music isn't everything."

The grin vanished, and he gave her an apologetic look. "It is to some of us."

Isabel, sensing support from her parent with that statement, tugged at his sleeve. "It's been the most horrid day, Papa." She continued to stare at Grace with animosity as she went on. "She made me do multiplication tables this morning, over and over. Then we went shopping, and she was so mean. She wouldn't buy anything I liked."

"Crimson is not an appropriate color for a young girl's dress. And you do not need a pet lizard."

"She wanted the modiste to put lace on my dresses," Isabel said with disgust.

"You don't like lace?" Dylan asked her, looking bewildered, and that earned him a groan of exasperation from his daughter. He turned to Grace for enlightenment.

"She says it itches," Grace told him.

"Then," Isabel went on as if Grace hadn't spoken, "when I said I was hungry, she wouldn't let me have anything to eat."

"As I told you before, Isabel, you would not have been hungry if you had eaten your meal before we went out."

Isabel folded her arms again with a great show of indignation and leaned back against the piano behind her, causing the keys to clang. "You see, Papa? She's mean and stingy and she's going to starve me. She is just like the nuns."

Dylan looked over at Grace, and those lines of laughter returned to the corners of his eyes. "She isn't like a nun," he told his daughter. "She just seems like one sometimes."

Grace found no humor in that. She gave Dylan a pointed look that said more clearly than words he was not helping the situation.

"Papa, you should have seen the nannies she interviewed at the agency today. I saw them lined up outside the door, and I was scared to death thinking one of them might be tucking me in at night. It was a jolly good thing she didn't hire any of them. I said I'd run away if she did."

"Don't be absurd, Isabel," Grace said smoothly. "That would not be sensible at all. If you ran away, your father would have to send one of Peel's constables to drag you back, and they are much more frightening than any nanny could be."

"Why do I have to learn embroidery?" the child demanded. "I am sure I should hate it!"

They had been at this all day. Lord, the child was stubborn. Grace drew in a deep breath, then let it out slowly, counting to ten. "You have not even tried it. You cannot hate something you have not yet tried."

"I tried sewing once, and I hated that. I know I'd hate embroidery just as much." Once again, she appealed to her father, who had listened to this exchange in silence. "Please, Papa," she implored. "I don't want to stitch samplers and read stupid poetry and learn German, and I am hungry, really. Mrs. March has lovely comfits, but she"—Isabel paused and pointed at Grace—"she told Mrs. March not to give me any. She wouldn't let me have any dresses I liked, and I haven't been able to play piano all day."

"One cannot play piano and eat candy all the time." Grace turned to Dylan. "Unless that is what you wish me to do with her?"

He looked at his daughter, who was gazing back at him as if Grace's regimen were the most barbaric of tortures.

Dylan was not impressed. "I understand your passion for music, Isabel, better than anyone, but Mrs. Cheval is right. Young ladies need more education than the piano. In the mornings, you will do your mathematics, geography, German, and embroidery—whatever Mrs. Cheval deems appropriate. In the afternoons, you may play your piano until your dinner."

Isabel began to protest, but he cut her off. "That

will be enough," he said, in a voice that dismissed any further argument, and Grace gave a sigh of relief. "You are sleeping in the nursery," he told his daughter, "and you will obey Mrs. Cheval's instructions. If you do not, she has my permission to punish you by whatever means she sees fit. Is that clear?"

Isabel did not reply. Instead, she bit down on her quivering lip and allowed the tears to spill down her cheek again. She seemed the perfect picture of misery.

The quirk of a smile at the corner of Dylan's mouth made it clear what he thought of this emotional display. "It seems you have something in your eye," he teased her gently. "Would you like a handkerchief?"

Any other child would have responded with frustration that the ploy didn't work, but Isabel was cleverer than that. She switched to a different battleground. "I'm very hungry, Papa," she moaned, still looking as pathetic as possible. "I didn't eat before we went out because shepherd's pie has peas in it, and I hate peas, and it's two whole hours until dinner. Can't I have something to eat?"

"Heaven help us," Grace muttered, pressing her fingers to her temples. "She never gives up, does she?"

Dylan glanced up with a grin. "I told you she was just like me. I hate peas, too." He looked back at Isabel again. "You are going to do what Mrs. Cheval tells you, aren't you?"

There was a long silence.

"Yes," she finally answered.

"Promise me."

Isabel sighed, giving in. "I promise. I promise." She gave him a hopeful look. "Can we have something to eat now?"

"You do not want her to get in the habit of eating between meals," Grace felt impelled to caution him. "If you let her have something now, she won't eat her dinner."

"Perhaps," he answered, "but I remember how long it always seemed until dinner. And after a day of shopping and trying to order my governess around, I would need sustenance, too." Dylan slid an arm around his daughter and rose from the piano bench, lifting the child with him. Isabel gave a cry of delight, any pretense of suffering gone. She put her arms around her father's neck, and they started for the doorway.

"Where are we going, Papa?"

"Where the food is, of course," he answered as he carried her out of the room. "Get you to the kitchens, Beatrice! Get you to the kitchens."

"It's heaven, Papa," she corrected, laughing. "Heaven, not the kitchens."

"Well, I never can remember my Shakespeare. Besides, when you're hungry, what is the difference between heaven and the kitchen?"

Grace followed them, glad that Dylan had supported her side and happy that he was taking a bit of time with his daughter. A spoiled dinner later was worth the parental attention the child so desperately needed.

Just around the corner from the kitchen, Dylan paused with his daughter in his arms, and Grace halted behind them. Keeping the child out of sight, he stuck his head around the doorjamb to take a look in the room, then he pulled back.

"This is a perfect opportunity," he whispered to his daughter, just loud enough that Grace could hear him, too. "Mrs. March is alone in there with a dozen brandy snaps. I'll distract her while you grab the plate. Go out through the butler's pantry, and I shall follow you."

He set his daughter on her feet and sauntered into the kitchen to greet the cook. Isabel slipped out of her shoes and waited, peeping around the doorway to watch for the right moment.

Grace also watched as Dylan charmed Mrs. March with compliments about her cooking, moving about her kitchen and slowly maneuvering the stout little woman away from the brandy snaps. Only then did Isabel tiptoe up behind the cook and take the plate of sweets from the table. Grace pressed her fingers to her mouth, smiling.

Isabel did not make a sound as she escaped out of the kitchen with the plate of sweets. Dylan lingered a few moments more, making culinary conversation, listening as if fascinated while Mrs. March explained in her thick Scottish burr that the secret of a good fool was in finding the sharpest, tartest gooseberries. When he could see that Isabel was safely gone, he excused himself from the cook with a bow, and Mrs. March returned her attention to rolling pastry dough as Dylan traced his daughter's steps out of the kitchen, beckoning with one hand behind his back for Grace to follow him.

She picked up Isabel's shoes from the floor and started to comply, but she was obviously not as accomplished at skulking as the other two, for Mrs. March glanced over her shoulder at the precise moment she was crossing the kitchen and stopped her. "Ah, Mrs. Cheval, would you be having a moment to speak with me about Miss Isabel's meals?"

Grace hastily hid the child's shoes behind her back as the cook turned to face her. Mrs March asked if she should be choosing Isabel's menu from now on, or would Mrs. Cheval prefer to take on that task herself? The cook added that she had prepared mulligatawny soup and fish pie for Isabel's dinner tonight, with brandy snaps for dessert.

"That sounds perfectly acceptable," Grace replied, trying to maintain a serious expression and not give the show away, hoping the cook wouldn't notice that the dessert in question had just disappeared. "If it is easier for you to plan her menus yourself, please do so," she said with a little cough. "Pardon me, but I must go."

The cook turned back around with a nod, returning her attention to her pastry crust. Grace started through the butler's pantry, then stopped. "Mrs. March?"

"Yes, ma'am?"

"I only have one requirement for Isabel's food. No peas. She hates peas."

The cook stared at her in astonishment that a child's wishes had anything to do with the matter of what she ate, but Grace did not stop to explain that some battles just weren't worth fighting. Instead, she continued on through the butler's pantry and escaped.

When she arrived back in the music room, she found that father and daughter together meant two loads of trouble instead of just one. They were a mess.

It was very difficult to eat a brandy snap in a tidy way, for each tube of pastry had the unfortunate tendency to fall apart the moment one bit into it, leaving most of the whipped cream filling all over one's fingers. But it seemed they had not even bothered to try being tidy. Crumbs and bits of brandied sugar were all over them and all over the table. There was a smear of cream on the rever of Dylan's black coat and another on his sleeve. More cream was slathered on the front of Isabel's lavender pinafore and all over her face. There was even cream in her hair.

"Oh, dear." Grace looked at them and started laughing. "If only Mrs. Ellis could see the pair of you. I shudder to think what she would say."

"You see, Isabel," Dylan murmured to his daughter in a confidential manner, "I told you she wasn't like nuns. She's not nearly mean enough for that."

"I think you're right, Papa. I already told her she was too nice to be a governess."

"I am back in your favor, I take it?" Grace turned her attention to Dylan. "Mr. Moore, you have my congratulations," she said. "You have now taught your daughter how to steal from the cook."

"I already knew how!" Isabel told her.

Grace gave a groan of mock exasperation, falling in with the game. "Hopeless, both of you."

"Spoken like a true nursery governess." Dylan picked up another brandy snap from the table and sent another shower of crumbs and sugar onto the mahogany table in front of him when he took a bite.

Grace glanced again at the brandy snaps that remained. She was getting hungry herself, and she had eaten her shepherd's pie—two helpings of it, in fact. Now that she lived in a house where food was plentiful, she couldn't seem to get enough.

"You may have some, you know," Dylan said, breaking into her thoughts, his voice amused. "A few brandy snaps won't spoil your dinner."

She tore her gaze away from the sweets, knowing she could hardly do such a thing after the stance she had taken. "No, thank you," she replied, trying not to look at the brandy snaps as she walked to the table and sat down.

"Didn't you ever sneak sweets from your family cook, Mrs. Cheval?" Isabel asked. "Not ever?"

"Heavens, no! I wouldn't have dared. Not from Mrs. Crenshaw."

She glanced at Dylan and noticed his skeptical look. "It's true," she said. "I never did. Dull of me not to steal from the cook, but there it is."

"Since I own the house and everything in it, including the brandy snaps, you could hardly call it stealing." He licked a dab of cream from his thumb and looked at his partner in crime. "Isn't that right?"

"Right-oh," the child agreed, her mouth full of cream.

"Please don't say 'right-oh,' Isabel," Grace admonished, "and don't speak with your mouth full." Grace returned her attention to Dylan, smiling. "I don't suppose you could have just told Mrs. March you wanted the snaps and taken them in a straightforward fashion?"

"How much fun would that be?" he countered. "It's much better when you can take them right from under her nose."

Isabel seemed to concur. "If we'd just asked for them, it wouldn't have been the same at all."

"I daresay, but don't be doing it every day, Isabel, or I suspect Mrs. March will stop making sweets for you altogether."

"No, she won't." Isabel popped the last bit into her mouth and stood up, then walked to the piano. "She won't catch me."

"The moment she discovers the snaps are missing, she'll know who did it, since you are the only child in the house." Grace glanced at Dylan again. "Well," she amended, "perhaps not the only one."

He grinned at that. She stiffened in her chair, watching as he began to lick cream from his fingers, one by one. An innocent enough thing to be doing, but the slow, deliberate way he did it and the laughter in his eyes told her he wasn't thinking about anything innocent.

Shameless man. She lowered her gaze to the table.

"Papa?" That word broke the spell as Isabel turned toward them. "May I play your Broadwood Grand? It's so much better than the pianoforte they moved into the nursery."

He glanced at the clock and shook his head. "I must work this afternoon. You may practice on it tonight before bedtime, if Mrs. Cheval has nothing else planned for you."

"That would be fine," Grace said. "Perhaps, Isabel, you should take your bath now. You have cream and crumbs all over you."

"Take a bath at three o'clock in the afternoon?" Isabel looked at her askance.

"Find Molly and tell her I said to draw you a bath now instead of after dinner. That way, once we have eaten, you will have a full two hours to play your father's piano before bedtime."

Isabel needed no further coaxing. She started toward the door, then stopped and gave her father a hopeful look. "It would be much better for both of us if I had a Broadwood Grand, too."

"I do not think so." Dylan pointed toward the door.

"Papa!" Isabel gave a heavy sigh. "I thought at least *you* would understand how important it is to have a good piano," she said with all the injured dignity an eight-year-old child could summon, then turned and left. The footman just outside the room closed the doors behind her.

"From the look of things," Dylan said, "I have fallen from grace."

"Never. You are her father. She adores you already."

"Only because I let her have a few brandy snaps."

"No, it isn't. Little girls always adore their fathers." Grace leaned back in her chair with a sigh. "All I know is that she has exhausted me. A whole day with her has left me feeling akin to limp lettuce."

"I suspect that is her intention."

"Oh, yes. She wants to wear me down, hoping I will find that giving in to her demands is easier than fighting with her about everything."

"Not a very effective strategy on her part, I'll wager. German, mathematics, no food between meals. What an excellent governess you are, for you are a bit like an army general."

Grace sat up straight in her chair, indignant. "An army general? No, indeed!"

"I am grateful I am not in your charge," he went on, ignoring her protest, "for I would never get away with anything."

"I am soft as butter compared to the governess I had when I was Isabel's age. Mrs. Filbert. She was very much the army general, very strict, and always emphasizing self-discipline."

"Ah, self-discipline! That explains why you keep staring at that last brandy snap with such longing, yet you will not just take it."

"I have not been staring at it."

"My apologies," he said gravely. "I don't believe you about your cook, by the way. No child goes through life without ever stealing sweets from the kitchen."

"I did," she said and began to laugh at his obvious disbelief. "Truly. I was always a very good girl."

"Were you, now?" he asked, his opulent lashes lowering as he looked at her mouth. "You never did anything naughty?"

"No," she said, refusing to get all flustered by that question and the improper way he asked it.

"Never?"

Not until I scandalized everyone, shamed my family, and ruined my reputation. "Never."

"Why not?"

The question was serious, and she blinked, disconcerted. "What do you mean?"

"It's a straightforward question. Why were you a good girl all the time?"

"I—" She broke off, unable to answer him, for she'd never thought about it. "I don't know."

He pushed the plate a bit toward her.

"No, I won't have any," she said with firm resolve. "I am attempting to set a good example for *your* daughter."

"I know. But Isabel isn't here right now, is she?"

Grace caught the movement of his hand and looked down as he took the last brandy snap from the plate. He leaned forward, bringing it close to her lips. She caught the scent of brandy and ginger and felt the sharp sting of hunger.

She looked up above the brandy snap just a bit, enough to see his mouth, enough to see that he was smiling at her.

"Go ahead," he dared, his voice low and beckoning. "I won't tell on you."

Her throat went dry, and she could not move. He was absurd, sneaking sweets from his own cook and pretending it was something forbidden. It was absurd that he could do this to her, hold out a brandy snap and make her feel as if it were the apple of Eden.

"You must have been very naughty when you were a boy," she accused, her words coming out in a choked rush, her fingers curling around the arms of her chair.

"Very," he agreed. "When I wasn't stealing brandy snaps, I spent my time—" He broke off and pressed the confection to her mouth, touching cream to her lips. "I spent my time trying to trick Michaela Gordon into letting me see under her petticoats."

"Who was Michaela Gordon?" she whispered, her tongue tasting cream as he pushed the end of the pastry into her mouth.

"A very pretty redhead," he said lightly. "The vicar's daughter."

"You would attempt to peek under the petticoats of a vicar's daughter," she said around the small pastry he had between her lips. She tasted whipped cream and took a bite before she could stop herself. It shattered in his hand, and she swallowed a mouthful of pastry and cream. He pushed the ends of two fingers against her lips, and she parted them, taking in what remained of the brandy snap—a few crumbs and lots of cream. Some of it must have ended up on her face instead of in her mouth, for Dylan began to laugh as he pulled his hand back.

She couldn't help laughing too, a laugh smothered by the fluff in her mouth. She swallowed it, but she could still feel the slick sweetness of cream on her lips, and she licked it off.

His lashes lowered a fraction, and his smile vanished. He reached out again, pressing his cream-covered fingertips to her mouth.

Oh, God.

Desire came over her like a wave of warm honey as she looked at him. Her eyes started to close, and she felt her lips parting against his fingers just as the thought crossed her mind that he must have done this sort of thing a hundred times before.

Grace jerked back, coming to her senses. He let his hand fall away, and he just looked at her, all amusement gone. Her breathing was a rapid rasp in the silence, and a hint of something undefinable came into his eyes, something that got past their opaque blackness, something almost tender.

"You have cream all over your face," he said, confirming her suspicion. He glanced down, reaching toward his breast pocket for his handkerchief, but his hand was still coated with whipped cream. He grasped the triangle of white linen carefully with the tips of two fingers, then pulled it out of his pocket and handed it to her.

She took it and dabbed at her mouth and chin. *At least a hundred times before,* she said silently, trying to harden herself against that look in his eyes. She handed the handkerchief back to him, watching as he used it to clean the whipped cream from his fingers.

Like Etienne, he was an artist, but his hands were not the long, fine-boned hands of her late husband. No, Dylan's were blunt hands, big, with wide palms and strong fingers, not like those of any other artist she had met. But they knew just how much force to use when playing a piano and just how much gentleness to use when caressing a woman.

"You have wonderful hands," she blurted out without thinking and could have bitten her tongue off.

"Thank you," he said. Several seconds of silence passed, but he did not resume his task. "Grace?"

She did not look up. "Hmm?"

"We are just friends now, aren't we?"

She forced her gaze up to meet his. "Yes."

Deviltry entered those black eyes once again. "Damn."

Chapter 9

The opening was brilliant, the rest was shit. Dylan groaned in creative agony and scratched out what he had just written. These chords should make the feminine theme richer, deeper, more sensuous, but they didn't. Something was wrong.

Exasperated, he dropped the quill onto the sheet of music that rested atop the piano, a sheet already marred by many ink blots and scratches— the pitiful result of this afternoon's efforts. He studied the paper before him, looking at something which could not by any stretch of the imagination be considered musical exposition. He wanted to tear it into pieces and throw it in the dustbin.

Instead, he reached for the bottle of brandy at his elbow. Staring at the blotched, stained screed on his piano, he downed swallows of brandy, and his thoughts drifted past the music itself to his muse. Three weeks now she had been in his home. That first afternoon with her had brought a wave of inspiration that had lasted him a week, taking him through the first half of the opening exposition, the masculine theme. The night after they had eaten brandy snaps with Isabel, he had begun the second half of the exposition, trying to create the feminine theme based on the vague bit of melody he had first heard that night at the Palladium.

He had spent countless hours at his piano during the past fortnight, yet he had nothing to show for his efforts but a great deal of frustration and a handful of half-formed ideas in his folio. The feminine theme was simply not coming to him. What little he did have felt so forced, pulled out of him by sheer will.

He glanced at the mantel clock and realized he'd been sitting here for nine straight hours. He looked around and noticed that daylight had come and gone, a servant had been in the room to light lamps and draw the draperies closed. Obsessed with his work, he hadn't noticed the time passing, and now it was almost eleven o'clock. By this time, he was usually out enjoying some of London's pleasurable diversions.

His preoccupation with this symphony had not diminished his need for distractions. He still spent his nights at gaming tables, parties, and his club. During the past two weeks, he had visited some of his more disreputable haunts, including two or three of his favorite seraglios and cock-and-hens, dallying and flirting with the courtesans, but never going upstairs with any of them. And why not? Because none of them were Grace.

Friends. Still an unappealing idea.

Dylan picked up the sheet of composition paper on the piano and studied it for a moment. Somehow, having his muse be merely a friend was not very inspiring. He crumpled the page into a ball and tossed it behind him onto the chaise longue, where it joined the dozen or so already there.

He could go out. Dylan downed another swallow of brandy. He didn't want a distraction, he told himself, not right now. He wanted to try again. Taking a deep breath, he put his hands on the keys, fighting to get past the noise in his brain and concentrate. He played chords over and over, tinkering with them dozens of different ways, trying to find a way to make them work in the theme, but they did not work. No matter how many ways he tried to improvise on them, they just did not work.

"Damn, damn, damn." Dylan plunked his elbows down on the keys, a discordant sound that matched his state of mind but was of little use to his composition. He rubbed his eyelids with the tips of his fingers, listening as the clock chimed midnight. Another hour gone, and still not a decent note to show for it. Five years of nothing but noise, then regained hope and a half-formed first movement, then nothing but noise again.

Perhaps he was fooling himself. Perhaps Grace was right and muses didn't exist. Perhaps he had been right five years ago, and what he heard now was only whispers, shadows of what had once been sonatas and symphonies.

With each passing moment, fear gripped him

tighter and tighter, until it clawed at his insides like the talons of desperate birds. He wanted . . . oh, God, what he wanted . . . to be himself again, to be the man who could sit down and write a flawless sonata as if he were writing a letter, to be the man who never struggled to bring out what he saw and heard and felt, the man who could say anything with notes and melody. To be again the man who had never needed to worry about failure and who had never known the meaning of self-doubt.

After the accident, he had sat here many, many times, just like this, trying for hour upon hour when it did no good, saying that if only he sat here long enough, something would happen, some key would unlock and everything would be right again. So many times he had walked away in despair, until one day, he had just not sat down, had just not hit the keys. He had stopped trying. That was the day his soul had begun to die.

From his earliest memory, he had always known what he was meant to do—to take all the turbulence of his soul and turn it into something finite, something of form and shape and substance that could be written down in notes and clefs on staffs of five and not be lost.

He was an egoist, no doubt, to believe with absolute conviction that what was in his soul was worth recording for mankind, but it had always been like breathing to him. He'd never had a choice. If he did not give voice to what was inside him, he would eventually cease to exist, not by putting a bullet in his head but by the death of his soul.

The clock struck quarter past midnight.

His hands ached, the whine was a searing pain through his head, and here he sat, staring at a row of black and ivory stripes. He had to finish the theme. Without theme, there was no exposition. Without exposition, there was no music. Without music, he had nothing. He was nothing.

What had he been thinking? He couldn't write a symphony. He didn't even have enough for a sonata. Those thoughts whispered to him, slithered through his mind like serpents, threatening to extinguish his hope. He would not let it happen. He rose to his feet with such force that he sent the piano bench toppling backward, feeling only the overpowering desire to get away, to replace pain, fear, and desperation with something else, something pretty or amusing or mind-numbing that would get him through yet another night.

He opened one of the doors leading out of the music room and started toward the stairs to go up and change clothes, but then he heard a faint, mournful sound that got past the noise and fear, a melody coming from down the corridor to his left. He paused, listening to Grace's violin.

Since that afternoon with the brandy snaps a fortnight ago, she had been avoiding him, and he had let her do it. He had no intention of leaving their relationship a platonic one, but she was not ready for more than that, and he was not ready for less. They had been at an impasse these past two weeks. Perhaps he could end that impasse tonight.

Dylan turned and headed down the long corridor to the library, and the music became louder as he approached. It was the poignant melody of *Pathétique*. He paused outside the closed door for a moment, then turned the handle and went inside.

She was sitting on the settee of ivory brocade under the window, her eyes closed, so absorbed in her music that she did not hear him come in.

She had retrieved her instrument from the music room a day or two after their dinner together, when she had played for him. He had noticed its absence, and he realized now that she must be using this room to practice in the evenings after Isabel was in bed.

The polished wood of her instrument gleamed in the candlelight, and her hair shone like gold against the aubergine velvet draperies behind her. Without making a sound, he closed the door and leaned back against it, then he shut his eyes and listened.

He remembered how afraid she had been to play for him that night they had dined together, and how unjustified her fear had been. She lacked the rare touch of brilliance and the driving egoism to be a true virtuoso, but she was a very good violinist, and it was a pleasure to listen to her.

The music stopped.

He opened his eyes to find her studying him, her violin tucked under her cheek, and her bow poised above the strings.

"Don't stop," he said as she lowered her instrument and bow to her lap. "Not on my account. I am thoroughly enjoying myself."

Somehow, without even smiling, her face lit up like a candle. Giving women compliments was second nature to him, and yet the pleasurable glow in her face at his words made him feel deuced awkward all of a sudden, and unexpectedly touched. "Please go on."

To his disappointment, she shook her head. "I have been practicing for some hours, and now that I have stopped, I appreciate just how long I have been playing, for my hands are beginning to ache."

"I know that feeling well." He clenched his fists and relaxed them with a grimace. "Especially today."

"Have you been composing since this afternoon?"

"Yes."

"And how is it coming?"

"It's not," he answered lightly. "I am quite put out that my muse has not given me any assistance."

"Hasn't she?" Grace set her violin and bow in the open case that lay on the floor beside her feet. "Most ungenerous of her."

"Indeed, it is, for during the past two weeks she has not come in once to see how I'm getting on, much less given me inspiration." He crossed the room and sat down in the chair opposite her with a long-suffering sigh.

She pretended not to notice the reference to their impasse. Instead, she closed her violin case, sat up, and brushed at her skirt as if removing a speck of dust. "Horrid muse."

He watched the movement and noticed she was wearing a new dress. It was periwinkle blue, with the fashionable dropped shoulders and sleeves that puffed out just above the elbows. The large, tiered collar around her shoulders was made of white lace, with gauntlet cuffs to match. "Grace," he said in surprise, "you are not wearing a scullery maid's dishrag."

She made a face at his teasing. "I ordered some gowns from the modiste when I took Isabel shopping. They arrived this morning. I must admit, it is nice to have some new and pretty things."

"They do you justice. I see that, unlike my daughter, lace does not bother you."

Grace laughed. "Perhaps Isabel will find lace to be like German. An acquired taste."

"Is she cooperating, then, with lessons in German?"

"Very reluctantly. She finds it an ugly language."

"But she is obeying you and doing her lessons?"

"She obeys me most of the time, but not willingly. She rails against things for no earthly reason except to be contrary. She is not accustomed to being gainsaid, and she doesn't like it when I do it. But I am taking this one day at a time." She smiled a little. "Rather in the nature of a long siege."

"If you need me to step in and discipline her, I will at any time."

"I would rather you gave her more of your attention," she said quietly.

Dylan looked away. "I am working on a symphony, and it is taking a great deal of my time," he said, and leaned back in his chair. It was an excuse, he knew it, but damn it, his work was important. It was everything. He looked at Grace, who was watching him with those eyes. "I'll try to make more time for her," he found himself saying.

"I am sorry to hear the composing is not going well."

He tried to make light of it. "I came to see my muse, yet when I seek her out, desperate for help, I find her playing Beethoven."

"It could be worse," she said, smiling a little. "You could have caught me playing Mozart."

"I have never been envious of Mozart, so that would not bother me quite so much."

"But surely you are not envious of Beethoven?"

"No, not at all. He only created the most brilliant piece of music ever written." Dylan paused, then with rueful admiration, added, "The bastard."

She laughed at that, taking it in the proper spirit. "So what is the most brilliant piece of music ever written?" she asked. "The Ninth?"

"Of course. Sonata form turned on its ear. Funeral marches, timpani crashes, adagio duets. It ought to be the most incoherent mess one ever heard, but no, it is exactly right and beautiful. Flawless, in fact, for one could not imagine it any other way. That is brilliance, Grace. I envy him like hell."

Her smile faded away at his last few words, which had been spoken with such vehemence. "You forgot to mention that he was deaf when he wrote it," she said gently. "Surely there is nothing to envy in that."

The irony of it almost amused him. He was not deaf, no. Instead he heard too much. One of God's little jests. "No," he said, "there is nothing to envy in that."

She did not reply. Those eyes studied him with

compassion and a strange sort of understanding. He did not like it, and he shifted in his chair, uneasy all of a sudden. "Why do you look at me like that?" he demanded. "What are you thinking?"

Her gaze shifted past his shoulder, almost as if someone else had entered the room. "I am thinking," she said, "of my husband."

He tensed, and he had to resist the urge to turn around. It was almost as if the other man were standing there.

My past is a painful subject for me.

He remembered those words, and he wanted to know why. "Where is your husband?"

Grace returned her gaze to his. "He is dead. He died two years ago."

That must be the reason for her pain, but she imparted the news with such detachment that she might have been talking of a stranger. There was no discernible feeling in her face or her voice. That in itself was an odd thing. Dylan had never cared one way or the other if she had a husband, and since the man was dead, there was no reason for him to be curious now, but he was.

The obvious question hung in the air, and he asked it. "Why were you looking at me and thinking of your husband?"

"In some ways, you remind me of him. That is all."

"Is that a good thing?" he asked, not sure he wanted to know. "Or a bad thing?"

"Neither. I was simply making an observation to myself."

She had asked that he not inquire into her past, but there was something he needed to know. Dylan relaxed his grip on the arms of his chair and leaned forward. He reached out and took her hand in his, then pulled it toward him, his thumb brushing back and forth across her knuckles. "And after two years, do you grieve for him?"

"Grieve?" she repeated, drawing out the word as if trying to determine whether or not that was quite the right way to put it. "I—" She drew a deep, shuddering breath, the only hint he had that she felt any emotion at all. "I stopped grieving a long time ago."

"Your hand is like ice." He could have been chivalrous and built up the fire, but there were better ways to warm her than that, and he wasn't chivalrous. He cupped her hand and lifted it in both of his, feeling it curl into a fist as he bent his head. "Relax, and let me warm you."

"I don't want you to," she said, but there was a breathless sort of uncertainty in her voice that his mind and his body recognized as a sign things were looking up. His curiosity vanished in the wake of more exciting possibilities. She tried to pull her hand free, but he held it fast.

He looked up. "What is it you fear?"

"Being hurt." The admission was simple, straightforward, and unassailable.

"I won't hurt you."

She closed her eyes. "No, you won't. I won't let you."

"Did your husband hurt you?"

"He—" She swallowed hard and opened her eyes, but she did not look at him. Instead, she stared past him again, into space. "My husband gave me some of the happiest moments of my life."

How queer her voice sounded as she talked

about powerful emotions with such reflective detachment, yet she was not detached. Dylan hated that she was looking past his shoulder as if seeing another man's ghost. Still, she was letting him touch her, and that was enough.

He moved to sit beside her, and he put his arm around her shoulders, still clasping her hand in one of his. She did not turn toward him, or away; instead, she stared straight ahead and did not move. There was nothing in her stiff pose that could honestly be called encouragement, but he would take what he could get.

"I would like to make you happy." Dylan bent his head over her hand, grazing the back of her fist with a kiss, then he opened his lips over the knuckle of her middle finger to taste her skin. He felt her fist unfold, and he turned her palm upward to kiss it. "I could do it, Grace. I could make you happy."

"Yes, I think you could," she murmured, a hint of surprise coming into her voice, as if she were admitting it to herself, as well as to him. "For a while."

He looked up from the hand he held in her lap. "Isn't that enough? God knows, there is little happiness in life. Can we not seize it where we find it, enjoy it while it lasts?"

"And find pleasure in the memories when it is over?" she countered, her voice suddenly hard. If that bitter tinge was due to her thinking about her husband, he intended to drive the other man out of her thoughts right now.

He straightened and let go of her hand, then lifted his own to cup her cheek. He turned her face toward him and tilted his head to kiss her.

She closed her eyes, but her mouth did not open at the touch of his. He ran his tongue back and forth over the closed seam of her lips, trying to coax her to part them.

After a moment, she did, opening them with a wordless sound, and shards of pleasure fissured his body, threatening to break apart his control in an instant. He slid his hand to the back of her head, and her hair felt like silk against his palm as he deepened the kiss, exploring the softness of her lips, the hard line of her teeth, her sweet taste.

As he kissed her, he moved his free hand down, grazing her with his fingertips in a light exploration along her throat, over her collarbone, and between her breasts. She had gained some weight during the three weeks she had lived in his home, he noticed as he continued down along her ribs to her waist, and he was glad of it.

He curved his palm over her hip and felt her body tense. He stopped, leaving his hand there, waiting. She did not push it away. He took advantage of that tacit agreement, curling his hand beneath her thigh. She stirred in his arms and turned her face away with a little gasp, breaking the kiss. An inarticulate sound came from her throat.

Was that a no? He decided it wasn't. He slid his hand down her thigh and eased his other arm around her shoulders again. He ran his lips along her cheek, then kissed the velvety skin of her ear and caressed the back of her knee through her dress.

Her breath was coming faster now, and he could feel fluttering shivers in her body, but she would not touch him, and that restraint was more erotic than he could have imagined. He lifted her legs across his own and eased her down until her head rested against the arm of the settee. He leaned over her and nuzzled her ear as he slid his hand back up her body to her breast. He embraced the shape of it, small and perfect in his hand. He could not feel her nipple against his palm through her clothing, but he could imagine it, and that alone was enough to inflame him. He made a rough sound, a groan in his throat smothered against her ear as he shaped her breast against his hand.

She touched the side of his neck, a light, tentative move, and the lust inside him ignited like brandy on fire. "Grace," he groaned, his hand reaching for the button of her lace collar. "Grace, you are so lovely. So sweet."

The button came free, and her hand curled over his wrist as the lace fell away.

Don't say it, for God's sake. His body was heavy, aching for her. *Not now, not yet.* Her fingers still curved around his hand as he unfastened the top button of her dress at her clavicle. "Let me do this," he murmured against her ear. The button came free and he moved to the next one. "Just let me love you."

She froze in his embrace, as if he had just thrown icy water over her. "Love, love!" she cried, and before he could gather his wits, she pressed her palms to his shoulders and pushed at him, succeeding just enough to roll off the settee and onto the floor. Scrambling to her feet, she was out of his reach before he could even begin to come to his senses.

Dylan sat up, his body thick with desire, his

mind unable to quite comprehend her sudden withdrawal.

"How lightly you talk of love!" She was still panting, but there was no soft warmth in her now. Those green eyes were as cold as any arctic glacier could be. "You do not even know what love is."

He forced his body out of chaos and into some semblance of control. He leaned back against the settee, and he did not care that his erection was flagrantly obvious through his tight trousers. "You know far more about love than I, of course."

"Yes, I think I do." She looked above his head, as if she could see through the velvet draperies and past the darkness outside. She went somewhere else, somewhere he could not follow her, somewhere that made her face soften in the fire's glow with a wistful sort of tenderness he had never seen before. He hated that look because it wasn't for him.

He stood up. "Forgive me. I did not know you had buried your heart along with your husband."

"What do you know of my heart!" she demanded. "I loved my husband, loved him in a way you could not possibly understand. You do not know what it feels like to love another more than yourself. I doubt you know what love really is or what it means."

He stood up, his body burning, anger growing hotter as desire grew cooler. "Now it is you who presumes to know what is in another's heart. I was in love once, Grace, as hard as that may be for you to believe."

There was a heaviness in his chest, a weight that made it hard for him to breathe. "I had been in love with the same girl since I was seven years old, a girl who was all the things I have never been, the only girl I ever wanted. I was twenty-one the summer after Cambridge when I came home and asked her to marry me. But I was the wild, younger son of the squire, marked with the tar brush even then. It was quite understandable, everyone thought, when she refused me. Over a decade has passed since then, and my romantic illusions about what love is may be gone, but I remember with painful clarity how it felt—every glorious, shining, agonizing moment of it."

Dylan took a deep breath, feeling as if he were sinking in quicksand, smothering in memories of a pretty, auburn-haired girl, a village green, kisses stolen and a proposal offered in the shadows of horse chestnut trees on a warm summer night. "Her name was Michaela Gordon. Yes," he added as her eyes widened in surprise, "the vicar's daughter."

He gave Grace a grin of self-mockery. "Shameless libertine that I have become, it seems I still possess a special weakness for virtuous women. What would people say?"

He bowed, then walked away, slamming the door of the library behind him. There was no satisfaction in the loud, resounding bang.

Chapter 10

~⁓◉⁓~

Sponsored by Whig families, Brooks's was the club of liberals, particularly the Devonshire set, but it was not really a club for those interested in politics. In truth, it was a club for radicals, artists, and heavy gamblers. The perfect club for Dylan.

He wasn't here for any of those reasons now, however. He was looking for Hammond, who was also a member. The viscount was always in the mood for less-than-respectable amusements, and Dylan needed a great deal of amusement just now.

The viscount's butler had proved to be accurate about his master's whereabouts, and Dylan found Hammond ensconced in a corner of Brooks's with a pair of their wilder acquaintances, Lord Damon Hewitt and that bold young pup, Sir Robert Jamison. A perfect group for his purposes. After that scene in the library an hour before, he had forced his turbulent emotions under control, but it would not take much provocation for them to erupt again. He badly needed to let off steam. The pubs and taverns near Temple Bar sounded like an excellent start, and these three would be more than willing to participate in alcoholic excess, skirt-chasing, and making sport of anything or anyone they came across.

Viscount Hammond was a long, lean, well-muscled fellow whose skill and quickness with a sword matched Dylan's own skill. He had brown hair, brown eyes, and was at the moment sporting a short, precisely groomed goatee. Since it went against current fashion, Dylan approved.

"Moore, you devil!" Hammond cried at the sight of him. "We were just talking of you."

The men were drinking port, a wine Dylan did not care for. He signaled to a waiter, who knew his drink of choice and nodded he would bring it. Dylan then sat down. "Talking of me, are you? What a dull subject."

"Exactly so!" Hammond cried. "I haven't seen you at Angleo's in ages."

"I've been working on a symphony. I've had little time for it."

"Make time, dear fellow. I have no decent swordsman with whom to spar."

"Spar?" Dylan countered. "I could slice you to ribbons any time I liked."

"You only wish," Hammond said, laughing. "I trounced you last time we fenced."

"Only because I stepped on a loose capstone and fell off the wall."

The last time he had gone out for wild sport with Hammond, the two had sparred with swords on top of a stone wall by Regent's Park, much to the fascination of the passersby. Like most of Dylan's exploits, it had made the scandal sheets.

"I am being serious about your absence, Moore," Hammond said. "Nearly a month into the season, and you've given the gossips nothing to talk about."

"Not a word of you in the society papers," Sir Robert added. "None of your naughty limericks heard at dinner parties. Not one steeplechase through Hyde Park. No reports of you with triplets in a seraglio—"

"Twins," Dylan corrected. "And it was not in a bawdy-house, but a bathhouse. Bagnio, Sir Robert, not seraglio."

"Moore, you must admit that you have been a bit dull this season," Lord Damon pointed out. "Not one scrape to your name. Is it not time for you to do something outrageous?"

"Does tonight suit you?" Dylan asked as a waiter set a bottle of his favorite brandy and a glass on the table before him. "I am amenable to the most outrageous adventures you can dream of," he went on, pouring out a generous measure of the liquor. "Particularly if it involves a pretty bawd or two." And virtuous women could go to the devil, he thought, lifting his glass and swallowing the brandy in one draught.

"So what shall we do, gentlemen?" Hammond asked. "Go slumming in Seven Dials, or perhaps Dylan and I should fence atop the rail on Westminster Bridge."

Dylan refilled his glass and opened his mouth

to concur with both suggestions, but Sir Robert spoke before he could do so.

"I say, there's Sir George Plowright. Yesterday, Givens tried to break his record, but only lasted eight minutes. Plowright is still the pugilistic champion at Gentleman Jackson's. Three years now, he's had the title."

"Fencing requires far more skill than boxing," Damon declared, earning himself toasts from both Hammond and Dylan.

"I'm not good at either one," Robert said gloomily.

Dylan leaned over and gave him an affectionate swipe across the head. "You're a young one," he reminded him, "scarce two and twenty. Give yourself a few years, and you'll surpass us all."

Sir George came swaggering by, his massive frame sheathed in a set of the gaudiest evening clothes imaginable. He was as well known for his colorful dress as he was for his boxing prowess.

"I believe he has surpassed himself tonight," Dylan commented, observing the subject of their conversation in the mirror on the wall behind Damon's head as Sir George and his companion, Lord Burham, sat down nearby. "A pink waistcoat and a bright blue coat? Ye gods."

"Shame the devil," Hammond said with a chuckle, "that a strutting peacock in pink-and-blue striped trousers and a pink waistcoat should weigh fifteen stone and be the undisputed champion of boxing in all Westminster."

"Bit of an irony, what?" Sir Robert added. "Anyone would think to look at him he favors the boys."

Dylan chuckled. "No, my young friend. There's

nothing so queer as that about Sir George. He has quite a different problem."

Robert glanced at Sir George, then back at the men seated with him, his eyes wide with curiosity. "What problem?"

Lord Damon was the one who chose to explain. "The demireps say he's a bit quick with his trigger," he said, striving for a straight face. "He cannot seem to get his pistol in the correct position before he fires it."

Comprehension dawned in the younger man's eyes, and he began to laugh. "Dash it, you're having me on."

The others shook their heads, and all four men began to laugh at once, so heartily that the subject of their conversation raised his voice to be heard over them.

"Burham, I say, it is a disgrace that Moore refuses to box. Can you imagine? I begin to think his reputation for daring is a great hoax."

Dylan met the other man's gaze in the mirror and lifted his glass, smiling. He said nothing.

"This is the man everyone thinks so brave." Sir George waved a hand in Dylan's direction, his voice becoming louder. "And why? Because he lives a degenerate life? Is that to be so admired?"

"Have a care, Moore," Sir Robert murmured. "He is baiting you on purpose. And in public, too."

Dylan took another swallow of brandy without taking his gaze from the beau in the mirror. "It's understandable," he assured the younger man. "Sir George and I are none too fond."

"The idiot challenged Moore at swords a few years ago," Lord Damon explained. "Of course, he was slashed to pieces. He still hopes to have his revenge by persuading Moore to box."

"Or by having me ostracized from society," Dylan added. "Preferably both."

"A life," Sir George continued, his voice growing louder, "of ridiculous displays, grandiose gestures, and defiance of moral principles. Yet people tolerate it because he is said to be so gifted with music. Is that acceptable? I say no."

The room was silent now, tense and waiting. Still speaking as if to Burham, Sir George went on, "Moore's life is of debauchery and excess, a contemptible mode in this Age of Reform." He turned and looked around the whole room. "Is it a harmless thing to kiss young ladies at public balls? To live openly with actresses and keep company with prostitutes? I call it whoredom."

Dylan stiffened, his fingers curling around his glass, wondering if word had gotten out about Grace. And what of Isabel? He didn't care about his own reputation, was rather proud of it, in fact. But if Dylan heard one disparaging word about either Grace or his daughter, he'd have Sir George's head.

He turned in his chair, putting on his most mocking smile. "Why Sir George, do you intend to become a clergyman, that you speak so?"

"You appear to need an excess of feminine companionship, sir. You live in Cock Alley."

"How would you know?" Dylan countered at once. "From what I hear, you cannot manage to enter the gates, much less live there."

His words caused a ripple of shocked laughter to echo through the room. As if struck by a sudden thought, Dylan added, "To be so afflicted, yet have the name Plowright. Most unfortunate."

The laughter got louder, and Sir George's face flushed dark red.

"No need to look so distressed, dear fellow," Dylan went on. "I have heard there are certain herbs one can take to assist one's . . . er . . . endurance."

Sir George took a predictable step forward, then stopped, his hands curled into fists at his sides.

Dylan saw the gesture, and stirred in his chair. He felt Hammond tug at his coat.

"Moore," he cautioned in a low voice, "this is piffle, not worth fighting about. Let it go."

Dylan didn't want to let it go. He was spoiling for this, especially tonight, and so was Sir George. He looked over at Hammond. "I don't believe I will," he said pleasantly.

The viscount placed his hands on the edge of the table and moved them as if playing piano. He shook his head.

Dylan let out his breath in a hiss of exasperation. Hammond was being sensible for once. He turned once again to Sir George, and with regret, he began to disengage. "I fence, and you box, Sir George. We are both Corinthians of different sport and, like all men, we enjoy the company of women. Pray, do not make a row of it."

Sir George stepped closer to his table, tapping his ivory walking stick on the carpet in three thumps. "You call yourself a Corinthian? You are nothing of the kind. You refuse time and again to engage in the true sport of honorable gentlemen, no matter the provocation. I am offended by your claim to be among Corinthians when you lack the bravery to prove it. You are no gentleman, Moore. In fact, you are a coward."

That was enough for a duel, but he'd settle for a fight. Dylan slammed his glass down, shoved back his chair, and rose. "By God, sir, you go too far!" he shouted as he faced Sir George. "I will not be called a coward by any man, especially not by a strutting pink peacock!"

He started forward, as did his challenger, but cooler heads intervened. Hammond rose and wrapped his arms around Dylan's shoulders to hold him back. Burham grabbed Sir George by the arm. They attempted to put a safer distance between the two men, but it was not going to work.

Dylan shook off the restraining arms wrapped around his shoulders. "I will not suffer this insult, Hammond," he said over his shoulder. "Plowright's craved this fight for years. This time, he shall have his way. And by fisticuffs, too, if that is what he wants."

Sir George gave him a smile of triumph. "When and where?"

"Moore!" Hammond caught his arm and turned him around. "Don't be stupid. You haven't boxed since Cambridge, and even then, never seriously. Think of your hands, man!"

Dylan yanked away again. "Would you allow any man to publicly denounce you a coward?" He looked at Sir Robert and Lord Damon. "Would you?"

None of them answered, and Dylan went on, "What is the record time with this pettifogging prick?"

They still said nothing.

He turned and glanced around. "Any man here," he shouted out, "tell me what the record is for standing against Sir George Plowright in a match."

"Twenty-one minutes, four seconds without going down for the count," someone shouted back to him.

"Easily done." Dylan looked at Sir George and gestured toward the doors. "Shall we?"

The other man raised his eyebrows. "Now? In the street? How like you, Moore."

"The mews then, if the street will not suit your refined sensibilities. I'll not stand with this insufferable accusation against me one moment longer. What's the matter, Sir George?" he added as the other man hesitated. "Are you afraid your pretty ruffled shirt will get a bit of horse dung on it?"

"Now it is, then. In the mews." Sir George bowed and walked away.

"I shall mark the lines," Burham said with a sigh and turned to follow his companion out of the club.

The moment they were gone, the silence ceased, and talk began to buzz all around the room. Odds were laid and bets were made. Brooks's was the club of deep gamblers, after all.

"Moore, don't do this," Lord Damon advised. "You could damage your hands."

Dylan did not reply. He shrugged out of his coat and began to undo the buttons of his waistcoat. He'd only come out for diversion, but this was far more than that. It was a matter of honor. Besides, his blood was surging through his body like thunder rolling, and he wanted the storm to break. He didn't mind breaking it over Sir George Plowright's head. He tore off his gray-and-black jacquard waistcoat and his cravat, then unbuttoned his shirt as his friends continued their attempts to talk him out of this course.

"Think, man," Hammond pleaded. "It means nothing. No one here but Sir George would ever brand you a coward, and everyone knows he's been itching for this ever since you thrashed him with a blade. The fellow's drunk, to boot."

"Is he? Good, for I'm sober as a parson." Dylan pulled his shirt over his head. "That gives me an advantage, I think."

"I doubt it, but if you are determined to do this, at least use practice gloves."

"Hammond, don't be tiresome," Dylan admonished. Seizing his narrow cravat from the table, he caught back his hair and knotted the silk. "No man uses practice gloves unless he is practicing. Will you act as second?"

Hammond lifted his hands in a hopeless gesture. "Of course. Do you remember the rules?"

"You'd best remind me quick." Dylan started for the door, and Hammond walked beside him, outlining Broughton's Rules. Sir Robert and Lord Damon followed them.

All the other men in the club followed them out of Brooks's, into St. James' Street, and around the corner to the mews behind. Word must have gotten across the street, for men were also coming out of White's to watch the fight. They reached the mews, where space had been cleared in the stable yard and Sir George, Burham, and a few men of their acquaintance were gathered, waiting for Dylan.

"Moore, don't!" someone cried, a voice he recognized, and he turned around, easily catching sight of the Duke of Tremore, who was tall enough to stand several inches above the other men in the crowd. His old friend was trying to wave him off, but he pretended not to see. He turned back around and walked to the wobbly square of chalk powder that marked the dirt in the center of the stable yard.

He faced Sir George. The other man had also stripped down, but only to his shirt. His sleeves were rolled back. True gentlemen, Dylan supposed, didn't bare their lily white chests to the fresh air.

It had been years since he'd fought with his fists. Words of training from Cambridge about the rudiments of proper boxing went through his head, and he remembered to tuck his thumbs. Just in time, too, for his first opportunity to strike came the moment the two men chosen to umpire lowered their arms and stepped back. Sir George was still waving to some of his friends when Dylan struck, landing a hard blow that snapped the other man's head sideways and sent jarring ripples of pain through his own arm.

Christ, he'd forgotten how much boxing hurt. He ducked Sir George's attempt at an answering blow, then he landed a second punch, this one to his opponent's thorax.

After that, however, his victories were few. When Sir George knocked him off his feet, Hammond tried to make him stay down. "Let it go, Moore," he said as the umpire counted. "Let it go."

"Damned if I will! I'll have at least twenty-one minutes and five seconds with this cock of the walk." He jumped to his feet, the umpires and seconds moved back, and the fight continued.

Plowright's fist came soaring toward his cheek, and he ducked, then struck upward with his own fist as he straightened, landing a blow to the chin that sent the current boxing champion staggering sideways. But Sir George got his revenge only a moment later in a series of punches to Dylan's head that made the whine pierce his brain in a series of shrill, ear-splitting whistles. With each blow, he felt as if his skull were splitting apart like a melon.

He lashed back, landing six hard, quick blows of his own across the other man's ribs, and he had the satisfaction of hearing a crack that sounded like a twig snapping.

His satisfaction didn't last. A moment later, Sir George laid him out for the second time. He heard one of the chosen umpires begin to count again, and he heard Tremore's hoarse voice shouting somewhere to his left.

"Hammond, for God's sake! You're his second. Haul him off!"

He felt the viscount's hands beneath his armpits to pull him back and end the fight. "Sod off!" he cried and tore himself away from the other man's grip. He got up and faced his opponent again, oblivious to the pleas of his friends.

On and on it went, and Dylan had never before realized just how long twenty-one minutes and five seconds could be. Until three weeks ago, it had been his custom to engage in swordplay and weights at Angleo's six days a week, and these were the moments that served to remind him why. He vowed that symphony or no, he would make time for that daily practice again.

Despite the excellent shape he was in, he could feel his body beginning to wear down against his massive opponent's continual onslaught and superior boxing skill. He ducked when he could, parried when he could, and took the blows when all else failed. Every time he was knocked down, he got up. It got harder and harder each time.

The sound of blows and the shouts of the crowd faded away, until the only thing he could hear was the whine in his head, and it enraged him that even now, when he was getting his organs pounded into mush, that damned noise wouldn't go away.

He took out his fury on the face in front of him. Moving his arm in an arc, using his entire body for momentum, he hit Sir George right on the jaw. Plowright's head whipped sideways, and in the halo of a streetlamp behind the mews, Dylan saw drops of blood and sweat scatter in an iridescent ring around the other man's head. He got in a second blow, to send Sir George's skull jerking the other way, but before he could strike a third time, something slammed into his solar plexus, a shattering pain hit him beneath his jaw, and he felt himself moving backward through the air, slowly, as if he were floating.

He hit the ground, and his back slammed into the hard-packed dirt. Every bone in his body shivered with pain.

Dylan blinked, but he couldn't see anything except stars flickering in a sea of black. Odd, he thought, for coal soot and gas streetlamps made seeing stars in town impossible. He blinked again, but this time, even the stars disappeared into blackness. He felt hands dragging him out of the marked fighting square. He closed his eyes and let them. He didn't know how much time had gone by since the fight began, but he'd better have gone twenty-one minutes and five seconds.

After a moment, the hands stopped dragging him. He willed himself to get up, but he could not seem to move. He could not open his eyes. Striving to concentrate, he slowly clenched his hands into fists, then relaxed them. They hurt, but he could tell from the feel of them that they were not broken.

Damned lucky, he thought, and almost wanted to laugh. Somehow, no matter what happened, no matter what outrageous thing he did, no matter how much he abused his body or his mind, he always managed to come out all right. Laudanum never addicted him, wicked ways never ruined him, stupid stunts never maimed him.

Even the hated whine had now receded enough that he could hear the crowd again. He discerned voices right above him. He opened his eyes, and it felt as if he were prying live oysters apart, but this time, he could see.

Two familiar faces were bent over him. He greeted the man of higher rank first as both men knelt down, one on each side of him. "Tremore," he croaked, ignoring the pain that shot through his jaw. "Back from the country estates for the season, I see. How are you, old friend?"

"Better than you at present, I think."

Dylan glanced at the man to his right. Hammond. He once again looked at the duke, and seeing both men together was so damned amusing that this time he did laugh, a low chuckle that hurt his ribs. "Now here we have a wager for the betting books. How long will the Duke of Tremore and Lord Hammond be able to linger here and not kill one another?"

Neither of them answered, but he could feel them examining him for broken bones and other injuries. He knew his hands were all right. Any other injuries he didn't care about. He'd probably care tomorrow, but now, there was only one thing he wanted to know. "Did I break the record?" he asked Hammond, frowning as the other man's face began to blur, then sharpen, then blur again.

"You did."

"How long?"

"I don't know. After the time was up, I kept shouting to you that you were done, but it was as if you couldn't hear me."

Dylan licked his lips and tasted blood. "I want the time."

"We'll find out later."

He tried to shake his head. "I want to know now."

"Even if you didn't break the record," Tremore interjected, pressing a handkerchief to the side of his face, "you put on a fine show for all of us. They'll be talking about it for years."

Dylan blinked two or three times, then narrowed his eyes on Hammond's face, trying to keep him in focus. "I want the goddamned time."

"Deuce take it, Dylan," another voice entered the conversation, one he had not heard for quite a long while, one that sounded decidedly irritated. "What difference does it make right now?"

"I want the time written in the betting book,"

he told the viscount, ignoring that other voice. "And I'll have Plowright recant his accusation in front of witnesses."

"I'll see to it." Hammond straightened and vanished from view. Another man took Hammond's place at once, and the sight of the disapproving face above him made Dylan wish it weren't too late to pretend he was unconscious.

"Ian," he greeted. "Aren't you supposed to be in Venice?"

"I docked at Dover this morning." His brother shook his head with a heavy sigh. "I have business in Devonshire, and I had intended to go straight on, but then I changed my mind, thinking to stay the night in London and pay a call on you. I can't think why, since even after six months away, I find that nothing has changed."

Dylan tried to grin, but his face felt stiff, as if glue had been spread over it and left to dry. "Reassuring for you, what?"

Ian did not answer but instead knelt beside him. "Of all the stupid, reckless, foolhardy things you have ever done," his brother said, beginning to help Tremore examine him, "this tops the lot."

"I have a reputation to maintain."

Ian did not reply. He glanced at the man opposite him. "Your Grace."

"Excellency," Tremore answered. "Congratulations on your successful negotiations in Venetia."

"Thank you."

"Well, Moore," the duke said after a few moments, "I do not believe you've broken any bones. Still, I believe a physician should examine you."

Before Dylan could answer, Hammond's face once again appeared in his line of vision, upside down this time. Dylan lifted his chin to have a better look at the man standing behind him. "Well?" he demanded. "How far did I get?"

"Twenty-two minutes and seventeen seconds, you amazing bastard." Hammond shook his head, laughing with him. "Not only did you set a new record, but the members forced Plowright to recant his accusation of cowardice."

"Cowardice?" Tremore and Ian asked at once.

"He called me a coward," Dylan confirmed, his voice sounding as cracked as he felt. "Because I don't box."

Ian groaned. "And because you are the most pigheaded, exasperating, contrary man in England, you just had to prove him wrong."

"He did it with a vengeance," Hammond said. "As we speak, Sir George is being trussed by his friends as if he's a Christmas goose. A cracked rib, they think."

"Bloody hell," Dylan choked, laughing in spite of how much it hurt. "That'll be in the society papers, I warrant." He took a deep breath. "Gentlemen, help me up."

"I believe you should be carried," Ian advised.

"I won't be carried anywhere until it's shoulder high." Before Ian could argue, he sat up. Pain shimmered through his body, and he sucked in air through his teeth. He counted to three and hauled himself to his feet, then wrapped one arm around Tremore's shoulders and the other around Ian's. He grinned at his brother. "Another escapade for my scandalous, someday-to-be-published memoirs."

"Memoirs?" Ian muttered as they began walking to an elegant carriage marked with the Tremore insignia. "Over my dead body."

There were twenty-four rosebuds embroidered on the edge of her counterpane. Grace knew that because she had counted them three times, recognizing each one in the darkness of her bedroom by its feel against her fingertips. There were also eighteen full-blown roses and thirty-six leaves.

She gave a frustrated sigh and folded back the counterpane, wondering if perhaps she should light a lamp and read for a bit. She had lain here in the dark for what seemed like hours, counting rosebuds and leaves and even sheep, but none of it had made any difference. She still could not fall asleep.

It was all Moore's fault. The wretched man and his kisses. Her body still burned everywhere he had touched her.

I have a weakness for virtuous women.

Grace bit her lip. She wasn't virtuous. Not at all.

There had been a time when she had thought herself to be. She had taken such pride in being the good girl—the dependable older sister who had loved watching over six younger siblings, the good friend who had kept confidences and remembered birthdays, the pupil who had always done her assignments, the serious-minded daughter who had never given her parents a moment of worry. A sweet, steady girl, people in Stillmouth had always said, their approval appealing to her vanity in a way no comments about her looks ever could. She had sung in the church choir. She had done good works for the poor. She had said her prayers every night. And she'd done it all so smugly, too, with the firm conviction that she was good and virtuous, when her goodness and her virtue had never been tested.

Then a wild French painter with eyes like the sky had come to Cornwall. Of all the places in the world to paint, Etienne Cheval had chosen Still-mouth, the tiny village on the cliffs of Land's End where strangers never came, nothing ever happened, and it was easy to be good.

On a hillside when she was seventeen, she had met the great Cheval, and in that instant, her whole world had changed. Ten years her senior, Etienne had known all about life and even more about love. Seventeen years of being responsible and serious had vanished the first time he'd made her laugh. Virtue had been given the first time he'd kissed her. A week later, Grace Anne Lawrence, the sweet, steady, sensible girl so admired by everyone, had eloped with a French painter of no fortune and dubious reputation and changed her life forever.

Her first two years with Etienne had been the happiest time she had ever known, two years of sweet, piercing love and wild, crazy lovemaking. Then, it had all gone wrong somehow. In the bleak, dark moods when he had not been able to paint, he had blamed her. Day by day, he had grown darker, she had stopped laughing, and the love had died.

Grace wrapped her arms around her pillow. How did one hang on to love and happiness? For those first two years of joy, she had paid a high, high price. During her years away from England, no member of her family had answered any of her letters. When she had returned to Stillmouth last autumn, she had discovered that her parents had died and her brother had inherited the estate and the burden of her scandal. The woman James had loved had broken their engagement, and he had wed a woman well beneath his position in life. Her sisters had never married. All five were spinsters because she had ruined the family name.

Eight years had passed since that day on a Cornish hillside. Her girlish notions of virtue were gone, her reputation was shredded beyond amendment, and her family was disgraced to this very day. She had seen the world beyond Land's End and had found it wasn't nearly as wonderful as she had thought it would be.

She wanted to go home. That wasn't possible in a literal sense, but if she could stay here for a year, just one year, she could have a home of her own and the sort of life that ought to suit an ordinary English woman. A stable, proper, mundane life.

Let me love you.

Love. The man didn't have the foggiest notion. Perhaps he had been in love with that vicar's daughter as a boy growing up, but he wasn't capable of it now. Artists loved their art. Everything and everyone else was a distant second.

Dylan Moore was not a boy in love with a girl and dreaming to marry her. He was a man, and Grace knew precisely what he wanted from her. She'd known it the moment she had seen him in that alley. He wanted her, yes. For an amour. That wasn't love. Not even close.

She wasn't cut out of the cloth to be a man's mistress, for sweet words about love and money put in an account for bedroom services rendered.

She wasn't hard enough for that life, and she didn't want to be. After Etienne—and even while she had been with him—there had been no shortage of men trying to beguile her with money and talk of love. A pretty woman always got offers of that sort.

This was the first time she had ever been tempted to accept. Despite Moore's reputation and what she knew about men like him, she still yearned for him to touch her again. His every kiss drew her closer. She pressed her fingers to her lips and hugged her pillow tight.

It had been so long, so long, and she was so lonely. Grace couldn't love with her body alone, but there were times, like right now, when she wished she could.

Chapter 11

It looked worse than it really was, Dylan supposed, staring at his reflection in the mirror on the wall of his bedchamber. Torn trousers, a nasty cut over his eye, bruises forming on his face and chest, but the doctor had cleaned away the blood, and there was no concussion or other serious damage to his body. He would be sore for perhaps a week, he'd been told, but after that, he would be well. The bruises would take a bit longer to disappear, perhaps a month or so.

"Damned lucky," Ian muttered.

"Yes, indeed," the doctor agreed and glanced at Phelps. "I recommend treating the sorest muscles with the application of ice or a soak in icy water," he told the valet. "Twenty minutes or so, several times a day, especially the hands. After a day or two, the soreness should ease, and he may use his hands again."

"Thank you, Doctor Ogilvie," Ian said. "I'll show you out."

The two men started toward the door, but the doctor paused on his way out the door and turned to Dylan once again. "Mr. Moore, before I go, I would like to say that my wife and I so enjoy hearing performances of your work. We saw you conduct your Twelfth Symphony at Saddler's Wells some years ago, and it was a wonderful experience. Quite moving."

"Thank you." Dylan was always gratified to know people appreciated his work, but he hoped the physician would not ask the inevitable question—when he would conduct again. "I am glad you enjoyed it."

The doctor departed with Ian, and Dylan dismissed Phelps from the room. He then turned to Tremore, who was seated in one of the velvet chairs by the fireplace. Hammond, being on hostile terms with his brother-in-law, had not ridden with them to Portman Square in the duke's carriage.

"Well?" Dylan asked as he sat down carefully in the padded bench at the foot of his bed. "Which do you want to know first, why I got into a stupid pugilistic contest with Sir George, or why I was with Hammond?"

"No man should stand down when another man publicly calls him a coward, but you could have called him out another way, my friend. Boxing? You are damned fortunate that your hands are not seriously damaged. As for the other, I recognize that carousing with Hammond has an appeal for both of you, but I do not understand it.

When this news gets out, Viola will know you were with Hammond, yet—"

"The unhappiness between a man and his wife is not my business, nor is it yours, Tremore, as much as you love your sister. Hammond and I are acquaintances, not friends. We both need men of good character to be our friends." Dylan smiled. "How are you, my friend of good character, and how is my sweet, violet-eyed duchess?"

"My duchess," Tremore answered with the pointed emphasis that always amused Dylan when he needled his friend about Daphne, "is in excellent health. A bit queasy in the mornings, of course," he added, his face taking on that rather sheepish expression of a man whose wife was pregnant, "but otherwise, she is well."

"I've already wagered on a son," Dylan told him. "I do not believe you would have it any other way."

"A daughter would make me equally happy, I assure—"

"Heavens!" a horrified voice interrupted from the doorway. Grace was standing there, one hand on the doorjamb and the other holding the edges of her white dressing gown together. She looked more beautiful than ever, with her hair in a thick plait over one shoulder and her bare feet peeping from beneath the hem of her plain white nightdress.

Both men stood up. Dylan did it too quickly and grimaced, aware of every place Plowright had danced fists across his ribs. She gave a cry and ran to him at once, glancing over the bruises on his face and bare chest with alarm.

"Are you all right? I heard all the commotion, servants running up and down the stairs, and I got up. Osgoode told me you had been in a fight." Grace lowered her gaze to his hands. "Oh, no," she choked. "Dylan, what have you done?"

That was the first time she had ever said his name. She had been so angry with him only a few hours before, yet here she was, soft, tousled, and pretty, smelling like pear soap and looking worried. Worried about him. A grin spread across his face.

"Steady on, Grace. A few bruises, I grant you, but nothing broken. I shall be right as rain in no time. Look."

He held out one bandaged hand, flexing it to show her there was nothing broken. She hesitated, then gently took his hand in both of hers, staring down at the white linen strips that bound it, touching a smear of dried blood on his finger the doctor had missed. The noise in his head quieted, and he forgot all about the pain in his body.

Suddenly, she let go of his hand and looked up at him, frowning. "Have you no common sense?"

"None," he confessed, liking the way she got that little dint in her chin when she frowned. He began to smile, watching her.

"You are a composer, in heaven's name! What are you thinking to engage in fisticuffs? You could have been . . . you might have . . . your hands . . . oh, Dylan, really!"

She was angry now, angry enough to be sputtering. She pressed her lips together, and her frown deepened. He knew she was trying to impress upon him just what a stupid thing he had done and how angry she was about it, but try as she might, she just could not look stern. Her mouth was too full, her eyes too soft. She looked ferocious enough to intimidate a puppy.

He wanted to plant a kiss right on that pursed-up mouth. The thought of it was enough to raise the heat in his blood and ease away the pain in his body with much more pleasurable aches, and he knew he was on the mend already.

A polite cough reminded him there was someone else there. He looked up to find Tremore standing by his chair a dozen feet away, watching them.

Grace gave a little gasp. She clutched the edges of her dressing robe together, realizing that they were in Dylan's bedchamber and that she was in a state of dishabille. She ducked her head, her cheeks flaming. "Forgive me," she mumbled and turned away, rushing past Tremore and out of the room.

The duke watched her go, then turned to him, one eyebrow lifted as if in inquiry.

Dylan's grin vanished at once. "Believe it or not, she is not what you think."

"It is not my place to think anything."

Perhaps, but Dylan could read his honorable friend's mind like a book.

Another one.

Given what he had just witnessed, Tremore's conclusion was inevitable and accurate, given Dylan's intentions. Despite that fact, he was angry at the implication and felt compelled to deny it. "She's not my dollymop."

"I did not say she was."

Dylan ignored the mild reply. "She is not anything of the sort. She is a respectable widow of good family." What was he saying? He didn't know anything about her family. "Nothing is going on."

"Moore, you do not have to explain anything to me."

"Of course I don't," Dylan snapped. "I know I don't." Then why was he? The duke was looking at him with an impeccably neutral countenance. "Damn it, Tremore, must you always be so damned polite? How we remain such excellent friends baffles me."

Before the duke could answer that, another voice spoke. "Politeness is generally regarded as a favorable trait, Dylan," Ian said as he walked through the open doorway. "Some of us work to cultivate it."

Dylan ignored that, still looking at Tremore. "She is not my mistress."

"Of course not."

"What mistress?" Ian looked from one man to the other. "Of whom are you talking?"

"You missed the angel in a white nightgown who floated through here a few moments ago," Tremore told him. "Lovely eyes," he added with a sudden grin. "Compose a sonata about her yet?"

Dylan saw no humor in that question. He remembered full well the night two years before when he had teased and goaded the duke about Daphne, actually provoking Tremore to a fight just for the fun of seeing the other man lose control. Tremore had not found it amusing at the time, though he seemed to be taking enjoyment in turning the tables.

"Not a sonata," Dylan replied, answering the question in all honesty. "A symphony."

"Good," the duke said unexpectedly. "About damned time you composed something of substance again. If that young woman inspired it, so much the better."

"What is all this about?" Ian demanded. "Do you have a woman living with you again?"

"A very lovely one," Tremore put in. "Blond. Green eyes."

"I'm shocked," Ian said, sounding anything but. "As I said, some things do not change."

"She is not living with me!" The statement was so ridiculous that he amended it at once. "I mean, she is, but not that way. Not the way the two of you are thinking."

Ian gave a laugh of disbelief. "And pigs fly."

Dylan let out his breath in an exasperated sigh. Perhaps this was the right moment to tell his brother and his best friend what would inevitably become common knowledge anyway. Hell with it. "Not just a woman," he corrected. "Grace is governess to my daughter."

"Daughter?" the two men said together.

He rather enjoyed their momentarily shocked faces. "Yes, gentlemen, my daughter. Isabel is eight years old, her mother is dead, and she was placed on my doorstep by a French Catholic nun two weeks ago."

Ian started to speak. "But how—"

"I have hired a governess for her," he went on, cutting off his brother's inevitable questions before they could be asked, before Ian could tell him what he thought was right for Isabel, what was wrong with Grace living in his house, before he could be tiresome and proper and inconvenient. "I intend to make provision for the child out of my allowance from the family estates as well as my own rents and income, so it is a good thing you are back from Venice. We shall both need to sign documents with the attorneys. I shall have them drawn."

"Before you do that, it has to be established for certain that you are the father of this child," Ian said.

"She is mine."

"How do you know?"

"If you met her, dear brother, you would not ask such a ridiculous question. And I do not wish to discuss the issue of her paternity any further."

"If you expect additional funds from the family estates to pay for her, you had better be willing to discuss it. How can you possibly know this child is yours?"

"I am his daughter! I am!"

The voice that spoke caused all three men to turn to see another female in white nightdress standing in the doorway, one much darker, much younger, and much more fierce when she scowled than the previous one. Isabel's small hands balled into fists as she looked at Ian. "He is my father, and don't you dare say he's not!"

Dylan grinned. *Take him on, my girl*, he thought with approval. *Take him on.*

"I'll be damned," Tremore said under his breath.

"Good Lord!" Ian said, staring at her. From the sound of his voice, no additional convincing would be required.

Isabel ran to Dylan. She wrapped one arm around his hips and glared at her uncle. "I look more like him than you do," she cried and pointed an accusing finger at Ian. "How do we know you're really his brother?"

Tremore choked back a laugh. "Excellent point."

Ian stared at her for a moment, then lowered his face into his hand. "I suppose something like this was bound to happen sooner or later," he muttered against his palm.

Isabel looked up at Dylan and frowned at him. "You got in a fight."

"Yes, I did. I am going to be well again though, thank you for asking."

"What about your hands? Are they all right?"

"Yes."

"You look awful, Papa."

Dylan knelt to her eye level. "Are you not supposed to be asleep at this hour? What are you doing down here, eavesdropping on conversations?"

"I always eavesdrop on conversations. How do you think I find out things? Besides, it's your fault I'm not asleep. Who could sleep with all this excitement going on?"

"Nevertheless, it's back to bed for you, little one. I have to tell your uncle Ian all about you."

Her chin quivered. "I am your daughter!" she cried, as if she needed to convince him when he was looking into a face so much like his own. "I am."

He lifted his bandage-wrapped hand and smoothed her hair back, feeling deuced awkward. "I know."

She glanced at Ian with resentment. "Don't let them say different."

"I won't." Dylan turned her toward the door. "Back to bed," he ordered with a gentle push, watching her go out the door.

Ian closed the door behind her. "Well . . ." he began, then stopped.

"Astonishing," Dylan murmured. "Isabel has managed to do something I have failed to do all our lives, Ian. Render you speechless."

Tremore spoke. "Moore, I vow I thought that child was going to go at your brother with fists flying. She looked just like you with Plowright earlier."

"She did," Ian admitted. "By God, she did."

Dylan smiled a bit ruefully. "Did I mention she composes brilliantly?"

There was a long silence, then Ian drew a deep breath. "Well," he said again, sinking down in the nearest chair, "that settles the matter, I think." With his usual diplomatic talent for understatement, he added, "This has been quite an evening."

"Here. I've finished this silly assignment." Isabel thrust the slate toward Grace and walked away, her shoes thumping on the floor as she returned to her small rosewood desk. She flung herself in her chair, crossed her arms, and gave her governess a resentful glare. "Are we done yet?"

"After over a month as my pupil, you should know such conduct does not work, Isabel," Grace reminded her, refusing to be provoked. The child was still fighting against the structure of her new life, a life with rules that were enforced. Today, Isabel had decided to test that enforcement by reverting to her former behavior, being insolent with both Grace and Molly, and being a thorough brat.

Grace glanced toward one corner of the nursery, where Molly sat doing some mending. Molly was looking at Grace, and when she met Grace's eyes, she shrugged as if she, too, was baffled by the child's behavior.

After several more trips to the agencies, Grace had made Molly the child's nanny on a permanent basis, for the housemaid had proven to be kind, patient, and stubborn enough not to give in when Isabel tried to rule her. Surprisingly, or perhaps because she feared the dragons that she'd seen Grace interview at the agencies, Isabel had accepted the arrangement.

"She was like this when she woke up, Mrs. Cheval."

Isabel sat up straight in her chair. "Like what?"

"Cranky," Molly answered.

"I'm not cranky." She gave Grace a pointed stare and yawned. "I'm bored."

Grace ignored that challenging look. "I think we are going to finish our lesson on Shakespeare."

The child's chin lifted a notch. "No, I'm going to play piano. I want to work on my new concerto."

"No," Grace answered with quiet firmness. "This morning, we are going to study Shakespeare. And take the insolence out of your voice, if you please."

Isabel inhaled a deep breath, then pushed the air out between her closed lips, making a sound that would have banished any young lady from good society for weeks. "Moderate your tone, dear," the child mimicked, her voice cracking in a way that sounded nothing like Grace. "Sit up straight. Eat your carrots. Walk, don't run."

"I am happy that you have been paying attention to what I say," Grace answered, sounding well pleased. "That is excellent."

Isabel stuck out her tongue, then walked over to the window in a huff. She turned her back and stared out the window at the mews and the busy London street beyond it.

Grace turned her attention to the slate, reading the lines scrawled there.

You can't blame Iago for Desdemona. Othello killed her because he wanted to. Iago was only saying what Othello already suspected. He wanted to kill his wife, and Iago couldn't make him do it. Nobody can make you do something if you don't already want to do it.

Grace pressed her lips together, trying not to smile. A true and unusual analysis of Iago's character. Isabel really was a clever girl. Not that she needed to use her lessons in Shakespeare to express her rebellious mood. It was quite clear.

Grace wished Dylan would spend more time with the child. It had been two weeks since that night in the library when he had promised he would try to make time for his daughter. He now came up to the nursery in the afternoons before he started composing, but these visits were brief, fifteen or perhaps twenty minutes. He listened to her at the piano and talked with her about her lessons, but he did not play with her, or take her anywhere, or eat any meals with her. But then, how could he take her anywhere or dine with her when he stayed out all night and didn't go to bed until eight or nine in the morning? Sometimes, the servants told her, he did not come home at all.

Grace would have discussed it with him before now, but except for the late afternoon and early evening hours when he locked himself in the music room, he was seldom home long enough for her to discuss anything with him. Isabel needed his love and affection and fifteen or twenty minutes a day was not enough.

Grace set the slate aside and looked over at the girl by the window. "Take your seat, Isabel, and we shall continue with our discussion of Othello."

The girl did not move. "We've been here forever. It must be nearly three o'clock by now."

"It is barely half past two."

"Oh, heavens!" Molly cried at the mention of the hour. "I promised Mrs. Ellis that recipe for Irish soda bread hours ago, and she wanted it for tonight's dinner." Molly set aside her mending and stood up, looking at Grace. "If you don't mind, ma'am."

"Of course not," she answered, and the nanny left the room.

Grace looked over at the window again. "Your father will probably be coming in half an hour or so. Until then, we are going to do Shakespeare. After your father leaves, you may go into the other room and work on your concerto."

The child did not turn around. "I already told you, I'm not doing any more Shakespeare. I hate him."

"You don't hate Shakespeare. You've studied him enough that you were able to correct your father's quote from *Much Ado About Nothing* just three or four weeks ago. If you hated his work, you wouldn't know it so well."

Isabel turned and gave her a scowl. "It was fun with Papa. It's not fun with you." She returned her attention to the view outside. "What are you going to do about it? Take away my piano privileges? Do it. I don't care."

There was another option available for this sort of behavior, one she remembered from her own girlhood, one she had used on her own younger siblings, one that if, judiciously employed, was far more effective than taking away privileges. Grace decided it was time to use it.

Setting her jaw, she marched across the room, grabbed Isabel by the ear, and pulled. The result was predictable and immediate. The child gave a loud yelp of protest but was incapable of doing anything more as Grace hauled her back to her desk.

She pushed the little girl down into her chair, none too gently. Isabel rubbed her ear with another scowl. "I hate you."

"I am sorry for it," Grace answered, "since I happen to like you very much, and I will continue to do so despite moments such as this."

Grace turned toward her own desk and picked up the slate. "I trust that we may now return to Othello? In your essay, you make a valid point, Isabel. If one cannot be made to do something one does not want to do—"

"Then," Isabel interrupted, "one has a very inefficient governess."

The sound of a chuckle caused both Grace and her pupil to turn toward the far end of the room, where Dylan stood in the doorway, one shoulder against the frame, arms folded across his chest, watching them. The bruises on his face from that fight a fortnight ago were fading from purple to yellow, making him look even more disreputable than he already was.

Caught by surprise, Grace tightened her grip around the slate in her hand. He was early today.

"Papa!" Isabel shoved back her chair and ran to him. He straightened away from the door at once and leaned down, opening his arms to his daughter as any father might do. He gave the little girl a smile, and the faded bruises made Grace think that must be what fallen angels looked like when they smiled—charming, handsome, and battered.

He lifted the child up in his embrace without showing any pain, so he must have fully recovered from his pugilistic adventure.

"I'm so glad you've come!" Isabel cried.

"Lessons difficult today?" he asked.

"She's had me locked up in here for hours with Othello," Isabel answered with a shudder. She wrapped her arms around Dylan's neck with exaggerated drama. "Please take me away!"

He glanced over at Grace as he set his daughter on her feet. "Has she been an army general again?" he asked, turning that smile on her.

Grace ignored that and glanced at the clock. "Isabel, you have spent exactly forty-two minutes on Shakespeare. Please do not exaggerate."

"Don't believe her, Papa," Isabel told him in a stage whisper loud enough for Grace to hear. "It's been hours. She is being very cruel to me."

"Cruel?" He shot Grace an amused glance. "I don't believe it."

Isabel proceeded to tell him just what a dictatorial horror Grace was for making her read *Othello* and why it was one of Shakespeare's dullest plays. "It's the worst, Papa," she summed up. "Worse than all the Henry plays put together. I like the comedies ever so much better."

"You won't have to worry about Othello much longer," he consoled her. "Isn't it nearly time for your piano practice?"

"Yes. Can I use your piano today?"

"May I," Grace corrected.

Isabel let out a heavy sigh as if to show her father how tedious governesses were. "May I use your piano today?"

"Yes, you may," he answered.

"I am writing a concerto. Come and help me with it."

"Isabel," he said, "you do not need my help. You compose beautifully."

"Duets, then?" she suggested. "Will you play duets with me?"

"I should love to play duets with you, but I cannot. Not today." He bent down and kissed the top of her head. "I have to go. I have an appointment this afternoon."

He started to turn away, but the child reached out and grabbed his hand. "Papa!" she cried. "You just got here!"

"I know, sweeting, but I have to go or I shall be late." He withdrew his hand from hers, and he did not see the hurt on her face, for he was already walking away. "I won't be back until very late tonight, but perhaps we might play tomorrow."

Grace glanced again at the clock. Today he had stayed exactly four minutes. These moments in the afternoon with him were the happiest part of Isabel's day, and all he could give her was four minutes. Grace set her jaw. Tonight, she was going to speak with him about this. She would wait until he came home, all night if necessary. This could not continue.

"Tomorrow, then." Isabel walked in the other direction, back toward the window, ducking her head as she passed Grace to hide her expression, but it was too late. Grace had already caught a glimpse of the child's face. There was no scowl, no tears, just horrible, crushing disappointment. Isabel walked to the window and stood with her back to the room, looking out at London.

Grace could not bear it. She turned to follow him and stopped, for he had not yet left.

He was staring at Isabel's back, and he was not smiling. He took a step toward her, then stopped. His lips tightened, and without a word, he turned on his heel and left the room.

Grace ran out of the nursery after him. When she reached the stairs, she peered over the rail, just in time to see him turn on the landing. "Dylan!" she called after him. "Dylan, I need to talk with you."

He stopped on the landing and looked up at her, his expression unreadable. "It will have to wait. I have an appointment."

He did not wait for an answer but continued on down the stairs, where he disappeared from view.

Damn the man. Frustrated, Grace slapped the polished wooden cap of the newel post with her hand. *Tonight*, she vowed and returned to the nursery, where Isabel was still standing by the window.

With a heavy heart, Grace crossed the room to stand beside her, and she followed the child's gaze to the street below.

Dylan was on the sidewalk, waiting for his carriage, which had just entered the square. It stopped in front of the house, he stepped up inside, and the carriage rolled away.

The clock ticked away one minute, then two. Then Isabel spoke, still looking out the window. "He doesn't want me."

"You do not know that," Grace said at once. "He has not been a father very long. Give him a bit more time to get used to you."

"He's had a month."

Grace almost wanted to smile at that. To a child, a month was such a very long time.

Isabel gave a heavy sigh. "I hoped it would be different here."

That statement puzzled Grace, and she looked at the profile of the little girl beside her. "Different in what way?"

"I don't know." She sounded bewildered, plaintive. "Just different. Like real families are. Me and Papa, like a real family."

Grace thought of her own childhood. She'd had a real family once, knew how important it was. "I know what you mean. But you and your father are a real family."

Isabel shook her head. "He goes out every night

and he does not come home until almost the middle of the morning. Where does he go?"

Grace bit her lip. She didn't think either of them wanted to know.

"If he loved me, he wouldn't go. He would stay here, and we'd have dinner together. He would play piano with me and tuck me in. He'd take me to the country and we'd eat apples together and he'd teach me to fence. I could have a pony and learn to ride." She paused, then went on in a harder voice, "He goes out all the time, and he drinks a lot. He smokes hashish, and he takes laudanum. He gets in messes with women and has duels and fights and all sorts of things. I knew all about him before I came here. I thought once I was here, he would love me, and he wouldn't do those things. That he would change."

Oh, my dear little girl, Grace thought, looking at her with compassion. If only one could force another's affections. If only men could change. If only it were that easy.

Suddenly, the child tore her gaze from the view out the window and turned to her, lifting her chin. In her expression was that look of hard determination Grace was coming to know so well. "I shall make him love me!" she cried, slamming her fist into the palm of her other hand, her childish vehemence heartbreaking. "I shall!"

Grace pulled the little girl into her arms, moving her hand up and down Isabel's back in a comforting gesture. "I know you shall," she said and hoped with all her heart that the child would succeed.

Chapter 12

~~~~∽∽~~~~

Everything was in order. All the documents had been prepared in accordance with Dylan's wishes. They included his formal acknowledgment of his daughter, the change of her surname to Moore, the specification of Ian as her guardian should anything happen to him, and his new will leaving her everything he had.

Once he signed these documents, Isabel would be his legal daughter. Dylan stared at the sheaf of papers before him on Mr. Ault's desk, and though he knew the solicitor was waiting, he made no move to sign them.

It was not because of doubt. As he had told Ian that night two weeks earlier, there was no question that Isabel was his, and even his practical, sensible brother had admitted the truth of that. The question of her paternity was not what made Dylan sit here in the solicitor's office as the seconds went by.

It was that look on Isabel's face, the same look she gave him every day when he went up to the nursery. She wanted not just a few minutes a day and a duet or two at the piano, but so much more. She wanted him to love her.

Dylan stirred in his chair, restless and uncomfortable. He'd seen a similar look on other faces. Faces full of expectation and the wistful hope that he would change, be good, do what was right. Faces that reflected such eagerness to please him, such expectation of his love in return. Isabel was a little girl, but no matter their age, all females wanted too damned much. They pinned their hopes and dreams on a bad lot and expected to be happy as a result.

And he was a bad lot. He was obsessed, and by only one thing. He was ruthless, temperamental, and wholly selfish. He went in for the lusts of the flesh, and he enjoyed them. He made no secret of his nature—flaunted it, in fact. Yet it seemed to be his destiny to have yet another female giving him that look, wanting something from him that he could not give.

Isabel was his daughter. If any person in the world should matter to him, it should be his own child. What was wrong with him?

Dylan pinched the bridge of his nose with his fingers. God, his daughter's eyes, so like his in appearance and so unlike him in the emotions they reflected—eyes that were innocent, vulnerable, and full of faith, eyes that made him want nothing more than to get away. He was no good at living up to expectations. They smothered him.

You do not even know what love is.

Grace was wrong. He did know what love was,

he just didn't have enough of it to go around. Music took it all. There never seemed to be enough left for another person.

Had not Michaela herself rejected him for that reason?

I would always be second in your life, Dylan. I do not want to be second. I want to be first.

His daughter, looking at him, wanting to be first.

Impossible. No one could ever be first. Not even his own little girl, a precocious eight-year-old with a scowl like thunder and eyes that had too much hope in them.

Mr. Ault brought him out of his reverie with a little cough. Dylan looked at the dry, precise little man who sat behind the desk. "Excellent work, Mr. Ault. Exactly what I wanted, thank you."

"We hope to always give the best of service to you and all your family, sir." The solicitor held the quill out to him.

No matter what expectations his little girl had of him, it did not alter his responsibility. He took the quill from the solicitor's hand, dipped the point in the inkwell on the desk, and scrawled his name on each page where his signature was required.

When he finished, he handed back the quill and rose to his feet.

Mr. Ault also stood up. "I shall send any documents pertaining to your income from the family estate to your elder brother for his signature."

"Yes. Thank you, Mr. Ault. Good day."

The little man bowed, and so did he. Putting on his hat, Dylan left the solicitor's office and stepped out into the street, drawing in deep breaths of air. The deed was done, officially declaring Isabel his daughter. He wished he felt like a father.

That evening after dinner with Molly and Isabel in the nursery, Grace left the child in the nanny's care and went into the library to practice her violin while the little girl had her bath. She did not want to be angry about Dylan, worry about Isabel, or think about the emotional scene earlier in the day. Her employer was a complicated man, and her pupil was exhausting, and all Grace wanted right now was some quiet time to herself. She shut the door, shut out the world, and lost herself in her favorite pastime.

When she returned to her room an hour later, she found a surprise waiting on her dressing table, a bouquet of half a dozen early pink tulips from the park outside. They were tied with a white silk ribbon, and with them was a note. The slip of paper was small and had only one line of words written on it, words in a round, upright handwriting that was very familiar to her by now.

I am sorry I was so beastly today. Isabel.

Grace touched her fingertip to one of the opening flower buds in the vase and smiled. That child was a trial, true enough, but she also did the most unexpectedly sweet things. An encouraging sign, Grace thought, and she wanted to show Isabel how much she appreciated the child's thoughtful gesture.

Struck by an idea, Grace rummaged in her

valise and found her scrapbook. She pulled it out, along with a wooden box where she kept keepsakes until she could put them in the book. Then she picked up her bouquet of tulips and went in search of a footman. Twenty minutes later, she went to the music room.

Isabel was sitting at Dylan's Broadwood Grand, just as Grace had expected. Her hair was loose and still damp from her bath, and she was already dressed in her nightgown. She sat plucking the keys, but there was no sheet music on the stand. She did not seem to be composing, for she had no paper and no quill. She looked up as Grace entered the room. A footman came in behind her, carrying the wooden crate she had filled with the items necessary to her project.

"Put them over there, Weston, please," Grace said as she gestured to one corner of the room. "Then you may go."

"Yes, ma'am."

Isabel let her hands slide away from the keys in front of her. "What are you doing?"

"Putting some things in my scrapbook." Grace lifted the bouquet of tulips in her hand. "Thank you for these."

Isabel shifted on the bench, looking rather embarrassed, clearly hoping Grace wasn't going to fuss and get soppy about it. "Molly helped me," she mumbled. "We went out to the park and picked them earlier." She glanced at Weston as he circled the grand piano toward the doors and departed, then she looked back at Grace, puzzled. "You have a scrapbook?"

"Yes. These tulips are so beautiful that I want to keep them forever," Grace explained. "So I'm going to press them. I also have some other things to put in my book. Would you like to help me?"

Isabel's gaze followed her as she walked over to the table, pulled one of the chairs out of the way, and began to arrange the items the footman had laid out. It did not take long for the little girl to come over and have a look at what she was doing.

"You are going to press them with those?"

Grace looked up as Isabel pointed toward the four heavy marble slabs on the table. "I am," she answered and reached for the tulips. "First, we have to make sure the flowers are not wet."

After untying the bow, Grace laid the tulips out in a row on the white tablecloth, then she examined them one by one, using a scissors to snip off all but two inches of each stem. "Then," she went on as she laid sheets of blotting paper over two of the four slabs, "we have to arrange them so that they will look nice when they are flat. We put blotting paper over them, and put the two other slabs on top."

She suited her actions to her words. "There. In two weeks, we can take them out and put them in the book."

"Is there room?" Isabel asked, eyeing the fat volume with a grin.

"Probably not. I think I shall start a new book with these flowers. That is appropriate, since coming here is rather a new chapter in my life." Grace moved around the table to a spot where she had more room to work, and she pulled out a chair. "But I have some other things to put in this book first, so I thought I would do that tonight."

As Grace sat down, Isabel moved to stand beside her chair. "What things?"

"It has been so long since I have worked on my scrapbook, I can't even remember. Let's have a look." Grace reached for the wooden box she had brought down from her room, lifted the lid, and turned the contents out onto the table.

"Why do you keep these things?" Isabel asked, staring at the various items spilled across the white tablecloth.

Grace did not answer. Her gaze was caught on an old, worn paintbrush amid the motley assortment, a brush as thin as the stem of a quill. She stared at it, and she was astonished to discover that the sight of it brought no pain, only the sweet, faded pleasure of a memory from long ago that no longer had the power to hurt.

"Why do you keep these things?" Isabel asked again. "I mean, they don't seem valuable or anything like that."

"They have value to me. Each of these things has some special meaning for me." Grace looked at the child. "Don't you have a scrapbook?"

Isabel shook her head, surprised. "No, I never keep anything. Except my music, of course. I never throw any of that away."

"Why don't you keep things?"

The girl gave a shrug. "I don't have anything to keep."

Grace found that statement infinitely sad, but she did not show it. Instead, she smiled. "You might want to start a scrapbook, for now you will have things to put in it."

"What things?"

"I don't know. A lock of your father's hair perhaps. Or a bit of crimson silk to remind you of the dress your governess wouldn't let you buy."

"But why should I want to keep something like that?"

Grace laughed at Isabel's genuine bewilderment. Like her father, there was nothing of the sentimentalist about this child. "Believe it or not, Isabel, someday you might look at that crimson scrap of fabric, remember that first day we went shopping, and laugh about it, wondering why on earth you ever wanted a pet lizard. Lots of things happen to us that don't seem significant at the time, but then, when we look back, we are glad they happened, and remembering them makes us happy."

Isabel pointed to the items on the table. "Do these make you happy?"

"Some of them do." Grace reached for a gold tassel from the pile and lifted it in her fingers. "This is from a dress I wore to a ball at Schönbrunn Palace." She laughed, remembering that night. "I danced every waltz."

"You waltzed at Schönbrunn Palace?" Isabel demanded. "With who?"

"My husband. Appalling, everyone said, for a married couple to dance all the waltzes together. We did not care. We rather enjoyed scandalizing the aristocrats."

"You truly have a husband? You didn't make him up?"

A bit surprised, Grace tilted her head to one side, studying the little girl. "I had a husband, yes. He died two years ago. Why would you think I made him up?"

"Some women don't have husbands, but they say they do so people will think they are respectable."

"Isabel!" Grace cried, not knowing whether to laugh or reprove the child for such a remark. She knew the most unexpected things about life.

As usual, the reproof slid off Isabel like water off a duck. "You've never said anything about your husband, and I just wondered about him, that's all. I'm sorry he died." She lowered her head, staring at the items on the table. "Do you—" She stopped.

"Do I what?" Grace prompted, wondering what the child wanted to ask.

"Do you ever get lonely, Mrs. Cheval?"

Lonely? Grace closed her eyes, a heavy tightness in her chest. "Sometimes."

"Me, too."

Grace opened her eyes and looked at the child. Isabel was still standing with her head bent, hair falling over her face, shoulders slumped forward. She reached out and pushed the hair out of the child's eyes. "Everyone gets lonely, Isabel."

"I know." The little girl paused, then said in a hushed, confiding sort of murmur, "I didn't mean it, you know, what I said." Seeing Grace's puzzled look, she added, "I don't hate you."

"I'm glad, because I did mean what I said. I like you very much."

"You do?" Isabel grinned at her suddenly, showing one of those mercurial changes of mood so like her father. "Then you won't make me do embroidery any more, will you?"

"No," Grace answered at once, "if you stop complaining about having to learn German."

Isabel made a face, then capitulated, her expression brightening. "I suppose it would help me understand Weber's operas better, wouldn't it?"

"Yes, it would," Grace agreed, laughing, wishing she'd thought to point that out at the beginning. "Very true."

Isabel pointed to a blue velvet sack on the table. "What's that?"

"Ah." Grace put aside the gold tassel and picked up the sack. She untied the drawstring and pulled out a man's white glove, holding it out to Isabel. "This glove belonged to Franz Liszt."

"No, it didn't!" Isabel said, but she took the glove. "You're just teasing me."

"I'm not. I acquired it last year when he gave some concerts in Paris. He lives there, you know."

"Did he tear off the glove like they say he does before he plays?"

"Yes, he did. I was playing in the orchestra, and I saw him do it."

"You played with Liszt? Truly?"

"Yes. Three times."

That impressed Isabel, Grace could tell.

"I saw a portrait of him once," Isabel said. "Is he as handsome as he looks?"

"Yes, quite handsome. Probably the handsomest man I have ever met."

"Liszt is *not* more handsome than Papa!"

"That's my loyal girl!"

The sound of Dylan's voice caused both Grace and Isabel to look up as he walked through the open doors of the music room, surprising both of them with his unexpected appearance.

"You're back," Isabel said, but this time, she did not go running to him. Instead, she turned her back on him and sat down at the table, arms folded. "You said you weren't coming back until late."

"I changed my mind." His gaze slid away from his daughter, and Grace saw something in his countenance she would never have expected to see. A hint of guilt. She began to smile.

He caught that smile, and he did not like it. He frowned back at her, looking quite defensive all of a sudden. "My appointments finished earlier than I expected," he told her. "That's all."

Grace wanted to point out that neither she nor Isabel had asked him for an explanation. "Of course," she said, her smile widening. "Perfectly understandable."

He did not like being teased about this, Grace could tell. He turned away and pulled off his coat, tossing it over a chair. He moved to the piano and stood leaning over the keys, scanning the sheets of his music that were scattered across the polished walnut surface.

She was not, she told herself, the sort of woman who ogled men. But that did not stop her from taking a moment to indulge in a long, slow perusal down the length of his body, appreciating the view. His white linen shirt, black-and-gold striped waistcoat, and black trousers only served to emphasize his powerful physique. She let her gaze linger on the tight fit of those trousers. A woman would have to be blind not to appreciate a view like that.

Do you ever get lonely, Mrs. Cheval?

Lonely? Lord, she ached with it.

She remembered him standing half-naked in his bedchamber. Oh, yes, she remembered it too well. Every line of muscle and sinew on the hard, wide wall of his chest and shoulders was still

quite vivid in her mind. The bruises had only enhanced the appeal of his masculine strength and
power.

Grace studied him standing by the piano, and
she reminded herself that she could not go down
this road, imagining his naked body. If she did,
she knew what the result would be. The idea of
how it would feel to touch his bare skin and have
him touch hers sent waves of that honeyed
warmth through her.

She forced herself to look away, and she returned her attention to her scrapbook, opening it.

"I thought," Dylan said, "I would come home
for a bit and spend time with my daughter before
she goes to bed."

Grace glanced at Isabel, who was still sitting
with her arms folded, her lips pressed together,
not looking at all ready to forgive him.

Grace glanced over at Dylan to find he was
looking at her, not at the child. What did he think?
That she was going to jump in and smooth everything over for him? If that was what he thought,
he was sorely mistaken. He was on his own here.
She looked away and began to rummage through
the things on the table as if far more interested in
her scrapbook than his paternal difficulties.

It was a full minute before he crossed the room
to his daughter. He knelt beside her chair. "I
thought we could play duets. Unless she would
rather bash my piano over my head?"

Grace looked up just in time to see that smile
curve his mouth. Any female with half a heart
would forgive him anything.

It was wasted on Isabel, however, because she

wouldn't turn her head and look at him. She sniffed. "I couldn't lift a piano," she muttered.

"Good thing. Do you know how much that Broadwood Grand cost me?"

That did it. Isabel began to laugh, unable to resist all her father's devastating charm any longer.

"So, are you going to play duets with me?" He began to tickle her. "Or are you going to pout some more?"

"I'm not pouting." She turned her head, saw his smile, and laughed harder. "Oh, Papa!"

Final capitulation, and so easy. Grace didn't know whether to be happy for the little girl or feel sorry for her.

"Excellent!" He stood up and pulled out Isabel's chair. "Go," he said and pointed at the ceiling.

The child stood up, looking at him in puzzlement. "Go where?"

"Go get your sheet music. You don't think I would play any other duets but yours, do you?"

Isabel laughed, slid off her chair, and was out of the room quick as lightning.

"She was far too easy on you," Grace told him.

"You would have been much more stern with me, I know." Dylan moved around Isabel's chair to stand beside Grace's.

"Much," she agreed, but she did not look up at him. Instead, she grabbed the jar of glue and pretended to be wholly absorbed in pasting the gold tassel of her ball gown onto the page. "I would have truly made you suffer."

"How long, Grace?" His hand, still marked by bruises, came into her line of vision. He leaned closer to her and touched the tassel fringe. "How long will you make me suffer?"

She watched his hand toying with the silky gold strands, and the memories of those fingertips brushing her skin sent a rush of warmth through her entire body in an instant. He leaned down, closer to her. "How much suffering does a man have to endure?"

He wasn't even touching her, for heaven's sake, and her body was on fire. She closed her eyes. No woman with sense would ever become entangled with Dylan Moore. She said it three times before opening her eyes.

He had left off playing with the tassel fringe. Instead, he was holding the white glove in his hand, his thumb rubbing the black silk threads of another composer's embroidered initials. He straightened beside her chair. "Liszt gave you this, did he? If you were in orchestra, he probably threw it in your lap."

He must have heard a good deal of her conversation with Isabel. "Yes, he did throw it in my lap." She looked up at him with a provoking smile. "Is that so surprising?"

"God, no." He paused, his hand tightening into a fist around the glove, such a masculine contrast to the pure white fabric and satiny monogram. "You knew why he did it, of course?"

"Of course I knew," she said, widening her smile, playing with fire.

There was a long pause. "Did you accept his invitation?"

The idea that she might have done angered him, Grace realized. She could bedevil him, too, it seemed. "That is a very impertinent question," she said primly.

"Answer it anyway." He leaned closer to her. "Did you?"

Isabel's running footsteps thumped on the stairs, saving her from having to answer that question. Dylan straightened, tossed the glove back onto the table, and moved away from Grace's side before his daughter reentered the room.

"Grace," he said over his shoulder as he walked toward the Broadwood Grand, "will you come and turn the pages for us?"

She glanced at Isabel, who was looking at her father with such adoration that she could not refuse. She joined them at the grand piano, taking the proper place at Dylan's right, slightly behind him. Isabel propped the sheet music of her duet on the music stand and opened it.

"One, and two, and three," Dylan counted, and they began. The tempo was fast and the tune lively. Between turning pages for them, Grace watched their hands roam over the keyboard, his so large and Isabel's so small, side by side. They might have been playing piano together ever since the child was old enough to sit up, as beautifully as they did it.

Even without a practice run, they only made two mistakes, both from colliding as the music forced their hands to cross. Grace turned the last page, they pounded their last chords, then stopped. Both of them began to laugh. Grace applauded. "Bravo!" she said, laughing with them.

"Excellent duet," Dylan told his daughter. He grabbed her suddenly around the waist, and she shrieked with laughter as he placed her on his lap. "Let's play it this way," he said. "You take half of my part of the duet, and I'll take half of your part."

"Papa!" she cried, still laughing even as she protested. "That won't work!"

"Why not?"

She turned her head to look up at the face behind her. "We can't play a duet that way!"

"Who says so?" Dylan asked. "Let's try it."

They did, and it was such a mess that Grace didn't need to turn any pages for them. Father and daughter gave it up, for Isabel was laughing too hard to play anything coherently.

At that moment, Molly came into the room, and Isabel's laughter faded at once, knowing the nanny's arrival meant an end to all the fun. "Begging your pardon, sir," Molly said with a curtsy, "but it is Miss Isabel's bedtime."

"Oh, no!" Isabel cried, turning on her father's lap to lean her cheek against his chest. "Oh, Papa!" she cried and threw her arms around his neck. "Not yet, can't we play again? I'm having so much fun. Please."

A man would have to be made of stone not to be moved. Grace watched him close his eyes, watched his lips tighten, watched him reach up behind his neck and catch her wrists as if to extricate himself. Then, to Grace's surprise, he changed his mind, wrapped his arms around his daughter, and turned his head to bury his face against her hair.

Grace blinked and looked away. Perhaps Isabel had been right, and she was the one who had been wrong. Perhaps men could change. Some men. Sometimes.

After a moment, he pulled back and stood up with Isabel in his arms. "Little girls have to go to bed because they need their sleep," he said. "Hush now," he admonished as she began to protest. He started for the doors, carrying her in his arms. "There's plenty of time for more duets."

Grace and Molly followed him up the stairs to the nursery and into Isabel's bedroom. Molly pulled back the sheets, and Dylan placed his child in bed, then pulled the sheets up around her and sat down on the edge of the mattress. His large frame seemed to dwarf the small bed and the even smaller child.

Grace watched them from a few feet away as Molly moved about the room, putting things away. From where she stood slightly behind Dylan, Grace could not see his face, but she could see Isabel's, and she observed the child's suddenly pensive expression.

"Papa?" Isabel looked up at him with a frown. "Are you going out tonight?"

A second passed, then two. "Yes."

Isabel pulled one arm out from beneath the sheets and grabbed his hand. "Do you have to go?"

"I have engagements, things to do."

"Things like what?"

Grace saw him shift his weight on the mattress, but then he leaned down to kiss Isabel's nose. "What do you care?" he teased. "You'll be asleep."

To Grace's surprise, Isabel did not make any more attempts to discuss it. She gave a little nod and let go of his hand, still frowning abstractedly. Dylan rose to his feet, moved the child's arm back under the sheets, then tucked her in. "Good night, little one," he murmured and pulled the counterpane up to her chin.

Isabel did not reply, nor did she try to argue with her father about this matter any further. That made Grace a bit suspicious. She watched for a moment, but Isabel stared up at the ceiling, clearly lost in her own thoughts. Grace would have given a great deal to know what was going on in that child's clever mind. Whatever it was meant trouble. Grace was sure of it.

Chapter 13

❧

Grace and Dylan left Isabel in Molly's care and departed from the nursery together. Since he intended to go out, she expected him to take leave of her at the second floor and go to his room to change, but to her surprise, he did not. Instead, he continued down to the ground floor with her.

"Do you intend to work?" she asked, gesturing to the things she had left on the table as they entered the music room. "If so, I can move my project into the drawing room."

"No, leave it. I am going out."

He made no move to do so, however. When she returned to the table, he followed her, but he did not sit down. As she resumed work on her scrapbook, he circled the table, studying the fragments of her life that were scattered over the white tablecloth.

Grace watched him from beneath her lashes as

he moved around the table. He was the most un-predictable man. His moods shifted in an instant, and he could do the most unaccountable things. Tonight, for instance. If someone had told her this afternoon as he was practically running out of the nursery that tonight he would tuck his daughter into bed, she wouldn't have believed it. If some-one had told her he would feel guilty about any-thing he did, she would have called that person a dreamer.

She lowered her gaze to his hands as he paused across from her, watching as he brushed his fin-gers across something small and glittering gold. He picked it up. "A hairpin?"

She stared at the thin bit of gold wire in his fin-gers. "At one time, I had a whole box of them," she said. "I had to sell them, but I kept one."

"Why keep one? And why put it in your scrap-book?"

"The pins were a gift from my mother when I turned seventeen. I kept one because I did not—" She broke off and swallowed hard, not looking up, keeping her gaze focused on his hand and the hairpin. "I did not want to forget."

He took another step around the table, moving closer to her. "Forget what?"

He halted to her right, standing a little behind her. She forced her gaze up, turning her head to look into his face. He was studying her, his mouth a grave, unsmiling line as he waited for an an-swer, as if this were a matter of vital importance to him, when it couldn't possibly be. "I did not want to forget my mother, my childhood, where I came from. My home and my family."

Her voice broke, and she looked away from

him, staring at the items on the table. Her whole life was here, all of it, in this book and this little pile of stuff. This and memories were all she had left. It all blurred and ran together before her eyes into one unholy mess of a life.

"Grace, don't cry."

How on earth could he know she was getting stupid and weepy? He could not see her face from that angle, standing a bit behind her like that. "I'm not crying."

He moved closer and bent down to touch her lashes. She blinked, smearing a tear against his fingertip, making herself a liar.

"No," he said gently as he pulled his hand back, "you're much too sensible, of course, to get all sentimental over a hairpin. Forgive me for thinking anything of the sort."

He was smiling a little, she could hear it in his voice.

Dylan Moore was a rakehell, she reminded herself. She knew all about him, how easily he could get any woman he wanted. He had the money to buy her, the smiles to beguile her, the charm to win her, the prowess to pleasure her, whichever was required at any particular moment. He had the knowledge to mix those things like notes, making a melody that many women would fall in love with.

His reputation made her aware of the other women to whom he had given his potent attentions. Now he was doing it to her. The worst part of it all was that she did not want to believe it was a farce. She wanted so badly to think he was giving her that attention because he cared about her. It was a dangerous illusion.

His love affairs were legendary, and so were their endings. He had never really cared for any of those women, she suspected, not deeply. Worse, he didn't think there was anything wrong with that.

His hand came into her line of vision, no longer holding the hairpin. She did not know what he had done with it. He reached across the table, bending close to her, his chest brushing the back of her shoulder as he grasped a pink ribbon she'd saved from a Viennese chocolate box.

He straightened with the thin strip of rose silk in his fingers. Her gaze followed the move, staring at his hand. The ribbon seemed an absurd, flimsy little falderal caught like that in his grasp. He lifted his other hand, and she watched as he twisted the bit of pink silk into a bow. Before she realized his intent, he was standing right behind her, putting the ribbon in her hair, probably along with her gold hairpin.

She remained perfectly still as he tucked the makeshift decoration into the heavy mass of braids looped at the back of her head. Once he was done, he did not move away. Instead, he spread his hands over the ribbon and the braids and was still.

What is he doing? she wondered as several seconds went by and he did not move. As if in answer to her silent question, he slid his thumbs over her temples and tilted her head back. He leaned down, his face upside down over hers, his black eyes and black lashes so close, a hint of a smile curving his lips. He bent closer, until both his face and mouth were out of her view and all she could see was the long, strong column of his throat and the pulse that beat there. Cupping her head, his thumbs caressing her temples, he kissed her.

It disarmed her, that contact, the tender press of his lips to hers in this upside-down kiss. It was all a game to him, but it was hard to care about that when he pulled her lower lip between both of his, sucking gently as if on a piece of candy, nibbling, tasting, savoring.

Grace felt herself unraveling. Her common sense and self-respect threatened to abandon her entirely in the thick, heavy haze of desire. Upside-down kisses, topsy-turvy emotions, and him, his hands, his mouth, his long hair a black curtain around her face. She was so mixed up that she didn't know what to believe about him anymore, but she knew what she wanted to believe. Cried out for it with a hunger she had not felt in years.

He straightened, his hands sliding down her arms, pulling her to her feet. "Grace?"

She felt the chair between them being pulled out of the way. "What?"

"Did you have an affair with Liszt?" he asked, his lips brushing against her hair. When she did not answer, he pulled her back against his chest, then his hands slipped beneath her arms and curved around her waist.

"Tell me," he said, bending his head to her ear. "If you don't," he added, his voice low and silky, "I'll have to just stand here kissing your ear until you do." He suited the action to the word, and Grace shivered, her body tingling from head to toe.

"You like that, don't you?" he asked. He was smiling, she could tell. He kissed her there again, teasing. "Don't you?"

"Yes," she gasped. "Yes."

"God, I love that word." When he pulled her earlobe into his mouth, she gave a strangled little moan, and something went wrong with her knees. He wrapped one arm around her, pulling her even more tightly against him, grazing her earlobe with his teeth. With his free hand, he began to unfasten the buttons at the front of her bodice. She ought to stop him. She didn't.

He was flagrantly aroused. Even through the layers of her clothing and his, she could feel the hard ridge of his penis against her buttocks, and she moved against it, savoring the feel of him, instinctively seeking what her mind kept telling her she did not want. He continued unfastening the buttons of her dress as he held her body tight against his, and she knew she had to call a halt now while she still could.

"Dylan—" she began and sucked in a deep breath, but he cut her off before she could tell him to stop.

"Did you have an affair with Liszt?" he asked again, his voice low and rough now, demanding an answer. "I want to know."

"Why should you care?"

"I care." He moved his hand beneath the edge of her unbuttoned bodice, the low square neck of her chemise, his hand pushing beneath the edge of her corset to embrace her breast. He cupped it in his palm against the tight fabric. "Did you?"

Grace could hear herself making little panting sounds. "I am not that sort of woman," she gasped, twisting in his arms, trying to remind herself of that fact at this very moment. "You know that. I do not have affairs."

"Virtuous." He sounded so pleased, the wretch.

He laughed softly, blowing warm air against the base of her throat. "Poor Franz."

His fingertips brushed the side of her breast within the confines of her corset, and he trailed hot kisses along the line of her shoulder to where the edge of her partially unbuttoned dress cut into her skin. He made an impatient sound and left off caressing her breast, lifting his hand to the buttons of her dress to unfasten more of them.

"I heard what you said earlier. Did you mean it, Grace?" His breathing was ragged as he unfastened the remaining buttons on her dress and untied the ribbons of her chemise with practiced skill, reminding her how many times he must have done all this before. He grasped fabric in his hands and pulled down her dress and chemise to bare her shoulders. "Are you lonely?"

Such an unfair question. She didn't answer, but then, she didn't really have to. He already knew, and he was exploiting it. She was letting him.

He cupped both her breasts, his thumbs brushing her bare skin above the corset. He edged his thigh between both of hers. Not at all hampered by the folds of her skirt, he moved his thigh, sliding against her where she burned the hottest. "Are you?"

"I . . . I do not believe . . . oh, God." Her voice trailed away. She was hovering on the edge of reason, and she knew she had to stop him now. Her loneliness would not be assuaged by one glorious, frantic rut. It was a loveless act that would only leave her aching more than she already did. If she waited, if she played with this any longer, Dylan would scorch away all vestiges of her self-respect. Even as his thigh slid provocatively back and forth against her, she forced herself to say it. "Dylan, stop."

Stop. Somewhere beyond the fire in his body and the roar of sound in his head, he heard that word. He didn't want to hear it, he tried to think he had not really heard it. Women said all sorts of nonsensical things at moments like this.

She couldn't mean it. Not really. Not now. Not when her breasts were in his hands and his head was spinning, not when he was rock hard and she was making erotic little sounds. Not when all he wanted was to pull up her skirts, impale himself inside her, and end this torture. Stopping now wasn't possible.

Dylan could feel her move against him again, but this time it was different. She was stiffening, pulling away.

He could not let her go. Everything inside him demanded completion. He grasped her shoulders to keep her there. "I get lonely, too, Grace." He could hear the hard, desperate need in his own voice as he spoke. "Come upstairs with me. Now."

She was frozen in his grasp, stiff as a board. "I thought you were going out."

"When I could spend my night with you?" If he wasn't in such desperate straits, he'd laugh at that. There was nothing on God's earth that could compare with what he had in his hands at this moment. He nuzzled her neck, knowing he had to get any crazy notions of stopping out of her head. "Go out now?" he groaned against her ear. "Not bloody likely."

He felt her flutter for a second, soften, wavering in his arms and driving him to madness. Then, without warning, she stepped sideways, twisting out of his grasp. "No," she said, her voice ringing with a sincerity that even his lust-filled senses could not ignore. "I cannot do this. I will not."

He made a low savage sound of protest, his body rebelling against this sudden, inexplicable withdrawal.

She was turned away from him, fastening buttons, her head bent. He moved to stand in front of her, and he saw that her hands were shaking. "Grace," he said, striving to sound gentle when there was nothing but seething masculine chaos inside him. "Grace, stay with me."

"I am staying." Her voice was prim and cool, infuriating in its normalcy. Only the trembling of her fingers as she fastened the last button of her dress gave her away. "I have to stay for a year."

"That's not what I meant." He reached for her, cupped her face in his hands.

"I said no," she reminded him. Her voice was soft, and she did not try to escape him. Instead, she looked straight into his eyes and said, "You gave me your word of honor."

He could have laughed at notions of honor at this moment, but those green eyes of hers were so steady, so unwavering as she looked at him, and it suddenly struck him that she was afraid. She should be. If he stayed here one moment longer, he did not know what he would do. The whine in his brain amplified to a screech, and he felt as if his head were exploding.

He uttered the foulest oath he knew and turned away, striding toward the doors, hating her, hating himself. He had to get out of here before he came apart. Never in his life before had he been close to forcing a woman. He flung back the doors with such violence that they probably dented the plaster walls. The footman in the chair near the door jumped to his feet. "Get my carriage," Dylan said as he passed the servant, knowing he was shouting over the noise screaming through his mind. "I'm going out."

He ran up the stairs to his room, sent Phelps scrambling for hot water, and less than fifteen minutes later, he had shaved, changed into evening clothes, and was downstairs in the foyer waiting for his carriage, his body still raging with unslaked lust, his head drowning in noise and static and the erotic sounds Grace had been making two seconds before she'd stepped right out of his arms.

He was finally going over the edge of madness, he must be. Grace, who was supposed to be his antidote, was making him insane. For weeks now, he'd been panting after that woman like a half-grown pup, rejected time and again but still coming back for more.

These past two weeks, while his body had healed, he had tried to keep thoughts of her out of his mind so that he could work on the symphony, but she'd kept getting in the way of it, invading his thoughts with such unerring persistence that hearing anything like music had been impossible. Things weren't all that different than before Grace had come, really. He still couldn't compose. He went out, caroused about town, sought his pleasures, indulged his whims, did all the things he usually did, with one glaring exception.

He hadn't touched another woman, much less

bedded one. He had not really wanted to. He had become too captivated by the woman living under his own roof.

How long was this going to go on? He'd been cooling his heels for weeks now, getting a few passionate kisses and any number of erotic fantasies. He wanted some erotic reality, damn it.

Before this evening was over, he was going to have a woman beneath him, by God, a woman eager and willing, a woman who didn't say no right at the moment when his cock was splitting his trouser buttons apart. A courtesan, a demirep, a bawd, a streetwalker—any was preferable to a woman of virtue. When the hell had he started to forget that?

When the carriage pulled up in front of the house, Osgoode set Dylan's cloak across his shoulders, a footman opened the front door for him, and he walked out into the soft air of a warm spring night.

He would have relief from this torment. He knew exactly what he needed right now, and a virtuous woman was not it.

It was a good thing Papa's house was on the corner of the square, Isabel thought as she crouched down in the night shadows, watching through the bars of the side gate as her father's landau drove from the mews to the front of the house. She breathed a sigh of relief that the tops had been lifted and the landau was enclosed.

The moment the carriage passed her, she grabbed the black wool blanket she'd brought with her, opened the gate, and followed the landau to the corner of the house, where the vehicle turned left.

Isabel did not continue to follow it around the corner. Instead, she stopped, flattening herself against the side of the house, waiting and listening as the landau stopped before her own front door only a few feet away. She heard the carriage door open, she heard her father give a direction to Roberts, then she heard the door close again. The moment it did, she peeked around the corner and saw that Roberts had his back to her and was walking toward the coachman's seat at the front.

Isabel knew this was her chance. She came out from around the corner and ran to the back of the carriage. She grabbed the bar and hauled herself up onto the footman's dummy board.

"Walk on," Roberts said, the landau jerked forward, and they were off. She wasn't tall enough to be seen by Roberts if he happened to look over his shoulder, but she did not want to be noticed by people on the street either, people who might be intelligent enough to see that the footman at the rear of the carriage was very short, very small, and didn't have any livery. The last thing she needed was for someone to call out to Roberts that he had a stowaway. She covered herself completely in the black blanket and curled herself into a little ball on the dummy board, hoping anybody who happened to look would think she was a bundle being transported.

Unless it made the society papers, like the fight two weeks before, she didn't know what her father did when he went out at night. She could make lots of guesses. He belonged to Brooks's and several other clubs, though precisely what men did in clubs she had no idea. Gambled, she knew that much, and drank. She didn't mind so much about those things. Papa did seem to win a lot at cards, and it wasn't as if he couldn't afford to lose. He drank, but he never became one of those horrible men who did mean things when they were drunk, so that was all right.

As for the other things he did, she was rather proud of some of those. It was exciting when you had a handsome father who fenced on top of stone walls and raced phaetons with other members of the Four-In-Hand.

His exploits with women, though, were a whole different matter. Isabel knew quite a lot about that sort of thing, and she was going to put a stop to it. If he was going to be the kind of father she wanted, he had to get married to a nice woman. Then she'd have brothers and sisters to play with and she wouldn't be lonely anymore. She wanted to live on Papa's estate in the country, where there were orchards, and baby chicks, and ponies.

On the trip from Metz, she had planned just how her life with her father was going to be, and she meant to have it just as she'd planned. Papa was just going to have to change, and she was going to help him do it.

She did not know how long they drove or how far they went, but it seemed to take a long time before the landau finally slowed, then stopped. She felt the carriage rock a little as the driver hopped down to open the door and her father got out. She listened to what the two men were saying, something about Papa intending to be here for several hours this time, and how Roberts could take the carriage around to the stables. He'd send word when he wanted to have the landau brought round.

Isabel squeezed her eyes shut and stayed utterly still, hoping neither man took a look at the back of the vehicle. If they did, they'd see her, certain sure. But when she felt the carriage rock again as Roberts climbed back up onto the seat, she took a peek out from under the blankets and saw her father go inside a house. It was a small villa, surrounded by a bit of park and trees.

The carriage circled around to the back of the house, and she pulled the blanket back over her face. When the landau was parked in the stables, Roberts was greeted by male voices of some other drivers, and Isabel concluded her father had been to this house before, because all six of the coachmen seemed to know each other well.

Isabel had to wait for a chance to escape without being seen, and it took a long time. It wasn't until the men began a game of dice that she saw her chance. From the sound of their voices, she could tell they were playing toward the front of the carriage, and when the dice game sounded like it was getting exciting, she peeped out from under the blanket. She saw nothing in front of her but the open stable doors, and she slid down from the dummy board and ran, hearing only the excited shouting of the winner of the dice game behind her.

Using the ivy to help her, she climbed over the garden wall of the villa. She tried several doors around the house, but all were locked, until she came to the conservatory on the far side of the house. That door was open. Thankful for careless servants, she slipped inside.

She could hear piano music, voices, and laughter coming from above. It might be that a party was in progress. She navigated her way through the house, dodging a few servants along the way, but she managed to find the stairs without being seen by anyone. By the time she reached the top of the stairs, she knew just what sort of party was going on.

Isabel had peeked in on parties like this. Her mother had given quite a few. She cast a glance around and down the stairs, then she took a quick peek around the jamb of the open door into the parlor.

Yes, it was just what she would have expected. Silk palm trees, lots of gilt mirrors, and red wallpaper. Why the houses of courtesans always had red wallpaper was something she didn't understand, but it had to mean something. There was smoke in the air, and she could smell both tobacco and hashish. Papa might be in that parlor, or he might already have gone upstairs with one of the women. She had to find out.

She stuck her head around the edge of the door for a longer look. There was a pianoforte in the corner, and a young man was playing it. There were several card tables in the room where men and women were playing poker and taking their clothes off. There were couples lounging about in chairs, on the settees, on the floor, and they weren't making conversation. A black boy was sweating as he waved a huge fan over the group, but the thick haze of smoke from the cigars and glass pipes made his task futile.

Isabel dodged out of sight again, and her lips pressed together with anger and disgust. Things weren't any different here in England than they'd been in Metz. Things were exactly the same. Only the parent was different. And she'd had enough of it.

Her father was here, somewhere in this house, and she was going to find him. She took another look, letting her glance sweep more slowly around the room this time, and that was when she saw him. He was in a far corner of the room, lying the wrong way on a chaise longue, his head toward the door, his hair partially caught back by the hand of the woman beneath him, a woman with long blond hair that spilled over the front of the chaise and onto the floor. Isabel watched as he smiled at the woman, and she felt as if she'd been kicked in the stomach. That was her papa, and no mistake.

He lowered his head, burying his face against the harlot's nearly exposed bosom, and she arched her body toward him. Her arm fell sideways, leaving his black hair to fall like a curtain over them both. With that, Isabel saw all her plans to be part of a real family disappearing into oblivion. She stepped into the parlor.

No one noticed her for several moments. Then the piano stopped playing, heads started turning in her direction, and the room began to quiet. Above the lowering voices and shocked murmurs, one woman's jaded laugh could be heard. "How, now?" she cried. "What have we here?"

Isabel didn't turn to look at the woman who had spoken. She kept her gaze fixed on Papa, folded her arms, and said in a loud, clear voice, "I have come to fetch my father home."

She watched as he lifted his head and shook back his hair. A grim, satisfied smile curved her lips at the appalled, stunned expression on his face.

His shocked baritone voice broke the silence in the room. "Good God!"

Chapter 14

 ❧❧

Dylan did not wait for his carriage to be called. He did not glance at the other people in the room. He did not even grab his evening coat from the floor. His only thought was to get his child out of this place. Silently, he picked her up in his arms and carried her out of the parlor, putting a hand over her eyes at the half-dressed and quite passionate couple on the stairs. Then he walked out the front door.

"Papa—" she began as he hauled her to the stables behind the house.

"Not a word from you, young lady," he said. "Not a word."

She seemed to take it meekly enough, for she didn't speak, and he was glad of it. He didn't want to discuss this, not when it was twisting his guts to know what she must have seen. He breathed in deep gulps of air, trying to get clear of the haze of hashish. His own pulse hammered like a staccato drum, and the whine in his brain began to get loud again. He did not think he had ever been more angry in his life.

"Roberts!" he bellowed, entering the stables and interrupting the coachman's lively dice game. "We're leaving, and I mean now!"

The young, good-humored driver lost his smile as he spied the bundle in his master's arms. "What in blazes?" he cried, then looked at Dylan's grim expression, pulled at his cap in a gesture of complete acquiescence, and started to hitch the horses. Dylan took Isabel out to the stable yard to wait.

It was not until they were both inside the landau and the carriage had begun the ride home that he found the ability to speak. "What did you think you were doing?" he demanded. "And how did you get here?"

"I rode on the back like a footman, and why does it matter? I wanted to know where you go at night, and I guess now I know, don't I?" Isabel looked at him, and the moonlight through the window showed her face. Her expression was one of both loathing and feminine contempt. His daughter, looking at him that way, did something to him, sliced him in a way no woman had ever been able to do.

"Do you know how dangerous London can be?" he shouted. "When I think of what could have happened to you—" He broke off, too furious, too appalled, too alarmed by the possible dangers to a little girl on a London street at night. "If you follow me again, I will peel the skin right off your back."

Isabel turned her face away, looking out the open carriage window. He caught the gleam of a tear on her cheek, a tear of genuine pain, and a force as powerful as a physical blow slammed into his chest. It made his heart hurt, and the pressure pushed up into his throat, trying to choke him. He'd known from the start he would be a bad father. Here was his evidence.

Dylan rubbed his palms over his face, not knowing what to do. If Grace were here, she could advise him, but considering where he had just been, he could hardly explain and ask for her help.

That blond courtesan had looked a bit like her, slender, with all that hair spilling down like gold silk. That was why he had chosen her, of course. Her eyes had been blue, not green, but since they had been closed and her lips had been parted in pretended ecstasy as he'd caressed her under her skirts, he had almost been able to believe the fantasy. A poor substitute for a desperate man.

Now he looked across at his daughter, who was the one suffering for it, and he did not know what to say. He reached out and touched her cheek, brushing the tear away. "Isabel," he began. "Don't cry."

She slapped his hand away. "Don't tell me I can't cry," she shot back with all the childish fury an eight-year-old could muster. Wiping away the tear herself, she added, "Nothing's different here. Wherever I was, I used to sit in my room and look out and dream that one day you would come and get me and I would have a real father. I thought you'd come and take me to England and we'd live at your house in the country, and I'd have a pony and an apple orchard and you'd take care of me." Her eyes bored right through him, accusing, angry, contemptuous. "You never came."

"I didn't know about you."

"You do now," she countered, a point he could not refute. "But it still doesn't matter." Her voice caught on a sob. "All you want is for me to be out of the way! You're just like all the rest of them."

Dylan frowned. "Who are the rest of them?"

She leaned back in the corner of her seat. Sniffing, she folded her legs up, wrapped her arms around her knees, and looked at him. "Mama's friends. Every time she'd get a new friend, we'd move into a house and he would come and stay, and Mama would say that he was going to be my papa, but none of them were my papa. *You* were, and you never came. When that new, pretend papa got tired of Mama, we'd move again. That place—" She paused to jerk her thumb back in a gesture to show where they had just been. "Mama was living in one of those when you first came to Metz. I heard her tell someone about it."

Vivienne. A vague memory brushed his mind of a pretty, dark-haired courtesan with brown eyes. They hadn't been able to come to terms. He'd had a night or two with her, but her price for exclusivity had been too high. He hadn't thought her worth her asking price.

The earth beneath him must have been cracking, for he felt himself falling down into a deep, dark cavern, headed straight for hell.

This wasn't my fault, he tried to tell himself. *I hadn't known.* But he could find no consolation in that. Sitting in front of him was a child, his child, and he understood with terrible clarity the life she had lived. The pain in his chest deepened.

Isabel began to sob, wrenching, inconsolable sobs. "I thought you'd be different. I thought since you were my real father, you'd take care of me and want me, but you're not my father. You're a pretend papa, just like all the others."

Each word flayed him.

"I'm not stupid, you know!" she cried. "Those men back at that house, I know what kind of men they are! The same kind I've known all my life. When they came to see my mama, I knew what they wanted!" Suddenly, she hurled herself across the carriage at him, her small fists striking out at him wherever they could. "You're just like them!"

Just like them. Dylan wrapped his arms around the flailing fury attacking him. He was sickened and ashamed in a way he had never been in his life before. *Just like them.*

And, God, he was.

He lifted the sobbing child up onto his lap and held her tight. He could not think of anything to say that would console her. He could only hold her and smooth her hair as she cried, each tear sending him further into the pit of hell.

As the carriage rolled back to London, a protective instinct Dylan had never known came over him, and he knew he had to do something to make up for the neglect she had suffered, for the lousy hand that her mother and he had dealt her. This was his daughter. His to raise, defend, and protect. His responsibility, and no one else's. He could not shirk this duty. He no longer wanted to.

"I'm so sorry, sweetheart," he muttered against her hair. "So damned sorry. I didn't know you were there. If I'd known, I'd have come. I vow on my life I would have come and taken you away." He wasn't completely sure of that, but he'd have said anything to stop the flow of her tears. Anything.

"All I ever wanted was a real family," she said, her sobs muffled by his shirt front.

"I know." He kissed her temple. "I know. We'll be a real family. You and I. We will."

Isabel didn't answer. She grabbed a handful of his ruffled shirtfront and burrowed her cheek into his shoulder, still crying. It wasn't until they reached Hyde Park that she finally cried herself to sleep. Dylan pressed his lips to the sleeping child's hair and whispered, "I'll change, Isabel. I'll be a real papa for you. I swear it."

Grace was in a panic, but so was every other person in the house, so she strived to be the calmest one. "Think," she ordered the handful of servants surrounding her in the foyer. "Where could she be?"

Molly began to cry. "Oh, ma'am, it's all my fault. I only left her for a few minutes. I couldn't sleep and came down for a cup of tea. I thought she was asleep."

Grace pressed a hand to her forehead, the bit of nightgown lace at her wrist tickling her cheek. "I know, Molly, but stop berating yourself. It does no good. Did she take any of her clothes?"

"No, ma'am. I checked twice to be sure. She just put on one of her old pinafores and her old white shirt that she wore with the nuns, you know. A pair of her shoes and her cloak."

Grace lifted her head, glancing at Osgoode,

then at Mrs. Ellis. "She's not in the kitchens or any of the servants' rooms? And she's not outside in the park?"

The butler and the housekeeper both shook their heads.

"It doesn't make sense," Grace said. "If she changed out of her nightgown and took her cloak, she must have run away, but why didn't she take any of her things with her?" No one answered her, but then, she hadn't expected an answer.

"We shall search the house once more, and if we don't find her, we'll have to call the constables. Osgoode, have the footmen search the park again, the north and south mews, and all around the square. If they see anyone outside at this hour, have them ask if they have seen her. Mrs. Ellis, take the maids and search the servant quarters. Work your way up. Molly and I shall take the nursery and do the same in reverse. Molly, come with me."

The group started to split up, when the bell for the front door sounded. "Oh, maybe someone's found her!" cried Molly as Osgoode opened the front door.

Molly proved to be right. It was Dylan, sans his evening coat and cloak, with a sleeping Isabel in his arms. Grace was so relieved at the sight of them that she went weak in the knees.

He glanced at the group in their nightgowns and dressing robes. "Looking for something?" he asked as he stepped into the foyer.

"Bless us and save us!" Molly cried. "She's been with the master all this time."

The servants began to ask questions, but Dylan cut them off. "Hush, or you'll wake her. She's all right, just worn out." He started toward the stairs. "Molly, come with me. Everyone else may go back to bed."

Molly went with him as he carried Isabel up the stairs. Grace, who had no intention of going back to bed without finding out what had happened, followed them to the nursery. She waited nearby as Molly pulled back the sheets and Dylan placed Isabel in bed. When the nanny reached for the sheet and counterpane to cover the child, Dylan stopped her.

"I'll do it."

Grace watched him as he tucked his daughter in for the second time that night. She studied his countenance and the grim set of his shoulders, and she knew something dreadful had happened. She suspected that Dylan had not taken his daughter with him voluntarily, but that was as far as her speculations went before Dylan straightened away from the bed.

He looked across at Molly, who was twisting her hands together in nervous agitation. "If you ever leave her alone again," he said quietly, "I shall send you packing. Do you understand, Molly?"

"Oh, yes, sir!" she whispered, so relieved by the second chance that her knees almost gave way. She grasped the bedpost. "Thank you, sir."

Dylan leaned down and kissed the unconscious child's forehead. "Sleep, little one," she heard him say. "And don't cry anymore."

He strode toward the door, and Grace followed him out of the nursery and down the stairs. "Why was Isabel crying?" she asked as they reached the ground floor. "What happened?"

"Go to bed, Grace."

She watched in astonishment as he opened the front door. "Where are you going now?"

"For a walk." He shut the door behind him.

Grace turned and went back up the stairs. Inside her own room, she blew out the candle, but she was still far too agitated to just go back to sleep. She walked to the window and looked down at the square. The moon was bright, illuminating the shrubs and trees of the park in the center of the square. She caught sight of Dylan almost at once, but he was not taking a walk. Instead, he was sitting on a bench in the park, his body slumped forward, his face in his hands.

Something was horribly wrong.

Grace pulled her black leather short boots from beneath the bed and hurriedly laced them up, then put her dressing gown back on. She grabbed her cloak, wrapped it over her nightclothes, and went downstairs. When she came outside, she found that he was still sitting in the same place and position, and he did not look up as she closed the front door softly behind her and walked to where he sat.

It wasn't until she was standing almost in front of him that he noticed her. He stiffened at once, pulling his hands from his face. He sat up. "I thought I told you to go back to bed."

"I do not do things just because you tell me to."

He didn't even smile. "True."

Grace sat down beside him. "Dylan, what's wrong? What happened?"

He was silent for so long, that she didn't think he was going to answer her question, but he finally did. "Isabel climbed onto the back of my carriage and followed me tonight." He paused, took a deep breath, and turned his head to look right into her eyes. "I was at a seraglio."

Grace stared at him in shock, yet she did not know why she should be shocked. After all his passionate kisses, after she had refused him, he'd gone to a bawd. Her body remembered every place he had ever kissed her or touched her, and he'd gone to a bawd.

"I see." She looked away. *It doesn't matter*, she told herself. *The child is what matters*. "Did Isabel—" she broke off, too appalled to continue.

"She saw me, yes."

The harshness of his voice caused her to look at him again, and she watched as he leaned forward, resting his elbows on his knees and his head in his hands, just as he had been before she'd come down.

"How she got into the place without anyone seeing her, I don't know," he said, his voice lowering to a hushed, agonized rasp. "She saw me with a—"

"Whore?" Grace supplied the word when he did not.

He did not flinch at the hard edge to her voice. "I do not blame myself for that part of it. I was on fire, and you know it."

"Are you saying I am to blame?" she asked quietly.

"No, damn it, that is not what I am saying!" He sat up, turning on the wrought-iron bench to face her. "I am saying that I wanted you so badly, I just could not accept not having you. So I went to the courtesan who looks the most like you!"

Grace stared at him, astonished by the revelation. After a moment, she asked, "Am I supposed to be flattered by that?"

"She is a poor substitute, I grant you, but there it is. I am a man, I am a bachelor, and I am accustomed to having a mistress. When I do not have a mistress, I seek out other feminine company, and that fact is hardly a secret. I am not going to defend myself for needs and desires that are natural and just."

Grace did not know how she felt about the fact that he'd gone to a courtesan who resembled her because he couldn't have her. How was a woman supposed to feel about something like that? Disgusted? Complimented? Appalled?

She reminded herself she had no claim on him. She had rejected him, her choice. He'd gone to a whore, his choice. Not much surprise there, except, of course, on the part of a little girl, who, if her father were a different sort of man, would not have felt the need to follow him out at night.

Another thought struck her, one that made her stomach lurch. "Did Isabel witness this um-interlude?"

"We did not have our clothes off yet, if that is what you mean!"

"Spare me the details, please." In her mind's eye, she could see him with some scantily clad blond, his hands roaming over her body in the very same ways he had touched her. Grace suddenly felt pain, like a bruise deep inside. "If you do not feel the need to defend your actions, then why are you so upset?"

"Why?" His voice rose. "Should I not be upset? I got Isabel out of there as quickly as I could, of course, but needless to say, she was devastated by the entire incident. She cried all the way home. She told me—" He stopped.

"What did she tell you?"

"She said—" He paused to take a deep breath, then he said quietly, "She told me that I was just like all the other men her mother knew."

"Dear God." Grace felt sick. She pressed a hand to her mouth. "Her mother was a courtesan."

"Yes." He looked away. "I remember her now. A French girl with brown eyes and brown hair. I wanted exclusivity, but I had not come into my inheritance yet, and though I was touring, I wasn't making enough at that time to keep her. We parted company after a week or so."

Grace did not want to hear any more. She rose from the bench. "So, now you know how your daughter spent her first eight years. It is up to you how she spends the rest of her life. What are you going to do now?"

"Be a real father. What else can I do?" He stood up and faced her. "We will leave London as soon as I can make the arrangements and the servants can pack. We're going to Nightingale's Gate, my estate in Devonshire. Isabel wants a pony and an apple orchard and a father, and by God, she's going to have them."

Chapter 15

When Dylan made up his mind, there was no diverting him. An express was sent to Devonshire to alert the skeleton household staff that the master was coming down and the Broadwood Grand had better be tuned before he arrived. Half the London servants were sent on ahead to complete the staff, while the servants remaining in London got everything packed, and Grace and Molly tried to keep Isabel from coming out of her skin from the excitement of really going to the country.

Within a week, the three of them were in Dylan's landau with him, heading west along the South Devonshire coast. They traveled past Seaton toward the small fishing village of Cullenquay and Dylan's property, Nightingale's Gate.

"But what does it look like?" Isabel demanded for the hundredth time. She stood up in the open carriage and flung her arms out in a sweeping gesture that encompassed the countryside around her—the hedgerows and rolling hills to the north and the sea coast to the south. "Does it look like this?"

"Perhaps."

"I know we're getting close. We must be by now. When shall we arrive?"

"Soon."

"Papa!" Isabel threw herself at him and pounded his shoulder playfully with her fist. "Why won't you tell me?"

Dylan grinned. "Because you keep asking me."

Grace and Molly both laughed, but Isabel gave a huff of exasperation. She resumed her seat beside Grace and was silent for a few minutes. But then, with the incredible persistence that only children can manage, she tried again. "It really has apple orchards?"

"Yes. Apples, pears, plums."

"That's all right, then. Why is it called Nightingale's Gate? Are there really nightingales?"

"Yes."

"Papa!" she said when he did not elaborate. "Will you not tell me anything?"

He shook his head. "I don't have to," he answered and pointed over his shoulder toward a wooded headland that rose on the other side of the small, shallow bay directly ahead. "There it is."

Isabel jumped up again with a cry and moved to kneel on the carriage seat beside her father, her tummy pressed against the back, leaning as far forward as she could in the open carriage.

Grace also leaned forward for a view, leaning around her pupil to look toward the headland, where a large brick house was nestled high up the cliff amid the trees. "It is beautifully situated. What a prospect it has of the sea."

"Bless me," Molly murmured. "A person could get giddy looking down at the sea from up there."

Still on her knees on the seat, Isabel turned toward her father. "Can we go sea bathing, Papa?"

"Do you know how to swim?" he asked.

"Yes." When her father shot her a pointed stare, she bit her lip, then admitted, "No. But you will teach me, won't you?"

"I will," he promised and looked at Grace. "Do you know how to swim?"

"Of course!" she assured him. "I don't ever remember not knowing."

"Spoken like a true Cornish girl!"

Those words brought a painful wave of homesickness, and she looked out at the sea. As they had made this journey into Devonshire, Grace had refused to think about her visit home last autumn, but now her last trip into the West invaded her mind with brutal clarity, of how she'd stood in the drive of the house where she had grown up, staring up at the faces of her five sisters peeking down at her from behind lace curtains at the windows, feeling their hate for her at what she had done.

"But I can't see the house." Isabel's excited voice interrupted Grace's thoughts, and she put the past out of her mind.

The child bobbed up and down on the seat, more impatient than ever. "How are we ever going to get up there?" she asked as the carriage curved inland around the bay.

Dylan didn't answer but instead pointed ahead

where the road split into two. One went straight on, ending at the bottom of the jutting headland, where steps had been cut into the cliff face, and a steep path led up to the house. The road to the right curved away from the sea, and the carriage followed that, winding up a series of grass-covered hills that led them northwest in a meandering, gradual climb. They passed through the farm, the dairy, and acres of orchards, where apple, plum, and pear trees were covered in blossoms and cattle grazed in their shade. Isabel wanted to stop, but Dylan said no, they would come down tomorrow. They passed the stables and paddocks, and when Isabel spied a pair of Devonshire ponies, she nearly jumped out of the carriage.

The carriage merged into a thick grove of trees, and the road wound up for another mile or so until it crested the top of headland. From there, the road sloped down to a graveled drive that swept in front of the manor house of red brick, a house nestled amid trees, fronted with windows, and trimmed with climbing vines of wisteria and clematis. May flowers were blooming, and the brilliant blue of the sea beyond glimmered through the trees.

The carriage had barely come to a halt before Isabel jumped down. To Grace, the rest of the afternoon was a blur of frenzied running as she tried to keep up with the child, who kept moving from one eye-catching sight to another. She had to see her room, and even though it was the nursery, she didn't seem to mind, for she had a view of the stables and could see the ponies from her window. Satisfied, she grabbed her father's hand and dragged him outside so she could see the grounds.

She also wanted to see the sea, so Dylan took them down the steep path through a terraced garden and down the wooded path that led to the steps they had seen earlier. As they made the climb back up the path, Isabel raced ahead, up the flagstone steps of the gardens to the house, calling for Molly to come out and see the starfish she'd found washed high on the shore down below.

"I feel as if we have walked a hundred miles," Grace told Dylan in a breathless voice as they climbed the steepest part of the path. "Have you shown her everything you own yet?"

"Everything?" He shook his head. "Even at the speed that little girl can run, we couldn't show her seven hundred and sixty acres in a day."

"No," Grace said, smiling, "I suppose not. Where is your family estate?"

He pointed northwest over his shoulder. "Plumfield is up toward Honiton, about ten miles from here. There are orchards there as well. I don't know if Ian is in residence now. We do not keep each other informed."

"When your brother was at the house in Portman Square, he did not stay even for the night. I never had the chance to meet him. You and he are not close, are you?"

"No." Dylan paused, then said, "We were, when we were boys."

"What happened?"

"He disapproves of me. He has no tolerance for my artistic passions and my . . . peccadilloes, shall we say? He feels I bring disgrace upon my family name. Nor do I have patience with him. He is very conscious of propriety and position. He talks in the language of diplomats, a dialect which is incomprehensible to me." He shrugged. "Chalk and cheese, that is all."

Grace stopped midway up the flagstone steps to look around her. "This is a beautiful place."

He stopped beside her. "Thank you. I had been looking for a property for some time. The family estates are entailed, but Ian and I each received substantial inheritances. Mine included funds for the purchase of an estate of my own." Dylan gave a laugh as he looked out over the sea. "I think it was the only way my father could think of to make me settle down and be respectable."

"Dylan?"

He glanced at her. "Hmm?"

"I do not think it worked."

He grinned at her. "The men of my family have always been the epitome of English gentry—upright, honorable country gentlemen. I am certain you know just what sort I mean."

She thought of her own father. "Yes, I do."

"The Moore men have all been like that—loved their horses and their dogs as much as they loved their women. They were the hunting and fishing sort, getting into a few scrapes at Harrow and Cambridge before marrying the right country girl with the proper dowry and settling down to life as country squires. My father messed up everything by falling inexplicably in love with a sweet, penniless Welsh girl, whose head was full of romantic ideas. She played the flute. Very different from anything the Moores had in the family tree, I assure you."

"You are a mixture, then, of both sides of your

family, musical like your mother, fond of sport like your father. Where does the wild side come in?"

He gave her a pirate smile. "That's all mine."

Grace watched the wind carry his hair across his cheek, and as he shook it back, she wondered what it was about men who were wild and disreputable that attracted her so much. It seemed to be her lot in life. "Since your mother was musical, she must have understood your passion for it."

"Yes. I adored my mother. She knew what music was, you see, she comprehended it in the same way I do. She wrote symphonic poems before there was a name for them. She was the only person who supported my talent. My father could never understand why we both had this passion for music. Despite the fact that he loved my mother until the day she died, he never understood her. He never understood me. Ian doesn't either. He is a great deal like our father. My mother died when I was a boy of eleven."

"That must have been hard for you."

"Yes." He bent down and began to collect some of the small stones beside the path. "When she died," he went on, "I had no one in my family, or anywhere really, who understood what I do and why it is so important to me. I began to rebel and do what I pleased, and my father could not really control me. He did not care about my music, and because of that, I did not care what he thought of me." Dylan straightened, stretched his arm back, and threw one of the stones in his hand. It cleared the cliff and arched out to the sea. "After Cambridge, I went to Europe for four years. I toured. First, piano concerts, then conducting." He tossed another rock over the cliff.

"I understand why you do not tour now," she said. "You do not need the money. But why do you not conduct?"

"I just don't." He did not elaborate, and she did not press him. After a moment, he said, "Anyway, my father and I never got along. I only came home to see him once before he died."

Grace took another look at her surroundings. "Yet, when you were looking for an estate of your own, this is the one you chose," she pointed out gently. "One near where you grew up, one that has orchards, one like home."

"Yes." Dylan looked over at her and laughed a little. "By God, I did, didn't I? I never thought about it that way. All I knew was that I loved this place from the first moment I saw it."

"Then why do you not live here all the time?"

He was silent so long that she thought he wasn't going to answer her. "London is . . . easier. I haven't been here in quite some time. Two years, at least."

"But why not?" Grace gestured to the prospect spread out before them, the trees on either side, the white rotunda that gleamed a few feet away from where they stood, and the terraces of garden and lawn that sloped down into a wild tangle of shrubs and trees before it dropped over the rocky cliff to the ocean below. "How could you stay away?"

"I had forgotten how much I used to love it here," he murmured without answering her question. Then, with a shake of his head, he turned and started up the steps toward the house.

"Used to love it?" she echoed, following him. "Do you not love it now?"

"I don't know." He stepped up onto the terrace and took several steps along its length, then stopped to look out at the view again. "It is so damnably quiet here, so serene. I had forgotten that."

"You talk as if quiet and serenity are bad things. Would not those very things help you write music?"

"No." She watched his lips tighten as he turned his back to the sea. He sat on the edge of the short wall that surrounded the terrace, his hands curling over the stone edge on either side of his hips. He closed his eyes. "I don't even know what serenity is anymore."

Grace thought of Etienne and his erratic mood changes. "What is the turbulence all about?" she asked him, almost as if to herself. "Does everything have to be exciting all the time?"

"You do not understand." He opened his eyes, but he did not look at her. Instead, he straightened away from the wall and started back toward the house.

Grace watched him go, and something made her call after him, "Dylan?"

He stopped, but he did not turn around. "Yes?"

"I would like to understand."

"I doubt you ever could." With that, he went inside the house.

It wasn't until Dylan was lying in bed that night that he fully appreciated why he never went to the country anymore. No diversions. No distractions. Country hours. Nothing to distract his attention at this hour of the night but the nightingale singing outside his window. Nothing to take him away from the hated, grinding sound inside himself.

I'd like to understand.

How could anyone understand what this was like, this maddening sound, day after day, night after night? Unless one heard it and lived it, one could never understand it.

He tried to shut it out, but as usual, the harder he tried, the louder the sound became. Laudanum was nearby, ready to dull his senses into an opiate-induced haze that might pass for rest. He had brought hashish with him as well, but he was strangely reluctant to take either of them. He thought of Isabel and the hashish he had smoked that night at Angeline's, and for a reason he could not quite define, he did not want to dull his wits anymore. It wasn't something a father should do.

He rolled onto his side, staring out the open French door onto his balcony, watching the cool ocean breeze play with the sheer white gauze curtain in the moonlight. If only he could spend the night like an ordinary person; how blissful to simply lay his head down, close his eyes, and drift into sleep.

He knew from experience that eventually his mind would surrender to his body's demand and sleep would claim him. Tomorrow perhaps, or the next day, but not tonight. He shoved back the sheet, got out of bed, and walked naked out onto the balcony.

Nights in early May were still a bit cool here on the coast, but he scarcely noticed the chill in the breeze. He inhaled the fragrance of the herbs in the garden below and the tangy smell of the sea beyond. The moonlight reflected off the caps of the waves in the distance like sparks in the night.

Dylan went back inside and shut the door. He walked into the dressing room. Careful not to wake Phelps, and fumbling a bit in the dark, he located a pair of black Cossack trousers, took his favorite dressing gown off the hook on the door, and left the dressing room. He slipped on the loose-fitting trousers and shrugged into the robe of heavy black silk, not bothering to tie it. He couldn't sleep, he might just as well work on the symphony, he decided and went downstairs. Since the music room at Nightingale's Gate was on the ground floor, a fair distance from the bedrooms, he probably wouldn't wake anyone.

The moonlight enabled him to see well enough to find an oil lamp and friction matches in the drawing room before he passed through one of the three wide arches that led from there into the music room. He poured himself a glass of claret, opened the French door that led into the garden to let in the cool air, and he sat down on the upholstered velvet bench of the piano, placing the lamp in the holder on the right side of the music stand. Phelps had already placed a stack of composition paper, a desk set, and his folio on the closed lid, ready for him whenever he chose to work. To dampen the volume, he left the lid down.

Given a choice, he preferred the Broadwood Grand in London to the one here in Devonshire, for the tone was just a bit richer, but one couldn't just toss a grand piano onto the rack of a traveling coach and take it along. This instrument was almost as excellent, and when he ran his hand over the keys, he found that Mrs. Hollings had followed his instructions. It was in perfect tune.

He played scales for ten minutes, then took a swallow of his wine as he scanned what he had already written.

He was in the midst of the second movement, and as his gaze ran across the notes he had scrawled on the staff lines, he remembered why that was so. He was stuck. The chords he had finally worked out for the feminine exposition didn't work here in the slow, lyrical second movement. He didn't know quite why. He tried several different variations on the theme, but none satisfied him, and that was the problem. He was never sure what worked and what didn't anymore, and as a result, he could not feel satisfied with what he had and just go on. He was constantly getting stuck.

Dylan stopped playing. He rubbed his hand over his eyes and made a grinding sound of exasperation through his teeth.

"Not going well?"

He looked up at the sound of Grace's soft voice. She was standing in her nightclothes under the middle arch that opened into the drawing room, a lamp in her hand, her hair caught back in that heavy braid across her shoulder, her feet bare beneath the unadorned hem of her nightclothes. She had very pretty feet.

He took a deep breath and looked into her face. "Did I wake you?" he asked.

She gave a yawn and nodded.

"I'm sorry. I didn't think anyone could hear in the bedrooms."

"I had my window open a bit for the ocean air,

and I heard you." She glanced around at the slate blue walls, the creamy white columns and moldings, and the solid, unpretentious furniture. "These are nice, these two rooms."

"How is your bedroom?"

"Pretty. Willow green paper and a soft rug. I like it. In fact, I like your house, Dylan." She walked around the piano as if to stand behind him and have a look at the music, but then she paused and glanced at him. "May I see it, or do you not let anyone see your work?"

Dylan made an open-handed gesture toward the sheet music on the stand. "Just do not critique it," he said with a short laugh. "I hate that."

She did not laugh with him. "I shan't criticize," she promised and moved behind him to peek over his shoulder. She set her lamp in the holder on the left side of the music stand and leaned forward. She put her right hand on the keyboard and awkwardly played a few bars. "Despite my lack of skill at piano, I think it's lovely."

"Thank you." He looked at it and frowned, thoroughly dissatisfied. "But it's all wrong."

"Wrong? But it sounds beautiful."

"It isn't right. I cannot explain why." He pressed his hands to his skull with a heavy sigh and closed his eyes. "It just doesn't sound right."

She put a hand on his shoulder. "Perhaps you should stop and relax for a bit." She leaned down closer to his ear. "It always helped Liszt."

She laughed and started to walk away, but he grabbed her around the waist and hauled her back. "Oh, no," he said, "you are not getting by with that. How do you know what worked for Liszt, hmm?"

"I was teasing," she said, laughing, grabbing his wrists at her waist and trying to push his arms away. "I was only teasing, I swear it."

With that admission, he let her go, and she walked away. "I am going to the kitchens to make myself a dish of tea."

"You don't have to do that. Ring for a maid."

"Wake up a maid at this hour? For tea?" She shook her head. "Maids work very hard and need their rest. I shall make my own. Would you like a cup?"

He shuddered. "I loathe tea," he told her and lifted his glass. "Besides, I have claret. I do think I shall take that pause you suggested, though."

"You don't like tea?" As he stood up, she stared at him, looking baffled. "How can you not like tea? Everybody likes tea."

"I don't."

He followed her to the kitchen. While she went into the buttery and searched among Mrs. Blake's kitchen stores for tea, he stoked the boiler of the stove and put a pot of water on for her tea.

"Would you like anything to eat?" she asked from the interior of the buttery. She appeared in the doorway with a cannister of tea in one hand and a smile on her face. "There is a tin of short-bread in here."

"Bring it out."

She laughed. "Somehow, I thought that would appeal to you."

She fetched it from the buttery and set it on the worktable in the center of the kitchen. While she made her tea, he helped himself to shortbread and watched her.

"You don't put anything in your tea," he com-

mented as she lifted her cup to blow on the
steaming beverage.

"I used to, and then—" She stopped and
looked away with a little laugh, as if she was embarrassed. "It has been so long since I put milk
and sugar in my tea, I cannot remember how it
tasted."

Dylan knew what she meant and why she was
embarrassed. He had not thought much about her
destitution and desperation, and even when he
had, it hadn't been because he had been ponder-
ing their effect on *her*. He was angry at himself for
that, angry and a bit ashamed.

"Why don't we go down and sit in the garden?"
he suggested, picking up his glass of wine and
gesturing to the door out of the kitchen.

"Now?"

"Why not? You should know the best time to sit
by the sea is at night, and you like gardens, especially roses. Let's sit in the rotunda. If memory
serves, there are chairs down there."

"There are. I noticed them as we walked past
the rotunda this afternoon."

They left the house through the French door in
the music room, guided by the moonlight down
the winding flagstone steps of the garden until
they reached the domed structure, where four
iron chairs, painted white, were set around a
matching table.

Grace did not sit down. Instead, she took a sip
of her tea, set the cup and saucer on the table, and
walked to the edge of the rotunda, where the path
continued to slope down through more trees and
gardens down to the cliff. She looked at the shim-
mering, moonlit waves in the distance. "I always

missed this," she murmured. "London, Paris, Florence, Vienna—wherever I went, I always missed the sea."

He moved to stand behind her. "Grace, are you ever going to tell me why you were selling oranges and living in a garret in Bermondsey?"

She hesitated, then she said, "My husband had died, and I had no money."

"But you come from a gentry family. I knew that from the beginning—it's in the accent of your voice. It's in the way you move, as if you spent a good part of your life carrying books on your head and practicing your curtsies. There is something very . . . fine about you. You were gently bred."

"Yes."

"Then why didn't you return to Cornwall after your husband died? Why didn't you go home?"

She did not answer him, and several minutes passed. Just when he thought she wasn't going to tell him, she spoke. "I did once. It was a mistake. Now I can't go home again."

She looked at him, pain in her moonlit face that hurt him, too. It reminded him of when he had dragged Isabel home in the carriage a week ago. He had that same tight squeeze in his chest, that same feeling of helplessness, the same outrage. Hurt on another's behalf, something he hadn't felt in years.

"Grace," he murmured and reached over to touch her face, brush his fingers over the little wet streak on her face that glistened in the moonlight. "When I ask you about your past, it always upsets you. God, love, what happened to you? Did your husband do something to you?" Just asking the question constricted his chest even more. But she shook her head, and he guessed again. "Your family, then. What did they do to you that is so painful you cannot talk about it?"

"They did not do anything to me. I'm the one. It is what I did to them. That is why I can't go home."

Somehow, the idea of Grace doing anything to hurt anyone was absurd, impossible. She felt guilty if she ate her dessert in the afternoon. Grace, by her own admission, was never naughty. "Stuff," he said, not believing it. "What could you possibly have done that was so awful?"

"I eloped eight years ago."

"What?" Given what he knew about her, it was so out of character that he almost laughed, but the look on her face stopped him. "You're serious."

She nodded and bit her lip, looking for all the world like a guilty child who wasn't going to get any supper. "He was French. I'd known him a week. He was disreputable, poor, and ten years older than I was. I was seventeen and the most serious girl you could ever meet. No one ever dreamed that Grace Anne Lawrence, the most high-minded, sensible, and—yes—virtuous girl in Stillmouth would cause the biggest scandal in Land's End in fifty years."

"So you eloped. Many girls elope. It's always a scandal, but the brides and grooms are usually forgiven."

There was a long pause. Then she said, "Not when they don't get around to actually saying vows for nearly two years and go gallivanting across Europe together with no marriage lines. That sort of thing doesn't go down well in my family, or in Stillmouth. Respectability and reputation mean everything for a woman, especially in a small village."

"You lived with your husband for two years before you married him?" He was getting more surprised by the moment. "Grace, you never even stole sweets from your family cook. You were never naughty, you told me yourself. How did you go from that to eloping with a man you barely knew and not even marrying him for two years?"

"I went mad."

Startled, he looked over at her. "What?"

"I mean, I fell in love. I fell in love with my husband the first time I saw him." Her lips tilted up in a wistful sort of smile that twisted his guts in a knot. "He made me laugh. I felt alive for the first time in my life. I never knew how much joy there could be inside one's own heart until I met my husband."

Dylan looked away. He didn't want to think about her being in love. He didn't want to think about her making love with some other man, especially a Frenchman, especially her husband, a man who had waited two years to marry her. "Did he love you?"

"Yes, he did."

Dylan scowled. "Then why didn't he marry you up front and do the honorable thing? He was a bastard. A French bastard," he added for good measure.

"Listen to the man!" She began to laugh through her tears, wiping them off her face with the backs of her hands. "How many women have you lived with?"

"Seven."

"Did you marry any of them?"

"That is not the same thing. I did not love any of them. They did not love me."

"Are you sure they did not?"

He thought of each mistress with whom he had lived. He could not really imagine that they had felt any love for him, but he could not be sure. "Can anyone really be sure of another person's true feelings? In my case, there was never a question of marriage. Surely you expected marriage?"

"Of course, and I knew we would get married when he was ready. He was not a settling-down sort of man. It took him awhile."

"I'm not a settling-down sort of man, and even I wouldn't live with a respectable girl of good family without marrying her. He should have married you."

"He did," she reminded him. "One day, he just said it over breakfast. 'We should get married.' Just like that. And we did."

"And six years after your wedding, your family will not forgive you?" he asked.

"Forgive?" She choked on the word and bent her head. "Dylan, I have five sisters. None of them have married, nor even had suitors. We never had a great deal of money. Enough from the estate to live comfortably, but there was never much in the way of dowry. All of my sisters live at home, and they shall probably die spinsters because of my disgrace. My brother married a respectable girl, but not the one he loved, who broke their engagement because of me. James gave me money when I asked for it, but I am too proud and ashamed and I—" She stopped and gave a deep sigh. "Oh, it was such a scandal. The consequences of my choice ruined so many lives, consequences I never thought about when I ran off. Both my parents died in the shadow of my disgrace. Their shock and grief, my brother told me. I was the apple of their eye, and I broke their hearts. My brother and my sisters just want to forget me and forget any of it ever happened. I don't blame them."

"I do." He was outraged, and he didn't bother to hide it. "Your parents died because we are all food for worms some time. Your sisters need to stop being bitter about their lot in life and find men of backbone, men who won't give a damn what society has to say. Your brother sounds like most of the high-principled, noble-minded men I know. They accept only the distinguished invitations, go to the club to get away from their wives, and go to the brothels because they married respectable girls instead of girls who actually loved them. And if his fiancée left him because of you, she wasn't worth marrying in the first place. As for you—" He stopped to draw breath. "Grace, I think you are the kindest, most compassionate person I have ever known. You're far too good for the lot of them."

She stared at him, blinking back tears, utterly astonished by his long, furious speech. "Thank you," she managed to say after a moment.

"You're welcome." He looked at her, and all he wanted was to get that awful pain off her face and out of her mind. In an attempt to divert her, he grinned. "I'm rather glad you told me about this."

She drew her brows together with suspicion at that grin. "Why?"

"Until now I was beginning to think I should write to the Archbishop of Canterbury and nominate you for sainthood. It's quite a relief to know I don't have to. Writing to bishops makes me queasy."

She laughed, a series of giggles mixed with hiccoughs.

He reached into the pocket of her robe. Sure enough, there was a handkerchief in there. He pulled it out. "Here."

"How did you know there was a handkerchief in my pocket?"

"Good girls always have a handkerchief. Blow your nose, and don't shed one more tear over doing what you truly wanted to do and enjoying some happiness. And for God's sake, stop wearing a hair shirt and lashing yourself because you fell in love with somebody your family and your neighbors didn't like. A girl can't help who she falls in love with, I suppose."

She smiled at him, an unexpected smile. "And shall you still feel the same when Isabel falls in love with a man you loathe?"

Nonplused, he stared back at her and felt as if he'd been kicked in the stomach. Hells bells, he'd never thought of that. "She wouldn't."

"Oh, wouldn't she?"

"No. I'll lock her in her room. Will twenty years be enough?"

"I doubt it. Besides, what makes you think locks would stop her?" She wrapped her arms around herself and shivered. "I'm getting cold. Let's go in."

Instead of answering, he pulled off his dressing gown and wrapped her in its heavy silk folds.

Then he put his hands on her shoulders, turned her toward the ocean, and slid his arms around her. She stiffened at once and tried to pull away, but he did not let her go. "Take a bit of your own advice and relax. I know I'm the greatest scapegrace England's ever had. Except for Byron, of course. But I won't try anything dishonorable. I promise."

She curved her hand around his wrist at her waist. "Like I said once, you could be a very nice friend."

"No, I couldn't. I would always want a peek under your petticoats." He pulled her back against his chest and held her for a long time, keeping her warm in the circle of his arms. His cheek against her hair, he listened to the sea in front of them and the nightingales in the trees above their heads, inhaling the scents of the garden and the ocean, and feeling the rise and fall of her breathing beneath his arms. He couldn't remember the last time he'd held a woman just for the sheer pleasure of it. A long time ago.

It wasn't until they were walking back to the house that he realized he hadn't noticed the whine in his head for the entire time they had been out here. It was only a dim hum in his brain right now, and he knew that had something to do with Grace, who made him feel a peace he hadn't felt in years. If only she could keep the noise in his head hushed all the time, but he knew she couldn't. It would come screeching back, again and again, probably for the rest of his life.

When they went back inside the house, she returned to bed, and Dylan went back to the piano. The moment he sat down and looked at the sheet music, he knew what was wrong.

It's too much, he realized, all his earlier frustration vanishing in sudden clarity. Chords were too heavy for this bit. He needed something lighter. Without conscious thought, he tapped a minor key—gently, not pushing it all the way down, but instead making the delicate sound of a grace note. That was right, exactly right.

He seized his quill and dipped it in the inkwell, then scribbled down a series of notes, alternating main ones with the shorter, lighter ones of an adjoining tone. After a few moments, he paused to study what he had just written. It was exactly right. *Grace notes*, he thought. *How fitting*.

Chapter 16

During the week that followed, Grace did not even attempt to resume Isabel's lessons. Being in the country was all so new and exciting that it could not be anything but a holiday to the child, and her father's attentions were far more important than German lessons or mathematics. In the light of this new world she was in, Isabel even put her music in second place.

She picked out her pony and promptly changed the animal's name from Betty to Sonata. Dylan began teaching her to ride. He took both of them to the orchards and showed them the mill and distillery, where cider, perry, sloe gin, vinegar, and scented soaps were made. The eighth day after their arrival, they went on a picnic.

Taking a blanket and a basket of cold ham, fruit, cheese, and bread, they went down to the shore. After their picnic, it was low tide, and they explored the tide pools. Grace showed Isabel how to gently use a stick to seek out the tiny animals disguised in the rocky pools. The child was fascinated by this exotic environment—its crabs and sea urchins and tiny fish.

Afterward, they spent most of the afternoon exploring the caves beneath the cliffs, then Dylan took Isabel for a walk along the shore. Grace sat on the blanket and watched as father and daughter walked together, hand in hand, barefoot, and looking for shells. Grace watched them from beneath the wide brim of her bonnet as they stuffed the pockets of Isabel's dress with shells and starfish.

Grace thought of that awful night in London ten days ago when she had asked Dylan what he intended to do with the child.

Be a real father. What else can I do?

He had meant it. He spent whole days with Isabel now, instead of minutes. He spoke of her as something more than simply an obligation. He was becoming a real father, a father in the most important sense of the term. She smiled as she watched him lift Isabel onto his wide shoulders. He waded out in the surf up to his hips, his arms lifted with his hands on his daughter's waist.

Days like this were what the child needed so much. Attention, care, and love. Grace wondered what would happen when the year had passed and her agreement with Dylan was over. The cottage he had promised her was somewhere here on his estate, and she would be willing to remain Isabel's governess, but what of the child's father? If he remained in Devonshire, could she stay?

Grace forced such speculations out of her mind.

She knew they were useless. She returned her attention to father and daughter, watching as Dylan carried Isabel out of the surf.

When they returned to where she sat, Isabel dumped the contents of her pockets on the blanket to show off her treasures to Grace, but it was not long before the child's attention was once again diverted. She started to explore the area behind them, wading into the mass of sea pinks, white stitchwort, and other May flowers that covered the hillside.

"Careful," Dylan warned her as she bent to pick a handful of the white flowers. "If you pick that stichwort, you'll be pixy-led."

"What does that mean?" The child straightened and looked at him, puzzled. "What is pixyled?"

Grace and Dylan looked at each other and laughed, but it was she who answered Isabel's question. "To be pixy-led is to be mad, bewildered, or lost. Even bewitched."

Dylan added in a murmur, "Or intoxicated."

She ignored that and explained to Isabel, "The piskies don't like it when people pick the stichwort, and they shall put a spell on you and lead you astray."

Isabel looked at her father, eying him with doubt. "Is that true?"

"Of course," he said, straight-faced. "Everyone knows about the *pixies*."

Isabel was not convinced. She folded her arms. "Have you ever met one of these pixies, Papa?"

"Yes, I have. They are very sweet things."

"What?" Grace protested, trying to sound as serious as possible. "Piskies are not sweet! They are devilish green creatures, and small enough to ride on snails. And," she added to Isabel, "they don't like children who misbehave. If you are naughty, they will come and turn your nose into a sausage."

"I don't believe it!" the child said stoutly. "If that was true, Papa would have a sausage nose. He always misbehaves."

Dylan laughed, but Isabel was serious. She walked back over to the blanket and plopped down on the sand beside it. She shook her head with disapproval. "You two are not very good at making up stories," she said, sounding wise. "When you try to fool someone, you should make sure your stories match."

Dylan's lips almost curved into a smile, clearly amused by his daughter's advice. "What do you mean?"

"Mrs. Cheval calls them *piskies*. You said *pixies*. And you said they are sweet, and she said they are not. She said they are green, and you didn't say that. You see, you are making this up as you go along."

"No, no," Grace assured her. "I come from Cornwall, where we call them *piskies*." She glanced meaningfully at Dylan. "And they are not sweet. They are mean."

He ignored her. "Not mean. Sweet. Pretty."

"You two are teasing me," Isabel said with a sniff.

"We're not teasing," he assured her. "Every person sees different kinds."

She rolled her eyes. "It all sounds silly to me. I don't believe pixies are real at all."

Grace and Dylan looked at each other.

"Grace," he said as if astonished, "my daughter does not believe in pixies."

"They get very angry when little girls don't believe in them," she replied. "They'll cut off all her hair when she's asleep," she added ominously, moving her fingers like a pair of scissors. "They might paint her face green and we'll never be able to wash it off."

"They wouldn't!" Isabel cried, suspending disbelief for a moment in the face of Grace's warning. "Would they, Papa?"

"No, no," he reassured her. "You're my daughter, and the pixies like me."

Grace turned to Isabel. "The piskies may like him, but little girls are different, so you'd best be good." Grace shot him a warning look from beneath the brim of her bonnet not to contradict her about that, and he took the hint.

"Sir?"

Dylan glanced past her, and Grace turned to see Molly standing on one of the steps carved into the side of the cliff. "It's time for Isabel's dinner," the nanny told them.

The child gave a cry of dismay. "Oh, no! Do I have to go in?"

"All of this will still be here tomorrow," Dylan reminded her. "You live here, remember? Go on."

Reluctantly, Isabel stood up, brushing sand from her backside as she walked to where Molly stood on the stone step waiting for her. She grasped the woman's hand but paused before starting up to the house. "Papa?" she called and turned to give Dylan a mischievous smile. "Does this mean next time I do something naughty, I can say a pixy led me to do it?"

"No!" Grace said before he could speak.

When Isabel started back toward the cliff steps with Molly and vanished from view through the thick shrubbery and trees, Grace returned her attention to Dylan. "I was trying to persuade her to be good and you ruined it!" she said in good-humored exasperation. "Nice piskies, indeed!"

"Sorry. I couldn't bear to let her think her face could turn green."

"Oh, heavens!" she cried, laughing. "You do have it badly!"

"What do you mean?"

"You are smitten, Dylan Moore, thoroughly smitten, with your little girl."

"Perhaps I am," he admitted, laughing with her and looking a bit stunned by the notion. "Who'd have thought that was possible?"

"I never doubted it for a moment," Grace lied.

He reached behind him, plucking a handful of sea pinks and stichwort from a clump nearby. He turned toward her, rising on his knees. Before she realized what he intended to do, he lifted one of the pinks above her head and pushed it into the ribbon band of her bonnet. Grace stared into the white wall of his shirt front. His shirt was wet, and through the fine linen she could see the hard lines of his body.

"Now you've done it," she said and shook her head in an attempt to deter him. "You picked that stichwort, and now you're the one being pixy-led."

"Too late. I became pixy-led five years ago."

Those words startled her and she tried to look up, but he placed his hand firmly on the crown of her head. "Don't move," he said and pushed a white flower into the ribbon of her bonnet, then leaned back and reached for another flower from the handful he had picked. This time, instead of putting it in her hat, he brushed the pink tuft of the flower beneath her chin, with a faint, knowing hint of a smile. "Pixies are sweet," he pronounced. "Pretty."

Grace felt the delicate edge of a flower petal tickling her chin and shredding her notions of virtue. He brushed the flower along her jaw, up her cheek, and over her bonnet, then added it to the other one he'd already tucked into the ribbon band.

The sun was low in the west behind him, and his arms were raised, making his torso a dark shadow inside the fabric. From beneath her hat brim, Grace lifted her gaze as high as she could without moving her head, then let it fall across him again—the beard stubble beneath his chin, the strong column of his throat, the unbuttoned opening of his shirt, and the barest hint of the black chest hair beneath it. Her memory filled in the rest—a dark triangle that tapered down with his torso and disappeared beneath the waistband of his trousers.

She closed her eyes, and her fingers curled into the blanket on each side of her hips, digging into the sand. She was utterly still, feeling the pull of him like Newton's gravity, trying to hold off natural laws by grasping fistfuls of sand.

He lowered his arms and bent sideways to look into her face beneath the stiff overhanging brim of her bonnet. "Nice hat," he said and ducked his head beneath it.

If he kissed her, if he pressed her down into the

sand, she would let him. In the space of a heart-beat. His every kiss eroded her resistence just a little bit more, until now it was as easy to tear apart as paper, and she knew she was the one under a spell. His spell. He wasn't touching her, but his mouth was only an inch away and his gaze was like a caress. She felt herself teetering on the edge of a cliff. Last time she'd felt this way, she'd jumped off that cliff. She had floated and soared like a bird on the wing, only to come crashing to the ground in a painful, broken mess.

If he kissed her right now, she would take that foolish, foolish step, fall right off into space, and forget the hard, painful lessons she had learned about wildly attractive, disreputable men. If he kissed her, she would drag him off the edge with her. She would pull the long, heavy length of his body over hers, feel his weight, his mouth, his beautiful hands.

Dylan did not kiss her. Instead, he moved back, putting a bit of distance between them. "Were you really trying to use pixies to make Isabel behave?" he asked in the most ordinary, conversational voice imaginable as he sat back and stretched his long legs out beside her hip, still not touching her.

Grace fought her way back from that high, dangerous cliff to a safe, sensible place on solid ground. She forced herself to concentrate on the conversation they had been having. Parental discipline, a good subject, a safe one. "It worked when my governess did it."

"Too well, in my opinion."

"You just demolished my best weapon," she told him, ignoring that comment. "The best weapon anyone in the West Country has with children. Fear of the piskies is very handy sometimes, Dylan."

"We shall need to find other ways to keep her out of trouble."

"It's too late. I fear that now, any time she wants to do something, she can say she was pixy-led."

"I cannot blame her for that." Dylan reached for another sea pink. He stripped away the flower and tossed it aside, then stuck the stiff stem between his teeth, leaned back on his hands, and grinned at her like a Penzance pirate. "It has always worked for me."

He was downstairs. Grace knew because the piano woke her again. This had been happening every night for a week now. She never knew when he slept, but it had to be for only a few hours at a time, for he spent much of his time during the day with Isabel and herself.

Grace had drifted off to sleep every night to the sound of his piano. In London, he went out at night, but here, she realized, there was nowhere to go. He did not seem to like the quiet and serenity of the country, but that did not make sense, for he had bought an estate in the country.

Grace listened, recognizing the part of his composition she had played the other night and the variations he had invented on that theme. There was more, pieces of music she had never heard before. She closed her eyes, and as she listened to him work, she remembered how it felt whenever he touched her, the hot, wild joy he evoked with each caress, each kiss.

She tried to talk herself into being sensible. He had gone to a courtesan. Though he was sorry Isabel had seen him there, he wasn't at all sorry he'd gone. That should have put some sense in Grace's head, but it didn't.

She tried to remind herself that women were playthings to him, trifles to be enjoyed for a time, then set aside. What would it be like to be his plaything, just for a little while?

Grace groaned and pulled the sheet over her head. She wanted to be respectable and virtuous, she reminded herself, but that wasn't any fun. She tried to remember Etienne, but he was a dim memory in her heart now, vanquished by a man to whom second place did not exist.

Dylan Moore made being a respectable widow seem as satisfying as . . . well . . . porridge. She had fought against this for weeks now, but no woman could be expected to hold out longer than that against a man like him. He was over six feet and fourteen stone of pure dessert.

But he was a man of much deeper character than that, complex, mercurial, and a better father than he had ever given himself credit for. She thought of the infinite tenderness with which he treated his child, showing a patience with Isabel that Grace would not have thought he possessed. Though he had not wanted the responsibilities of fatherhood, when they had hit him in the face, he had taken them on completely. More than that, he had come to love his daughter. And that, Grace knew, was the thing that was sending her over the edge of that cliff.

Grace was afraid of it, she had not wanted it, she had fought so hard against it, but she could not stop it. She was falling in love with him.

The music stopped. She waited, but when she

heard no more music, and she did not hear him coming up the stairs to go to his bedchamber, she pushed back the counterpane, put on her dressing robe, and went downstairs.

She found him staring at the opened folio on the music stand, his arms folded. Across the closed lid of the piano were more sheets of music, along with quills, ink, and a jar of blotting powder.

"Awake again, I see," she murmured.

He stirred and glanced at her. "I'm afraid so."

Grace walked over to the stand beside him and put a hand on his shoulder. "Why do you not sleep well?" she asked. When he did not answer, she ventured a teasing guess. "Guilty conscience?"

That got a hint of a smile. "No."

He did not elaborate, and Grace glanced at the sheet music in the folio. "How is the music coming?"

"Right now it is not making me happy. This third movement is supposed to be a minuet, but I keep writing it like a scherzo. It wants to be a scherzo, and I am fighting it."

"Shall I leave you two alone?"

That made him chuckle. "No, don't, I beg you. If you do, it will continue to torture me." He closed the folio and looked up. "Tea in the rotunda, ma'am?" he suggested.

"No, I think—" She hesitated, then she jumped off the cliff. "I want to see my cottage."

"What, right now?"

"Do you have something else to do?" Her voice quavered a little.

He noticed it. He turned toward her, tilting his head back, and looked at her thoughtfully. "You truly want to see it tonight?"

"Yes." She ran her hand along his shoulder, the silk of his dressing gown slick beneath her palm. Her hand curled at the side of his neck. "I want to see it right now."

He leaned forward and looked down at her toes, then looked up at her again and smiled a little. "You had best put shoes on. It's about a half-mile walk."

She went upstairs, slipped into stockings and her short black boots, then wrapped her shawl around her shoulders. When she came back down, she saw that he had put on boots as well, the stirrups of his black-and-tan striped Cossacks tucked beneath.

He took her out into the garden, where he turned down a side path. He reached back for her hand and led her down a sloping, narrow dirt path through the trees and shrubbery. When they came out of the trees, he pointed down the hill, where she saw the shadowy lines of hedgerows and silvery patches of meadow in the moonlight. Nestled amid them, she saw the line of a roof and the whitewashed stone walls of a cottage.

They walked down the hill, and as they approached the front door, she could see that it looked like thousands of others all over the West Country, with the thatched roof and fat dormers she had always envisioned, but it was different in one very important way. It was going to be hers.

"It has glass windows," she said, and looked at him, a wave of joy bubbling up inside her. She began to laugh under her breath.

"Do you like it?" he asked.

In the moonlight, the red dragons on his dressing gown were barely visible, but she knew they

were there, and she thought of the stories brought
to Stillmouth by the sailors who declared they
had been to the edge of the earth.

Beyond this place, there be dragons.

She wasn't afraid of dragons, not tonight. Grace
knew that right now, there was nothing to either
hope or fear. She had only the hungry need to be
with him. She could bear another night alone, but
she did not want to, and she did not have to. However many nights she had with him, she would
enjoy them all. Grace had no illusions about the
aftermath. She would crash somewhere, sometime, but oh, the sweetness on the way down.

"Do you like it?" he repeated.

"It is perfect." She grabbed his hand. "Let's
go in."

They went inside the cottage, where there was a
front parlor to her right and a dining room to her
left. Each room had its share of castoffs—old
chairs, stacks of wooden crates filled with bric-a-
brac, and a few rickety tables. Dylan went into the
parlor, making his way through the maze of stuff
on the floor. He walked to one of the windows
that flanked the stone fireplace, and Grace followed him.

"Out there is the cottage garden," he told her
over his shoulder as he pointed out the window.
"And yes," he added, looking out, "it has roses
in it."

Grace walked over to him. She glanced past
him and saw an arbor with pale, half-opened
rosebuds that gleamed in the moonlight. She put
her hands on his shoulders. The silk of his dressing gown was smooth and warm from his skin,

the muscles beneath her hands taut and powerful. She would look at the roses tomorrow.

At her touch, he turned around, and she lifted her hand to his face. The strands of his hair tickled the back of her hand as she curved her palm across the nape of his neck. "Thank you," she whispered. "Thank you for this."

She leaned closer, rising up on her toes. "I wanted to come out here for another reason," she said and used her free hand to tug at the sash of his dressing robe.

"What reason is that?" He was rigidly still as her fingertips caressed the tight tendons at the back of his neck.

"There is something I need to say to you." She touched her lips to his. Against his mouth, she whispered, "Yes."

Chapter 17

Y_es._ To Dylan's ears, the whispered word reverberated through the room like a shout. When she'd told him she wanted to come down here, he had hoped this was what she had meant, but he was not going to assume anything. He let her lips touch his, but he did not move.

He remembered in vivid detail that night two weeks ago, and this time he wasn't taking anything for granted. Last time, it had been agony to walk away with his body in anarchy. He wasn't going to let that happen again. If she wanted him, she had to prove it.

Grace's lips were brushing his as lightly as that flower he'd caressed her with earlier. He parted his lips just enough to encourage, but he did not return her kiss. He closed his eyes, balled his hands into fists, and waited.

She lowered her heels to the floor, her hand

pressed against the back of his neck, and she expected him to follow her move. He did not.

She shifted her weight a bit, doubtful now. "Dylan, is something wrong?"

"Wrong?" He tilted back his head and laughed a little. "God, no."

"Then . . ." Her voice trailed away, the question hanging in the air.

"Are you sure you want this?"

She nodded. She seemed sure. Perhaps she meant it. Desire flickered dangerously in his groin. He lowered his chin and looked at her. "You're not going to change your mind in the midst of everything?"

She shook her head and slid her fingers beneath the edges of his dressing gown, fanning her hands across his chest. "I'm not going to change my mind."

Triumph flooded through him, and he wanted to shout it, but Dylan merely allowed a smile to play across his lips. "Then go ahead," he murmured, daring the virtuous woman to be a bad girl. "Take what you want."

He watched her bite her lip and slant a thoughtful look at him, tilting her head. Moon glow spread across her cheek and jaw. She smiled, liking the idea.

Quick as that, with just a smile, she made him thick and excited, rock hard. He wanted to have her right now on the floor and take thorough, debauched pleasure in it.

Grace pulled the edges of his dressing gown apart and leaned forward to press a kiss to the flat, brown circle of his nipple. He tilted back his head, inhaling sharply, shudders of pleasure rippling through his body. She laved his nipple and the flat, brown circle around it lightly with her tongue, a provocative tease. Dylan groaned, felt his loins tighten. When she slid her hand down to his belly, she almost annihilated his control. Almost.

Grace kissed his other nipple, caressing him just above the waistband of his trousers. "I want to undress you."

This agony was going to kill him. He set his jaw. "Do it, then."

She lifted her hands to slide the dressing gown back off his shoulders and down his arms. It fell to the floor, a heavy whoosh of silk in the quiet room. She touched him, exploring his shoulders, his back, his torso. She rippled her fingers down over his abdomen. He endured it all in silent, exquisite agony.

He felt the flap buttons at the top of his Cossacks come undone. Then Grace knelt in front of him, and the sight of her in this submissive pose, with the tip of his jutting erection beneath her jaw and that knowing, feminine smile on her upturned face was a combination so erotic that he unclenched his fist and spread his hand over her hair, but that wasn't what he wanted. He let his hand fall away, and he thanked fate he hadn't been wearing a full suit of clothes when she'd begun. That would have been too much torture for any man.

Without moving her gaze from his face, she lifted his heel to pull back the trouser stirrup and remove his shoe. First the left one, then the right.

She had undressed her husband. She must have, with the sureness of her hands. Jealousy hit him like tiny stabs from the point of a knife, an unexpected emotion, one he almost never experienced. But it was gone as quickly as it had come, for she was pulling his trousers down his legs. Dylan stepped out of the Cossacks and kicked them sideways with his foot.

She stood up, her gaze looking him as if he were a brandy snap. He liked that look. He liked it a great deal.

Dylan reached for her, pulling her hard against him in a sudden movement that made her give a startled gasp. This time, he did kiss her, a full, open contact against her soft, full lips that tasted her mouth and stole away all her control. He savored that kiss. He let his arms fall to his sides, loving it when she wrapped her own around his naked body, pulling him closer, but he knew this couldn't go on much longer.

He broke the contact with her lips and turned his head to kiss her ear the way she liked. "Grace," he groaned low, his lower lip brushing against her ear, "take off your nightclothes."

She gave a shaky laugh and slipped the dressing robe from her shoulders. "Who are you to be giving orders? I thought I was in charge of this."

"You take too long." He reached for the top button of her nightgown. He slid each of the five buttons through their holes, then lowered his hands to her hips, bunched linen folds in his fists and dragged her nightdress upward. "I want you naked, and I want it now."

"Patience is a virtue," she said, even as she raised her arms over her head.

"Virtue is the last thing on my mind. Remember who you are talking to."

"We are supposed to do what I want," she went on, her voice muffled by the linen he was pulling over her head.

He tossed the nightgown aside. He took a moment to step back and look at her, at her sweet, pretty breasts, fuller now than before. Her skin was pale and translucent in the moonlight, and the sight of the dark blond curls between her thighs made everything in him tighten and pull with the effort of holding back.

He pressed his lips to her ear as he cupped her breast in his hand. Yes, it was fuller now, but still exquisitely shaped. His thumb rubbed across the hard, plump swell of her nipple and the puckered, velvety aureole. "Don't you want this?"

She made a sound of accord, but it hushed and caught in her throat. He smiled, a loose tendril of her soft hair tickling his cheek.

Bending his head, he parted his lips over her nipple, pulling it into his mouth. It was his turn to tease this time, and he took full advantage of it, his tongue gently drawing the tip of her breast against his teeth over and over. He cupped her other breast, embracing its shape in the palm of his hand.

She grasped his shoulders and her hips twitched instinctively against him, the curve of her hip barely brushing his erection, like a flutter of silk. He laughed against her skin and slid his hand down her ribs and over her navel. His fingertips grazed the soft triangle of hair, the tip of his middle finger creasing the seam of her sex. "You don't want this?"

She moaned his name, her knees sagged, and she wrapped her arms around his neck. Her thighs tightened convulsively around his hand.

"Or this?" He eased the tip of his finger inside her, and she cried out. She was wet, and so soft. He pulled back and she arched toward his hand, wanting more and ready to receive it. He bit his lip, feeling the painful bruise of his teeth as he fought to keep himself in check just a bit longer.

"This is what you want, isn't it?" He dipped into her and out again, stroking the folds of her opening, spreading moisture with the mere flex of his hand.

"Yes," she gasped, frantic, her face buried against his shoulder, her panting breaths hot on his skin. "Yes, yes. Oh, yes. Ohhh."

Her hips jerked, and she climaxed with a long, low moan of feminine ecstacy, her thighs clenching around his hand again and again as she said his name.

He moved his hand again, caressing her inner thigh. "It's time, I think."

"Yes," she agreed on a groan. "Is there a bed in here anywhere?"

"No." He put his hands on her shoulders and took her with him as he turned around. His back faced the corner, each shoulder supported by a wall, giving him leverage. He cupped her buttocks. "Do we need a bed?"

Before she could answer, he tightened his grip. "Part your legs," he ordered as he lifted her. "Wrap them around me."

She complied, making a smothered, ardent sound as the head of his penis grazed her and he inhaled deeply of pear fragrance and womanly scent. He paused, pressing himself to the soft, wet folds of her opening without entering her. His breathing was ragged. "This, too, Grace?" he rasped. "This, too?"

Her legs tightened around his torso. "Yes," she gasped.

Dylan pushed his cock into her, just a little way. "Are you sure?"

His voice sounded rough, brutal. He could hear it himself. No time left to be gentle.

"Do it," she panted against his neck, giving orders now. "Yes, oh, please, yes. Do it."

His hands tightened their grip and he pulled, impaling her on his shaft. Driving out the ghost of the man she had known before. *Mine*, he claimed her. *Mine*.

Arms and legs wrapped around him, she followed his rhythm, crying out at her peak, tightening around him again and again as he held her buttocks in his hands and thrust deep within her, all his own passion finally unleashed in a rough, frantic cadence. With the hoarse cry of full possession, he came in a rush, his body jerking with the unbearable pleasure of his own release.

He leaned his head back in the corner, and she rested her forehead against his shoulder. He held her suspended, keeping himself inside her, and both of them were still. The whine in his head was a far distant hum, overpowered for now by his savage breathing and hers, and by the sweet warmth of her body enveloped around him.

After a few moments, he withdrew from her and set her on her feet again. "Do you want a tour of the place?" he asked, and kissed her mouth. He kissed her cheeks, her bare shoulders, her chin, her hair.

All she wanted right now was for him to hold her, caress her, move in her again. She shook her head and kissed his chin, snuggling up closer.

"No sense of adventure in you now, hmm?" He was smiling against her hair, she knew it from his voice. Suddenly, he lifted his head and took a look around. "I have an idea," he said. "Don't move. I shall be back in a minute or two."

He walked away, and Grace turned, leaning back against the wall as she watched him walk across the moonlit room, weaving his way amid the various odds and ends scattered about.

His body was magnificent, strong and solid. Beautiful in that utterly masculine way. She smiled, feeling as tipsy and delighted as if she'd had a bit too much wine, caught up in a blissful sort of euphoria that made her want to laugh and weep and do it all again.

She could hear him rummaging about in another room, and she wondered what he was doing. She didn't have to wonder long. When he returned, he was carrying a long, rolled-up tube on his shoulder, and as he drew closer, she could see in the dim light that it was a carpet.

"I thought there might still be one or two in here," he said and shrugged, rolling it off his shoulder and onto the floor. He bent and held the fringed edge with one hand as he pushed the carpet away from him with the other. It unfurled, and when it was fully open, the edge at her feet immediately began to curl up again.

She stepped onto the thick Axminster to stop it, and the moment she did, she chuckled. He sank to his knees, shaking back his hair and looking up at her with a quizzical glance.

Staring down at her feet, she said, "I thought it was only men who left their boots on."

He gave a shout of laughter, then tilted his head, thinking it over as he studied her. "I like it," he said, then slanted her a wicked look. "But I think I'd like it better if you came over here and let me take them off."

"Would you, now?" She licked her lower lip. She walked to the center of the carpet, sat down, and stretched out her leg toward him.

He moved closer, and sat back on his knees, taking her foot in his hands. He removed her short boot and tossed it aside, then took off her garter, peeled away her stocking, and settled her foot on the carpet beside his hip. He repeated this procedure with her other foot, spreading her thighs apart. But when he was done, he did not stretch out between them. Instead, he rested his palms on his knees and looked at her. "Your hair, Grace," he said, his gaze lowered to the muslin ribbon that held her braid together. "Let me see it loose."

She was melting beneath that dark, heated gaze. Her fingers fumbled with the end of her braid, where the ribbon lay against her bare breast. She untied the strip of muslin and began to unravel the plait of hair.

Dylan moved to stretch out and lowered his weight onto his elbows as he watched her fan her hair out loose around her shoulders.

"That," he said unsteadily, "is a sight I've dreamed about a hundred times. God, I wish it was daylight, and I could see all the colors in your hair. Come here."

She did, her palms sliding up his long, strong body as she moved to spread her legs wide over his hips, and he laid his head back against the carpet. She grasped his thick shaft and lowered herself onto him, crying out when he pushed up to meet her and his erection pushed hard all the way into her. He was big and filled her in that one, quick surge, then he sank back into the carpet as he lifted his hands to cup and cradle her breasts.

She flattened her palms on his chest and rode him. He moved with her, their gazes locked together. One of his hands toyed with her breast as he brought the other down to where she joined to him, flattening his hand across her stomach, the edge of his thumb brushing her in her most pleasurable place. She rocked up and down on him in quick, frantic moves to reach her peak.

She came first, and he followed her, his body going rigid as he thrust up into her one more time, then shuddering as she collapsed down onto him. Her hair fell all around his face.

He began to laugh, an exalted laugh and no mistake. She lifted her head, smiling as she brushed back her hair and looked at him through the blond curtain.

"If this is virtue," he said, his hands brushing her hair back to cup her face, "I could get used to it."

Her heart was filled with a warmth and happiness she had not felt in years. She had forgotten how wonderful falling in love truly was. "Thank you," she whispered and kissed him.

"What for, in heaven's name?" he asked as she pulled away and rolled to lay beside him.

"For—" She turned her face into his shoulder, oddly embarrassed. "I don't feel like a dried-up widow any longer."

"You never were." He pulled her against his side

and kissed her hair, but he didn't tease. Instead, he just held her there for a long time, one arm a pillow for her head, the other wrapped around her.

She couldn't sleep now, she was too full of tumbling emotions for that. But she felt his body slowly relax, and after a time, he slept.

She smiled, watching him, her face only a few inches from his. Even when his features were softened in sleep, he still looked the scapegrace. She reached her hand to his cheek, then stopped without touching. She didn't want to wake him. Instead, she lay on her back and looked up at the ceiling of the cottage. This was to be hers.

It was everything she had dreamed of during three long years of trying to find her way home. It was cozy and comfortable. It had a garden and a dovecot and everything else she could want. Yet, somehow, in a way she could not define, something was wrong with it.

Dylan shifted in his sleep, and with a sudden pang, Grace realized what was wrong with her cottage. She stared at the white coving of the ceiling, and she knew that when this love affair was over, she would not live here, for she would not be able to bear it.

When he woke, Grace was gone. He felt her absence before he even opened his eyes, the scent of her still filling his senses. When he did lift his lids, he blinked against the bright, unexpected sunlight that poured into the room.

"Grace?"

His call echoed through the cottage, and he looked around. Her nightclothes, stockings, and shoes were gone, but the ribbon from her hair still lay on the carpet, a strip of periwinkle blue muslin. He picked it up, rubbed it between his fingers.

He had slept. The realization whispered to him, sudden clarity in the daze of waking up. He had actually slept—for hours, he judged by the sunlight pouring through the windows.

With her beside him, he had slept the way an ordinary man sleeps, restful, contented sleep. Peaceful. The noise was there, of course, but it was softer than it had ever been before. He had no headache. He felt truly rested for the first time in years. Dylan rubbed the bit of muslin in his fingers and felt as if everything inside himself was right again. He pressed his lips to the blue ribbon, then put it in his pocket.

Chapter 18

The following night, Grace and Dylan camped out in the cottage again, but this time, Dylan was prepared. He brought a straw mattress for the floor, sheets, and a blanket, which would remain in here from now on. At some point, he would get the place decently furnished for her, but for now, these things would have to do.

He also brought fruit, wine, and the red silk bag in which he always kept a supply of French letters. He had brought one of the condoms with him in the pocket of his dressing gown the night before, but the moment Grace had kissed him, he had forgotten everything but the feel and taste of her, and he'd lost his head. To protect Grace from pregnancy, he had to remember to use them from now on.

He brought a lamp to the cottage as well, for he wanted to see Grace's body in true colors, not the silver and gray shadows of moonlight.

When he made love to her that night, it was with the fierce, hot intensity of absolute possession, driven until he was drowning in the waves of her passion, until she was sobbing his name as she came again and again.

The second time, he did everything with exquisite slowness, kissing her face, her nose, her cheeks, and making leisurely explorations of her body, as if time had stopped everything just for them. He sought out the secret places that gave her pleasure, and he exploited them. The backs of her knees, the sensitive skin on the underside of each breast, the base of her spine, and the back of her neck. He murmured words to woo her, pretty compliments, suggestive remarks, and blatant sexual indecencies, until she was blushing all over and moving beneath his caresses in ardent, purely feminine agitation. He entered her slowly and teased her with his body, flexing his hips to barely move within her, increasing the power of his thrusts only when she demanded it of him, arching upward in frantic desire for completion.

Afterward, he asked her if she wanted to sleep, and when she shook her head, they went outside. He teased her about putting her nightclothes back on, but she looked at him with such shock when he almost walked out the door naked that he slipped on his Cossacks and his dressing gown. They lay under the stars in a patch of soft grass, where they listened to the singing of the nightingales and the roar of the sea. "I'm not sleepy either," he told her.

"Is it because you are accustomed to sleeping during the day?" she asked.

"No. The time of day doesn't matter. I sleep only when I am so exhausted I can't stay awake a moment longer. I used to go out every night to drive myself to exhaustion."

"That is a hard way to gain rest." She leaned on her elbow and laid a hand against his cheek. "Do you know why you can't sleep?"

He didn't answer, and after several moments, she settled back into the grass and shifted the topic. "I always wanted to sleep outside at night and listen to the sea, but I wasn't allowed. This is heavenly." She reached for his hand, entwined their fingers.

"My ears ring," he said.

Grace turned her head. He was in profile, his face looking at the midnight blue drifts of a few clouds that passed over the moon and the stars, not looking at her. "That is why I do not sleep well."

"Your ears ring?" She didn't quite understand what he meant. "When?"

"All the time." He spoke through clenched teeth. "Twenty-four hours a day. It's not even ringing, not like bells or anything pleasant. No, it's a steady, unwavering whine. It sounds like an off-pitch tuning fork. The only thing that varies is the amplification. There are moments when I barely hear it. Other times, it is like a searing screech in my brain."

She sat up and looked into his face, her mind skipping back over odd things that had made no sense at the time. How he would press his hands over his ears. His headaches. How he said he did not like the quiet in the country. She tried to imagine what it was like to live with a noise like that all the time, how intolerable it must be to lay in bed, trying to sleep with that noise in one's head, but she could not imagine it. She did know it would be torture.

"It was a fall from my horse that caused it. In Hyde Park, five and a half years ago. I was racing far faster than I ought, took a tumble, and hit my head on a rock. My left ear bled for two days. And then the whine started. God, I hated it. I still hate it. I can hear it now."

Grace's hand tightened around his. "That is why you wanted to kill yourself, isn't it?"

"Yes. The noise was driving me mad. I could not hear music anymore. That was why I could not compose."

"But this happened five years ago. You have published some extraordinary works since then."

"No. I have not."

"How can you say that? What of your opera, *Valmont?* Your Piano Concerto Fourteen? What of your Fantasia On Sunrise? What of those?"

"Grace, have you not guessed the truth? Those are old pieces, some of them going back to my boyhood. I trot one out every now and then so no one will know the truth. I wrote Fantasia On Sunrise when I was fourteen. That concerto I wrote when I was twenty, I just hadn't named it yet. I completed *Valmont* just one day before the accident." He pressed the heels of his hands to his eyes. He gave a short laugh. "Pieces I never thought were good enough to publish."

"Not good enough? Dylan, they are beautiful." Her heart ached for him, for what it must cost him every day. "Not good enough for you, perhaps, but they are not just for you, you know. They are also for the pleasure and enjoyment of the rest of us. Some people think *Valmont* is your best opera."

He took his hands from his face and lifted one to brush back her hair. "Until I met you again, I had not written a single piece of music in over five years. Not one."

She remembered his words the night they had met. *I will never write music again.*

She thought of Etienne, who had forever been saying he would never paint again, only to be hard at work a few days or weeks later, passion renewed.

Her reply to Dylan that night at the Palladium had been so confident. *Yes, you will. One day.* She hadn't understood.

His hand tightened in her hair, fisted around the long, loose strands. "Then you came, and gave me hope."

"Oh, Dylan, it isn't because of me." She leaned over him and laid her hand against his cheek. "It is all inside of you. You do not know how strong you are!"

"Strong?" He shook his head. "The night you met me, I was trying to kill myself, for God's sake. That is as weak and cowardly as a man can be."

"We all have our weaknesses, Dylan, but you have proven that you are strong. You have the will to live when living is hell and hope is all you have left." She paused, then she said, "My husband was a volatile man, a man subject to abrupt, inexplicable changes of mood. He was a brilliant man, but he allowed the weaknesses in his character to take him over until they dominated everything he did."

"The same could be said of me, Grace."

"No. There is one great difference. I left my husband not because he had weaknesses but because he did not have the will to fight them. He lost his hope. If I had stayed, I would have lost mine, and he would have destroyed me. He died a year later."

"Grace." He pulled her down to him and kissed her. "Grace, you are the most compassionate person I have ever met. Whenever I am with you, you soothe me. Your voice," he said and touched her throat. "Your eyes, so green. Fresh and green." He touched her lashes with his fingertips. "Like spring, I thought, when I saw them in daylight. You quiet the noise in my head. Last night was the first night in five years I got a full night's sleep. When I am with you, the noise goes low and far away and I can hear music."

She smiled. "I thought you were just being torrid, and making love to me. Pouring the butter over me to get me into bed."

"Well, I was doing that, too." He lifted her onto him and smiled that pirate smile at her in the moonlight. "And it worked," he said, unbuttoning her nightgown. "Didn't it work?"

"Dylan, stop," she whispered, glancing around as she tried to pull the edges of her nightgown back together. It was futile, for he was already sliding it off her shoulders. "We can't! Not out here!"

Impervious to her sensibilities, he ignored the hands that pushed at him, and he cupped her breasts. "Yes, we can," he murmured, teasing her with his thumbs and his voice. "Come on, Grace. I dare you. Make love with me naked in the moonlight. I won't tell on you."

And she did. A pagan dance with him in the dark. Wicked man, to tempt her with such delights.

In the cottage afterward, he slept soundly beside her, lying on his side, one arm around her waist, his other arm pillowing her head. Grace watched him, glad he could sleep. She loved him. He made her laugh. He made her glad to be alive.

She turned her head and whispered her secret against his palm, her voice so low that she could barely hear it herself. "I love you."

She kissed his palm and folded his relaxed fingers over, gently, so as not to wake him. She did not fall asleep. Instead, she lay there with her lips pressed to his fist, where her secret was caught inside. She was alive in every part of her body and soul. She was thankful for each and every moment of happiness. But fear still cast a shadow over her, fear born of past pain and the dread of what she would feel if it all fell apart.

May turned to June. By tacit agreement, they were discreet. During the day, in front of others, they were polite and perhaps a shade more distant than they had been before. When they were alone, the things he did to her ignited the flames banked by daytime discretion and anticipation.

It was not only he who could inflame desire. She began to discover some of the secret things that drove him to ecstasy, and loving him as she did, she loved doing every one of them.

There were moments when it was hard to keep their secret. Sometimes, she would look up from one of Isabel's lessons and find him watching her, and she knew he was thinking about their nights together in the dark, of the words he murmured in her ear and the words he wrung out of her when he made love to her.

He liked that, she discovered, wordplay in bed. She discovered that she liked it, too. She had never known that such a wanton side of herself existed, but when he murmured hot, shocking ideas to her as he touched her, she wanted him to do them. He wanted her to tell him what she wanted, just for the sheer pleasure of hearing her voice. She did it and reveled in it.

He loved her hair. She put it up every morning, and he took great delight in taking it down every night. He ran it through his fingers, he pulled it down to fall over his face when she was on top of him. Sometimes, he would walk by her when no one was looking and snatch away a comb, bringing one of her braids tumbling down. Worse, he would walk away and leave her with the comb in his pocket and no way for her to put her hair back up.

When it was fine, they lay outside at night, talking, sometimes making love in the grass. When it rained, they remained inside the cottage, lying on the mattress with the window open, listening to the rainfall. Dylan liked rain, she discovered. He said the sound of it, like her voice and the ocean, soothed him.

Sometimes he slept, sometimes he didn't. When she had her courses, he slept with her anyway if she felt up to it, content to simply hold her. She loved that about him. Sometimes, if she had pain, she wanted to be alone, and he let her. Sometimes, he wandered away when he couldn't sleep, took long walks in the hills or along the sea by himself. She didn't know what he did or where he went, but he always came back to lie beside her. Slowly, day by day, Grace forgot what it was like to be all alone.

The pretty days of June went by and became the hot, sultry days of July. Dylan composed while Isabel had her lessons each morning. Most of it was a struggle, one note at a time. Occasionally, inspiration came in a flash—he'd see Grace walk by, or Isabel would laugh, or the ocean would call him, and he would have music to write. Those moments were precious and rare, and when they came, they were sweet satisfaction. Bit by bit, he worked his way through the symphony into the fourth and final movement.

The end of any piece had always been the easiest part for Dylan to write, but not this time. He just could not find the right way to bring this symphony to a satisfying close. This opus was a watershed, representing the beginning of a new phase in his life, and it was important. He wanted the finale to be just right, but perhaps he was simply trying too hard.

He knew now that when he felt like this, when he was exasperated by hours spent getting nowhere, it was time to stop and relax, and he decided to seek out his best two sources of inspiration.

Today, when he went up to the nursery, he found Grace teaching Isabel how to dance a waltz to the tinny sound of a musical box on his daughter's desk. Not wanting to interrupt, he paused by the door and watched.

Grace happened to glance up as she led Isabel across the floor, and she saw him standing in the doorway. He put his finger to his lips, and she carried on the lesson as he looked on, unobserved by his daughter.

Grace's golden head was bent slightly above Isabel's dark one. Dylan listened to her liquid voice count the cadence, a voice as melodious as the Weber waltz to which they danced. *Or tried to dance*, he amended to himself as his daughter stumbled.

A waltz was something Isabel understood from a musical standpoint, but actually dancing to one was something altogether different, as his daughter was now finding out. Grace tried with gentle patience to guide her along with the lilting melody, but Isabel was stiff and awkward, unable to relax.

Most people would have been surprised that someone with Isabel's ability at composition would be less accomplished with the dancing of it, but Dylan understood at once. She was frustrated by the notion of being led anywhere.

"I don't like this," Isabel said, and she confirmed his instinctive conclusion by asking, "why can't I lead this time?"

"A girl doesn't lead," Grace answered.

"You're leading me, Mrs. Cheval, and you're a girl. And anyway, who made up the silly rule that a girl can't lead?"

Dylan pressed a fist to his lips, smiling. So independent and strong-minded, his little daughter. Tenacious, too, forever questioning the world and everything in it just as he did, fighting its conventions and strictures with the same contrary nature he possessed. The reason for it was one he could not quite fathom, even for himself, let alone for his child. The need for drama to constantly replenish that creative well, or the restless, prowling energy that consumed him, too. Fighting the world, perhaps, because it was simply there, and life would be deadly dull if someone didn't fight it.

This was his connection with her, he realized, the true one, one deeper even than music. He understood her, and she made him understand himself. They shared character traits that were soul-deep, passed from him to her in a kinship beyond the loveless act that had created her.

She was so strong-minded, in fact, that it worried him. The life of a woman with his temperament would not be easy. He almost wished she had been born a boy. But then he looked at her in her white dress trimmed with a crimson ribbon—a ribbon of victory in the battle over proper colors for little girls. And the hem had ruffles of lace—*lace,* that hateful stuff that itched.

"Papa!"

She careened to a stumbling stop, her big, dark eyes looking at him, her absurd, pretty, rosebud mouth smiling at him. Dylan banished any thought of boys.

"May I lead?" he asked.

Grace stepped away and walked to the musical box to start the waltz again as he came forward and took his daughter by the hand. "Do you trust me?" he asked.

"Yes, Papa."

No hesitation in that reply but a conviction she did not easily give, an inexplicable trust he hadn't yet earned. *He would earn it,* he vowed. "If you let me lead," he said, "I will not let you stumble. I promise."

She nodded, and he looked over at Grace. She was watching them, looking like a warm spring day, with her gold hair and her green eyes, with her peach-colored dress and her radiant smile. She was the most beautiful thing he had ever seen in his life, and the sweetest dessert he'd ever had.

As he looked at Grace, Dylan felt his daughter's hand in his, how small it was, how vulnerable. His throat tightened, his heart constricted. It was too much, that feeling, it poured over him, sank into his bones, and welled up in his chest until he couldn't breathe.

He turned his head and looked through one of the open windows, seeing the pear trees in the distance. He turned his head again and saw the map of Devonshire on the wall. Right beside it was Isabel's rendering of Sonata, the pony—a rendering somewhat out of proportion. Nearby, his daughter's collection of seashells reposed in a clear glass bowl on a dark, cherrywood table. He had been in here countless times since they had arrived two months ago, and yet this time, he could only stand and look about him in a buffle-headed sort of daze, as if he had never seen it before. *Home,* he thought stupidly. *I am home.*

"Papa, are you ready?"

He looked down into his daughter's upturned face and touched her cheek, and he finally understood what Grace had meant that night five years ago when she had told him why he needed to live.

You might be needed for something important.

This was it. This, every day, for all his days until they put him in the ground. Dylan held his daughter's hand tight in his and drew a profound, shaky breath. "Yes, my darling girl, I am as ready as a father can be."

Chapter 19

Dylan and Isabel had been dancing for only an hour before their lesson was interrupted. "Sir?" Osgoode said from the doorway, raising his voice slightly to be heard above the musical box. "Sir Ian Moore has come to call."

Dylan brought Isabel to a halt and looked at the butler. He hesitated, not wanting to stop what he and Isabel were doing, but he couldn't very well leave his brother lounging about in the drawing room. "Tell him we shall be there directly."

He looked at Grace and Isabel, then he gestured to the door. "Shall we?"

Downstairs, Ian was waiting in the drawing room, and he rose to his feet as they came in. The moment he looked at Grace, Ian's eyes widened just a bit, and his usually impassive face flickered with surprised admiration of her beauty, and something more. But the smooth diplomatic countenance slipped back in place before Dylan could define quite what he had seen in his brother's face.

"Ian," he greeted him, "you remember my daughter, Isabel?"

"Yes, of course." Ian bowed to her. "Miss Isabel."

"Good afternoon, Uncle," she answered and dipped a curtsy, then took her father's hand in hers and gave Ian a look as imperious and gloriously superior as any queen his brother had ever met. Dylan could almost read the words *Told you so* above her head like a Rawlinson caricature. Ian's lips twitched with a hint of humor, but other than that, his face was politely grave.

"And this is Mrs. Cheval, Isabel's governess."

"Excellency." She gave him the full curtsy due his diplomatic rank as he bowed. "Will you take tea?" she asked.

"Certainly."

Grace rang the bell and, when a maid appeared, ordered tea be brought, then she moved to sit in one of the chairs that formed a pair of conversational crescents in the center of the room. She motioned Isabel to sit beside her. Ian took the chair opposite Grace. Dylan, forever restless, did not sit down.

There was a moment of silence. Grace shot Dylan a glance as if indicating he should take the lead in the conversation, but at that moment, Molly came in. "If you please, sir," she said to Dylan, "I am going down to the farm, and I thought Miss Isabel might like to come with me and see the new kittens. They've got their eyes open."

Isabel was on her feet at once. Ian, it seemed, had not yet been forgiven for doubting her paternity. "May I, Papa?"

Kittens sounded more fun than Ian, and he cast his daughter a glance of envy. "You may."

She was headed for the door quick as lightning, dragging Molly with her, and Grace had to stop her. "Isabel, have you not forgotten something?"

The child turned to her uncle, dipped another curtsy, and said good day. She received the appropriate reply and was gone in a flash. Dylan laughed, watching her go.

When he returned his attention to his brother, however, his amusement vanished at once. Ian was looking at Grace again, a longer look this time, a subtle perusal of her person. It was rather out of character for Ian, who never stared at anyone for a moment longer than scrupulous politeness demanded. Staring was rude.

Nor did Dylan miss the nuances of his brother's attentive gaze. Grace, in her tactful way, did not seem to notice this masculine interest, but Dylan noticed it, and it tore at something primitive and elemental inside him.

Osgoode came in with tea and placed the tray on the table between Ian and Grace.

"How do you take your tea, Excellency?" Grace asked, her soothing voice such a civilized contrast to what Dylan felt inside him. He leaned back against the window so that the bright light at his back could shadow his expression. He didn't usually feel this way about another man's interest in the women he bedded, but this was not any woman. This was Grace, with her virtuous intentions, her gentry-polite manners, and her generous heart. Grace, who had just looked at him an hour ago as if he were king of the earth. This possessive instinct that flared in him with such quick savagery was new, and strange, and he did not like it. He felt smothered by it. His mouth turned down as he watched his brother watch Grace.

She poured out Ian's tea, added the sugar and milk he had requested, and presented his cup to him on its saucer, her manner polite, composed. She seemed thoroughly at ease.

Ian accepted his tea with the same polite reserve, and Dylan wondered why he felt as if he were in a play and he was the only one who did not know his lines. Grace glanced at him, but she did not ask if he wanted tea, for she knew he did not like it. Instead, she simply poured a cup for herself.

"I have read of your diplomatic efforts in Venice," she said to Ian, "and I congratulate you for the success of your negotiations. Will the marriage of the Italian princess really prevent their war with the Austrians?"

While he went on about the negotiations of a royal marriage and Italian nationalism, Grace listened with interest, and Ian looked like a man staring at heaven wrapped in peach-colored silk.

Dylan moved from the window to stand behind Grace's chair. Meeting his brother's gaze over the top of her head, he deliberately put his hands on her soft, white shoulders above the rounded neckline of her dress.

Startled by such intimate contact in front of another person, she stirred a fraction, then was still. Ian raised a brow at him, dignified and proper and disapproving, but Dylan kept his hands where they were.

In the end, there seemed little purpose to the call, other than the usual one Ian had when he visited, the polite notion of paying respects. Ian always did that when they were in the same city at the same time because it was the right thing to do. Even when his thoughts were anything but proper, Ian was all about doing the right thing.

After about ten minutes of polite piffle, Ian rose to leave. Grace also moved to stand up, and Dylan let his hands fall away from her shoulders.

"It has been a pleasure, Excellency," she said and actually held out her hand to him.

Ian kissed it, the perfect way, of course, without touching his lips to her hand at all. He then glanced at Dylan. "Will you see me out?"

That surprised Dylan. "Of course," he murmured, and the two men walked out to the drive where Ian's curricle and groom waited for him. They stopped beside the vehicle, but instead of stepping up, Ian paused and looked at him. "I should like you to come see me tonight, if possible. Any time convenient."

"What?" Dylan could not believe such a request had come out of his brother's mouth. These days, he was never invited to Plumfield. If he had been, he would have declined.

"Yes," Ian said, looking earnest and serious and even more stuffed shirt than usual. He brushed back a lock of his dark brown hair with one hand. "I am not making this request lightly. It is important, Dylan. It concerns a matter of business, so I would like you to come alone, please."

Dylan sure as hell wasn't taking Grace with him. "Very well. Six o'clock?"

"Six, it is." Ian stepped up into the curricle and took the reins from his groom. Dylan watched the carriage pull out of the drive and start down the shaded lane, then he went back into the house. Dylan felt vaguely uneasy.

When he returned to the drawing room, he found Grace standing just outside it. "May we speak privately?" she asked him in a low voice, glancing around for servants. Without waiting for an answer, she walked to the small writing study across the corridor, and he followed her.

He closed the door behind them, and to his surprise, she shut the window. Then she turned round and spoke. "Dylan, I know it has not been all that long since we . . . became involved, but something about our arrangement must be understood." Her serene voice was low and cool. "Please do not ever touch me in that way again."

He cooled as well in the chill of eyes that looked at him like the Arctic Ocean. He planted a slight smile on his face as his insides clenched and the noise rose in his ears. "I love touching you."

"I cannot allow you to do that to me in front of another person. It is not decorous. I should not even have to point this out, Dylan, and you know it. What was that about? I know you and your brother do not get on, but—"

"Get on?" he interrupted. "I saw how he looked at you."

"He was scrupulously polite, which is more than I can say for you. You demeaned me, Dylan."

That lashed at him like the quiet sing of a whip, and he felt the sting. He could not defend himself on that score, he knew, so he veered to the other. "Polite?" he repeated. "Bloody hell, I knew what he was thinking. He was looking at you as if he wanted to get you out of your clothes."

To his amazement, she did not dispute it. In fact, she seemed indifferent to it. "And if he was?"

"You are my mistress, Grace, and not available to be his. I was simply reminding him of that fact."

"I am not your mistress, Dylan. A mistress is a possession, something bought and paid for, something owned. I will not allow you to treat me as if you own me. You pay me only in the capacity that I am governess to your daughter. In bed, there is no money between us. I am not your mistress. I am your lover."

"Either way, you are mine."

"No," she contradicted him, calm and poised in her defiance. "I belong to myself, and when and how I choose to give of myself to anyone is a choice I make. It is not for you to decide."

She turned to walk away and he reached for her, wrapping an arm around her waist to keep her there, burying his face against her neck. She stayed rigid in his hold, stiff and unyielding, and he gave it up. The moment he let her go, she left the study. The door closed softly behind her. He stared at the painted white surface, suffocating in the airless room. "Mine," he told her through the closed door as if she were standing on the other side, but when he opened the door, she was not there. He thought of her eyes and her smile and that afternoon in the nursery, and his chest ached with the rage of jealousy, possessiveness, and— God help him—fear.

Dylan stalked into the music room and sat down. He had never felt this way before, and he did not understand himself. He opened his folio and set to work, using his music to shred that sickening jealousy and fear and get it out of his system. There was no time to get mired in the agonies of composition that usually plagued him these days, and he pounded keys with such force that they overrode the noise in his head. He wrote fast and furious, ending the symphony with a rollicking finale that, when played with full orchestra, would bring down the house.

He grabbed the quill one more time. At the bottom of the last page, he wrote one word. *Finis.*

Breathing hard, he put the quill down and stared at that word, not quite able to believe what he had just done. He had finished it, after days of struggling to find the end, he had just sat down and written it in a way he had not done for years, without thinking, without struggling, without being blocked by the noise. He had completed an entire symphony, when only a few months ago, he had thought anything he wrote would be a miracle.

He laughed out loud with exultation. He had done it, by God. At last.

Dylan gathered up the sheets of music and tucked them into his folio, then he rose from the piano. He had to find Grace and tell her. She was probably still angry with him, but she would forgive him, she was too softhearted not to forgive him. She was just made that way, soft and sweet and way more forgiving than he deserved.

He started to leave the music room and go in search of her when he heard the clock chime. He glanced at the mantel and realized it was already six o'clock.

Christ, he thought, he was supposed to be at Plumfield. Ian would be steaming when he arrived an hour late, but he had to go. Tonight when he returned, he thought, he would patch up his quarrel with Grace. Tonight at the cottage he'd make up with her any way she wanted.

A horse was faster than a carriage, and Dylan rode to Plumfield, arriving at a quarter to seven. He expected his brother to be quite put out over his lateness, but Ian did not seem to mind. He accepted the explanation of losing track of time over a new symphony without even a hint of reproach. He seemed preoccupied with other thoughts, and Dylan realized whatever his brother needed to discuss with him truly must be of vital importance.

Ian had long ago accustomed himself to all manner of different cultures and delicate political situations, and however important the matter to be discussed might be, he never came straight to the point. Instead, he led Dylan into the drawing room and poured wine for them both, then they talked of seemingly trivial matters for over an hour.

They discussed estate business first, then Ian shifted the conversation to Isabel. He asked what Dylan intended to do with the child. Dylan replied that he was keeping her with him, and that in a year or two, when she was ready, they would do a tour together—a plan he decided on even as he spoke it.

Ian was cautionary. "A young woman cannot

hope to go beyond the restrictions of society," he pointed out. "Her future is inevitably that of all women, a suitable marriage and children."

The idea that his daughter's fate was to be inevitable was enough to make Dylan rail against it. He casually mentioned a few names, including Sappho and Maria Teresa d'Agnesi, and tried to tell himself it wasn't Ian's fault that he was as dull and conventional as a sermon.

"So until then, at least, she remains in the care of Mrs. Cheval?" Ian asked.

The question was bland, but Dylan set his jaw at the mention of Grace, and every muscle in his body tensed. He met his brother's inquiring eyes across the five feet of space between their chairs. "Yes."

The other man sighed and sat back. "Dylan, about this woman. You do know about her, do you not?"

"Know about her? I know she is from a good family in Cornwall, and that she is a widow."

"No, I mean do you know *who* she is? About her husband and all that."

"She eloped and disgraced her family," Dylan said irritably, "though I don't know how you came to hear of it. Your sensibilities are offended, I am sure, but mine are not. Nor am I concerned for Isabel's sake. Grace is an excellent governess, and Isabel has become fond of her."

"Yes, but Dylan, surely you know—" Ian broke off and took a swallow of port, looking like he needed it. "You've been here in Devonshire for two months," he said as if thinking out loud. "You have not heard."

Alarm began to prickle the tiny hairs at the back of Dylan's neck. He took a heavy swallow of claret. "Ian, for God's sake, let us not engage in endless rounds of diplomatic fencing. Whatever you have to say to me, say it straight out." He lifted his glass for another swallow of wine.

"She's Etienne Cheval's widow. You must know that. So . . ." His voice trailed away delicately.

Dylan froze, his glass midway to his lips. "Etienne Cheval, the painter?"

"Yes. The Great Cheval."

Dylan made a sound of derision. "You must be mistaken. Cheval is a common enough name."

"The paintings confirm it. I recognized her the moment I saw her."

He was French . . . ten years older than I . . . not a settling down sort of man . . . artists, why are you all so tormented?

It was true. In a sudden rush of certainty, he knew it. Of course she knew about artists. She'd been married to one. Why had she not told him who her late husband had been? Cheval, the painter. Did it matter? He closed his eyes, and something cracked inside him. If it did not matter, she would have told him.

"I do not care if she is your mistress," Ian said, his voice forcing Dylan to open his eyes, "if you are discreet. But there is your daughter to consider."

Grace was better with Isabel than any other woman could be, and Dylan didn't know how Grace's being the widow of a painter, however disreputable and famous he had been, affected Isabel. He set his glass down carefully. "Ian, what do you mean?"

"Even you must see that a woman like that cannot be your daughter's governess. When word gets out that she is living in your household—"

"I still do not see why you are concerning yourself with my mistress."

"Cheval killed himself two years ago. Starved himself to death, I understand, after she left him."

Dylan's grip tightened around his wineglass. He knew better than anyone the desperation that could drive a man to suicide, but that was hardly Grace's fault. Everyone had a choice.

"Cheval was always an unstable sort of fellow," Ian went on, "with no money. When he died in Vienna, his creditors took everything, including all the works in his studio. But several months ago, three paintings that had not been among his effects were discovered, when the Comte d'Augene died."

"So?"

"They were found in d'Augene's private art collection at Toulouse. His mother is English, you know. She has put her son's entire collection up for auction at Christie's. No one even knew these three Chevals existed, for there were no sketches with them, no record in his workbooks of them at all. They are being sold individually, and each will no doubt go for a very high sum. They should, for they are magnificent. I have seen them."

"By God, Ian, can you never come to the point? Tell me in specific terms what the hell you are talking about, or I shall throttle you, brother! What do Cheval's paintings have to do with me or my daughter?"

Ian rose and walked over to a writing desk along one wall of the drawing room. From the single drawer, he pulled out a pamphlet and brought it to Dylan, placing it in his hands. A Christie's folio of the upcoming auction. "Page nineteen."

Dylan opened the pamphlet, flipping past sketches of Louis XVI flatware, Elizabethan tapestries, and Roman pottery. On page nineteen was an engraving of a painting to be auctioned, one of three nudes by Cheval to be sold. The first description read, *The Girl with Green Eyes on a Bed*.

Grace. She was half-reclining on a bed, her weight on her hip and her arm, her hair hanging down. She was fully nude, her face so full of life and laughter that any man would climb into bed after her. He turned the page and found two more nudes of her. *The Girl with Green Eyes in a Bath. On a Swing*.

By now, Dylan knew her body so well. Images of her breasts and legs and buttocks, her pretty feet, and her hair, long and spilling over her shoulder, flashed through his mind. Here, in an auctioneer's folio for men to bid on. Now Dylan knew just what had made his brother stare at her so intently the day before, when Ian was never rude enough to stare. He'd been imagining her body like this.

Dylan's head roared. His heart wrenched. His eyes saw.

He looked up, and he wanted to hurl himself at his brother and beat him to a bloody pulp for even seeing Grace's body like this.

Ian sensed what he felt. He stared back at Dylan steadily, and Dylan closed his eyes for a moment, trying to get control of himself. This was not Ian's fault. Any man who had seen this would stare at her the same way if she was sitting across from him.

Oddly enough, it was not only her body, produced like this for public view, that enraged him, that caused the whine in his head to scream and his heart to be ripped out of his chest. No, it was her face. Her beautiful face showing an expression he had never seen.

He felt himself splintering into pieces. His hands shook, and the pamphlet fell to the floor, right side up. He leaned forward, his forearms on his knees, staring between them at her face. No wonder Cheval had been one of the great masters of his generation. His hand and eye had been true to his art, faithful to what he'd seen: the love and adoration for him in a young woman's face.

I loved my husband.

Now he knew how much. Love, the essence of it caught on canvas, frozen in time forever. Now available for any man to see, to lust after, to have for himself, if only in his imagination. Magnificent, Ian said they were, and Dylan could see why. Someday, they would be hung in museums for people to gawk at. Grace on public display, giving every man the look of love that should be his but was not his.

"My God," Ian muttered. "You love this woman."

Dylan was smothering. Rage was erupting inside him. His reason was dissolving. He had to go, walk, move, he didn't care where. He could not sit here one moment longer.

He snatched up the pamphlet, stood up, and

shook back his hair. He walked away from Ian, out of his childhood home, out into the fresh air, taking deep, gulping breaths. He got on his horse and he rode, as fast and as hard as he could. He did not know where he was going. All he knew was that he had never seen Grace look at him with all that love in her face. Not once.

Chapter 20

Dylan did not come to the cottage that night. Grace waited there for hours, but he did not come. He was not back the next morning, and she concluded he had stayed the night with his brother. They must have had a great deal of business to discuss.

It was late afternoon by the time he came home. Isabel was down at the farm with Molly, and she was bedding out geraniums in a sunny patch of the garden when he arrived. She did not know he had returned until his wide-shouldered shadow crossed the patch of dirt in which she was working.

"Finally!" she exclaimed in relief as she turned toward him and stood up, brushing dirt from her hands. "I was getting worried about you."

She looked at him, and the moment she saw his face, she knew. He was ending it.

Her heart rejected it entirely, but her head knew. It was inevitable. She'd always known. Grace felt herself shaking inside, and she wrapped her arms around herself so she would not come apart. She tried to tell herself she was mistaken.

"I want you to leave," he said. "Now. Today."

No mistake.

She lowered her gaze to a bundle of papers in his hand, and she watched as he dropped them into the empty basket beside the pots of geraniums. Papers and banknotes. Something else landed on top of them, something small and heavy. A key. "Why?" she said, trying to think, but her wits were muddled, thick like tar.

"I have a lodge in Wales I inherited from my mother. It's a few miles outside Oxwich, in Swansea. It's yours. The deed is here, with my signature. A manservant and his wife see to the place, and there is a letter with my seal that tells them you are the new owner and will be living there from now on. There is a billet of passage across the Bristol Channel in here, and five hundred pounds. I have sent an express to my agents in Oxwich, and they will have the other five hundred pounds deposited in an account for you by the time you arrive. The place has a . . . has a garden, I think."

The catch in his voice almost broke her. She drew in a deep breath and did the hardest thing she had ever done. Harder than leaving her husband. Harder than seeing her sisters' faces. She looked into Dylan's black, black eyes. "Why are you doing this? Why? Is it about our quarrel yesterday? If that is so—" She broke off, hearing a wobble entering her voice, sensing she was about to say things that were desperate, ask the pitiful questions of a cast-off mistress. She would not. This was not about their quarrel. She held his gaze and waited for an answer.

She was not to get it. He was the one who looked away, bending to pick up the basket. With his free hand, he straightened the papers and pulled the ten-pound notes into a neat stack. "If you need anything—" He paused, his hands stilled, and Grace felt herself beginning to panic.

"You have your cottage," he said, amending whatever he had been about to say. He shoved the basket toward her and said, "Here. Go."

She did not take the basket he shoved at her, and he simply set it back down on the turf. She had known he could be cold, but not as cold as this, to be so abrupt, to refuse to explain.

"I knew it would be over between us one day," she heard herself say. "I just did not expect it to be so soon." Her throat closed painfully, and she could not say anything more. He was setting her aside as he would any mistress. What was there to say?

This was the same man who had made love to her as if he worshiped her, who could smile and make a woman believe anything, who wrote music that was as beautiful and full of love as something not made by God could be. A man who could go to a whore without a thought, but loathe himself for it because it made his daughter cry. A man who could make her laugh and make her want to live, a man who could demolish her with only a few words and then look at her as if she were a total stranger. "You were going to shoot yourself," she said. "Why didn't I let you?"

Unable to bear looking at him a moment longer, she turned her back and looked down at the geraniums she had just planted. She knew that all her life, she would remember that exact shade of red. "You bastard. Oh, God," she choked, "you bastard. Why now? Why this way? With no explanation?"

Seconds went by, and he did not reply. She turned around and found that he was gone.

Grace sank to her knees in the dirt. She wanted so badly to weep, but the pain was too sharp for tears. Her sobs were dry, like hot, desert air through her lungs. She could still not believe what he had just done to her.

She had to get control of herself. What if Isabel came home and saw her this way? It took everything she had, but Grace forced herself to stop.

After a moment, she picked up the basket and rose to her feet. She stared down at the key that lay on top of the pile of papers, and she picked it up. It was a perfectly ordinary latchkey, but she studied it as if it were the most important thing in the world. As she held up the key in the sunlight, a strange sort of detachment came over her, almost as if she were watching herself in a dream. Numbness filled her limbs and Cornish common sense filled her head. Her hand curled around the key, and she put it in her pocket. She told herself that at least she had a place to go, and she tried not to think about how bleak that seemed.

She rifled through the deed and accompanying papers, papers with her name on them, and she looked at the tidy pile of notes. She wished she could go after him, throw it all in his face and call him a bastard again.

She did not do that. She took the papers, the sealed letter, and the key. That was what they had agreed to, and if he wanted to end their bargain early, she would be stupid to refuse it. She had to leave here, and where else was there to go?

Grace looked at the money. She would take only what had been defined in their agreement. Grace pulled out two ten-pound notes to pay for the clothes she had bought, and tucked the rest of the money in her pocket. She carried the basket of papers into the house.

She took the two ten-pound notes to his piano, wanting to put them somewhere he would find them. His folio was propped up on the music stand, and she opened it. She would put the money in here with the completed pages of his symphony. He'd be sure to find it there.

Grace started to get up, but then she caught sight of the title written at the top of the page, and she paused.

Inamorata. A woman who was a man's lover. This symphony was about her, she realized. About their affair. She flipped through the pages and counted four movements. She knew his symphonies were always four movements. She pulled out the final sheet, and she saw the proof at the bottom of the page, written in his hand. *Finis.*

He had finished the symphony, so he had ended the affair. Of course. She had known from the beginning that it would come to this. Artists and their art. Composers and their music. They were all the same. The work came first. First, last, and always, the painting or the symphony was everything.

That was when she began to cry. She felt the tears rolling down her face, blurring the notes of sheet music in her hand and smudging the ink. She dropped the page, heedless of where it landed, shoved back the bench, and picked up the basket of papers from the floor. She called for Osgoode and, bless the man, he did not say a word about the tears staining her face or the incoherency of her words as she asked him to send for the carriage. He did not even change expression. *He must be accustomed to crying women asking for carriages*, she thought as she turned away and ran for her room. Galling to think how many times the butler must have seen this sight before.

She packed heedlessly, shoving her clothes into her valise without bothering to fold them, her only thought to get away from here. She put in her scrapbooks, threw the deed, the key, and the money on top, buckled the valise, and was running for the waiting carriage. She did not take one look back. When the carriage passed by her cottage on the road into the village, she could not bear to look at it, and she turned her face away.

It was only after she was at the inn in Cullenquay, waiting for the post coach that would come the following day, that she realized she had not said good-bye to Isabel. She would write the child a letter, for there was no going back now. One could never go back. One did not get to do things over. That night, Grace lay in the hard bed of her room at the inn and cried herself to sleep for the first time in years. When was she going to learn the most important lesson about life? There were no second chances at anything, not even love.

* * *

By the time Dylan arrived back at Nightingale's Gate, it was twilight, but he did not go to the house. Instead, he left his horse at the stables with a groom and went for a walk. Twilight turned to dark, but still Dylan did not return to the house. During the hours that followed, he did not know how many miles he walked, but he went to every place he could think of that they had been, relived everything he could remember that they had done. He walked down to their favorite picnic spot along the shore. He went to the mills, inhaling the scent of pear oil until it made him physically sick. He lay on a patch of turf and looked at stars.

He went inside the cottage, lay on the mattress, and tortured himself with memories of all the things that had happened between them in this room. He tried to sleep without her. It didn't work, but he lay there a long time.

He planted those geraniums of hers by moonlight because she'd left them there outside their pots on top of a patch of dirt. He could have called for the gardeners, but they were asleep, and as Grace had once told him, servants work hard and need their sleep.

He could not shut out of his mind that look on her face in the paintings, and how jealousy was eating him alive because of how much she had loved another man. She would never love him like that. How could she?

There were some who would find this entire situation very amusing. How his enemies would laugh if they knew, and what a good joke it was. Dylan Moore jealous of another man, a dead man at that. As he shoved geraniums into the dirt, he realized that he had never known jealousy because he had never cared enough to get that worked up over another person. That was the bitter truth. He had never cared more about another person than he cared about himself and the music he made.

You don't know what love is.

Grace had been right about that. Michaela; he'd fancied that was love. The girl who had refused him had made a nice, tidy reason to explain why he'd never given his heart away, but really, that hadn't been it at all.

He flayed himself for what he had done, trying to figure out why he had just thrown away the closest thing to love he'd ever known. Six hours of wandering around the Devonshire countryside without purchase, and still, he did not know why. The look in her eyes. No, he would not think about her eyes.

It was just before dawn when he went back to the house. He went upstairs. He took a look in Grace's room, but found nothing there to see. All her things were gone.

He went to Isabel's room and peeked inside. He lifted the lamp high enough to see that she was asleep. To his surprise, he saw that Molly was in the bed with her, holding her tight, and he realized his daughter had cried herself to sleep, comforted by her nanny. Music and hurting others. His greatest gifts.

He went downstairs to the piano and sat down. He opened his folio, which was propped up on the music stand, and the moment he did, two ten-pound notes fluttered out and landed in his lap. He stared at them, and it took him a moment to understand why they were there. She was paying back the money with which she had bought her clothes.

Grace, he thought, staring down at the money. *Why didn't you tell me about him?* If he had known . . . if he had known. But he had known. She *had* told him.

I loved my husband.

He just hadn't been listening. He had not wanted to know, had not wanted to think that any man before him could be more important. The enormity of his own ego was something he had never thought much about, but he thought about it now, of how he had allowed that and his own self-ishness to hurt the most wonderful, most vibrant person he had ever known. He loathed himself.

"Papa?"

He looked up to find his daughter beside him. He hadn't even heard her come in. "What are you doing down here at this hour?"

"You woke me up with the lamp when you came in."

"You need to be back in bed," he told her and stood up. He lifted his daughter in his arms and started out of the room.

"Why, Papa?" she asked against his neck.

He was saved from answering by Molly, who was coming down the stairs, a lit lamp in her hand and a frantic expression on her face. "Oh, sir," she gasped, "I'm sorry. I woke up and she was gone. I'm so sorry."

She thought she was about to get the sack. Dylan looked over his daughter's head into the nanny's frightened face, and he said, "It's all right, Molly. It's all right. Just help me get her back in bed."

The servant followed him as he carried Isabel up the stairs. The child said nothing more as he laid her in bed, but if he thought it was because she had decided to let the matter drop, he was mistaken.

"Why did you send her away, Papa?"

He froze, the edge of the counterpane in his hand, and looked down into his daughter's face. *Don't cry*, he thought, looking at the awful glisten in her eyes. *Don't cry anymore or I'll come apart.*

Here was another person he had not thought about before doing what he wanted to do. He had not thought of how painful it would be for his child to lose her mother, and then her governess, a woman who had also become her friend. No, he had not thought of anyone but himself. What he felt. How he hurt. He watched his daughter's tears spill over onto a face already puffy from crying, and they brought him to his knees beside the bed.

Now I know, Grace. Now I know what love is.

"You made her leave."

He did not deny it. He could not, even though it came from the one so vulnerable, who adored him so much, who wanted him to be a knight on a white steed. He brushed tears away with his fingertips. "Yes."

"Why, Papa?" she cried. "Why?"

Dylan stalled. "I thought you did not like Grace very much."

"Is that why you sent her away?" She looked at him as if he were a hopeless pudding-head. "I didn't like her at first, but that was ages ago. I told you how governesses are, but she didn't let me walk all over her. And she wasn't stupid or silly, and I started to like her. Even though she's in charge of me, she doesn't treat me like a little girl. She treats me like a person. That's why I like her." Isabel sat up and grabbed his face between her hands. "*You* like her, Papa. Molly said so. I heard her tell Mrs. Blake."

From somewhere behind him, Molly sniffed. *Christ, almighty,* he thought, *is every female in this house going to cry?*

He pulled Isabel's wrists down and held her hands in his. He tried to find solid ground, but Grace was gone. He had no solid ground. "You overhear too many things."

"You like her and you sent her away."

"Why did you quarrel with her all the time?" he countered, letting go of her hands to pull the sheets up over her and tuck them around her body.

"She wants me to be good, and I know I have to be good, and it's hard." Isabel wriggled. "Papa, you're tucking me in too tight."

"I'm sorry."

She looked at him. "You understand what I mean, don't you, about being good?"

"Yes, sweeting," he said. "I understand."

"So why did you send her away?"

He looked at her helplessly. "I don't know."

"Sometimes I do things and don't know why. Everybody does, don't you think? You just have to fix it."

Fix it. Of course. Oh, to be eight years old and believe again that anything could be fixed, no matter how broken it was.

"You have to get her back," Isabel told him. "I had it all planned."

"Planned?"

She nodded. "I was thinking if you liked her, you could marry her, and then I'd have a mother. But you hurt her and made her cry and she left."

Shame consumed him. How many women had cried because of him? Too many, he knew. Far too many.

"You'll have to apologize," Isabel told him, "and that's always hard. Take flowers, too. That's what I do, and she always forgives me."

Apologies and flowers. How many times had he used those techniques with women? Dozens. How shallow they were. Easy, cheap, and shallow because he had never really cared whether they worked or not. Dylan leaned forward and kissed Isabel's forehead. "Go to sleep."

He pulled the covers up to her chin and left the nursery. He went downstairs and, because there was nowhere else to go, he sat down at the piano and began to play whatever came into his head. It was the only thing he knew to do. There were no other distractions left.

He could not go back to days of opiates and hashish, gambling and women. All the women. He could not go back. He was out in the open now, raw and exposed with nowhere to run and a daughter who depended on him. He stopped playing.

"Grace," he said in despair, "how am I supposed to raise her without you to help me? I don't know how to be a father."

There were so many things he didn't know. He didn't know himself, but Grace knew him. She had understood him from the very first moment. He looked at his folio on the stand. He stared at the symphony named for her. For the most generous heart he had ever hurt, for the girl with green eyes. Eyes that would haunt him for the rest of his life because of all the love in them that was not for him.

He loved her. He knew that now. Too late.

You bastard, she had said. And he was. He lowered his face into his hands. There was nothing he could say to get her back, nothing he could do to get what he wanted.

But perhaps there was something he could do for her. To give her what she really wanted. Dylan got up. Dawn was breaking, and he had a great deal to do.

Within two hours, he was back at Plumfield, insisting to the butler that Ian be woken at once and he didn't care if it was seven o'clock in the morning.

A few minutes later, Ian entered the drawing room in his dressing gown. "Dylan, what are you doing here?"

"I need something." He looked his brother in the eye. "I need the services of a diplomat."

Chapter 21

Grace tried to like living in Wales. As weeks went by, she tried not to compare it to Devonshire. Her cottage was small but cozy, nestled in a rocky cliff by the sea. It had a garden and a thatched roof. It even had furniture, something she had not expected. If she was thrifty, she could live for a long time on the thousand pounds Dylan had given her.

Best not to think of Dylan. Grace stopped snipping the dead flowers off the rosebush in her garden and closed her eyes, trying to force him out of her mind. He would not go. He was there, like a shadow over everything she did, like an open wound that would not heal. When she had left Etienne, she had never looked back, for in her heart she had left him long before she'd packed her things and departed. Dylan was different— she looked back dozens of times a day. It hurt every single time.

It was September now, and a chilly wind was in the air today. Two months since she had left Nightingale's Gate. It seemed like years. Never had days and nights been so long.

She should hate him. She tried, but hate was such a hard emotion to sustain. Especially when there were so many things about him that she loved. His creativity, his energy, the way he listened to what she said and remembered it, his love for his daughter and the way he had met that responsibility. She missed his charm, the way he could make her laugh, the way he had taken her side completely in her feud with her family. She missed his kisses; in fact she missed him so terribly that she ached with it. If she hated him, it would be so much easier to bear what he had done.

Grace gave up deadheading roses. It was silly to be doing it now, when she should be letting the last ones set hips, but she had needed something to do. Perhaps she should go for a walk instead.

She glanced back at the green, misty hills behind her, and up at the sky. It was going to rain again. It seemed to rain every day in Wales. She shoved the pruning scissors into the pocket of her apron and started up the hill. Yes, she decided, a walk would be better. What did a little rain matter?

A carriage came into view along the road and turned down the lane toward her cottage. Surprised, Grace watched as the closed traveling coach circled to her front door and pulled to a stop. She turned and retraced her steps down the hill, watching as the coachman opened the door and a man stepped down, a tall, thin man with fair hair.

She took a tentative step down the hill. "James?" she cried and began to run to the coach, staring at her brother as she approached. "James, it is you!"

Her brother stared back at her as she halted in front of him. He took in the threadbare maroon dress, work apron, and white kerchief tied round her hair. Some nuance of feeling touched his face, a hint of regret, something she had not seen the last time they'd met. "Grace."

"Oh, James, I cannot believe it!" They had not parted on good terms a year ago, but in her loneliness, she was glad to see her brother, more glad than she would have thought possible. She held out her hand, and more astonishing, he took it.

"How did you find me?" she asked.

"I received a visit from a friend of yours, a Sir Ian Moore."

"What?" she cried, more astonished than before. "Why on earth would His Excellency come to see you?"

"It is a rather long story." He gestured to the cottage. "Perhaps we should go inside?"

"Of course!" She led him into the cottage and into her small parlor. She reached for the poker and started to stoke the fire, but her brother took it from her hand and did it for her.

"Would you like tea?" she asked, and he shook his head. She sat down on her small settee, and her brother took the opposite chair.

"How are you, Grace?" James asked her.

"Well enough," she answered, looking into eyes as green as her own. "But quite bewildered, I confess. What are you doing here?"

"As I said, I received a visit in Stillmouth from Sir Ian. He came at his brother's request, and that prompted my trip here."

"What?" Something wobbled inside her, threw her off kilter, and she swallowed hard. Dylan had sent Sir Ian to her brother? She told herself she didn't care.

"Sir Ian and his brother were both very concerned for your well-being. You were governess to Mr. Moore's daughter?" her brother asked, a tiny hint of disapproval there. How could there not be, given her brother's fastidious nature and Dylan's wicked reputation?

"Yes, I was." She could not believe Dylan was concerned about her. Why should he be? Dylan had no interest in her any longer, and she could not fathom why on earth he would send Sir Ian to go to James about her. "Did Sir Ian indicate how Isabel fares?" she asked, stalling as she tried to get her bearings.

"He said his niece is perfectly well, but that she misses you terribly."

"And Dylan—" She stopped. So painful to say his name, but she wanted that sort of pain, she welcomed it and the exquisite hint of pleasure that came simply with saying it. "Was Mr. Moore well?"

"Sir Ian indicated that Mr. Moore was in excellent health. The reason His Excellency came to see me was that he and his brother were devastated to know of your estrangement from your family. He said they were both fully aware of the circumstances, and that it wounded them deeply that something which happened so long ago should still be causing all of us such sorrow. He explained that you were such a wonderful governess to Isabel, and they could not help but be concerned for your welfare. He came to Cornwall in hopes of facilitating a reconciliation between you and your family. Needless to say," James added, "I was astounded."

He was not the only one. Grace stood up and moved across the room to stand by the fire. Her back to her brother, she spread her hands before the blaze, so thoroughly confounded that she did not know what to say. She could not understand what would prompt Dylan to such actions after the cold, cold way he had treated her.

"Sir Ian assured me that your other friends, including Lady Hammond and her brother, the Duke of Tremore, were also very concerned to know of the sad situation of your disgrace and our estrangement."

Grace froze, not turning around. What was he talking about? From the society papers, she knew those people were friends of Dylan's, not hers. She had never met them. Well, except the duke. She'd met him that night in Dylan's room, but they hadn't even been introduced. She'd only known his identity from the servants the following day.

"My dear Grace, I had no idea you moved in such high circles," her brother said, interrupting her disjointed thoughts.

"I don't," she whispered into the fire.

"Eh? What was that?"

"Nothing." Grace pressed her fingers to her forehead, trying to think this out. If Sir Ian had said such a thing, it must have been to impress James, to increase the chances of reconciliation. "I am—" She coughed. "I am amazed that . . . they . . . should . . . umm . . . take such keen interest in my situation."

"They do. They are, in fact, working to amend your reputation and that of our sisters, now that they know of it. They all seem to be patrons of the arts, and were admirers of your . . . late husband." Those last words were said with such venom, and it saddened her. Etienne had been a lousy husband, true enough, but he had loved her as best he had been able, and he had given her so much happiness in those early years.

"Sir Ian asked if I was open to reconciliation," James went on. "The fact that you have such influential friends to plead your case is more than enough proof your reputation is not beyond amendment."

She bit her lip. Why were Dylan and his brother trying to save her reputation?

Whatever the reason, it seemed to be working. She could hear the impressed note in her brother's voice, but then, James had always been a bit of a prig. It wasn't his fault. He had been born that way. Titles, connections, and things like that had always impressed him. And she fully understood the pain he and their sisters had suffered because of what she had done so long ago. Grudges were a waste of time. If he was willing to make peace, she was as well. She turned around. "James, you are my family. I would like nothing better than to reconcile our differences. But what of our sisters?"

"They are amenable. Sir Ian offered to introduce them if they should go to town in the spring. Lady Hammond, as well as the Duke and Duchess of

Tremore, have offered to do the same. No doubt the season would be a delightful one for them, and Sir Ian commented that if they were as beautiful as their elder sister, they would have suitors lined up at their door in a week."

How could they not with a charming ambassador to help them, along with dukes and viscountesses?

"You seem bewildered by all this, Grace," James commented, "but this can bridge our estrangement, can it not? I hope so."

"Oh, James." Her voice broke. Turning around, she ran to her brother. She threw her arms around his neck and hugged him. "I am so sorry about everything, especially Elizabeth! I know how much you loved her, and I know she broke your engagement because of me."

"It was a long time ago," he said, enough stiffness in his voice to reveal that it hurt him to this day, "but I am quite content with my wife, Marianne." He did not hug her, exactly, but he did pat her back in an awkward sort of way just as he had done when they were children, and she remembered he never had liked being hugged. He stepped back with a little cough, clearly feeling uncomfortable. "Grace, do not distress yourself about me, not after so many years. It is our sisters we must think of."

They sat back down, and James leaned forward to take her hands in his. As if she had not had enough surprises today, he squeezed her hands with what might have been a sign of genuine affection. "I am glad this has happened, Grace. Truly." Still holding her hands, he looked away, and a dark flush came into his cheeks. "Our last meeting was most unfortunate, and I deeply regret that I was so cold and unforgiving."

"I am glad of this, too," she said and meant it. "How fare our sisters? So much time has passed, and I should dearly love to know what has happened to them and to you."

"Certainly, where would you like me to begin?"

"At the beginning. Tell me everything."

Dylan lay stretched out in the grass at the crest of the hill, looking down at Grace's cottage, his chin propped in his hands as he waited. Her brother had been in there for well over three hours before he finally came out. Grace followed him to the carriage in front of the house as Dylan watched.

He had been here before Lawrence's arrival, knowing the other man would come today. He wanted to see for himself how things turned out. He had come early, torturing himself by watching her as she pruned roses. She looked so lovely, and so alone, that it made him ache. His fault. He had forgotten how desolate a spot this was, a perdition to which he had sent her. He hoped her visit with her brother was going well and a reconciliation could be effected. Her family had treated her as cruelly as he had done, and she did not deserve it. She did not deserve to be alone. She deserved to be safe and secure.

From his position at the top of the hill, hidden in the grass, he watched as she wrapped her arms around her brother's neck and how the other man returned her embrace by putting his arms around her waist. Ian had done his job with his usual diplomatic skill, and as Dylan watched brother and sister, the sight twisted something inside his heart. He was glad, so glad, for her. She had been in such sorrow about her family and their estrangement, and now, with the help of Ian, Tremore, Daphne, and Viola, her reputation and that of her sisters would be saved.

She was wearing one of her old dresses, the red one, with an apron, and there was a white kerchief wrapped around her gold hair. It hurt to look at her, hurt deep in his soul to watch her from up here, unable to touch her and hold her. The money he had paid her would eventually run out, and her pride would never allow her to take more money from him, but as he watched her with her brother, he knew that now she would be taken care of. With her family, she would never have to sell oranges on the street or work herself to death as someone's charwoman or play music for anyone's pleasure but her own. Now, she could truly start a new life, the life she deserved.

He glanced beside him at the bouquet of roses he had brought. He was going to take Isabel's advice, but he doubted it would help. Roses and an apology meant nothing. She would never take him back. How could she? She did not love him. Now she did not need him. She certainly could not want him, not after the cruel way he had set her aside.

His gaze slid past the bouquet to the large, flat package he had also brought with him. The roses she would throw in his face, but that package was different. He didn't know what she would do with that.

Dylan returned his attention to the scene below, watching as James got into his carriage and brother and sister said their good-byes. Like himself, her brother was staying in the village of Oxwich nearby, though the other man did not know he was here. No doubt Grace would return with her brother to Cornwall; she would sell this cottage, and earn herself a dowry. She might then be able to marry. A good man, a respectable man who would take care of her. A man who deserved her.

The ache that had been in his chest ever since she'd left twisted, deepened. He could not bear to think about her marrying any other man. God, he was selfish to the end, even in his love for her.

Dylan waited until Grace had gone back inside, then he watched James's carriage pull into the lane and circle around to the road. He turned his head, looking down the other side of the hill at his own carriage parked by the side of the road. He watched James's vehicle pass it, going toward the village. Once the other carriage was out of sight, Dylan stood up. He tucked the roses under one arm, picked up the large, burlap-wrapped bundle in his hands, and walked down to Grace's stone cottage at the bottom of the hill.

He set the flowers on the ground beside her front door, propped the package against the stone wall of the cottage, and tapped the door knocker. He heard footsteps approach the door, and his heart began to pound in his chest as if he were a lovesick suitor. He rubbed his palms over his face and took a few deep breaths. He had never been more nervous in his life, and he fully expected her to slam the door in his face the moment she saw him, but he could not let her. He had to give her what he had brought with him, and he had to explain, he had to apologize. Then, when she told him to leave, he would go.

The door opened, and she froze, staring at him with all the stillness of a statue. Her lips parted, those pretty green eyes went wide, and her hand rested motionless on the door handle.

"Hullo, Grace." He tried to smile, a charming smile, the one he had always used to woo and placate women, but he couldn't manage it. Not with Grace. Not anymore.

"What are you doing here?" she asked, her hand lifting to her throat. She tugged at the worn white collar of her dress and looked away, as if unable to bear the sight of him.

"I came to bring you something."

That returned her attention to his face, though she did not quite meet his gaze. "What?"

"Something that belongs to you." He bent down and picked up the shallow package four foot square. Over the top of the burlap wrapper, he looked into her eyes. "May I bring it in?"

She did not move. "That doesn't belong to me," she said. "I have all I own right here."

"I vow it is yours. Please, Grace. Let me bring it in."

She hesitated, and he held his breath, waiting, but she stepped back and opened the door wider for him to enter. He tipped the package sideways to get it through the doorway, and she let him into the small parlor, where he crossed to set it on the table in the corner.

She followed him over to the table, placed her hand on the burlap, frowned, and glanced at him standing beside her. "I left nothing behind in

Devonshire, certainly not something of this size. Whatever this is, it cannot possibly be mine."

"It is yours. Now."

"A gift from you?" Her voice and her eyes were so cold. "I do not want it."

He raked a hand through his hair, not knowing quite how to do this. He had never truly been in love before, not like this. All he knew was the game. He didn't know how to set about the real thing. "I know I have no right to ask anything of you, but I am asking you to accept it." He could hear the desperate edge coming into his own voice. "I know it won't change anything, but please, Grace. Open it."

She could not imagine what he had brought her, but whatever it was, she would not accept it. She bit her lip, glancing from the package to him and back again. He stood there, his beautiful, powerful body framed by the doorway behind him, his long hair disheveled by the wind outside. The tenderness was there, too, that tenderness he could paste on his face anytime he liked, with any woman he was with to get whatever he wanted.

But what did he want? Why had he sent his brother to reconcile her family, and why had he asked his friends to save her reputation? Why had he come all the way to Wales to bring her a present? There was nothing in this for him.

Unless he wanted her back. She felt the icy hardness she'd been building around her heart for two months cracking, sliding away. She began to quiver deep inside with stupid, stupid hope. She felt her foolish heart trying to overrule her head yet again. Where was her pride? He had abandoned her so cruelly, without a thought, with no explanation. If he did want her back, it was to be his mistress until he got tired of her or had a change of mood. She had lived for six years with an erratic man like that. She would not do it again.

"Is that why you came?" Furious with him and even more with herself, she gestured to the package on the table. "To give me a present like any man would give his mistress? Are you trying to turn me up sweet? Get me to come back?"

"No. You are already sweet, and—" He broke off, and a shadow of something that might have been regret crossed his face. "I doubt I have a chance in hell of getting you back." He gestured to the package on the table. "And this is not a present that a man would give his mistress, believe me. I thought it was very important that you should have it, that's all. So I bought it, and I brought it here to you. What you do with it is up to you."

She made a sound of vexation and turned toward the table. She knew she might just as well open it. Then she would reject it and tell him to take his present and go away. She stared down at the burlap-wrapped package, pulled her pruning shears out of her apron pocket, and cut the twine. She began to unfold the layers of coarse fabric wrapping.

When she uncovered what lay beneath the burlap, she gave a gasp of shock, seeing the last thing she would have expected. It was one of Etienne's paintings. The nude of her on the bed.

Grace stared down at her own face laughing back up at her.

The Girl with Green Eyes on a Bed. Nearly eight

years ago when Etienne had painted this. She'd been so very young. So terribly in love—as only someone that young could be. Crazy love, immature love, the shallow, worshipful love of a seventeen-year-old girl for a man she had put on a pedestal.

Grace lifted the canvas, revealing a layer of tissue paper, and she could see another painting beneath—the one of her stepping into a bath. Below that was the one of her in the swing. All three of the nudes Etienne had painted of her were here. She laid them back down flat and stared at the top one. Her nude body, half-reclined on the bed, with nothing of her form or her feelings left to the imagination.

She pressed her fists to her mouth, feeling slightly ill.

"Etienne promised to destroy the paintings when I left," she murmured behind her hands. "When they did not appear anywhere after his death, I thought he had kept his word. I had almost forgotten these even existed."

She stood there for a long time, staring at the image of herself from so long ago. She thought of the girl she had been, and she hurt for that girl, who had loved so desperately, who had believed that one could fall in love in an instant and expect it to last a lifetime. But Dylan was proof that even when one took months to fall in love, it still didn't last. A sob caught in her throat.

"Don't cry!" Dylan's hoarse voice broke into her thoughts, and before she could turn around, he was behind her, his arms sliding around her waist, holding her tight against him. "Don't cry," he repeated, his lips on her cheek, kissing tears away.

It was so humiliating to cry in front of him. She struggled, but he did not let her go, and she gave it up, sagging in his arms. "Where did you get these?" she choked.

"I bought them." He hesitated, then added, "Grace, they were up for auction at Christie's."

"Oh, God," she moaned and buried her face in her hands. The idea that her body had been on public display, described and bid on in front of dozens of men was horrifying to her. She remembered that night in London when she had thought she would have to pose nude to a stranger for money, and she thanked God she had not been forced to that. She had done these paintings for her husband, the man she had once loved. Countless other men had seen them now, and the thought sickened her.

"No one will ever see them again," Dylan whispered fiercely in her ear as if he could read her thoughts. "I told you, they are yours now to do with as you wish."

She lowered her hands, turned around in his arms, and pushed at him. This time, he let her go, taking several steps back. "How much did you pay for them?" she asked.

"It doesn't matter."

"How much?" she repeated. No matter how long it took, she would pay him back. She did not want to owe him, not for these.

"Grace—" He broke off, studying her expression, and she could tell he did not want to tell her, but after a moment, he capitulated. "Eventually you will find out anyway, I suppose, since everything I do is in the scandal sheets," he muttered. "Thirty-six thousand pounds."

"Oh, good Lord," she said, wretched. "I can never pay you back. I will be in debt to you my entire life."

"Grace, damn it, you are not in debt to me." He stepped forward and grabbed her arms. "I don't want you to pay me back! I am giving these to you. They should have been yours in the first place, and your damned husband should have destroyed them when you asked him to."

Grace pulled away from him. Seeing him, having him here in front of her, letting him touch her and kiss her tears away, was too much. It hurt too much. God help her, she loved him too much. She twisted away and crossed the room to the fire. Her back to him, she stared into the blaze.

He had gone to that auction, and he had watched as each image of her naked body had been propped up on a stand and described by an auctioneer. He had bought every one, paying dearly for them, and he had given them to her. A thought struck her, and she whirled around. "I didn't even know these paintings still existed. How did you find out about them?"

"Ian told me."

"What?"

"He showed me a Christie's pamphlet—you know the kind I mean, that have engravings, sketches, and descriptions of the items to be auctioned. He had it with him in Devonshire, and when he was introduced to you, he knew at once who you were."

"That was why you made me leave," Grace said with a sudden glimmer of understanding. "You saw engravings of me without . . . without my clothes, and you set me aside. Without even an explanation!" A flash of pain crossed his face, but her own pain was too great to care. "Damn you, you set me aside for these stupid paintings?"

Horrified at all the hurt in her own voice, she fought hard to regain her control, but it was futile. She was splintering apart. "Because my own husband painted me nude?" A bubble of hysteria rose in her throat. "I didn't think Dylan Moore was such a prude."

"I didn't give a damn about that!" he shouted, stepping toward her. "I hated the idea of other men looking at you, ogling you in some collection or museum, I grant you that. But that was not the main reason! It was your face! It cut me to the heart, your face."

"What? I don't understand."

"Look at yourself, look at your face." Dylan jabbed a finger in the direction of the canvases on the table. "You loved him."

"Of course I did." She could only stare at Dylan, bewildered. "I told you that."

"Cheval was a great painter, wasn't he? Oh, yes, a very great painter. He painted what he saw— that love in your face, so much love, all the love in your heart, all the love in the world, for him."

"So?"

His face was ravaged, full of pain, like a wounded animal. "You have never, ever looked at me that way."

He loved her. She knew it in an instant, not from what he said but from the shattered way he looked at her. All her defenses came tumbling down as she stared at the proud, wounded man in front of her. She had never seen anything like this pain in a man's countenance before.

"Oh, Dylan," she said, lifting her hands in a helpless gesture. "I was a girl. I was a child. I scarcely knew what love was. When Etienne painted that, I was seventeen years old, and my infatuation for him was mixed up with admiration and physical desires. I loved my husband, yes, but it was such an insubstantial love, it didn't last more than three years. He was my lover, and I had never been in love before. It was all so new, so romantic, and so very exciting . . ." Her voice trailed off as she looked into Dylan's pain-filled face.

"I had only known Etienne a week when we eloped," she reminded him. "He may not have married me until two years after we met, but he did love me in his way, as much as he was able. He was a man of such violent moods, living with him was hell. He thought I was his inspiration." Dylan let out his breath sharply and turned away.

"As his moods got darker," Grace went on, "he became more and more unstable. When he couldn't paint, he blamed me. Then he turned to other women. Somehow, it all went wrong, and the love all died. I could not bear the blame he heaped on me, the affairs he flaunted in my face, and I left him. Oh, Dylan," she cried to his back, "I loved him, but I was not the woman I am now. Can you not understand that?"

Something, a sound broke from him, and he turned around. "I hate him, Grace. I hate him because he hurt you, he took your beautiful, generous, loving heart and he broke it, he forced you away. I did the same. I hate him because I hate myself. I did not appreciate what I had until it was lost to me."

"Dylan—"

"Wait!" he interrupted. "Hell, I almost forgot."

He strode out of the parlor, and when he came back, he had a bunch of roses in his hand, all mixed colors, tied with a ribbon. He thrust them into her hand. "I know roses are your favorite, and I tried to buy you a beautiful posy of them, but there's no florist in the village. I stole them out of some poor woman's garden on the way here."

Grace took them, and inside, she began to shake. "Why are you giving me flowers like a suitor at my door?"

"It was Isabel's idea. You see, she said I had to come and get you back. She had it all planned out, that you were going to be her new mother. Part of that real family business she wants. And she told me to come and get you, to give you flowers and apologize. She says that works on you when she misbehaves, and I thought it was worth a try. Grace, I'm sorry."

"You hurt me."

"Yes. I know." He did not even try to make an excuse. His mouth tightened, but he did not look away. "I saw you crying in the dirt. I know saying one is sorry is the most trite, stupid, inadequate phrase in the English language. But I don't know what else to say. I know how terribly I hurt you; and I'm so goddamned sorry."

She took a deep breath, inhaling the sweet scent of roses. In the rush of his words, she'd caught something about being Isabel's new mother, but she wasn't sure if he was proposing or not. There had just been too many unexpected things today, she couldn't seem to think straight.

"I never knew I could be a jealous man," he said, "but when Ian came, and he was looking at you, it started gnawing at me. You remember how we quarreled?"

"Yes, I remember."

"Then I saw the engravings of those paintings and that look on your face, and I can't explain what happened inside of me. I just . . . I just erupted. I was so afraid, Grace, so afraid, knowing you didn't love me. Not when you could look at the man you loved like that and hadn't ever looked that way at me."

He gave a harsh, humorless sound. "Not that I deserve it. I have hurt so many women in my life, and I never thought about any of them, not one. Most of them I can't even remember. I never thought about them or how they felt. Only how I felt. Now, I know what I did to them—I broke their hearts, and I know how it feels because mine is in pieces without you. I love you. I love you more than my life. I love you more than my music."

"Dylan—"

"Grace, don't say anything," he interrupted, a desperation in his voice she had never heard before. "I know you probably just want me gone, but I have to tell you about me. You were right. I didn't know what love was. I thought I knew, but even with Michaela, I didn't. I proposed to her, but I still didn't give my heart, not really. Music took it all."

"Dylan, I understand that. You don't have to explain that to me."

"I have never given my heart away," he went on

as if she hadn't spoken. "Never. Because I always knew that when I did, I would give it all, and there would be nothing for the music." His words were coming so fast now she could barely follow what he said. "Do you see? Without music, I would be nothing. For five years, without music, I was nothing."

"That's not true."

"It was true. Then you came back into my life again." He reached into his coat pocket and pulled out a sheaf of papers. "Here's the symphony. I wrote it about us, I named it for you."

"I know," she whispered. "I—"

"I want you to have it," he said. "Without you, I could never publish it. Without you, I don't give a damn about the music anymore. I know just saying these things doesn't mean anything. But I love you. And I want to get married. To you, I mean. Us, you and me. Post banns and do everything right. I wouldn't spirit you off to France and not marry you for two years like some Frenchman."

"I see."

"Well?" he prompted her to get it over, say it. "Grace, will you marry me?"

There was a long silence. He looked at her and waited, but when she still didn't speak, he lifted his hands to touch her. Then he changed his mind and let them fall back to his sides. "Say something, for God's sake," he ordered in a fierce, agonized whisper. "Aren't you going to say anything?"

She gave a shaky laugh. "Are you going to let me say anything?"

"Grace, if you're going to shred me to ribbons, do it. God knows, I deserve it."

"I'm not going to shred you to ribbons." She looked at the symphony in her hands, then at the painting on the table. She thought of what he had done for her family, and how he'd come to her this way to list all his faults for her like a litany with which to lash himself. "What am I supposed to do with a symphony?" she asked him.

"Burn it. I don't care."

"You and Isabel. With both of you, there always has to be drama in everything. Can you not just fall in love and propose like a normal person? Do you have to write a symphony about it all? I'm just a girl from Cornwall, for heaven's sake. You know, it is a very good thing for the two of you that I happen to be a sensible person. Or you would both be lost."

"What?" He looked at her, and there was no sound in his mind but the thud of his pounding heart. "What are you saying?"

"I'm saying yes. I love you."

"You do?"

She nodded, and he hauled her into his arms. He held her so tightly that he knew he must be smothering her. "Grace, Grace, don't ever leave me again. Ever."

"You are the most unaccountable man! You told me to leave, remember?"

"I never said I wasn't a fool." He kissed her lips, her cheek, her ear. "Grace?"

"Hmm?"

"Remember when I said I didn't do all those things to get you to come back to me?"

"Yes."

"I was lying."

She smiled and wrapped her arms around his waist. "I know."

Startled, he pulled back and looked at her. "You do?"

"Yes. You smile a certain way when you lie."

"I do not. I have never lied to you before."

"Isabel does, and she smiles just the same way you did when you said you weren't trying to sweeten me up and get me back. Like daughter, like father. That's how I knew."

"I was right about you all along. Army general. With you in charge of me, I shall never be able to get away with anything."

Grace laughed at that and brushed back a long, black lock of his hair. "As if I could ever be in charge of England's most notorious rakehell. You're the one in charge, because with every smile of yours I see, with every kiss you give me, you make me love you more."

He pulled her even closer. His hands slid along her hips, stopped, and he became serious again. He hoped she was right about that smile thing, because he wasn't smiling now. This was important. "From now on, every smile and every kiss and every symphony is for you. Only you. For the rest of my life. I swear it."

He resumed kissing her ear and began to pull at her skirt, but instead of giving in, she put her hands on his wrists. "Wait," she said with a little frown, trying to sound severe. "What about all the sonatas, the concertos, and the operas? What woman gets those?"

Dylan pulled his hands free of her grasp, gave up on the skirts, and tried an alternate route. He reached for the top button of her dress. "Isabel, of course. Oh, and I have to save some of my kisses for her, too."

"Well," she murmured, giving in at last, "you did write me a symphony."

"Yes, I did." He pulled the neckline of her dress back and kissed her soft, white skin. Then he lifted his head, looking at her in wonder, fully appreciating for the first time just what a miracle that was. "Damn. I really did. And you told me muses don't exist." His lips grazed her mouth. "They do. I'm going to marry mine and spend the rest of my life hearing music because of her."